Hakumei & Mikochi 4

Tiny Little Life in the Woods

Takuto Kashiki

Contents

Chapter 20

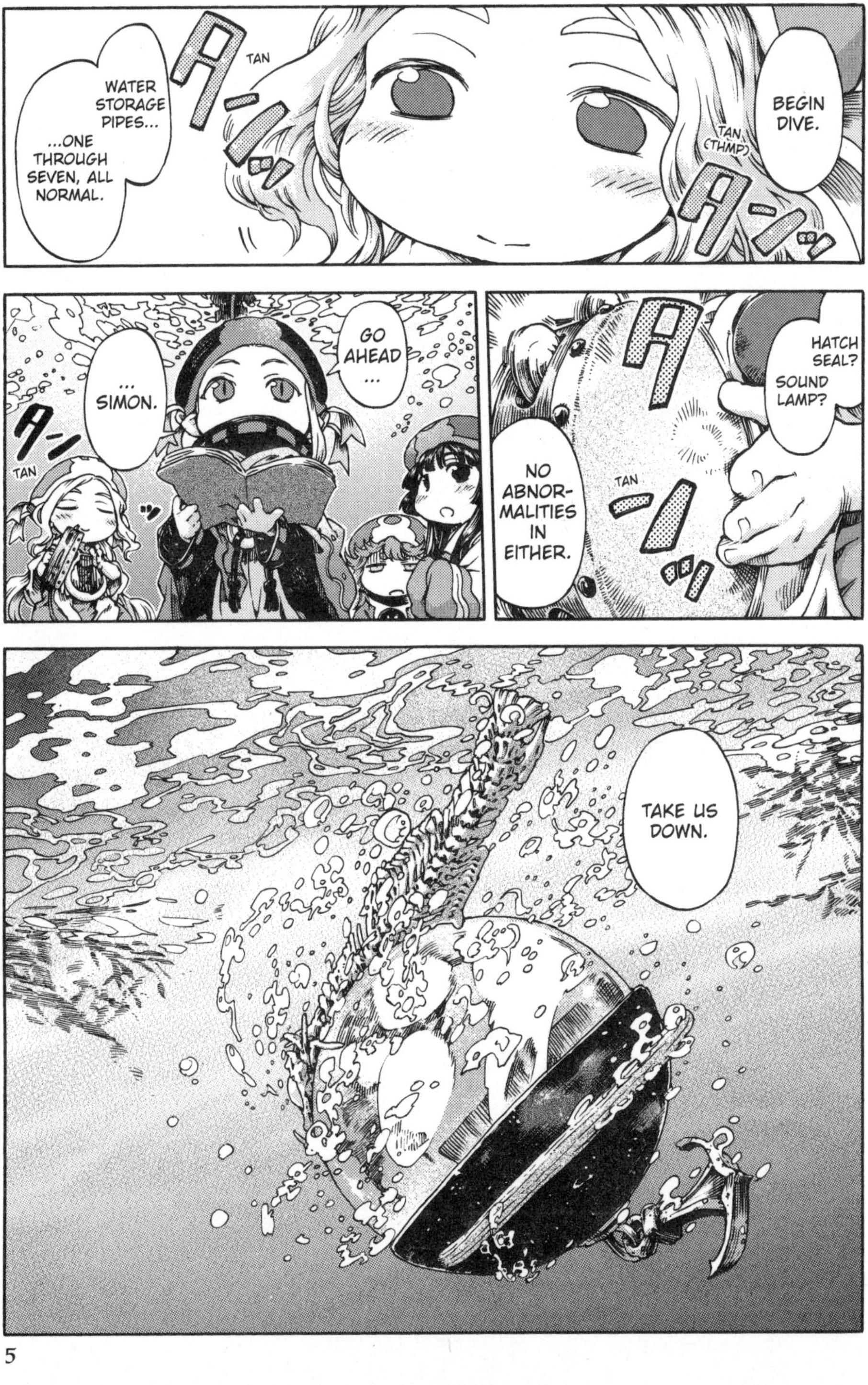

BEGIN DIVE.
TAN (THMP)
WATER STORAGE PIPES... ...ONE THROUGH SEVEN, ALL NORMAL.
TAN
HATCH SEAL? SOUND LAMP?
NO ABNORMALITIES IN EITHER.
TAN
GO AHEAD...
...SIMON.
TAN
TAKE US DOWN.

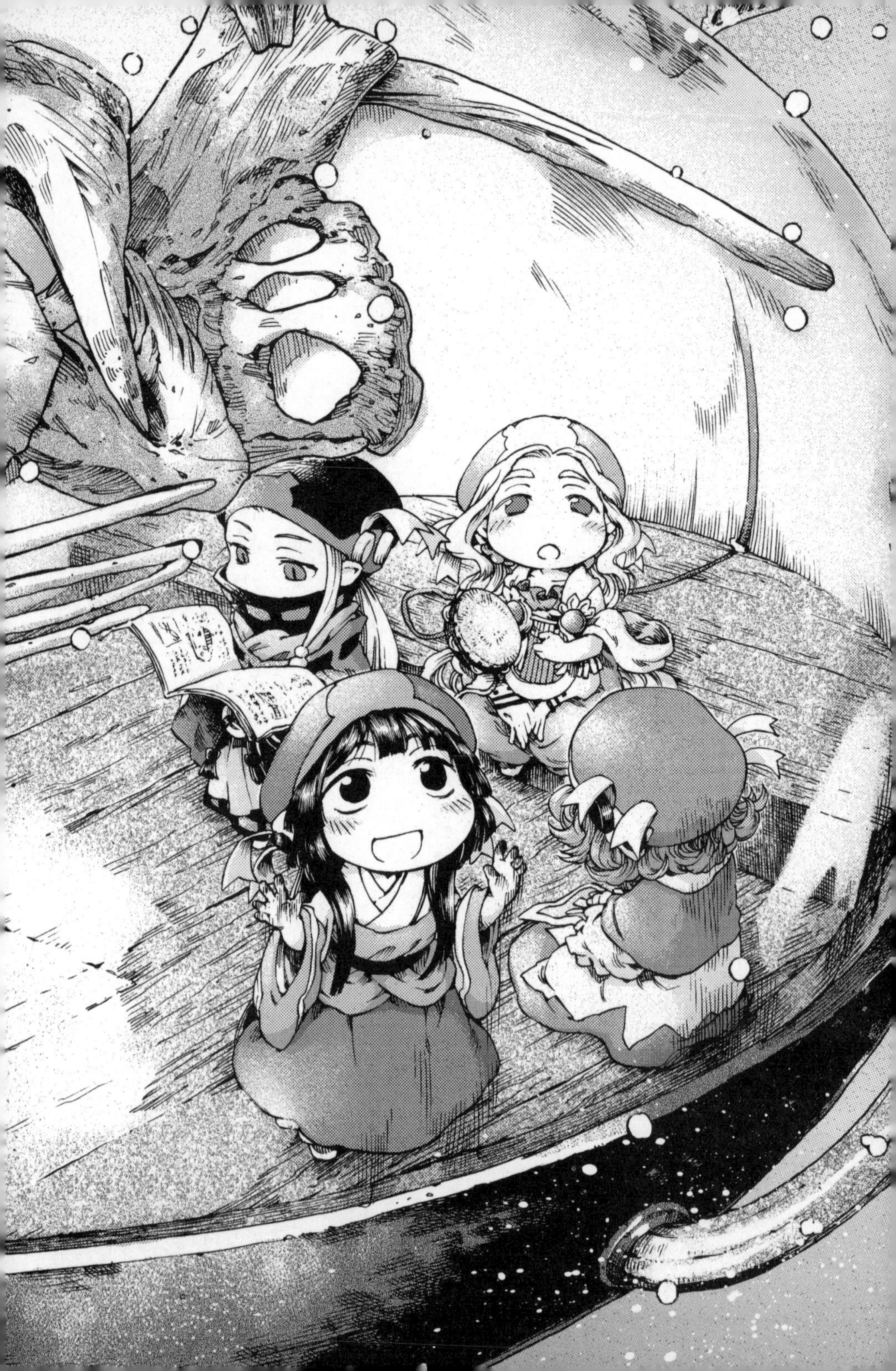

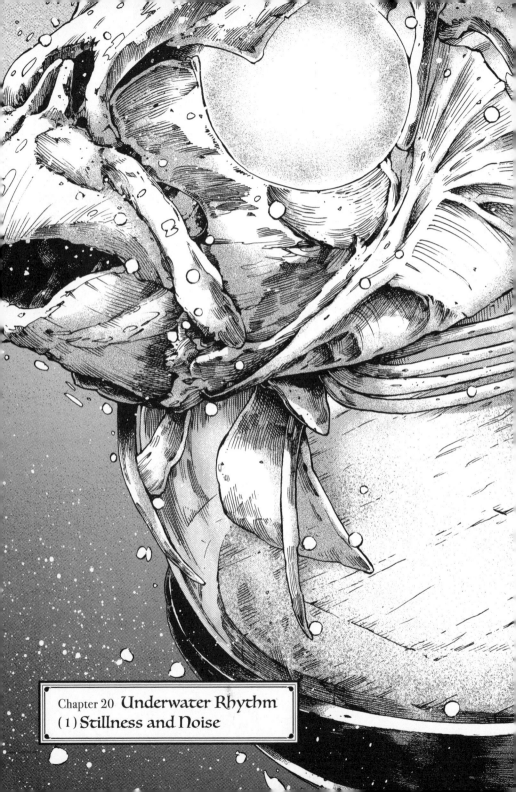

Chapter 20 Underwater Rhythm
(1) Stillness and Noise

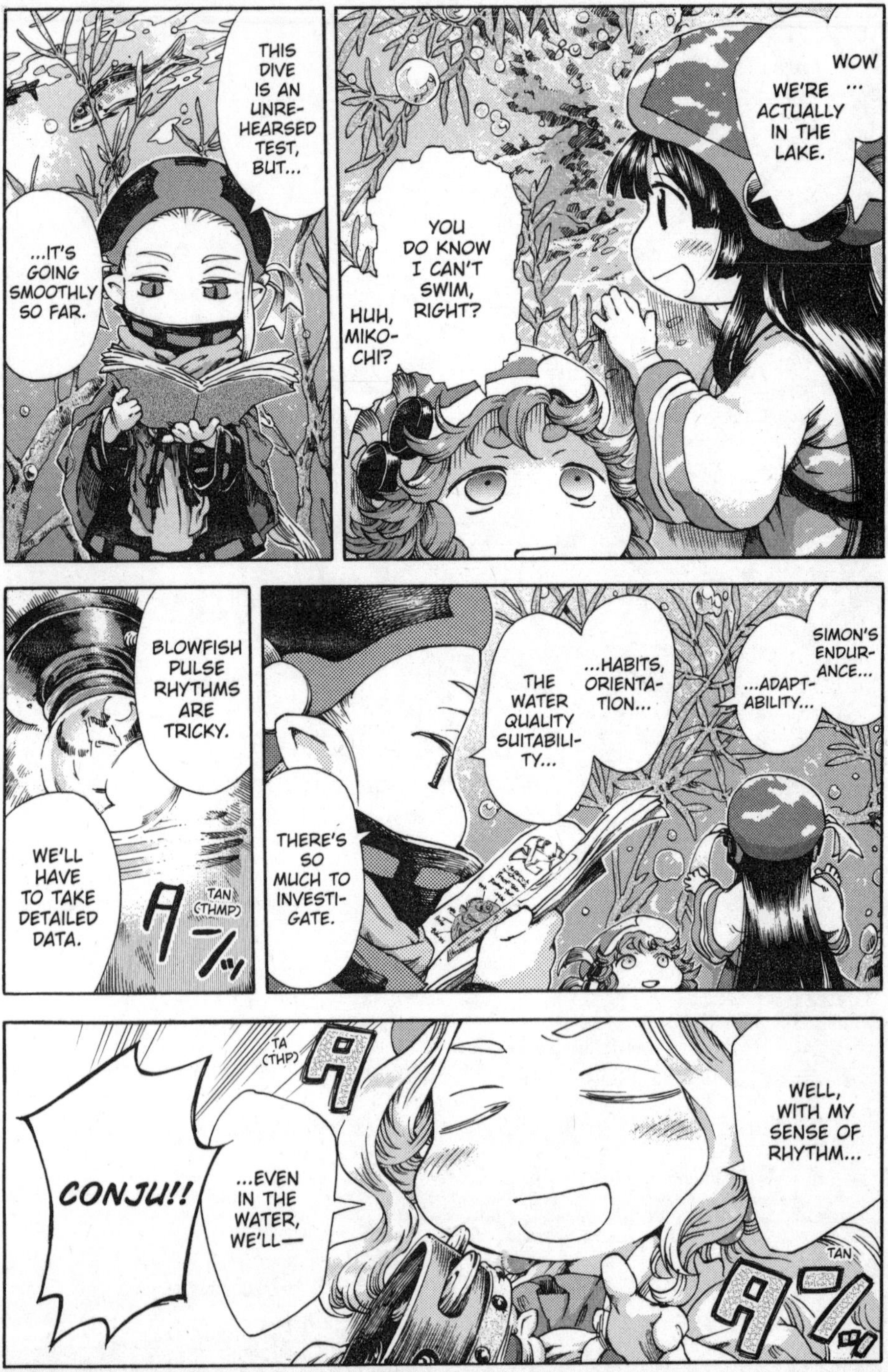
WOW ... WE'RE ACTUALLY IN THE LAKE.
YOU DO KNOW I CAN'T SWIM, RIGHT?
HUH, MIKO-CHI?
THIS DIVE IS AN UNRE-HEARSED TEST, BUT...
...IT'S GOING SMOOTHLY SO FAR.
SIMON'S ENDUR-ANCE...
...ADAPT-ABILITY...
...HABITS, ORIENTA-TION...
THE WATER QUALITY SUITABILI-TY...
THERE'S SO MUCH TO INVESTI-GATE.
BLOWFISH PULSE RHYTHMS ARE TRICKY.
WE'LL HAVE TO TAKE DETAILED DATA.
TAN (THMP)
WELL, WITH MY SENSE OF RHYTHM...
TAN
TA (THP)
...EVEN IN THE WATER, WE'LL—
CONJU!!

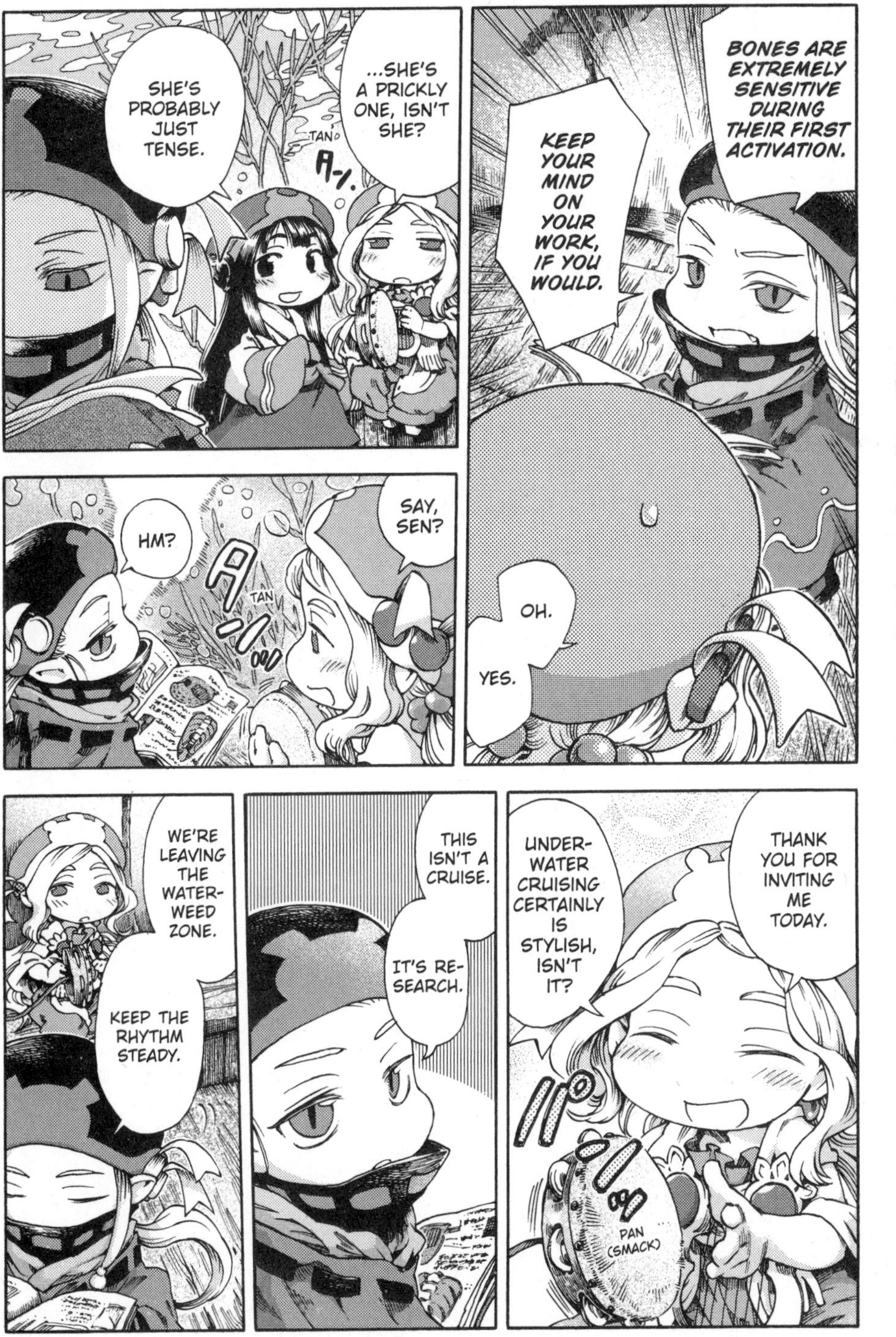
BONES ARE EXTREMELY SENSITIVE DURING THEIR FIRST ACTIVATION.
KEEP YOUR MIND ON YOUR WORK, IF YOU WOULD.
OH.
YES.
...SHE'S A PRICKLY ONE, ISN'T SHE?
SHE'S PROBABLY JUST TENSE.
TAN
SAY, SEN?
HM?
TAN
THANK YOU FOR INVITING ME TODAY.
UNDER-WATER CRUISING CERTAINLY IS STYLISH, ISN'T IT?
PAN (SMACK)
THIS ISN'T A CRUISE.
IT'S RE-SEARCH.
WE'RE LEAVING THE WATER-WEED ZONE.
KEEP THE RHYTHM STEADY.

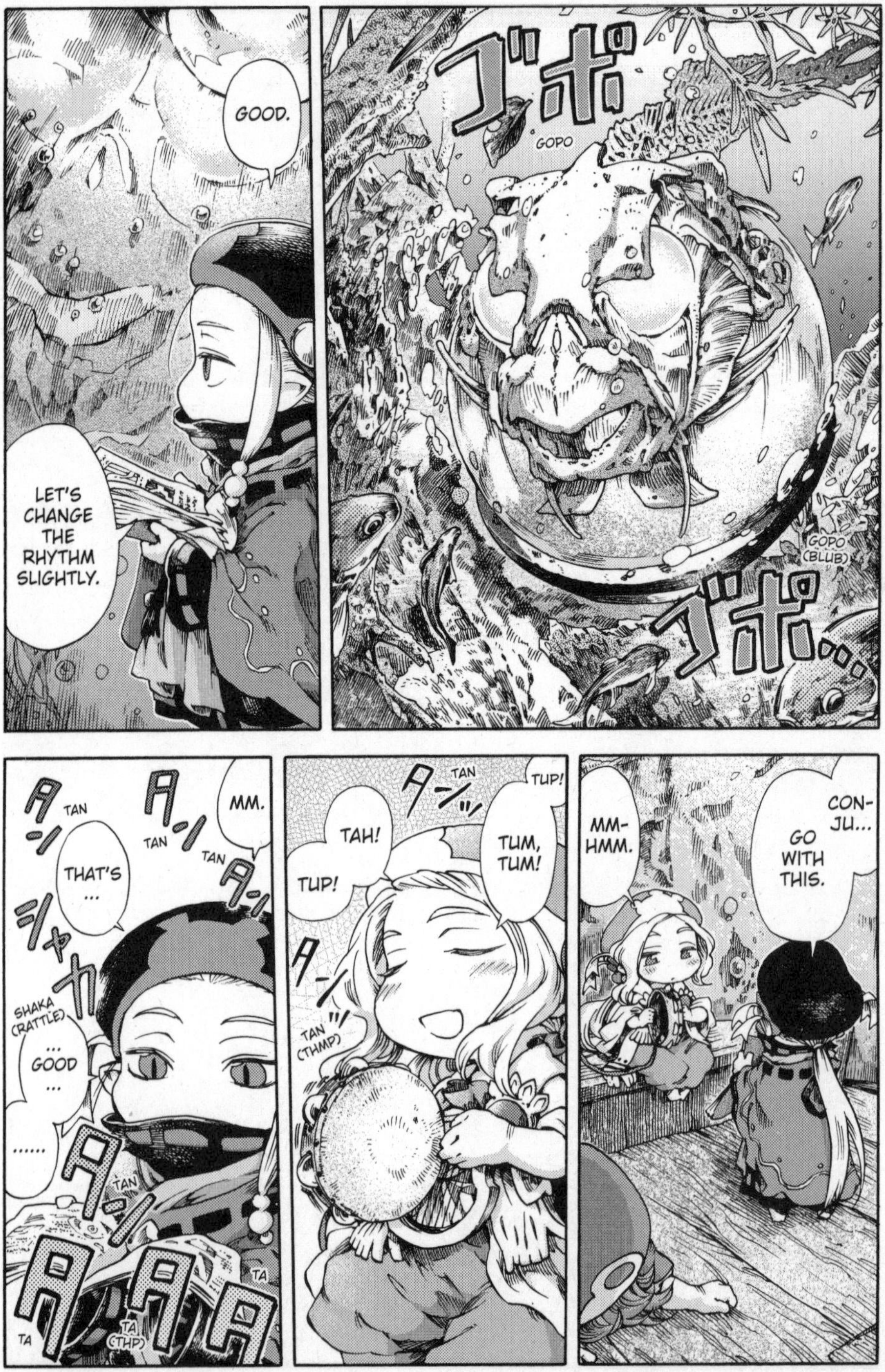
ゴポ
GOPO
GOPO (BLUB)
ゴポ…
GOOD.
LET'S CHANGE THE RHYTHM SLIGHTLY.
CON-JU... GO WITH THIS.
MM-HMM.
TUP!
TUM, TUM!
TAN
TAH!
TUP!
TAN (THMP)
MM.
THAT'S...
TAN
TAN
TAN
SHAKA (RATTLE)
...GOOD...
......
TAN
TA
TA (THP)
TA

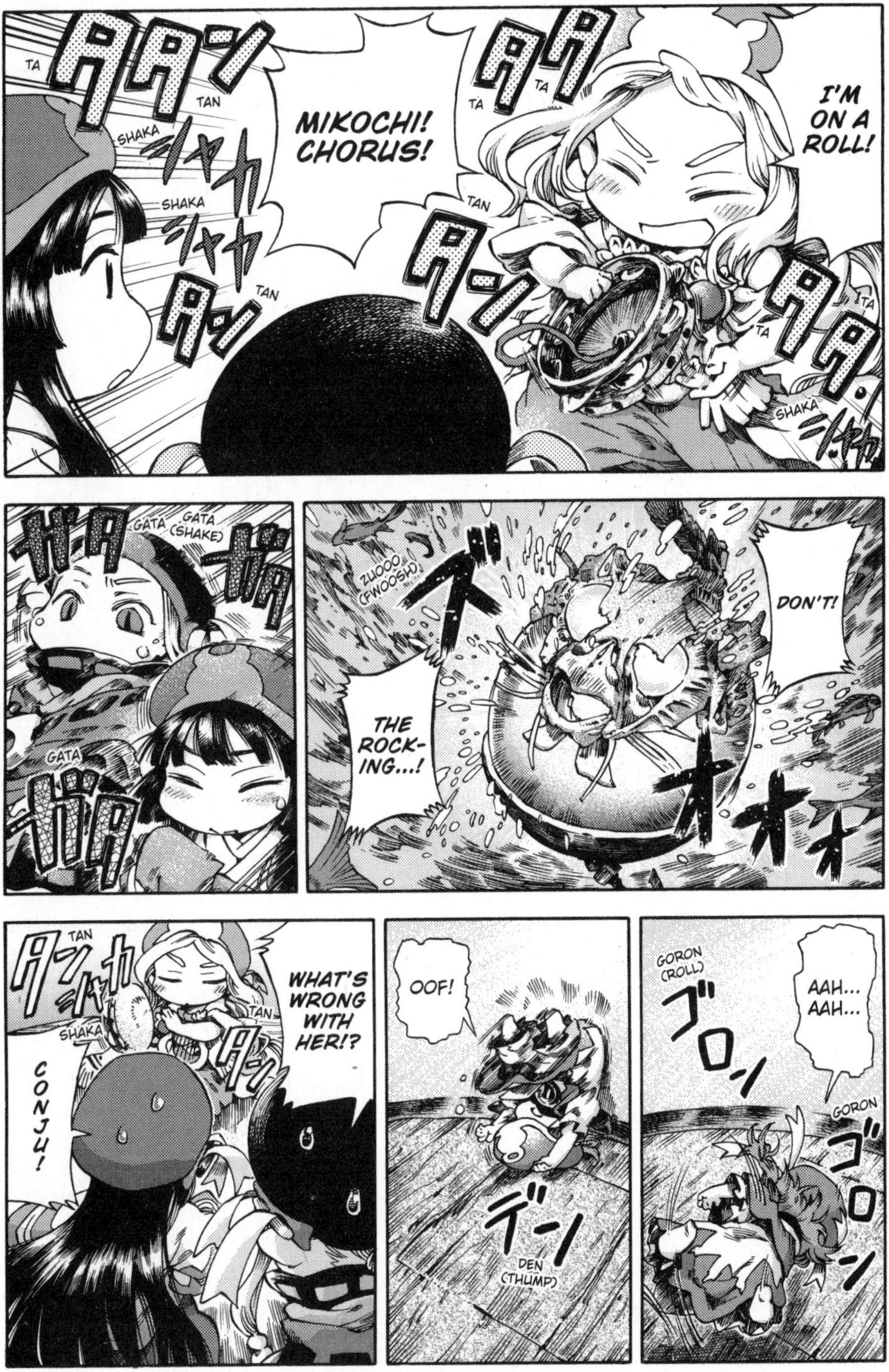
I'M ON A ROLL!
TA
TA
MIKOCHI! CHORUS!
TA
TAN
SHAKA
SHAKA
TAN
TAN
TA
TA
SHAKA
DON'T!
ZUOOO (FWOOSH)
THE ROCKING...!
GATA
GATA (SHAKE)
GATA
AAH... AAH...
GORON (ROLL)
GORON
OOF!
DEN (THUMP)
TAN
WHAT'S WRONG WITH HER!?
TAN
SHAKA
CONJU!

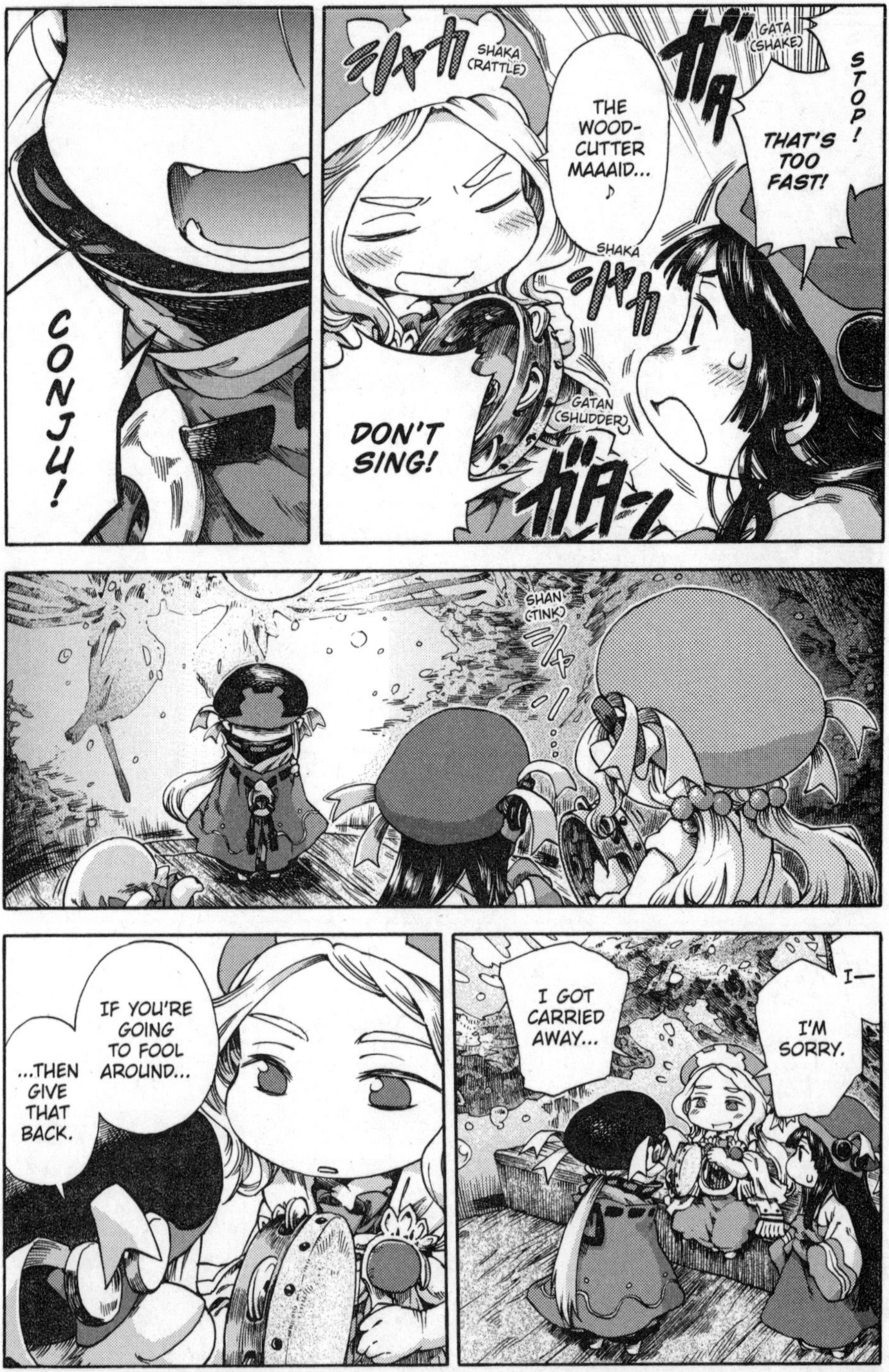
GATA (SHAKE)
STOP! THAT'S TOO FAST!
THE WOOD-CUTTER MAAAID... ♪
SHAKA (RATTLE)
SHAKA
GATAN (SHUDDER)
DON'T SING!
CONJU!
SHAN (TINK)
I—
I'M SORRY.
I GOT CARRIED AWAY...
IF YOU'RE GOING TO FOOL AROUND...
...THEN GIVE THAT BACK.

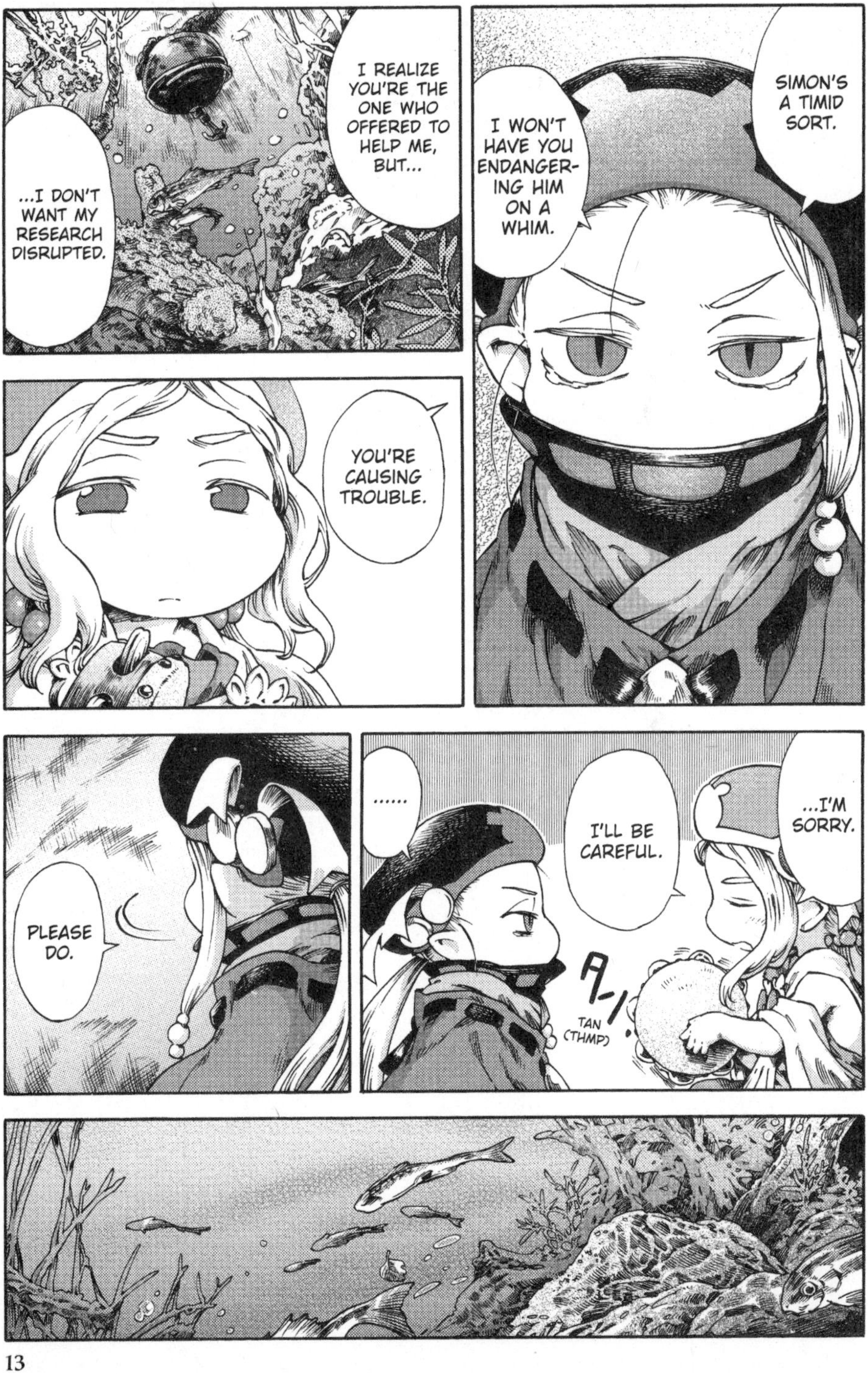
SIMON'S A TIMID SORT.
I WON'T HAVE YOU ENDANGERING HIM ON A WHIM.
I REALIZE YOU'RE THE ONE WHO OFFERED TO HELP ME, BUT...
...I DON'T WANT MY RESEARCH DISRUPTED.
YOU'RE CAUSING TROUBLE.
...I'M SORRY.
I'LL BE CAREFUL.
......
TAN (THMP)
PLEASE DO.

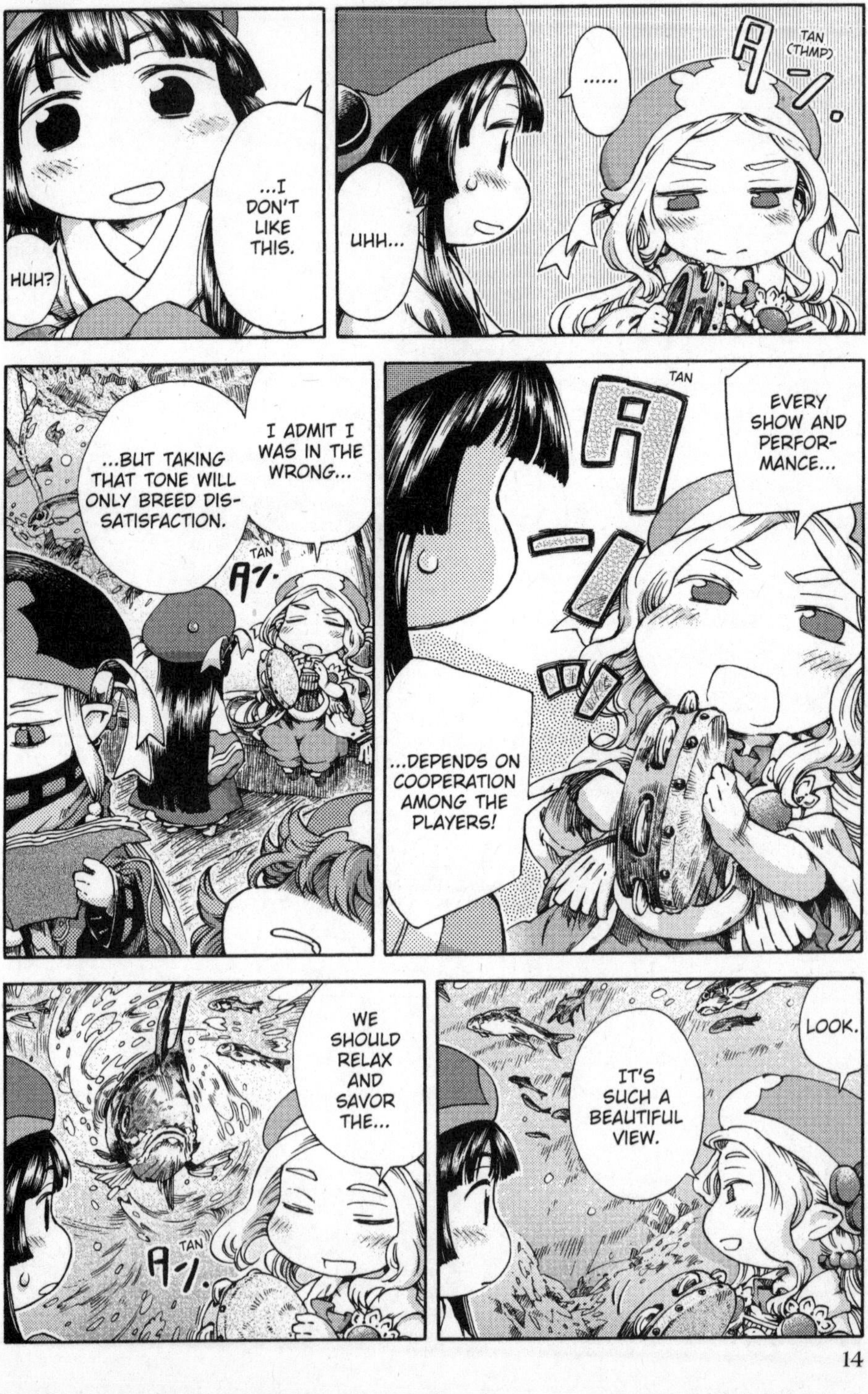
TAN (THMP)
......
UHH...
...I DON'T LIKE THIS.
HUH?
TAN
EVERY SHOW AND PERFORMANCE...
...DEPENDS ON COOPERATION AMONG THE PLAYERS!
I ADMIT I WAS IN THE WRONG...
...BUT TAKING THAT TONE WILL ONLY BREED DISSATISFACTION.
TAN
LOOK.
IT'S SUCH A BEAUTIFUL VIEW.
WE SHOULD RELAX AND SAVOR THE...
TAN

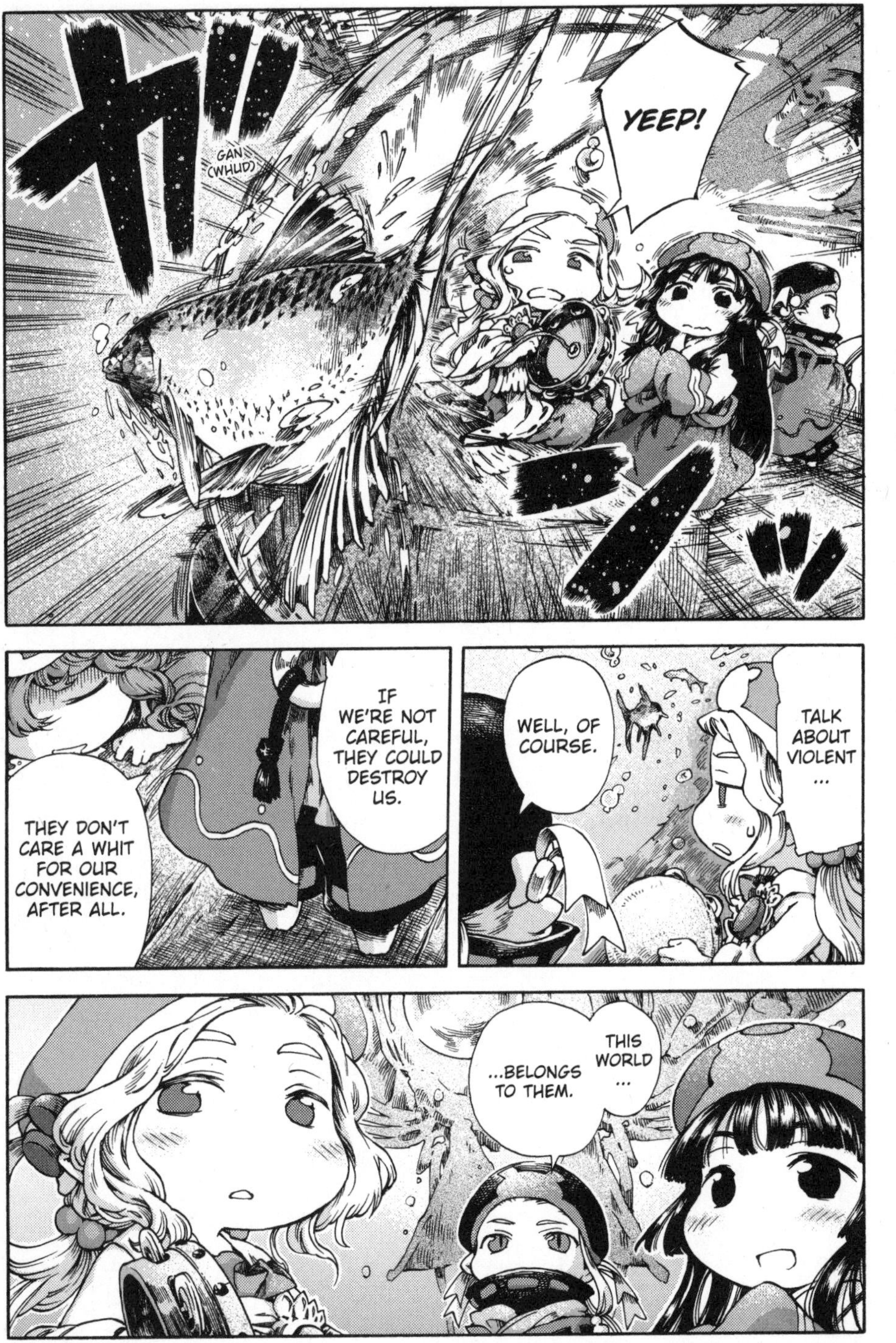
YEEP!
GAN (WHUD)
TALK ABOUT VIOLENT ...
WELL, OF COURSE.
IF WE'RE NOT CAREFUL, THEY COULD DESTROY US.
THEY DON'T CARE A WHIT FOR OUR CONVENIENCE, AFTER ALL.
THIS WORLD ...
...BELONGS TO THEM.

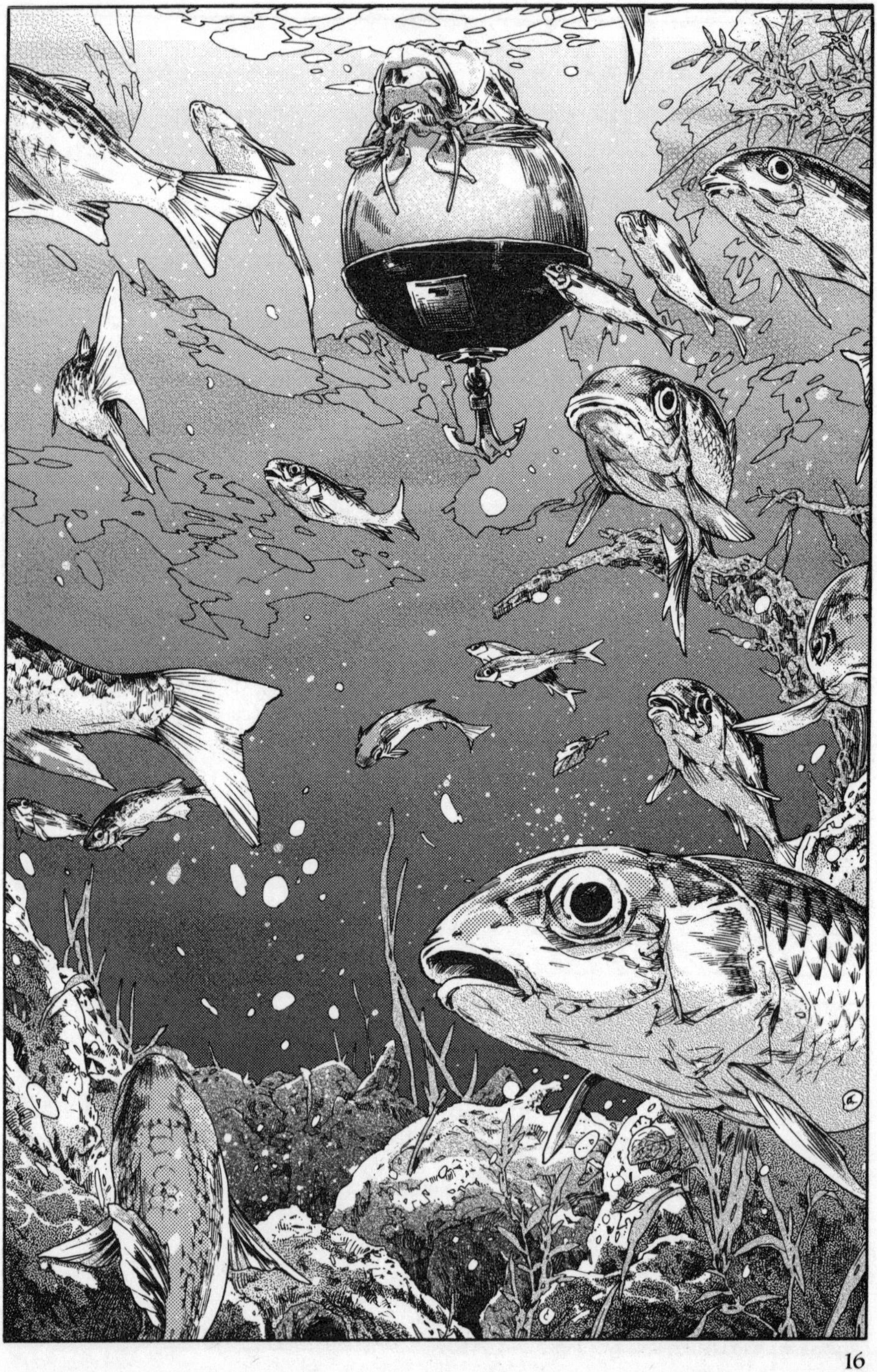

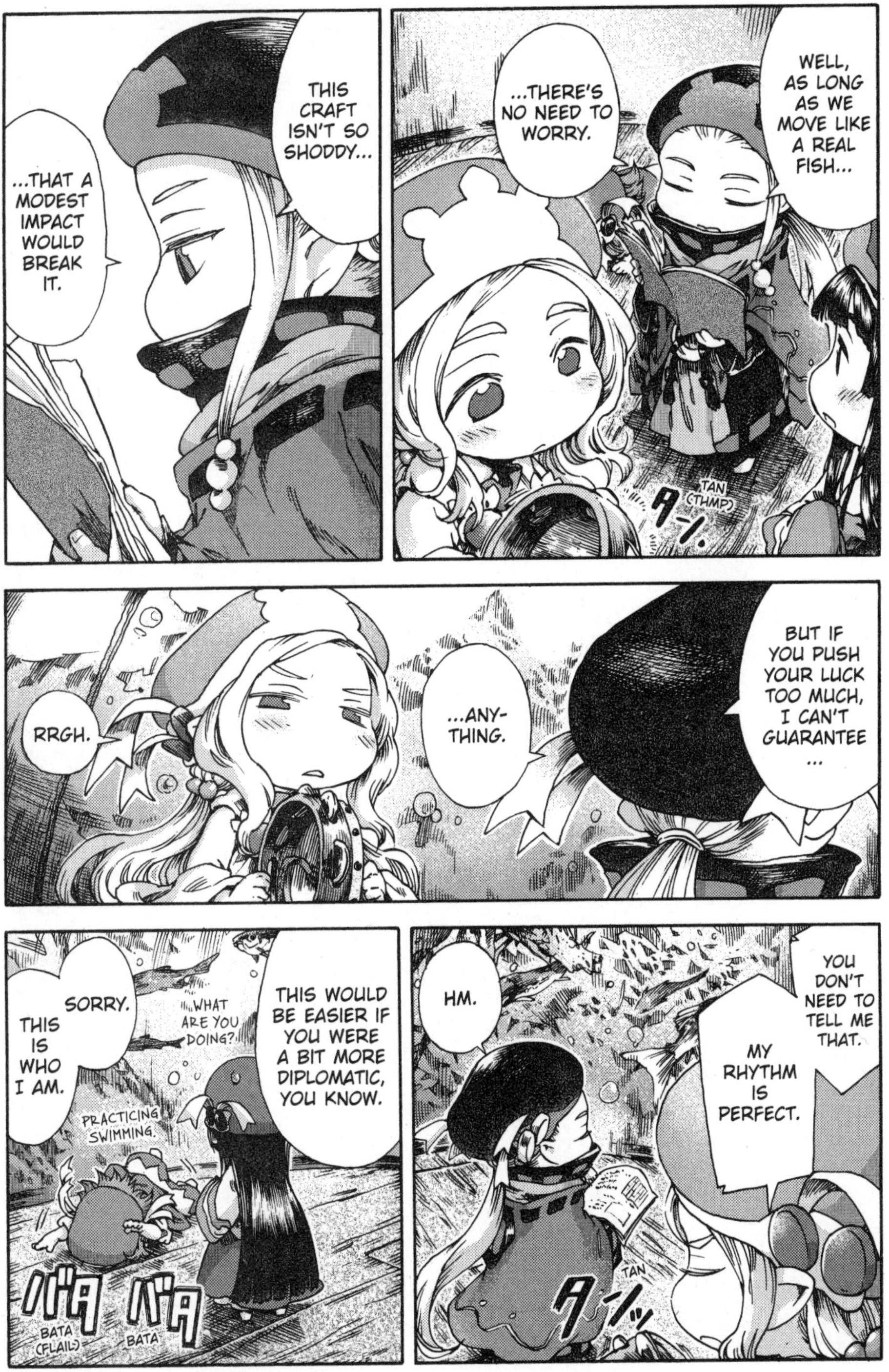
WELL, AS LONG AS WE MOVE LIKE A REAL FISH...
...THERE'S NO NEED TO WORRY.
TAN (THMP)
THIS CRAFT ISN'T SO SHODDY...
...THAT A MODEST IMPACT WOULD BREAK IT.
BUT IF YOU PUSH YOUR LUCK TOO MUCH, I CAN'T GUARANTEE ...
...ANY-THING.
RRGH.
YOU DON'T NEED TO TELL ME THAT.
MY RHYTHM IS PERFECT.
HM.
TAN
THIS WOULD BE EASIER IF YOU WERE A BIT MORE DIPLOMATIC, YOU KNOW.
WHAT ARE YOU DOING?
SORRY. THIS IS WHO I AM.
PRACTICING SWIMMING.
BATA
BATA (FLAIL)

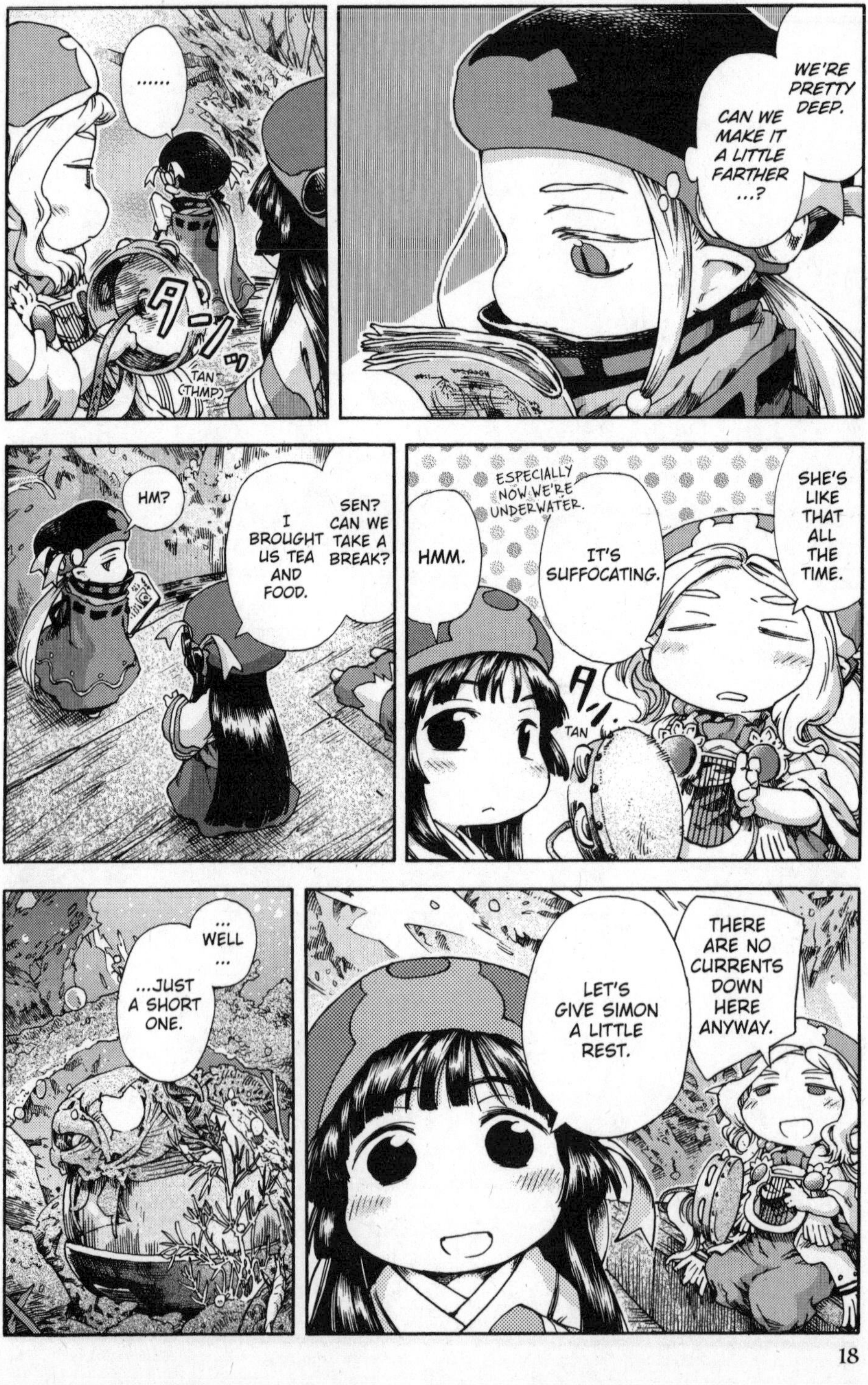
WE'RE PRETTY DEEP.
CAN WE MAKE IT A LITTLE FARTHER ...?
......
TAN (THMP)
SHE'S LIKE THAT ALL THE TIME.
IT'S SUFFOCATING.
ESPECIALLY NOW WE'RE UNDERWATER.
HMM.
TAN
SEN? CAN WE TAKE A BREAK?
I BROUGHT US TEA AND FOOD.
HM?
THERE ARE NO CURRENTS DOWN HERE ANYWAY.
LET'S GIVE SIMON A LITTLE REST.
... WELL ...
...JUST A SHORT ONE.

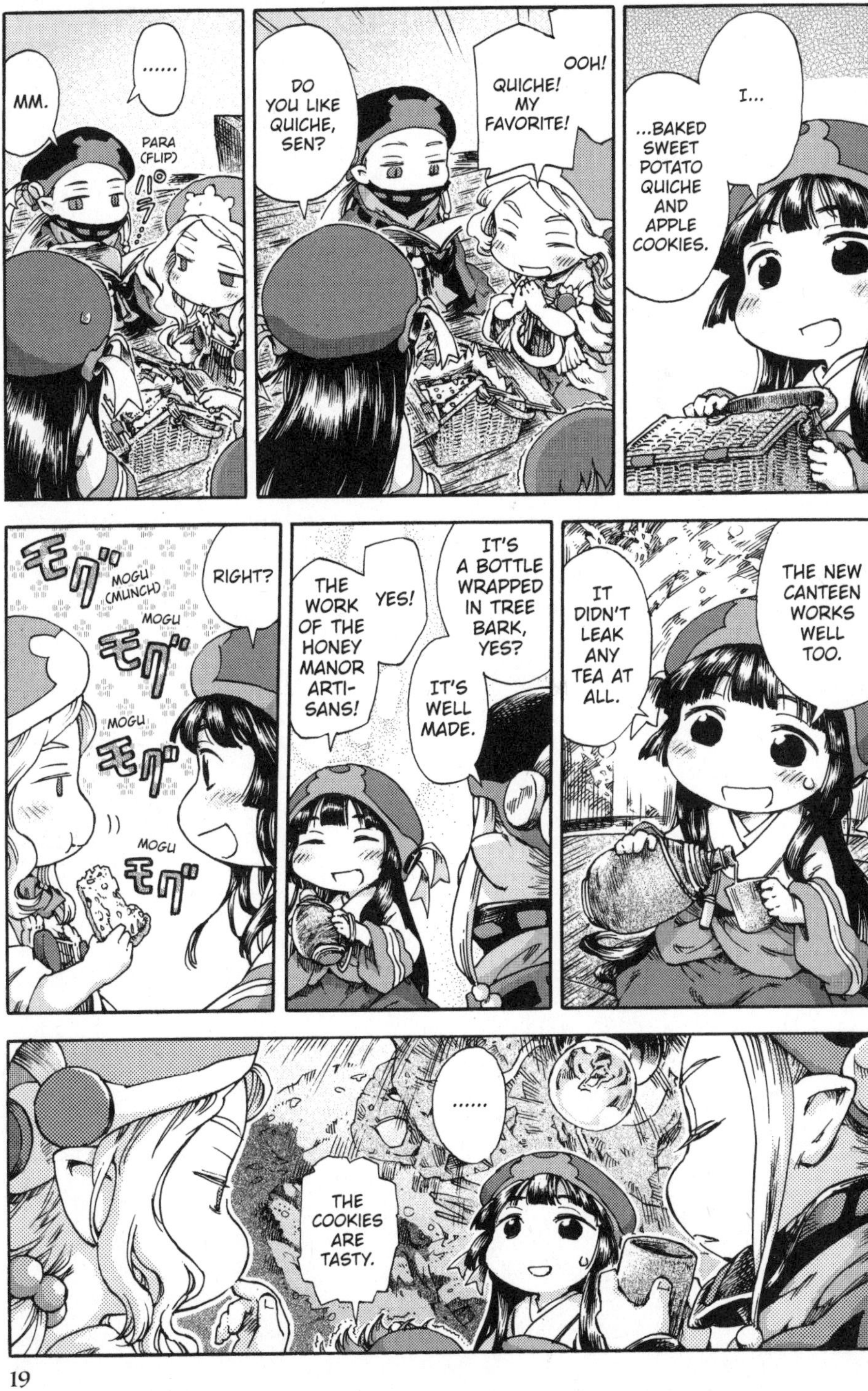

I...
...BAKED SWEET POTATO QUICHE AND APPLE COOKIES.
OOH!
QUICHE! MY FAVORITE!
DO YOU LIKE QUICHE, SEN?
......
MM.
PARA (FLIP)
パラ
THE NEW CANTEEN WORKS WELL TOO.
IT DIDN'T LEAK ANY TEA AT ALL.
IT'S A BOTTLE WRAPPED IN TREE BARK, YES?
IT'S WELL MADE.
YES!
THE WORK OF THE HONEY MANOR ARTI-SANS!
RIGHT?
モグ
MOGU (MUNCH)
MOGU
モグ
MOGU
モグ
MOGU
モグ
......
THE COOKIES ARE TASTY.

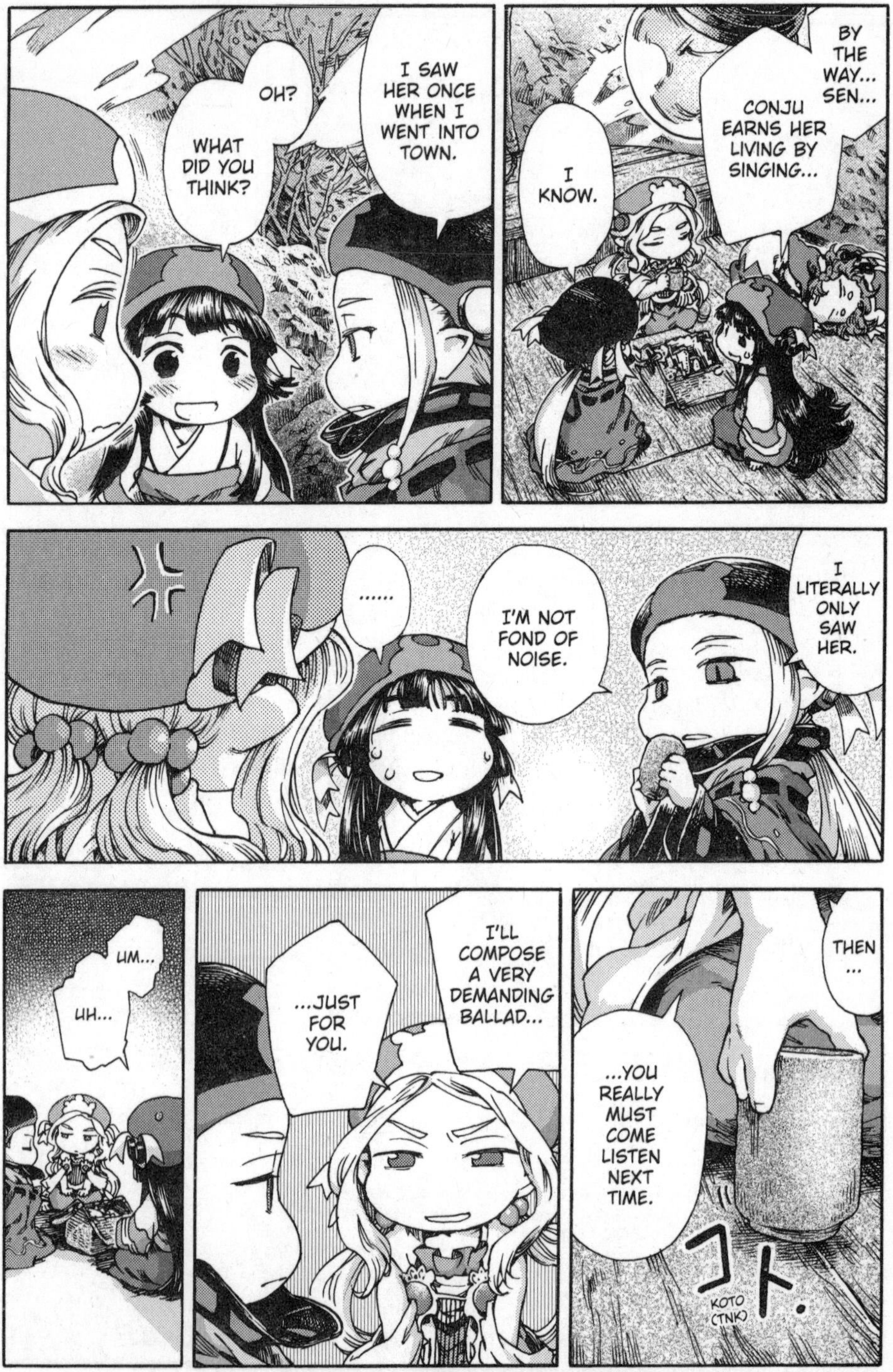
BY THE WAY... SEN...
CONJU EARNS HER LIVING BY SINGING...
I KNOW.
I SAW HER ONCE WHEN I WENT INTO TOWN.
OH?
WHAT DID YOU THINK?
I LITERALLY ONLY SAW HER.
I'M NOT FOND OF NOISE.
......
THEN ...
...YOU REALLY MUST COME LISTEN NEXT TIME.
コト.
KOTO (TNK)
I'LL COMPOSE A VERY DEMANDING BALLAD...
...JUST FOR YOU.
UM...
UH...

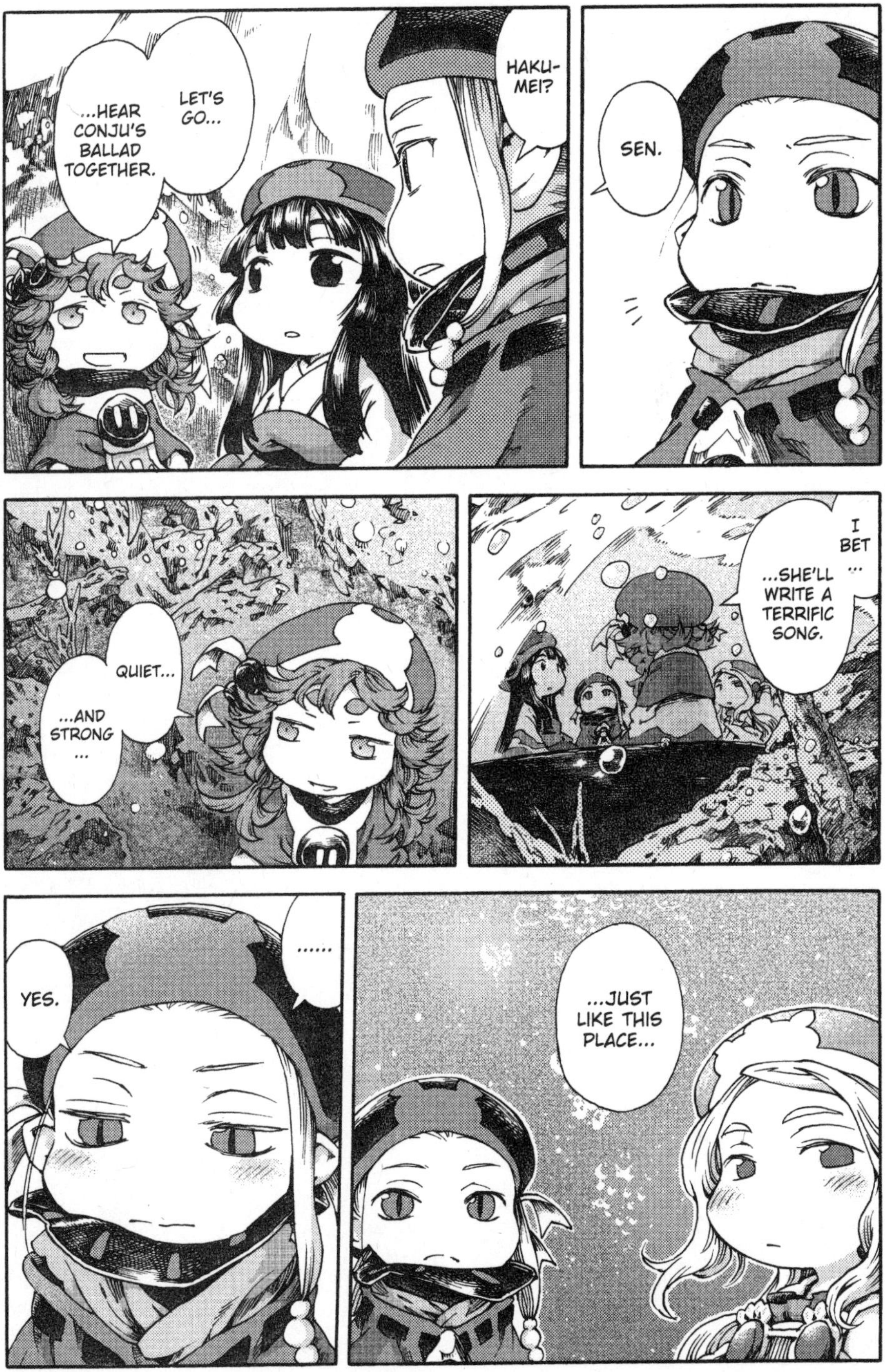
SEN.
HAKU-MEI?
LET'S GO...
...HEAR CONJU'S BALLAD TOGETHER.
I BET ...
...SHE'LL WRITE A TERRIFIC SONG.
QUIET...
...AND STRONG ...
...JUST LIKE THIS PLACE...
......
YES.

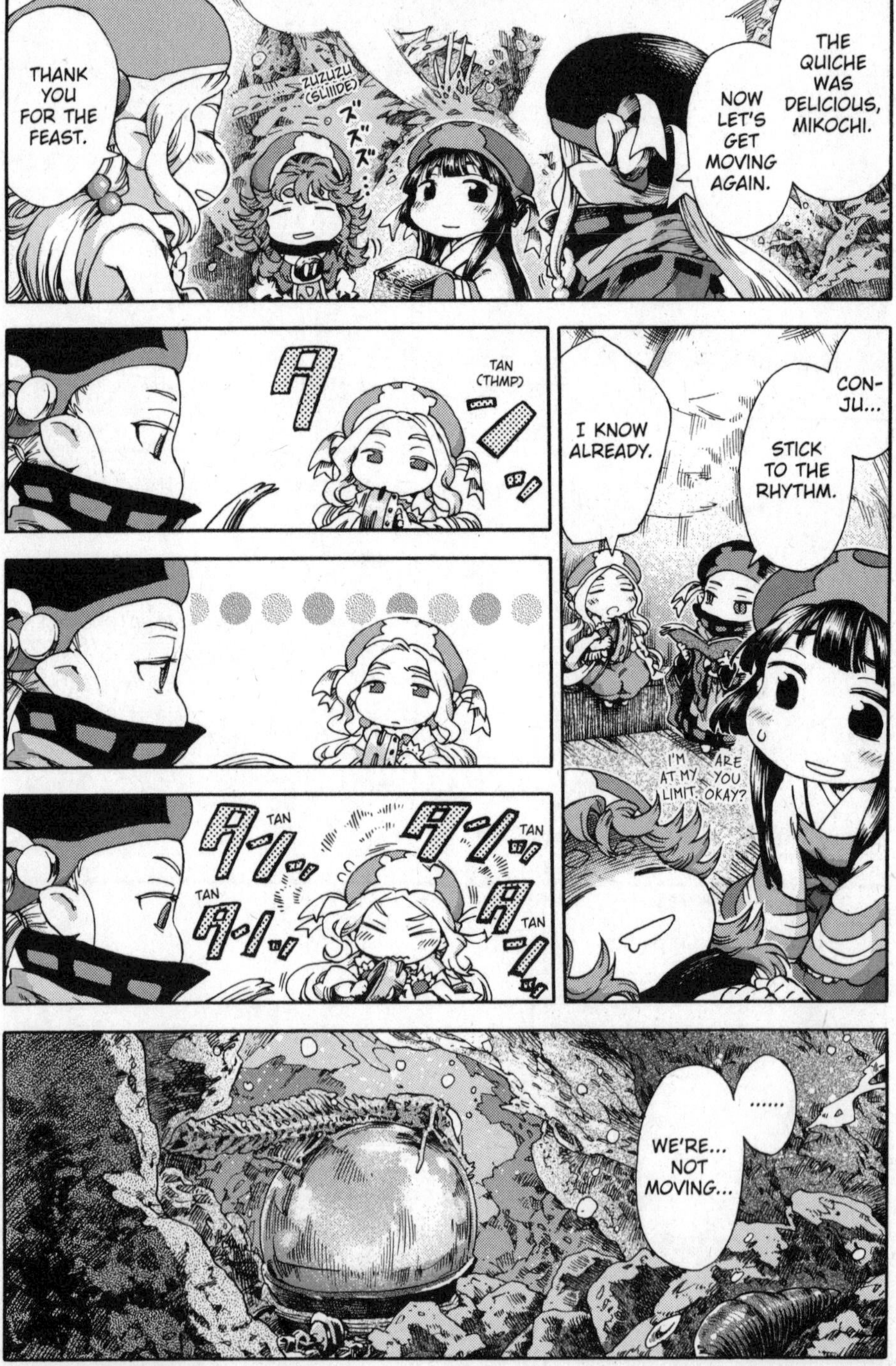
THE QUICHE WAS DELICIOUS, MIKOCHI.
NOW LET'S GET MOVING AGAIN.
ZUZUZU (SLIIIDE)
ズズズ…
THANK YOU FOR THE FEAST.
CON-JU...
STICK TO THE RHYTHM.
I KNOW ALREADY.
ARE YOU OKAY?
I'M AT MY LIMIT.
TAN (THMP)
TAN
TAN
TAN
TAN
......
WE'RE... NOT MOVING...

To Be Continued

(2) Diving Suit
and Tambourine

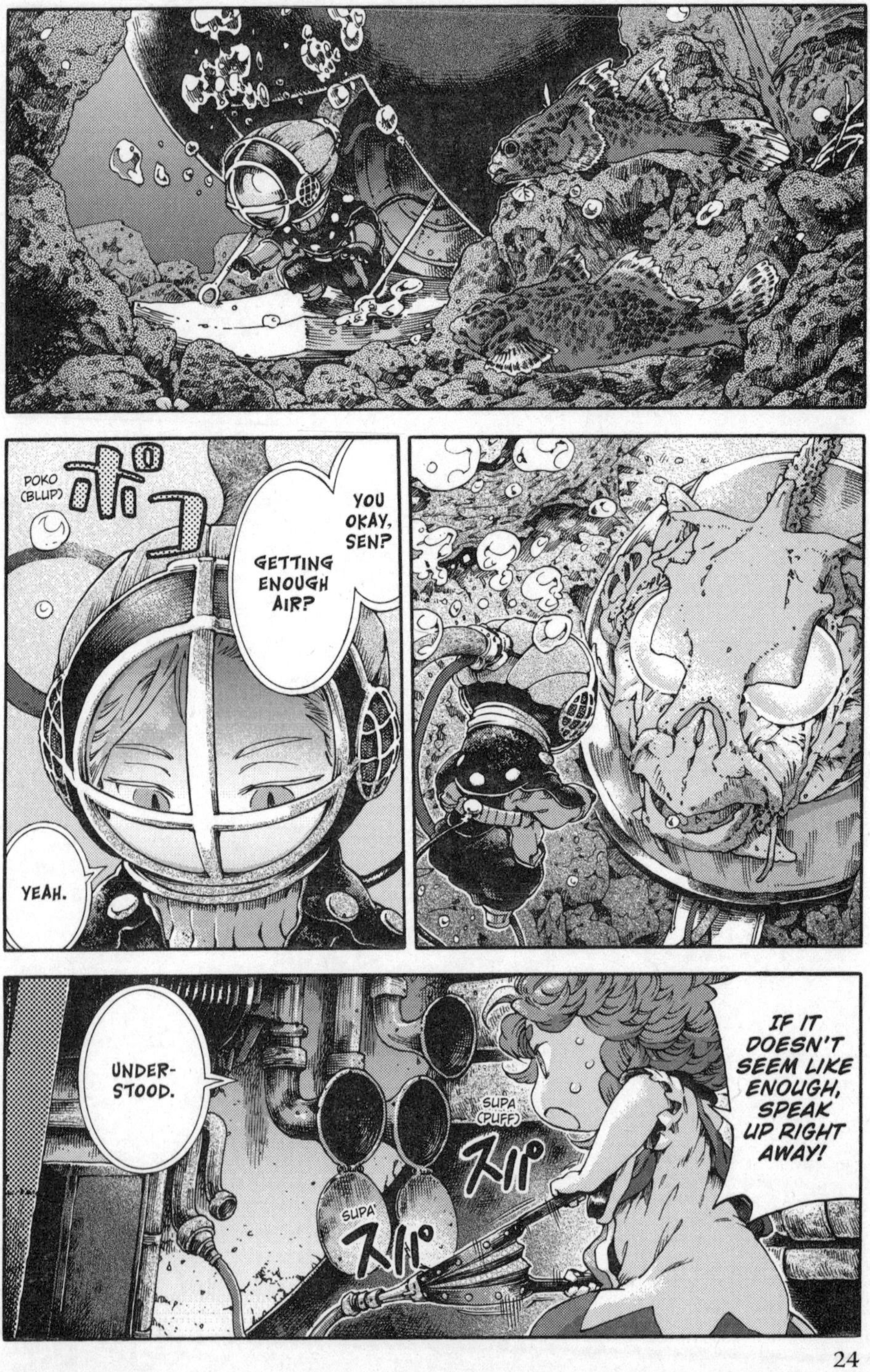
YOU OKAY, SEN? GETTING ENOUGH AIR?
POKO (BLUP)
ポコ
YEAH.
IF IT DOESN'T SEEM LIKE ENOUGH, SPEAK UP RIGHT AWAY!
SUPA (PUFF)
スパ
SUPA'
スパ
UNDER-STOOD.

NOW, THEN.

WHAT'S WRONG...

...SIMON?

SORRY FOR MAKING YOU HELP...

...WHEN YOU AREN'T FEELING WELL, HAKUMEI.

IF IT'LL GET US BACK TO THE SURFACE, I'LL DO ANYTHING!

I WONDER IF SEN'S...

...ALL RIGHT.

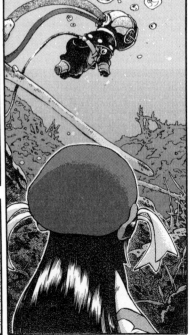

AND THEN...

...THERE'S THIS ONE...

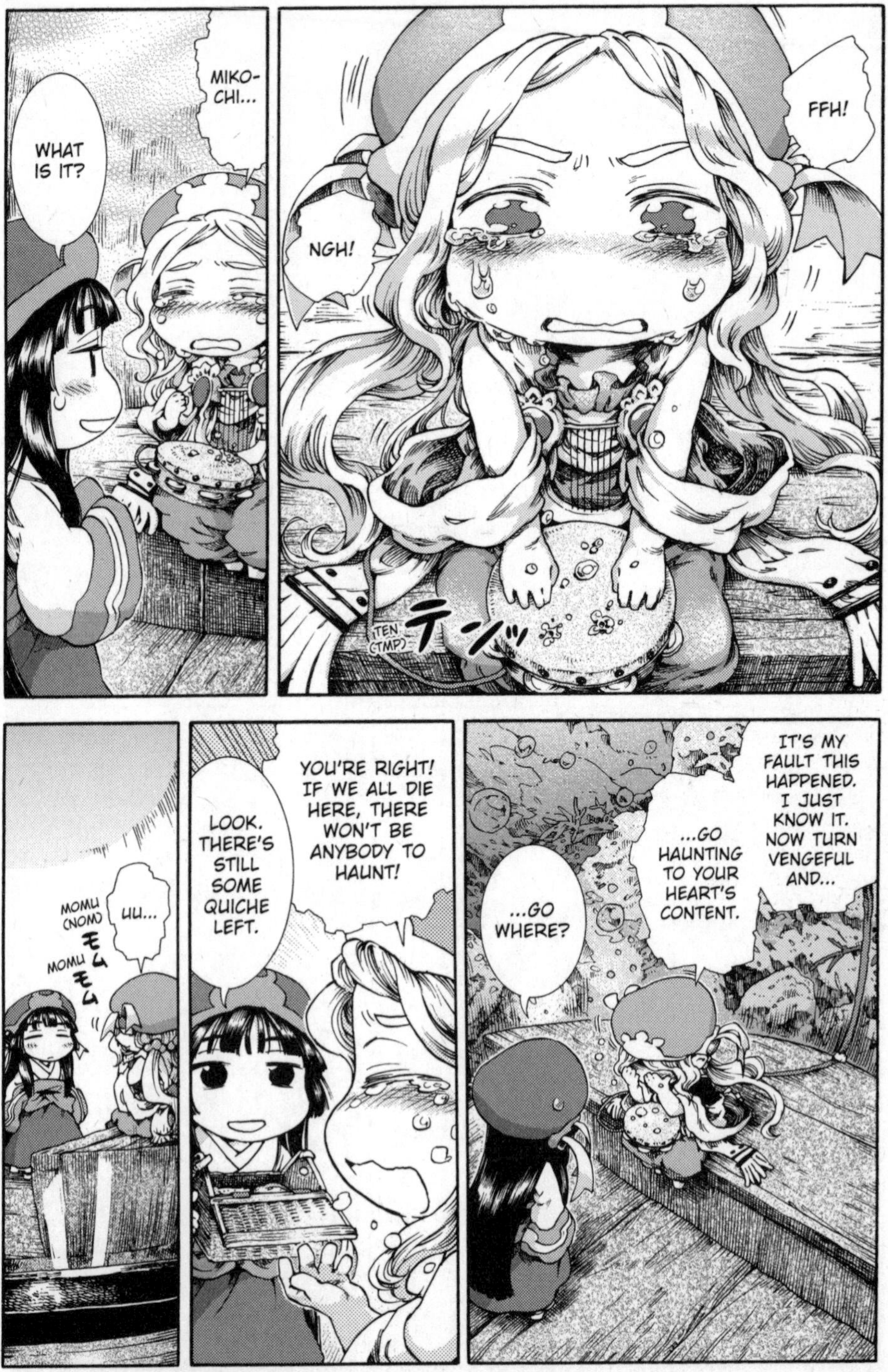
FFH!
NGH!
テンッ
TEN (TMP)
MIKO-CHI...
WHAT IS IT?
IT'S MY FAULT THIS HAPPENED. I JUST KNOW IT. NOW TURN VENGEFUL AND...
...GO HAUNTING TO YOUR HEART'S CONTENT.
...GO WHERE?
YOU'RE RIGHT! IF WE ALL DIE HERE, THERE WON'T BE ANYBODY TO HAUNT!
LOOK. THERE'S STILL SOME QUICHE LEFT.
UU...
MOMU (NOM) モム
MOMU モム

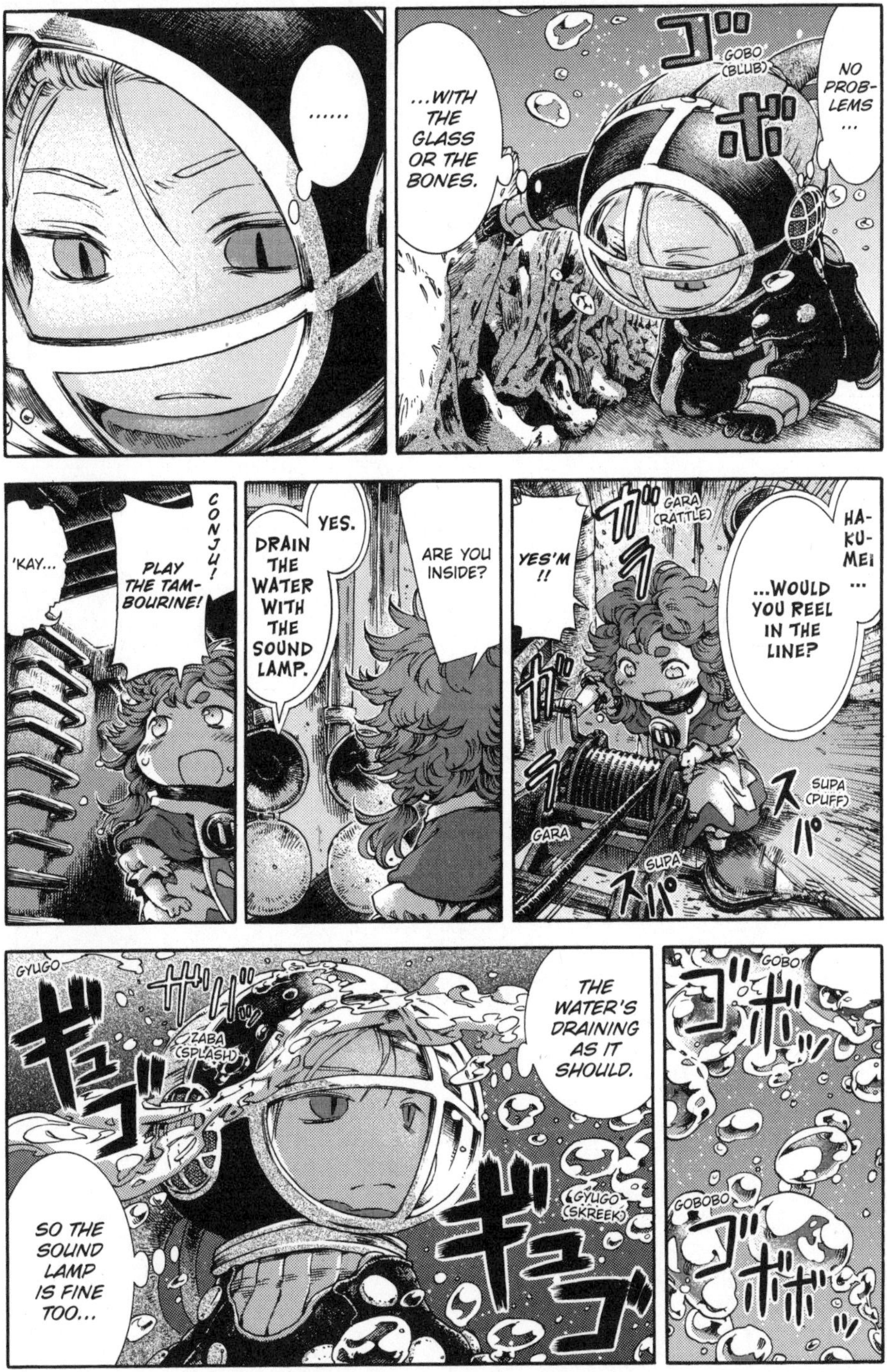

NO PROBLEMS...
GOBO (BLUB)
...WITH THE GLASS OR THE BONES.
......
HAKUMEI...
...WOULD YOU REEL IN THE LINE?
GARA (RATTLE)
YES'M!!
SUPA (PUFF)
GARA
SUPA
ARE YOU INSIDE?
YES.
DRAIN THE WATER WITH THE SOUND LAMP.
CONJU!
PLAY THE TAMBOURINE!
'KAY...
GOBO
GOBOBO
THE WATER'S DRAINING AS IT SHOULD.
GYUGO
ZABA (SPLASH)
GYUGO (SKREEK)
SO THE SOUND LAMP IS FINE TOO...

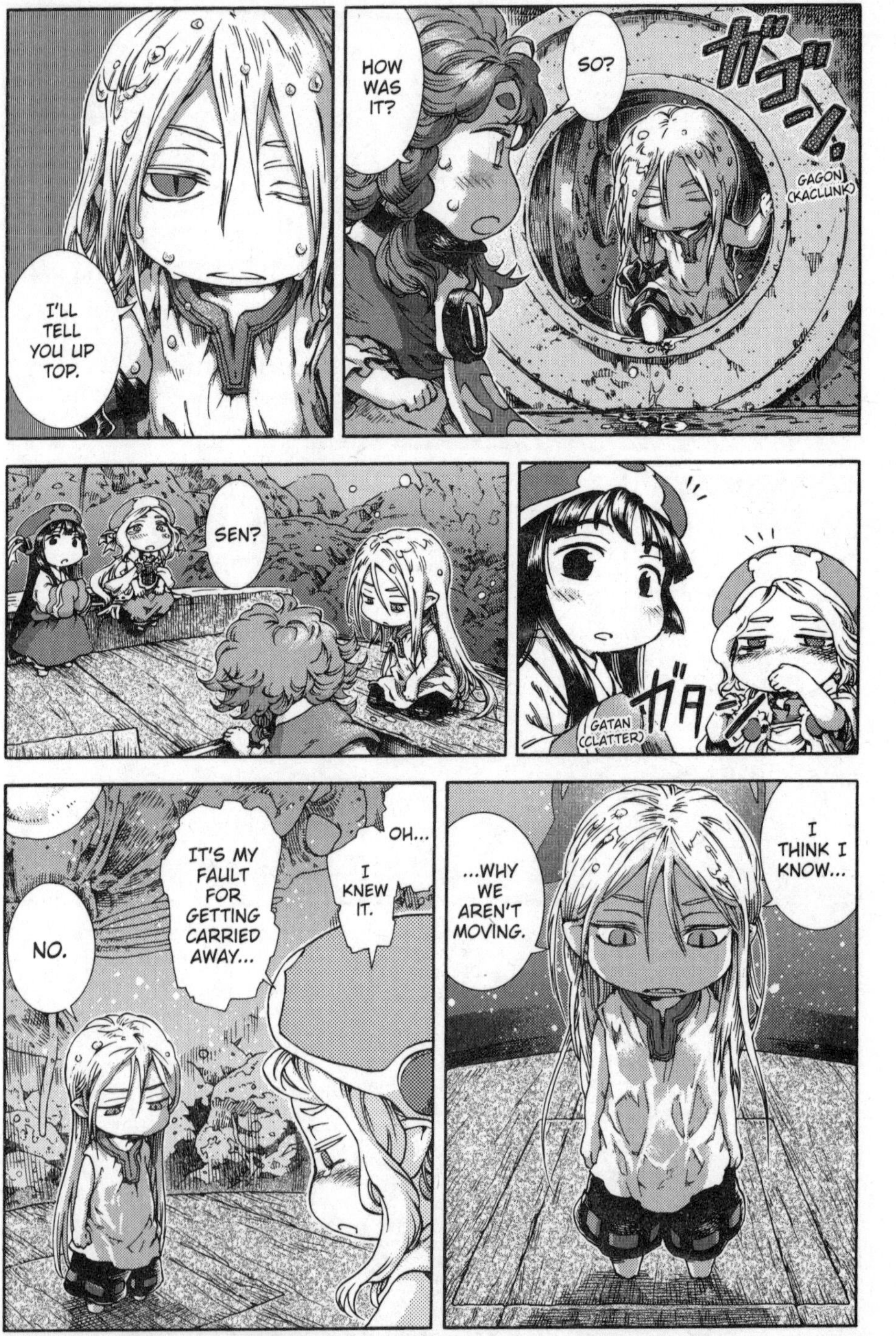
ガゴン。
GAGON (KACLUNK)
SO?
HOW WAS IT?
I'LL TELL YOU UP TOP.
ガタ
GATAN (CLATTER)
SEN?
I THINK I KNOW...
...WHY WE AREN'T MOVING.
OH...
I KNEW IT.
IT'S MY FAULT FOR GETTING CARRIED AWAY...
NO.

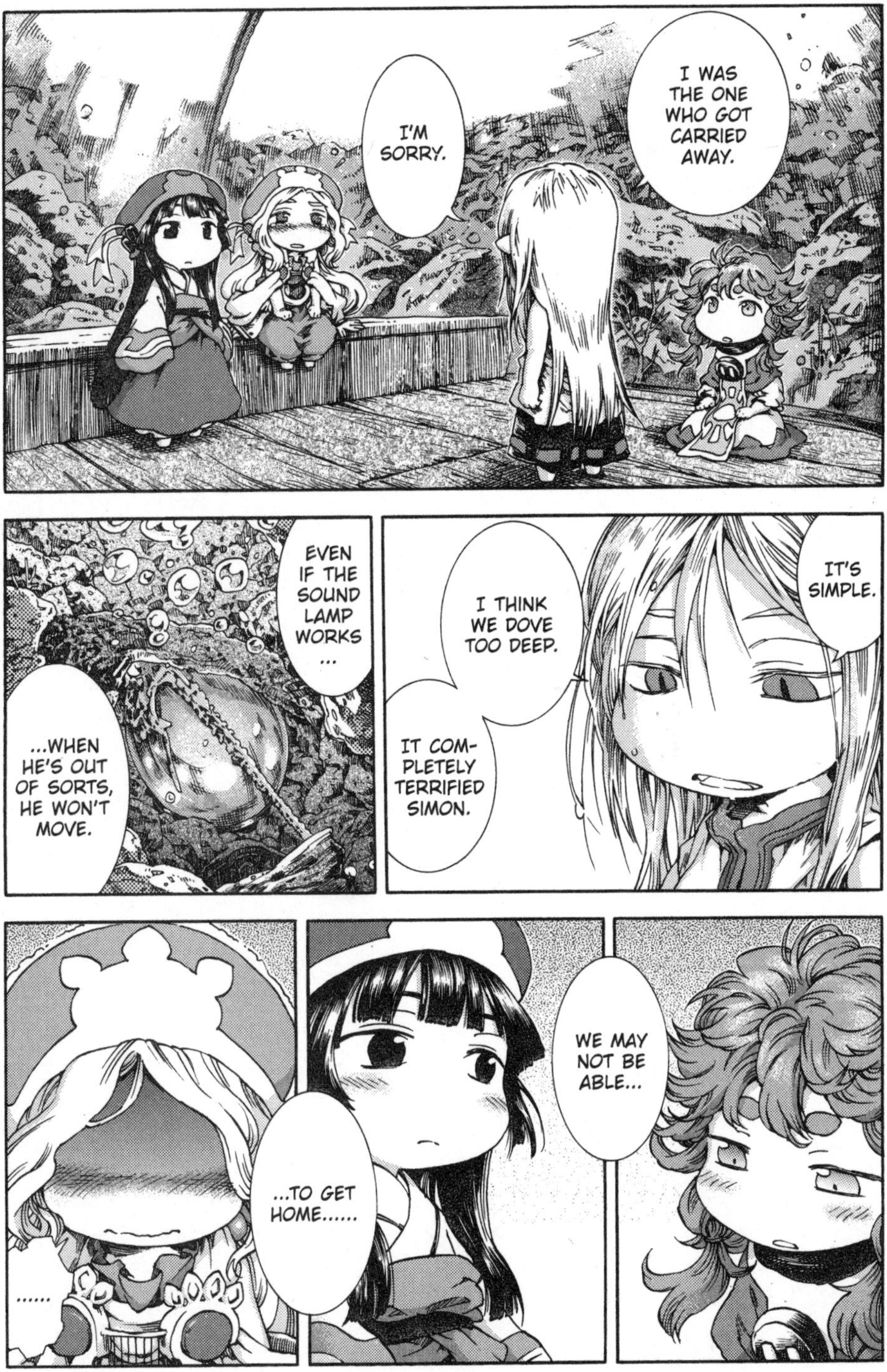
I WAS THE ONE WHO GOT CARRIED AWAY.
I'M SORRY.
IT'S SIMPLE.
I THINK WE DOVE TOO DEEP.
IT COM-PLETELY TERRIFIED SIMON.
EVEN IF THE SOUND LAMP WORKS ...
...WHEN HE'S OUT OF SORTS, HE WON'T MOVE.
WE MAY NOT BE ABLE...
...TO GET HOME......
......

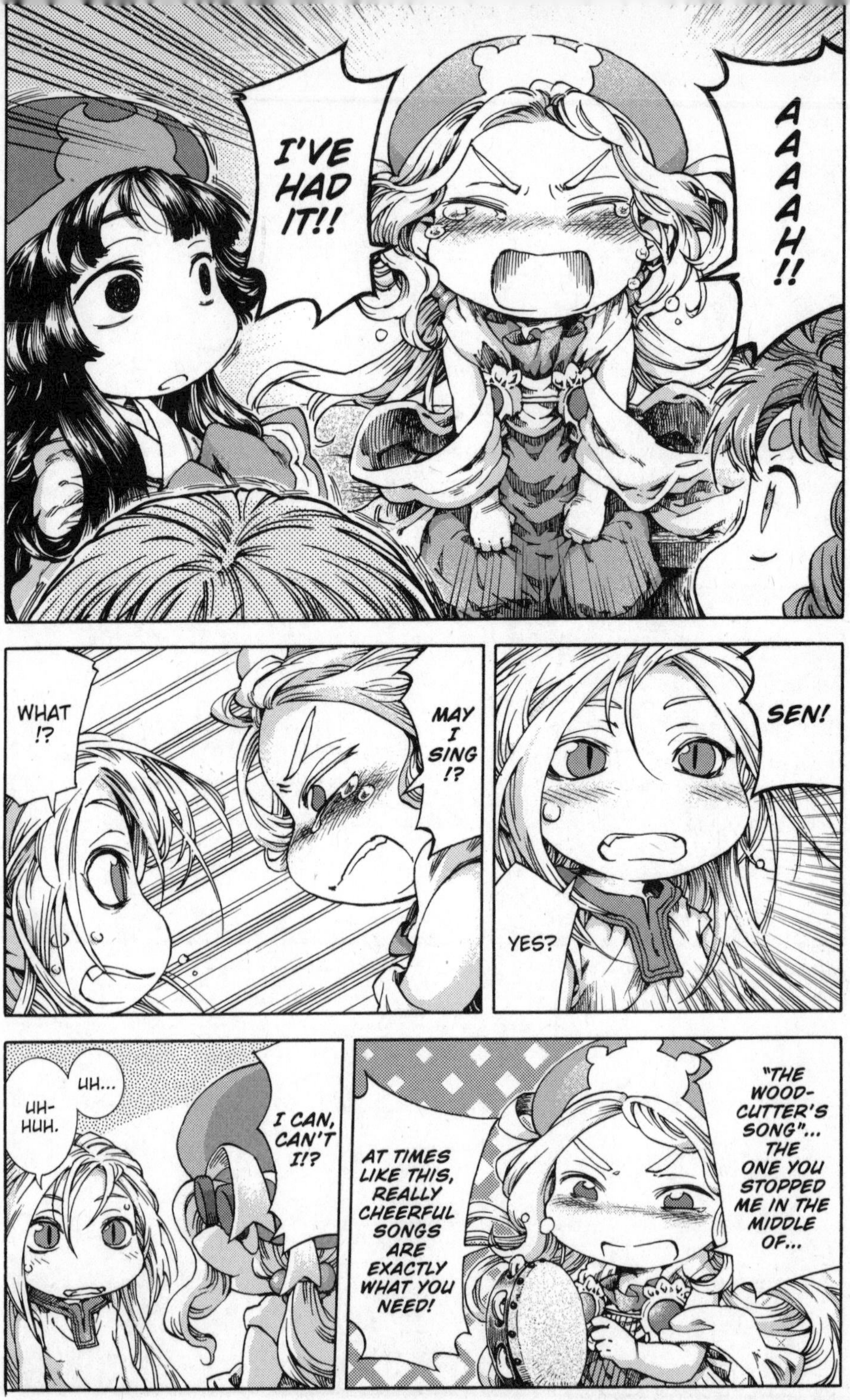
AAAAAH!!
I'VE HAD IT!!
SEN!
YES?
MAY I SING!?
WHAT!?
"THE WOOD-CUTTER'S SONG"... THE ONE YOU STOPPED ME IN THE MIDDLE OF...
AT TIMES LIKE THIS, REALLY CHEERFUL SONGS ARE EXACTLY WHAT YOU NEED!
I CAN, CAN'T I!?
UH...
UH-HUH.

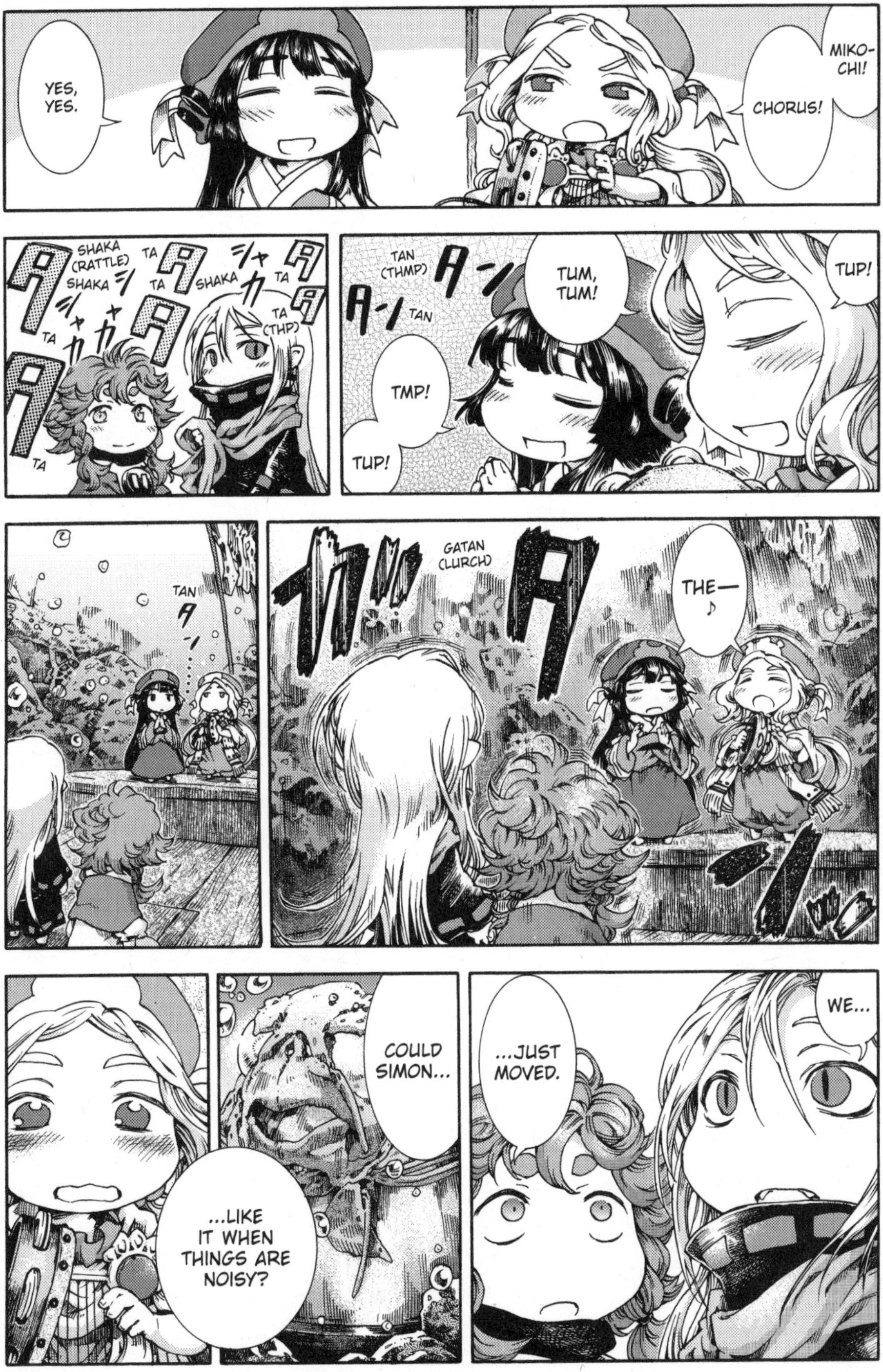
MIKO-CHI!
CHORUS!
YES, YES.
TUP!
TUM, TUM!
TAN (THMP)
TAN
TMP!
TUP!
TA (THP)
TA
SHAKA
TA
SHAKA (RATTLE)
SHAKA
TA
TA
TA
THE—♪
GATAN (LURCH)
TAN
WE...
...JUST MOVED.
COULD SIMON...
...LIKE IT WHEN THINGS ARE NOISY?

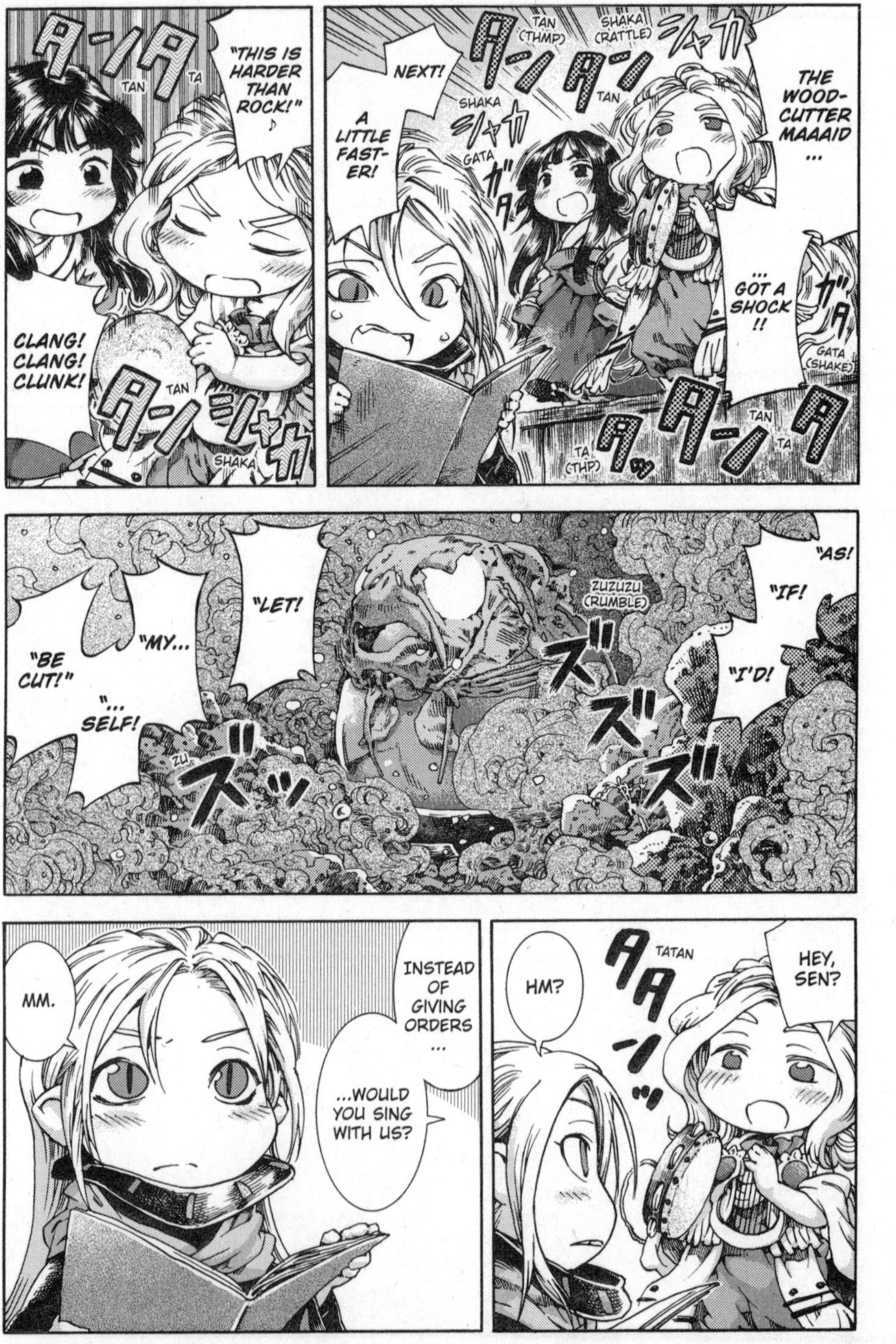
THE WOOD-CUTTER MAAAID ...
SHAKA (RATTLE)
TAN (THMP)
NEXT!
TAN
SHAKA
A LITTLE FASTER!
GATA
... GOT A SHOCK !!
GATA (SHAKE)
TAN
TA
TA (THP)
"THIS IS HARDER THAN ROCK!" ♪
TA
TAN
CLANG! CLANG! CLUNK!
TAN
SHAKA
"AS!
"IF!
"I'D!
ZUZUZU (RUMBLE)
"LET!
"MY...
"... SELF!
"BE CUT!"
ZU
HEY, SEN?
TATAN
HM?
INSTEAD OF GIVING ORDERS ...
...WOULD YOU SING WITH US?
MM.

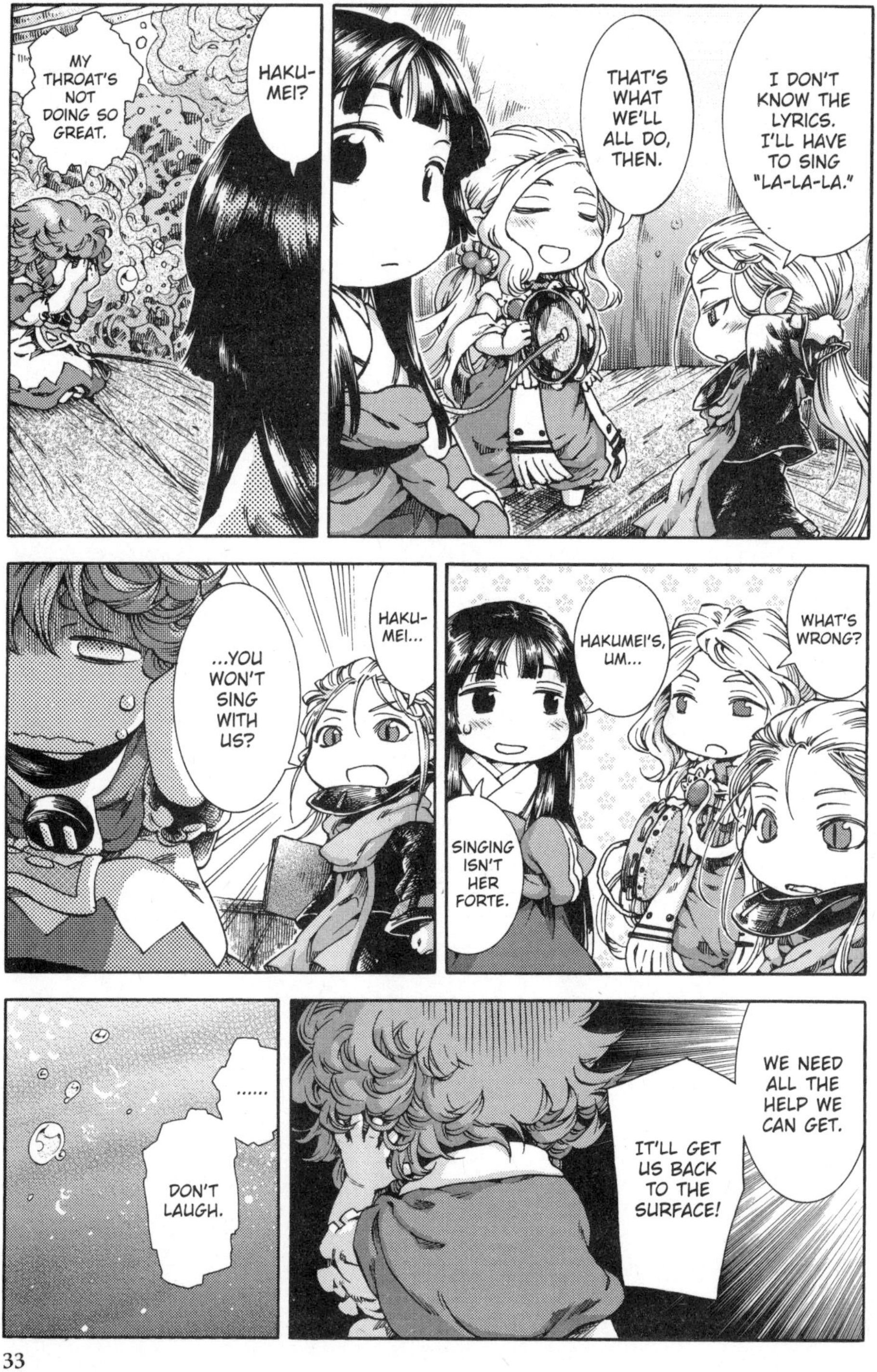
I DON'T KNOW THE LYRICS. I'LL HAVE TO SING "LA-LA-LA."
THAT'S WHAT WE'LL ALL DO, THEN.
HAKU-MEI?
MY THROAT'S NOT DOING SO GREAT.
WHAT'S WRONG?
HAKUMEI'S, UM...
SINGING ISN'T HER FORTE.
HAKU-MEI...
...YOU WON'T SING WITH US?
WE NEED ALL THE HELP WE CAN GET.
IT'LL GET US BACK TO THE SURFACE!
......
DON'T LAUGH.

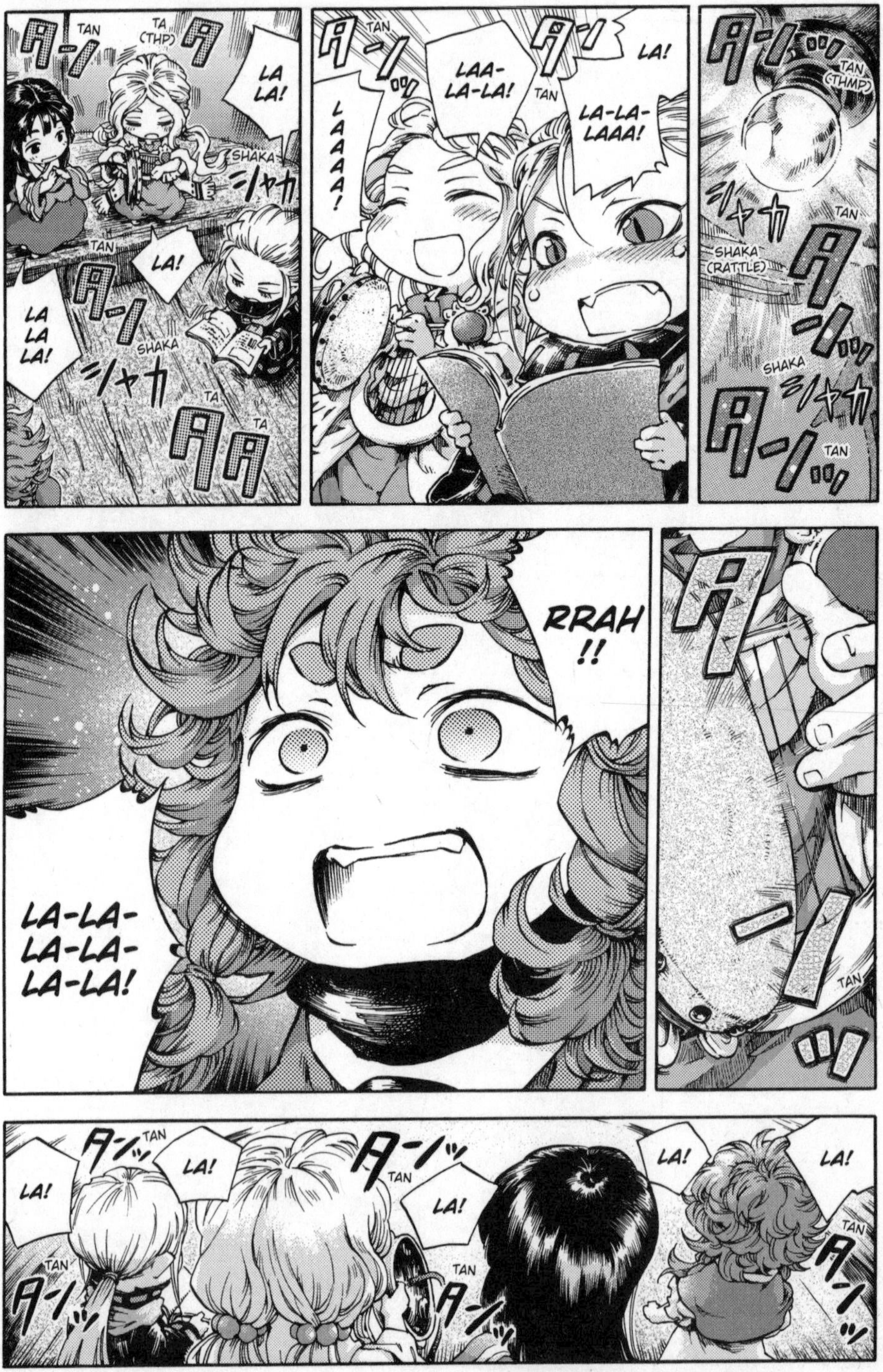
TAN
(THMP)
SHAKA
(RATTLE)
TAN
SHAKA
TAN
LA!
LA-LA-
LAAA!
TAN
LAA-
LA-LA!
LAAAAA!
TA
(THP)
TAN
LA
LA!
SHAKA
TAN
LA!
LA
LA
LA!
SHAKA
TA
TA
TAN
RRAH
!!
LA-LA-
LA-LA-
LA-LA!
LA!
TAN
LA!
TAN
LA!
TAN
LA!
TAN
LA!
TAN

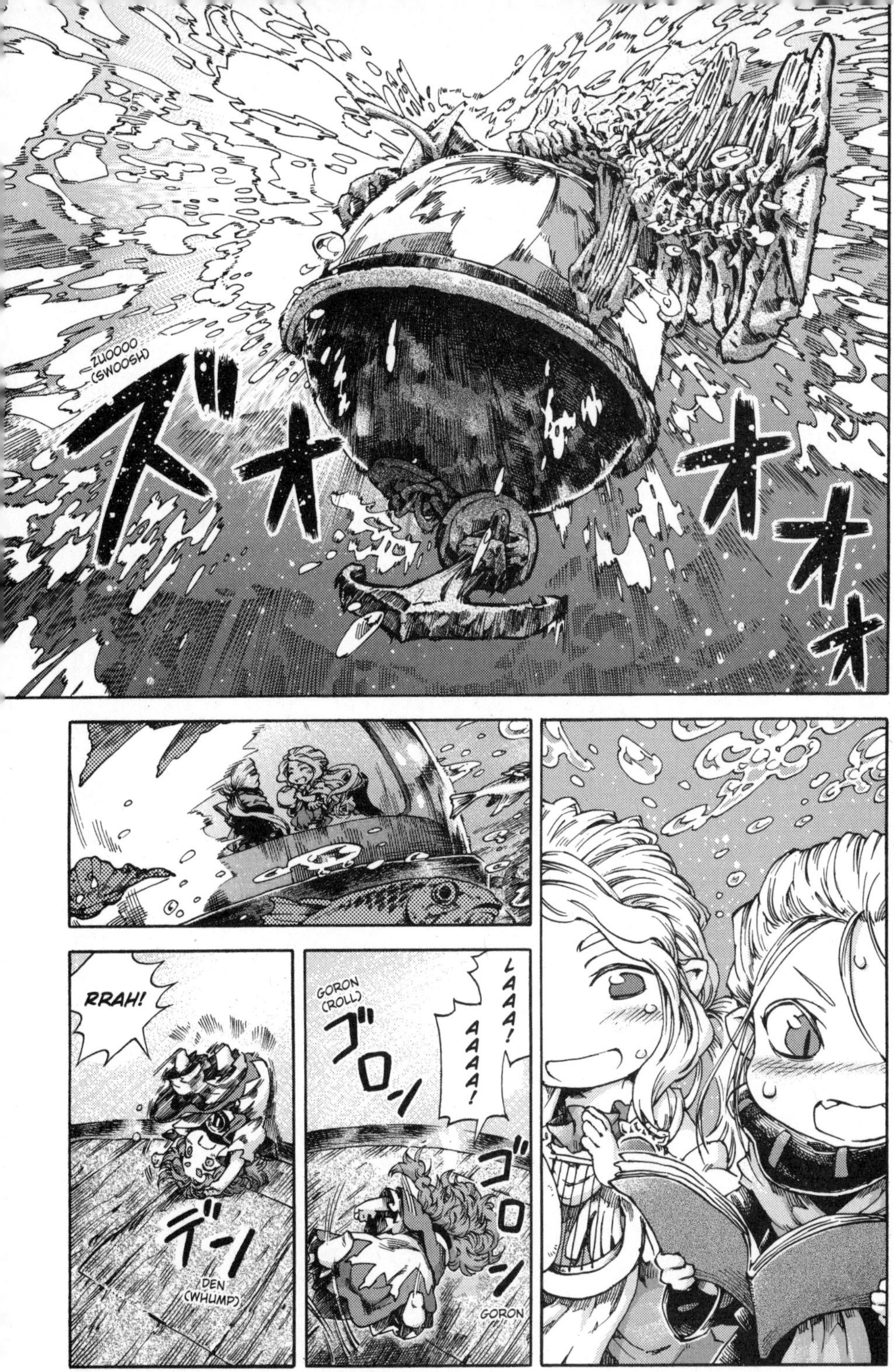
ZUOOOO (SWOOSH)
ズオオオオ
GORON (ROLL)
ゴロン
LAAAA! AAAAA!
ゴロン
GORON
RRAH!
デン
DEN (WHUMP)

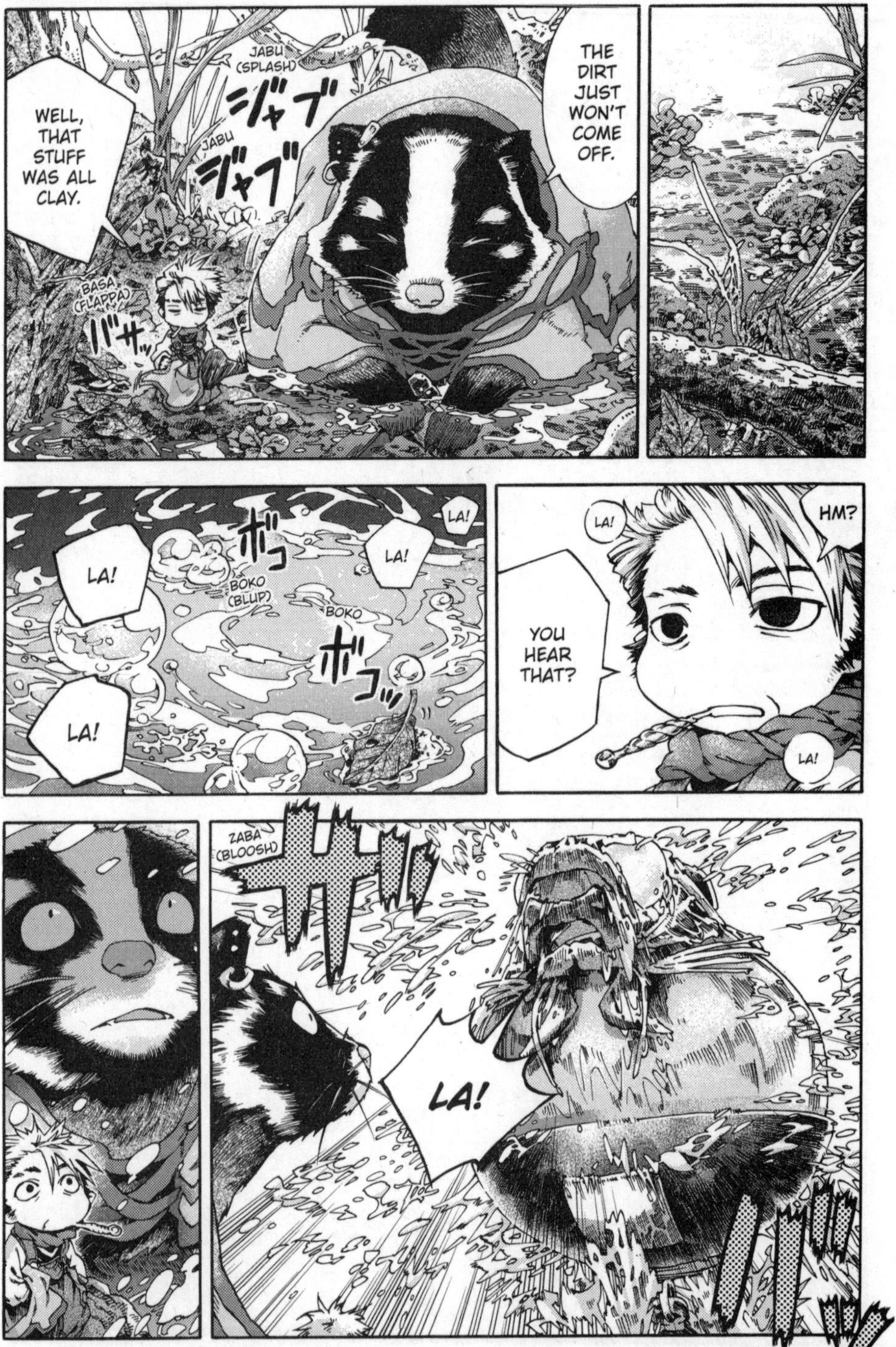

THE DIRT JUST WON'T COME OFF.
JABU (SPLASH)
ジャブ
JABU
ジャブ
WELL, THAT STUFF WAS ALL CLAY.
BASA (FLAPPA)
バサッ
HM?
LA!
YOU HEAR THAT?
LA!
LA!
LA!
ボコ
BOKO (BLUP)
LA!
BOKO
ボコッ
LA!
ZABA (BLOOSH)
LA!

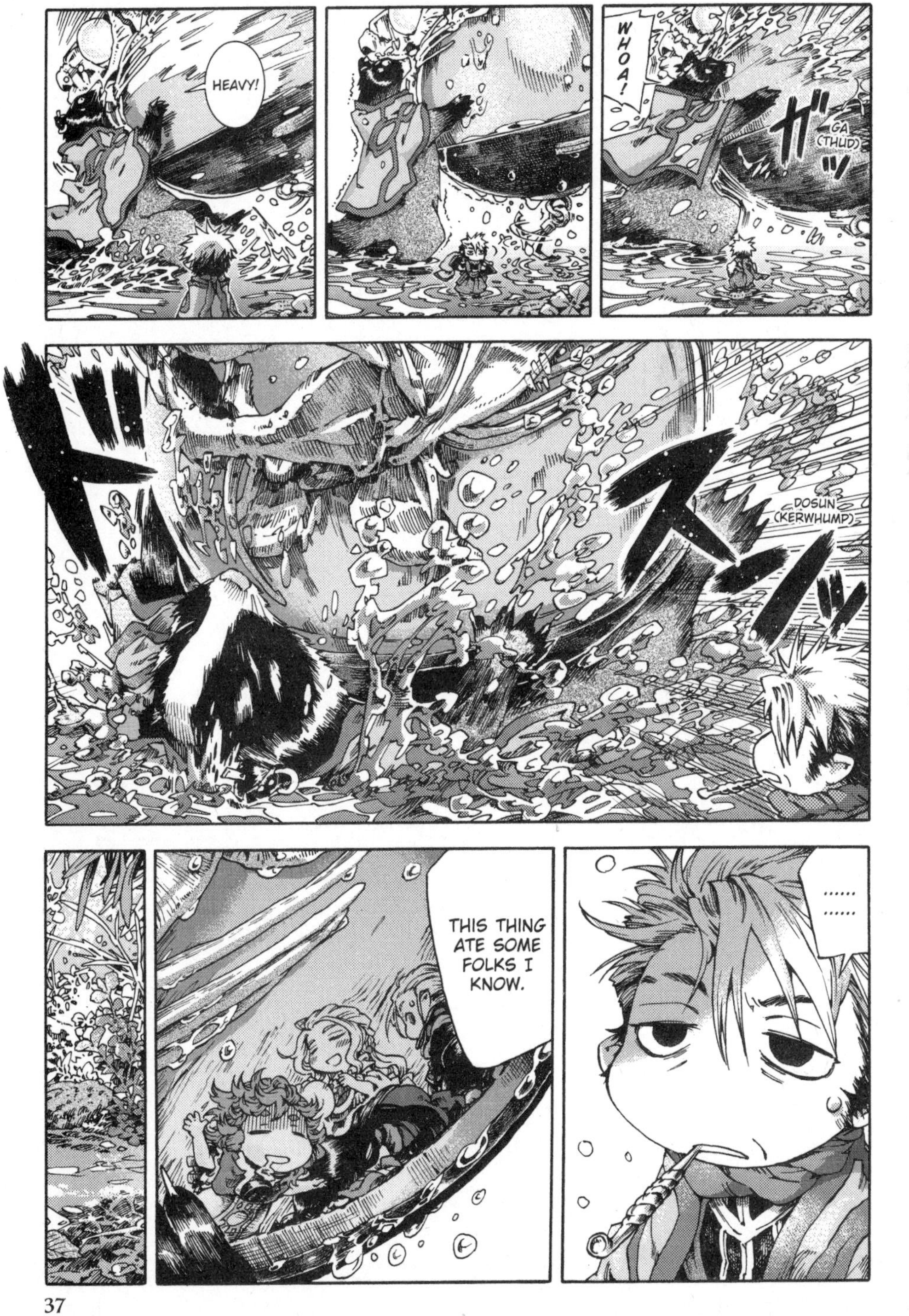
WHOA!
GA (THUD)
HEAVY!
DOSUN (KERWHUMP)
......
......
THIS THING ATE SOME FOLKS I KNOW.

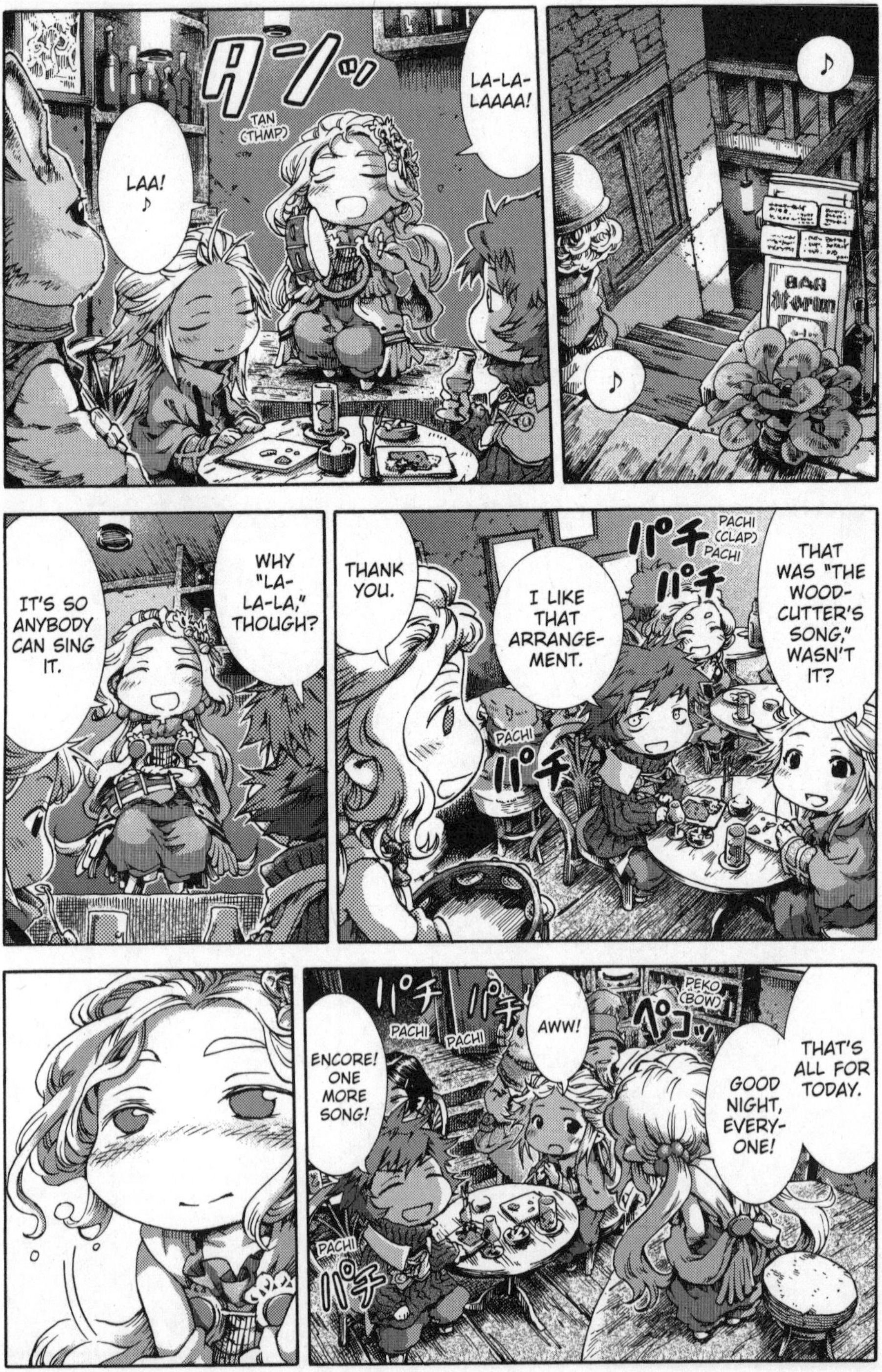
♪
♪
LA-LA-LAAAAA!
TAN (THMP)
LAA! ♪
PACHI (CLAP) PACHI
THAT WAS "THE WOODCUTTER'S SONG," WASN'T IT?
I LIKE THAT ARRANGEMENT.
PACHI
THANK YOU.
WHY "LA-LA-LA," THOUGH?
IT'S SO ANYBODY CAN SING IT.
THAT'S ALL FOR TODAY.
GOOD NIGHT, EVERYONE!
PEKO (BOW)
AWW!
PACHI
PACHI
ENCORE! ONE MORE SONG!
PACHI

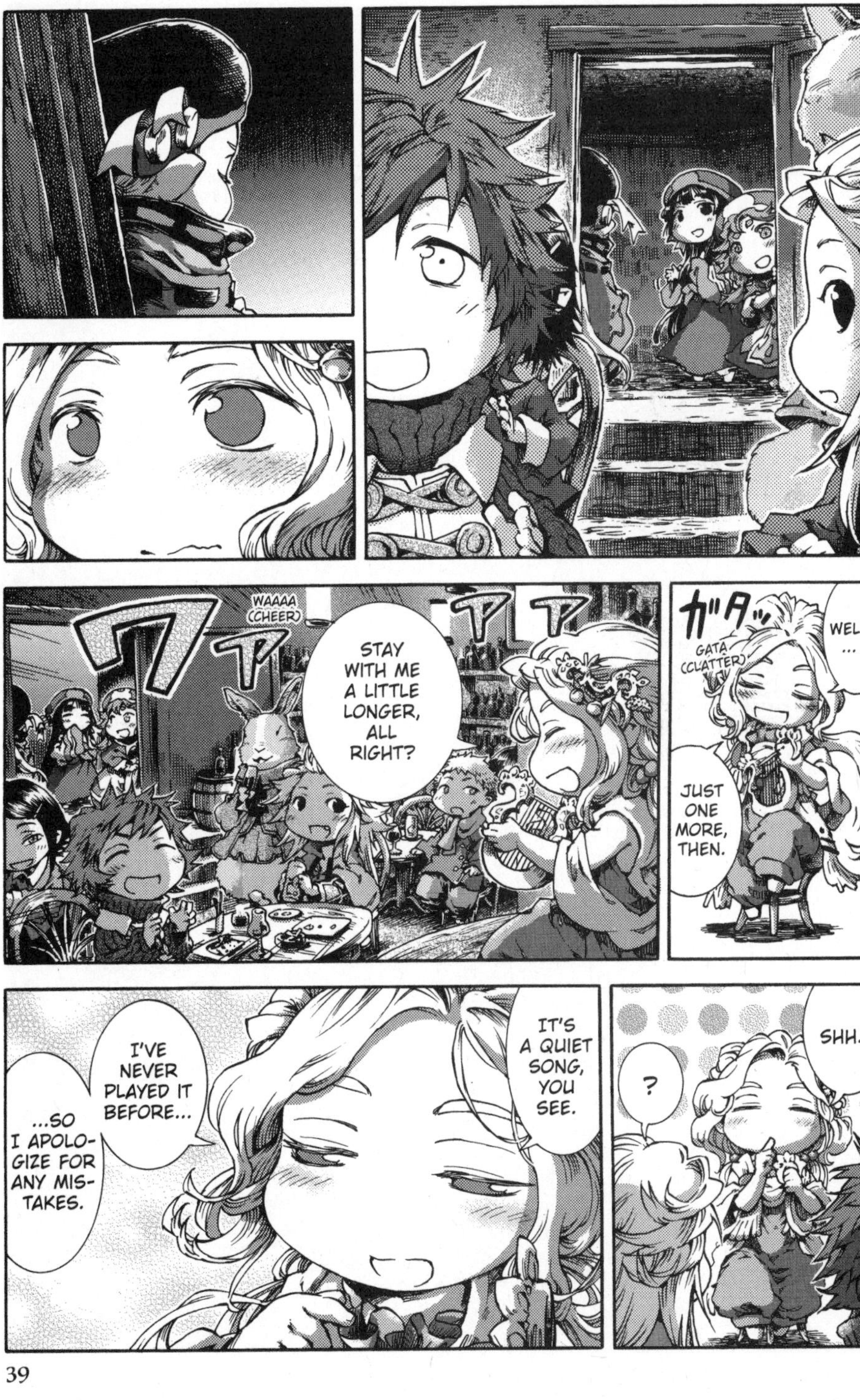
ガタッ
GATA (CLATTER)
WELL ...
JUST ONE MORE, THEN.
ワァァァ
WAAAA (CHEER)
STAY WITH ME A LITTLE LONGER, ALL RIGHT?
SHH.
?
IT'S A QUIET SONG, YOU SEE.
I'VE NEVER PLAYED IT BEFORE...
...SO I APOLOGIZE FOR ANY MISTAKES.

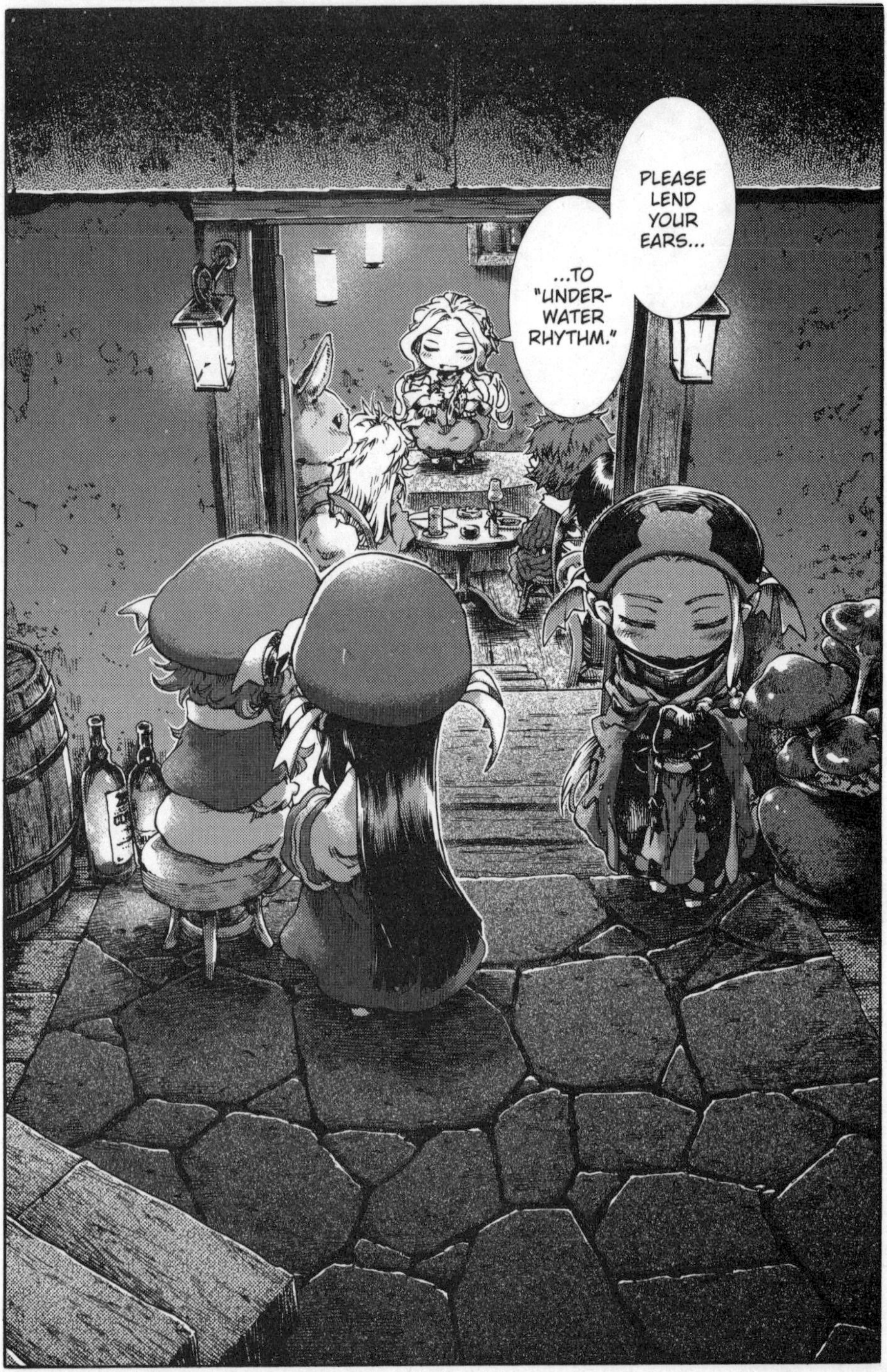
PLEASE LEND YOUR EARS...
...TO "UNDER-WATER RHYTHM."

Chapter 20 • End

"The Woodcutter's Song" is a folk ballad from the Yuen region. It has its origins in the call-and-response shouts between laborers, and it's believed that it didn't initially have lyrics. The tune is extraordinarily cheerful and jaunty, and it's still a favorite of workers.

As bards and artists from Yuen continued to sing it over generations, the ballad acquired lyrics, but the details vary from singer to singer. The most common version is a witty dialogue between a young female woodcutter and an old evergreen oak that has acquired a will of its own, but there are lyrics which recast the oak as a young male landowner. In this case, the melody changes dramatically, and it's transformed into a slow song of dark love and loneliness.

Chapter 21
A Scream and a Bed

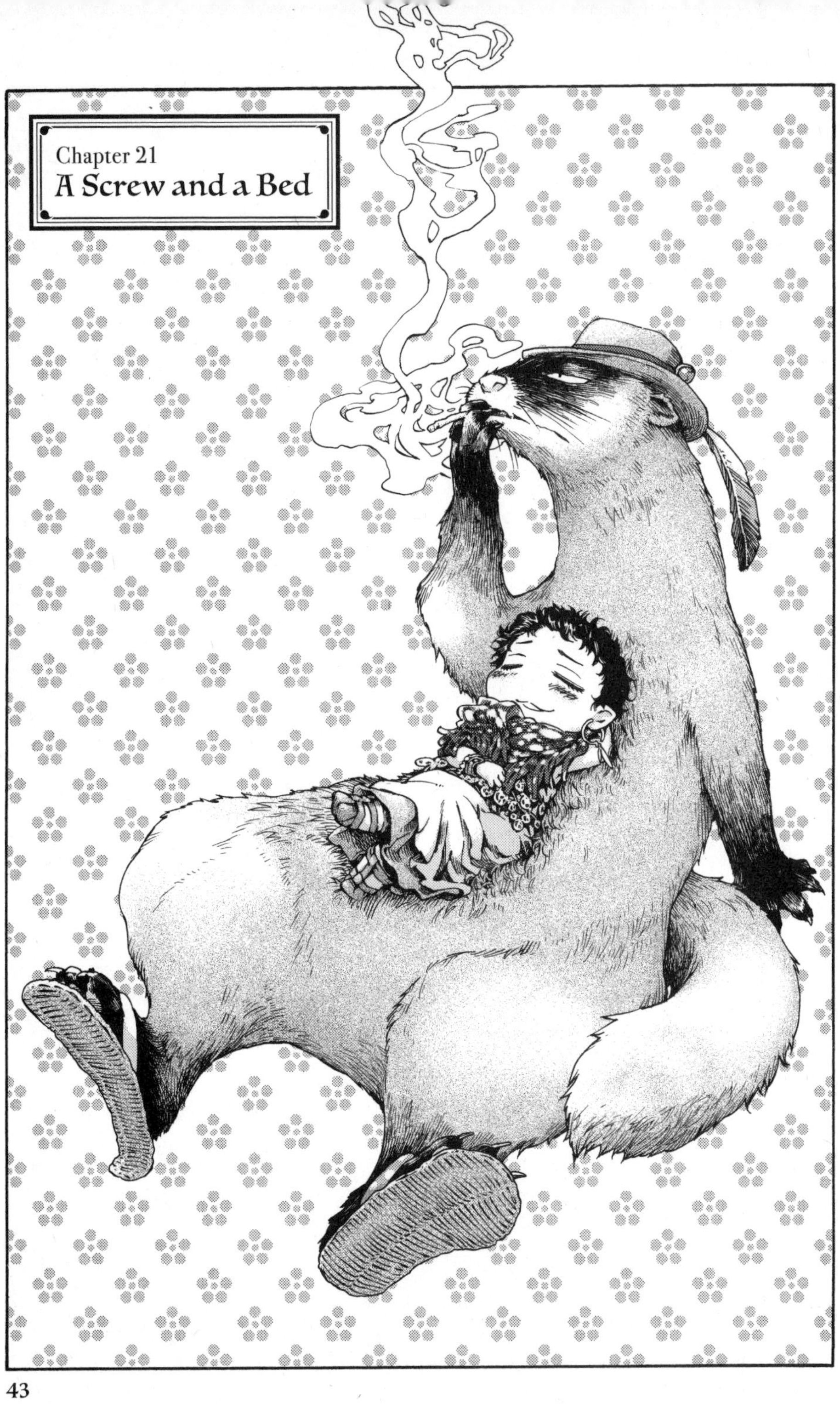

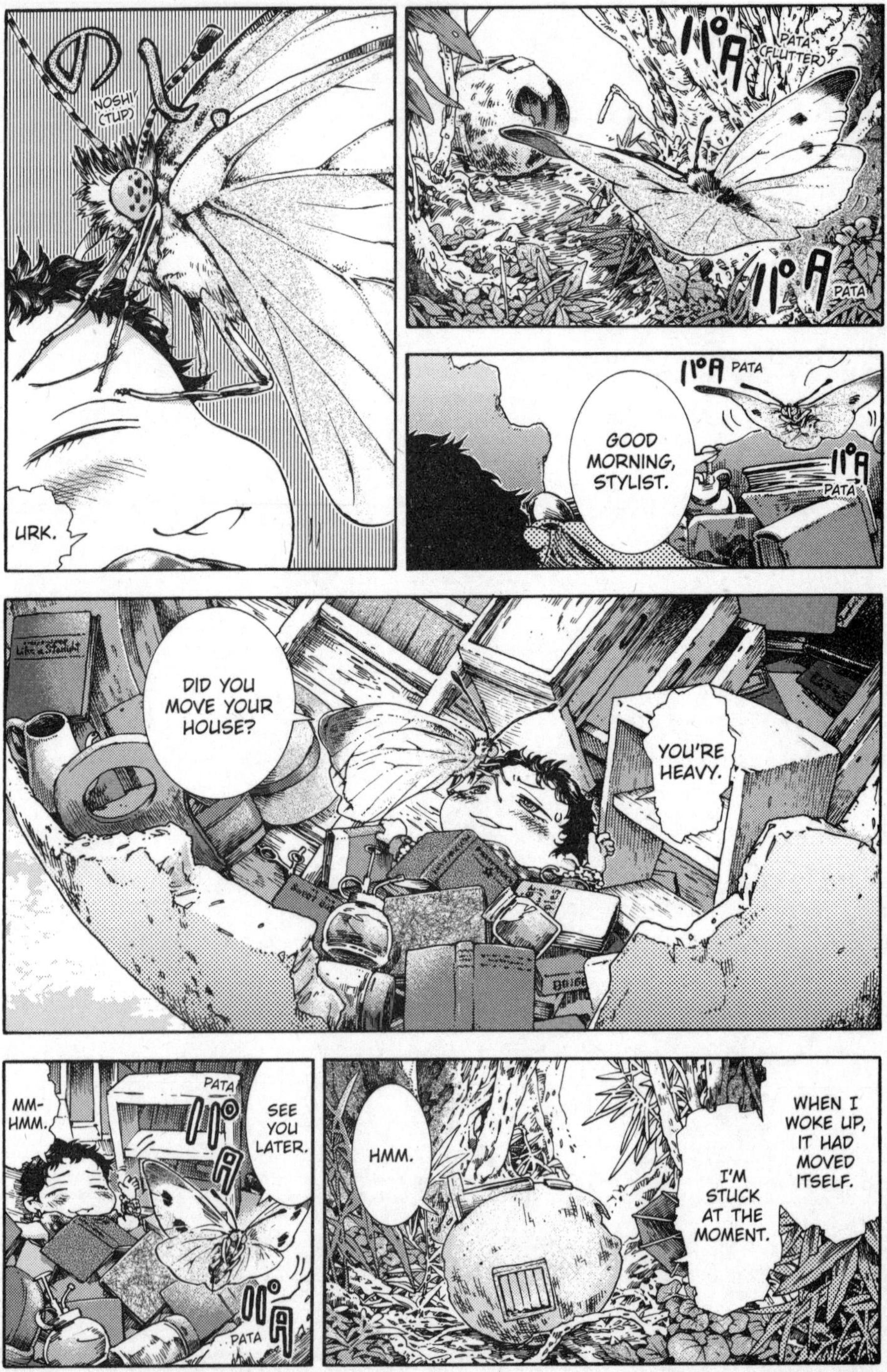
PATA (FLUTTER)
PATA
PATA
GOOD MORNING, STYLIST.
PATA
NOSHI (TUP)
URK.
YOU'RE HEAVY.
DID YOU MOVE YOUR HOUSE?
WHEN I WOKE UP, IT HAD MOVED ITSELF.
I'M STUCK AT THE MOMENT.
HMM.
PATA
SEE YOU LATER.
MM-HMM.
PATA

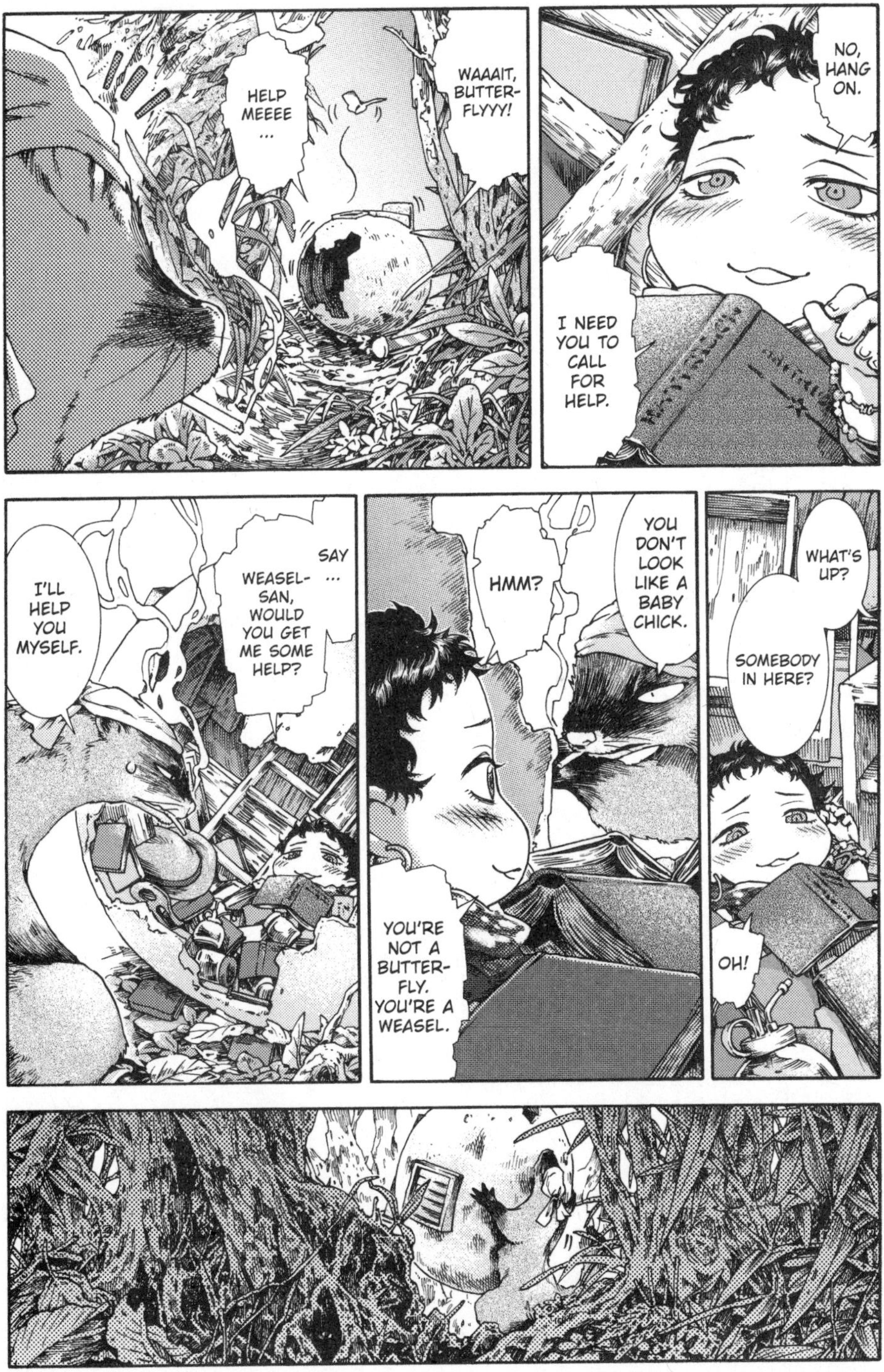
NO, HANG ON.
I NEED YOU TO CALL FOR HELP.
WAAAIT, BUTTER-FLYYY!
HELP MEEEE ...
WHAT'S UP?
SOMEBODY IN HERE?
OH!
YOU DON'T LOOK LIKE A BABY CHICK.
HMM?
YOU'RE NOT A BUTTER-FLY. YOU'RE A WEASEL.
SAY ...
WEASEL-SAN, WOULD YOU GET ME SOME HELP?
I'LL HELP YOU MYSELF.

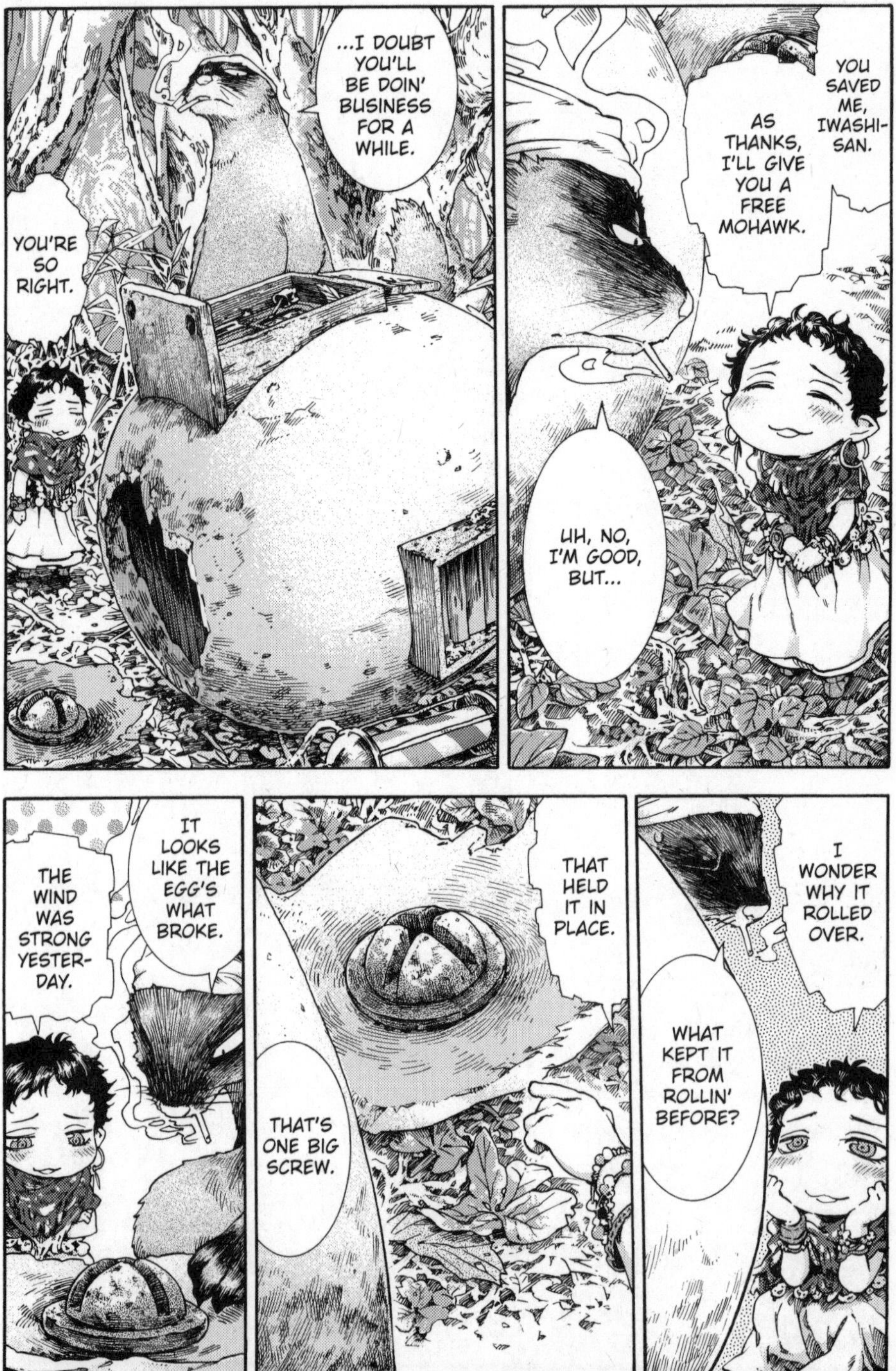
YOU SAVED ME, IWASHI-SAN.
AS THANKS, I'LL GIVE YOU A FREE MOHAWK.
UH, NO, I'M GOOD, BUT...
...I DOUBT YOU'LL BE DOIN' BUSINESS FOR A WHILE.
YOU'RE SO RIGHT.
I WONDER WHY IT ROLLED OVER.
WHAT KEPT IT FROM ROLLIN' BEFORE?
THAT HELD IT IN PLACE.
THAT'S ONE BIG SCREW.
IT LOOKS LIKE THE EGG'S WHAT BROKE.
THE WIND WAS STRONG YESTER-DAY.

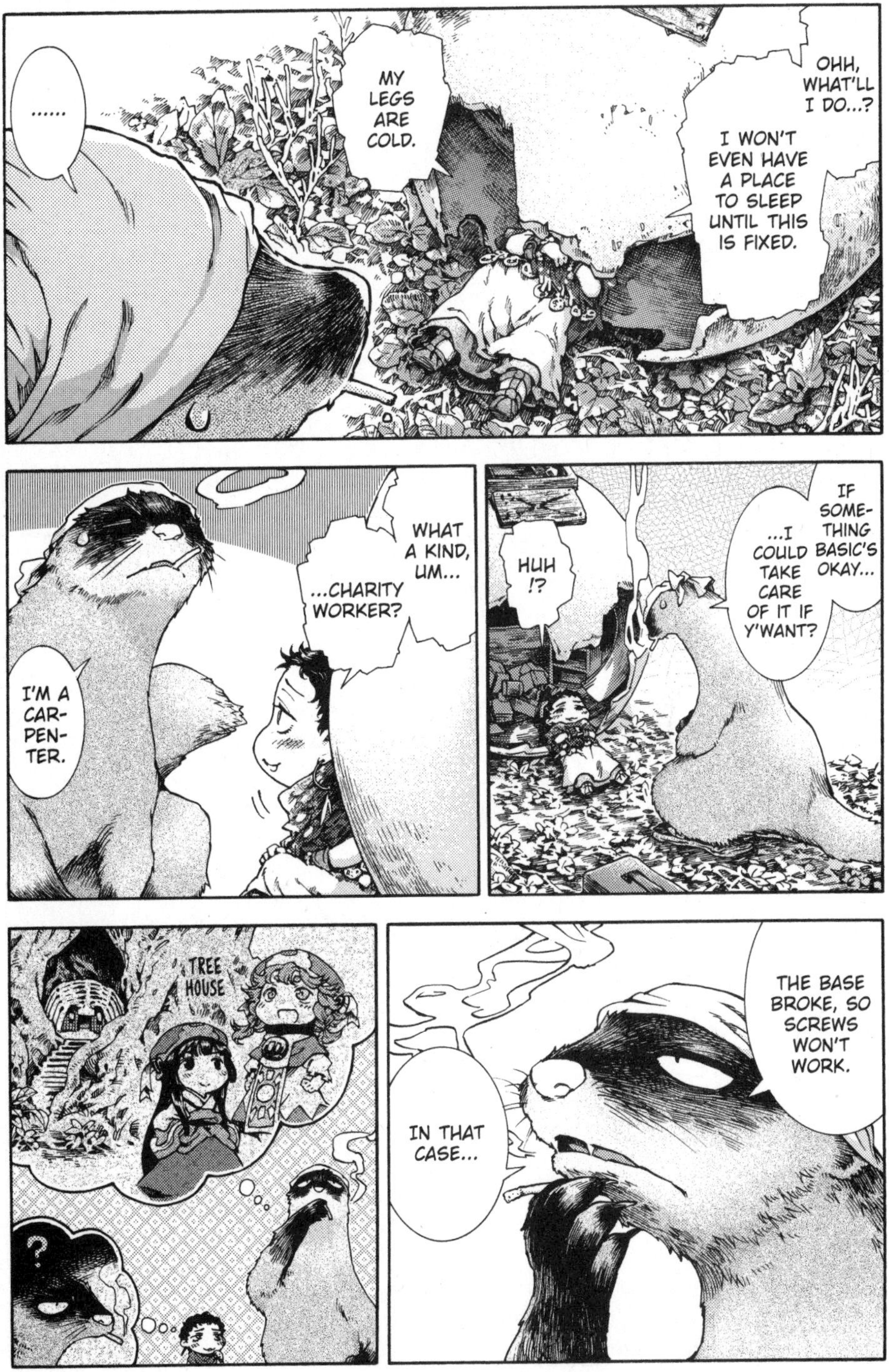
OHH, WHAT'LL I DO...?
I WON'T EVEN HAVE A PLACE TO SLEEP UNTIL THIS IS FIXED.
MY LEGS ARE COLD.
......
IF SOME-THING BASIC'S OKAY...
...I COULD TAKE CARE OF IT IF Y'WANT?
HUH !?
WHAT A KIND, UM...
...CHARITY WORKER?
I'M A CAR-PEN-TER.
THE BASE BROKE, SO SCREWS WON'T WORK.
IN THAT CASE...
TREE HOUSE
?

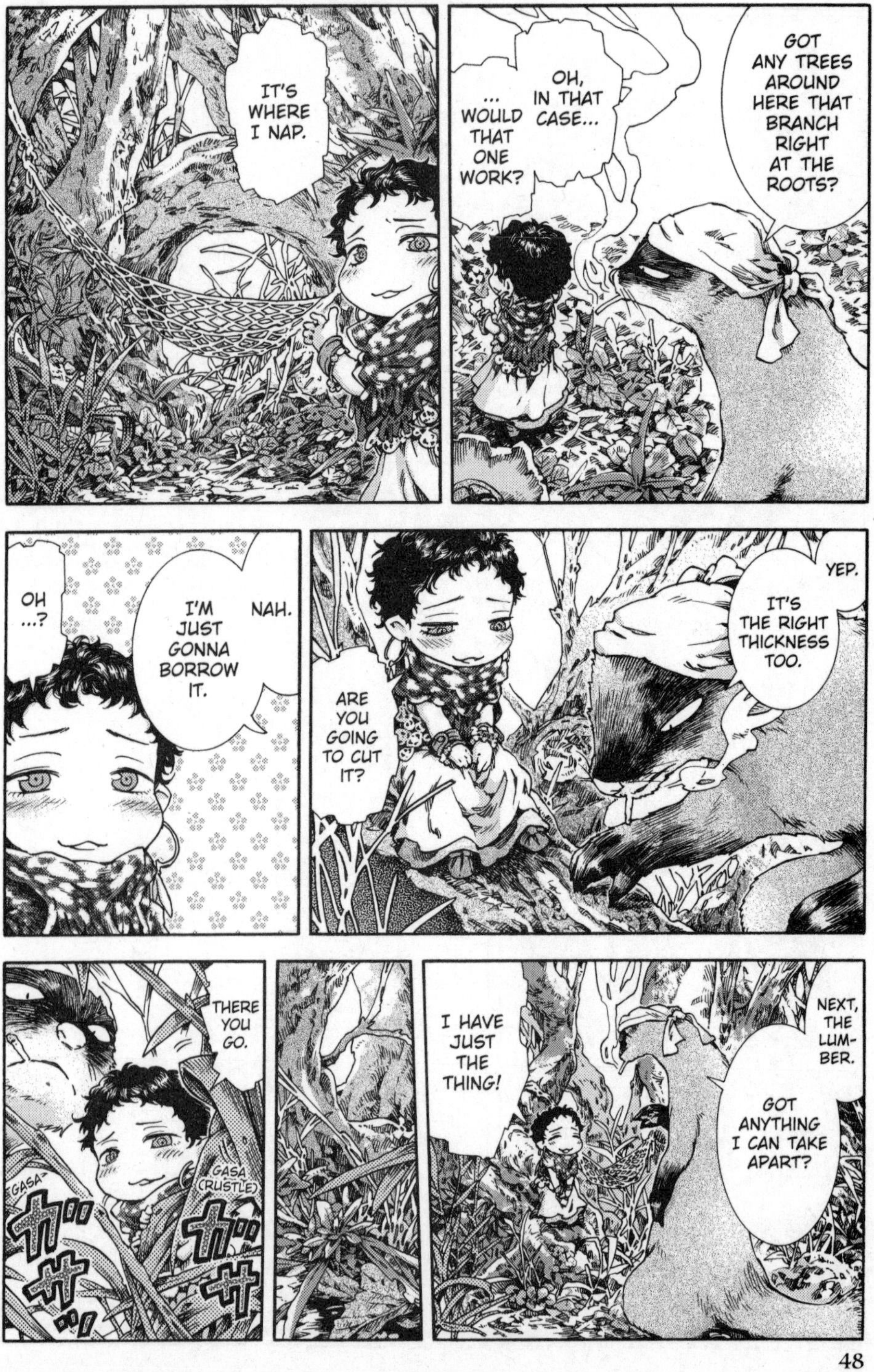
GOT ANY TREES AROUND HERE THAT BRANCH RIGHT AT THE ROOTS?
OH, IN THAT CASE...
... WOULD THAT ONE WORK?
IT'S WHERE I NAP.
YEP.
IT'S THE RIGHT THICKNESS TOO.
ARE YOU GOING TO CUT IT?
NAH.
I'M JUST GONNA BORROW IT.
OH ...?
NEXT, THE LUMBER.
GOT ANYTHING I CAN TAKE APART?
I HAVE JUST THE THING!
THERE YOU GO.
GASA (RUSTLE)
GASA

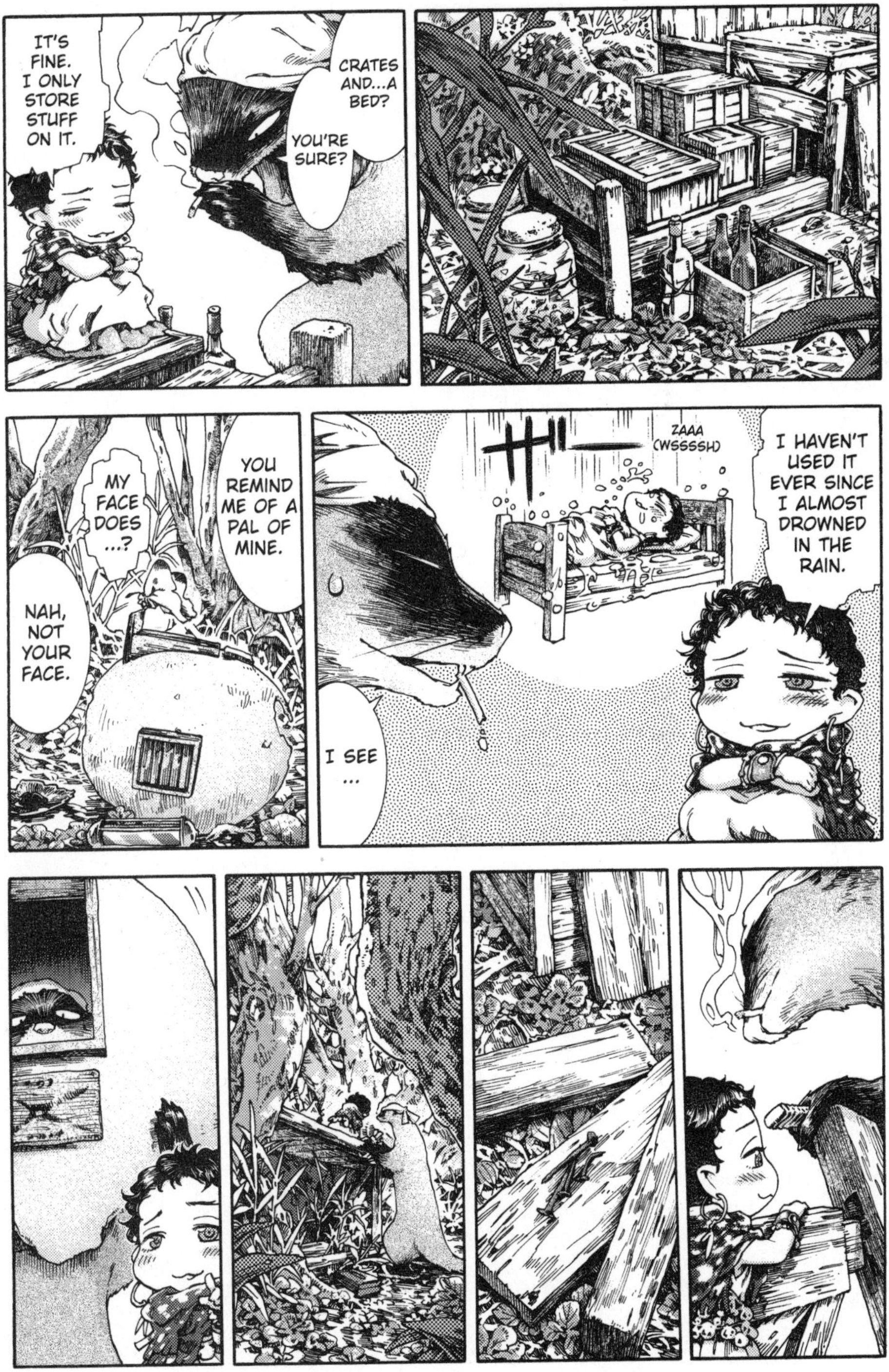
CRATES AND...A BED?
YOU'RE SURE?
IT'S FINE. I ONLY STORE STUFF ON IT.
ZAAA (WSSSSH)
I HAVEN'T USED IT EVER SINCE I ALMOST DROWNED IN THE RAIN.
I SEE ...
YOU REMIND ME OF A PAL OF MINE.
MY FACE DOES ...?
NAH, NOT YOUR FACE.

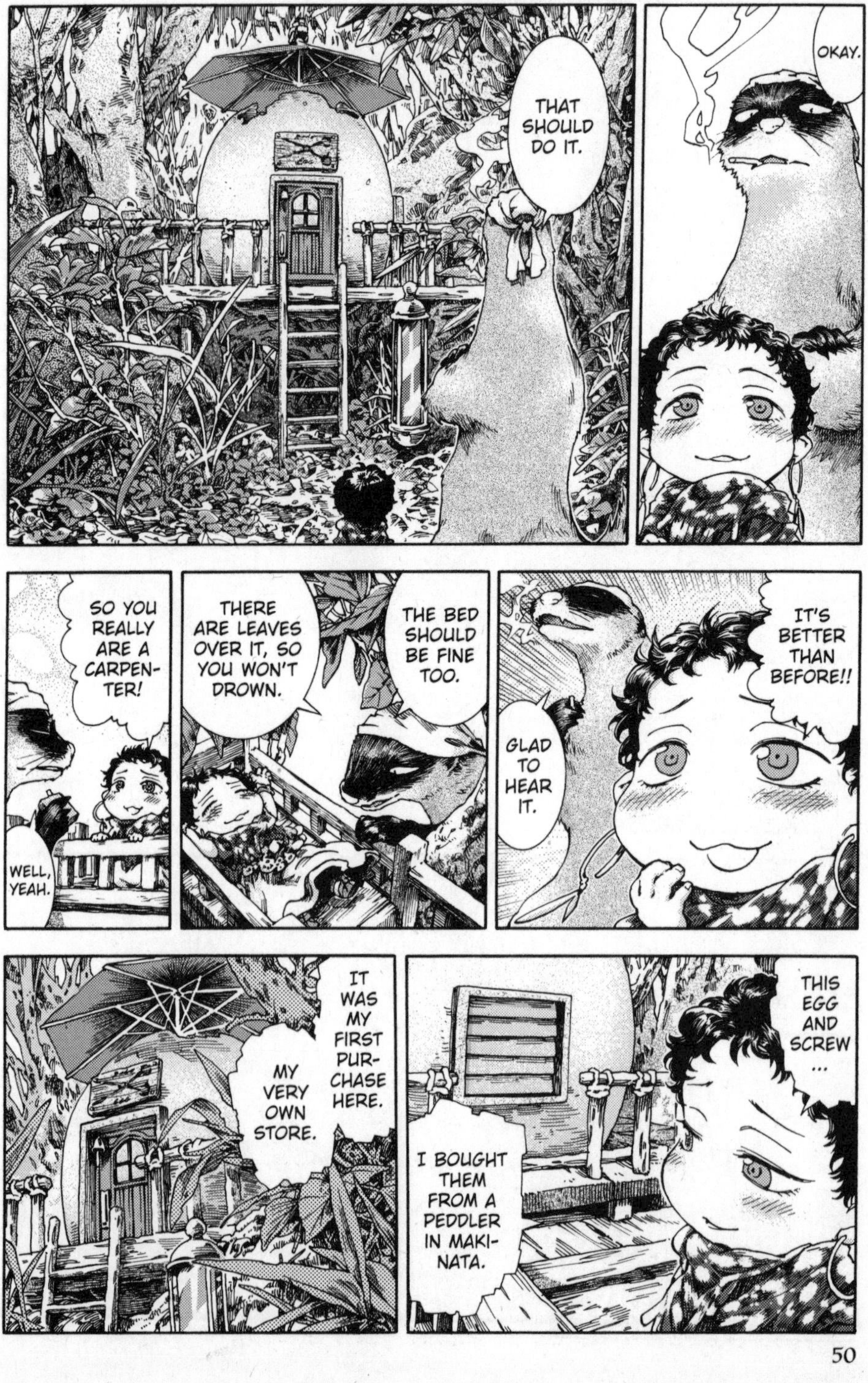
OKAY.
THAT SHOULD DO IT.
IT'S BETTER THAN BEFORE!!
GLAD TO HEAR IT.
THE BED SHOULD BE FINE TOO.
THERE ARE LEAVES OVER IT, SO YOU WON'T DROWN.
SO YOU REALLY ARE A CARPENTER!
WELL, YEAH.
THIS EGG AND SCREW...
I BOUGHT THEM FROM A PEDDLER IN MAKINATA.
IT WAS MY FIRST PURCHASE HERE.
MY VERY OWN STORE.

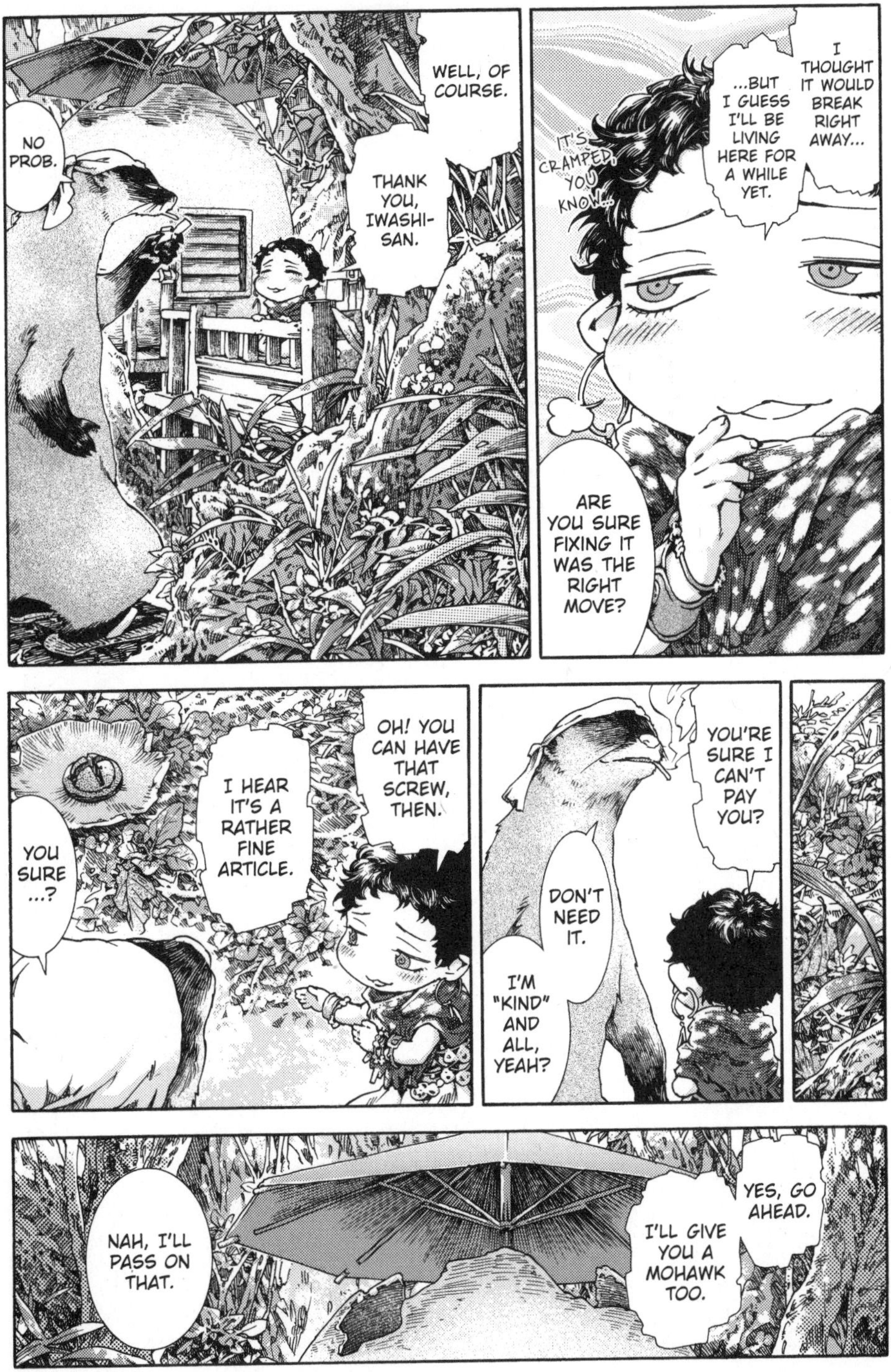
I THOUGHT IT WOULD BREAK RIGHT AWAY...
...BUT I GUESS I'LL BE LIVING HERE FOR A WHILE YET.
IT'S CRAMPED, YOU KNOW...
ARE YOU SURE FIXING IT WAS THE RIGHT MOVE?
WELL, OF COURSE.
THANK YOU, IWASHI-SAN.
NO PROB.
YOU'RE SURE I CAN'T PAY YOU?
DON'T NEED IT.
I'M "KIND" AND ALL, YEAH?
OH! YOU CAN HAVE THAT SCREW, THEN.
I HEAR IT'S A RATHER FINE ARTICLE.
YOU SURE ...?
YES, GO AHEAD.
I'LL GIVE YOU A MOHAWK TOO.
NAH, I'LL PASS ON THAT.

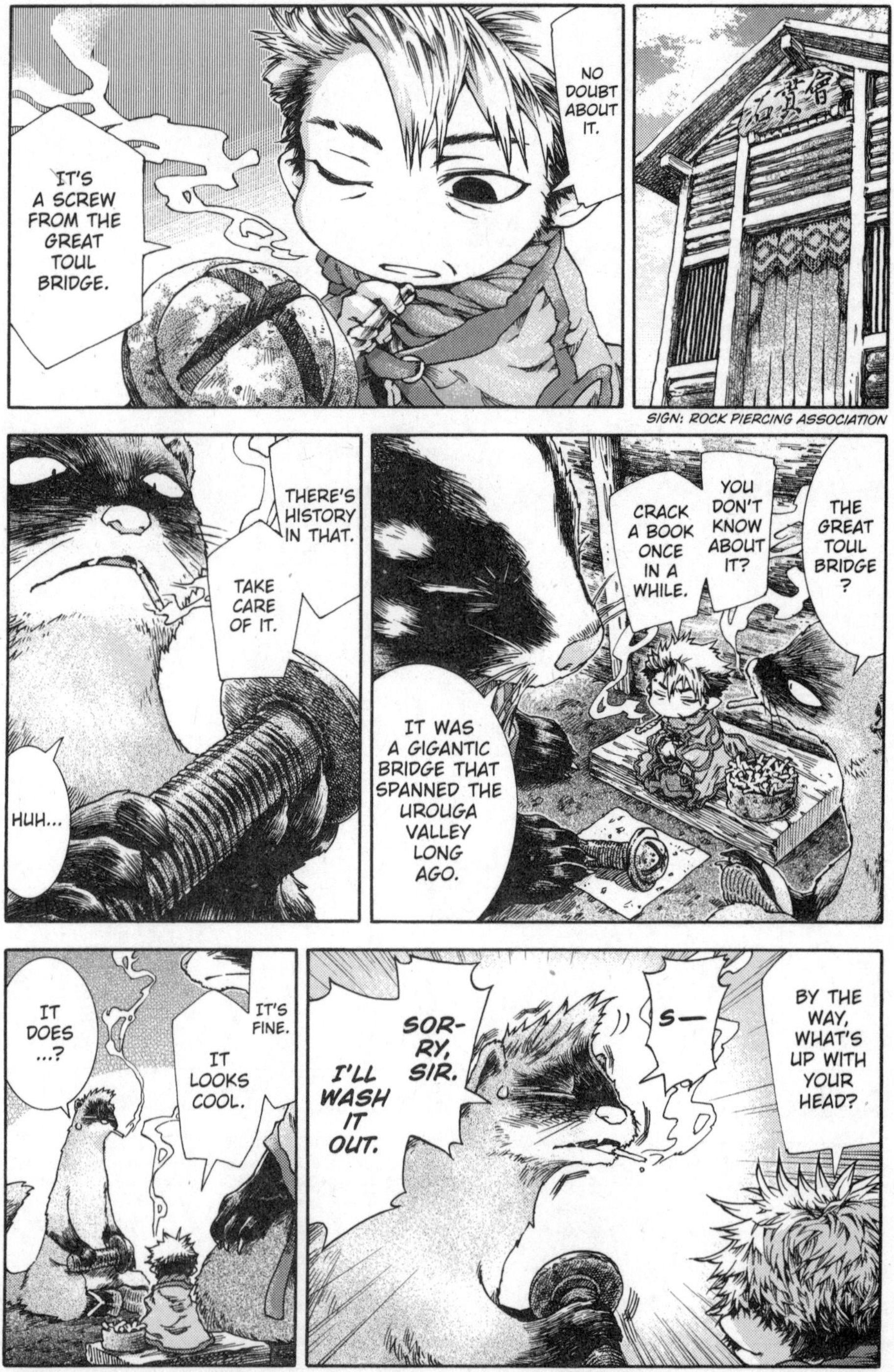
SIGN: ROCK PIERCING ASSOCIATION
NO DOUBT ABOUT IT.
IT'S A SCREW FROM THE GREAT TOUL BRIDGE.
THE GREAT TOUL BRIDGE?
YOU DON'T KNOW ABOUT IT?
CRACK A BOOK ONCE IN A WHILE.
IT WAS A GIGANTIC BRIDGE THAT SPANNED THE UROUGA VALLEY LONG AGO.
THERE'S HISTORY IN THAT.
TAKE CARE OF IT.
HUH...
BY THE WAY, WHAT'S UP WITH YOUR HEAD?
S—
SORRY, SIR.
I'LL WASH IT OUT.
IT'S FINE.
IT LOOKS COOL.
IT DOES...?

"Look, look, this hairstyle...Mohawks are cool, aren't they?"

"Ain't what I was picturing. Do you use oil to make it that stiff? The sides aren't shaved."

"It really looks cooler if they are shaved, but I wouldn't know where to stop with you, Iwashi-san."

"Nah, I think it's better without the shaving."

"Shall we shave you to see?"

"I said no shaving. Just make it stiff."

"Roger dodger. Would you like me to straighten up your whiskers while I'm at it? They're a little unkempt."

"I've never had that done..."

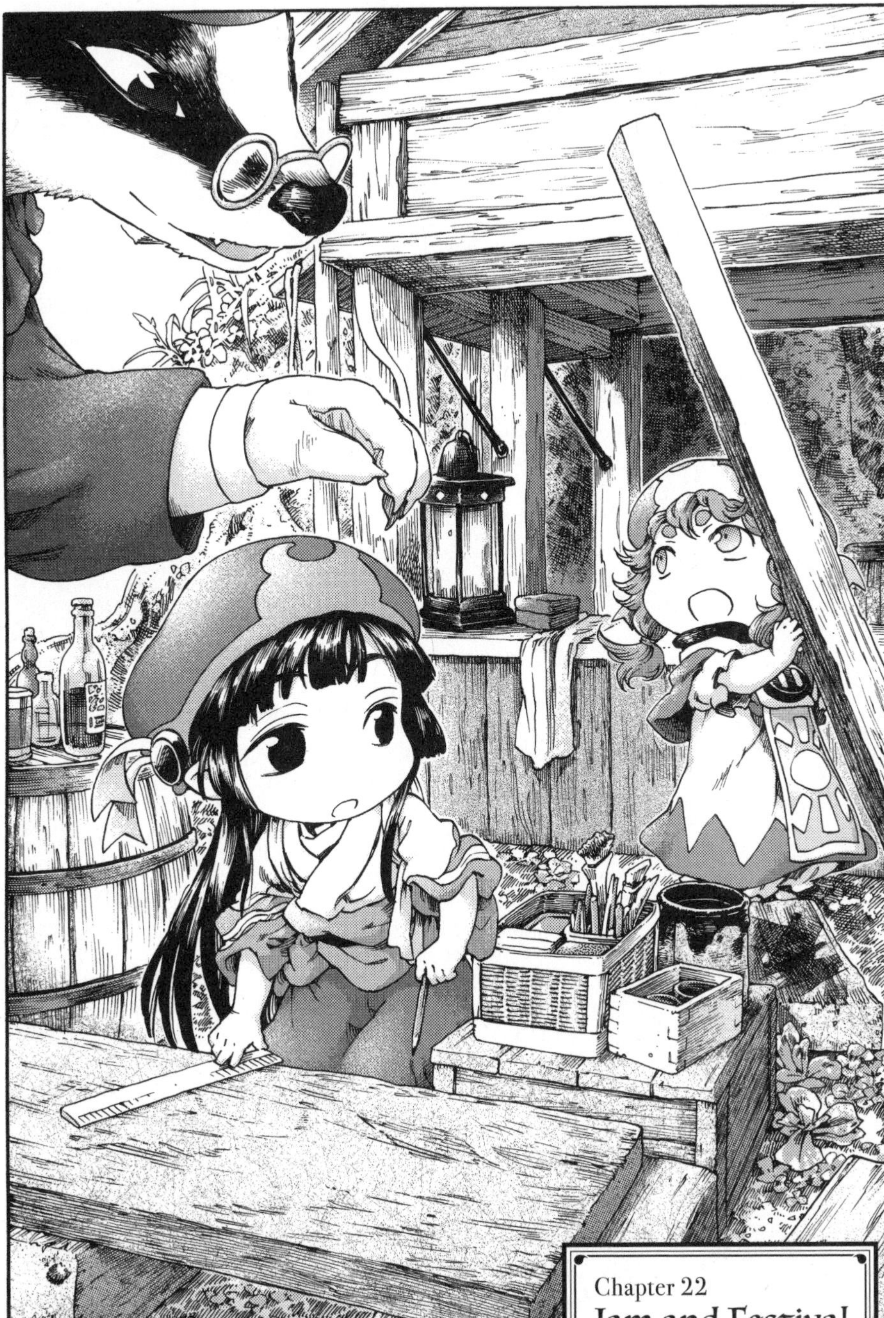
Chapter 22
Jam and Festival

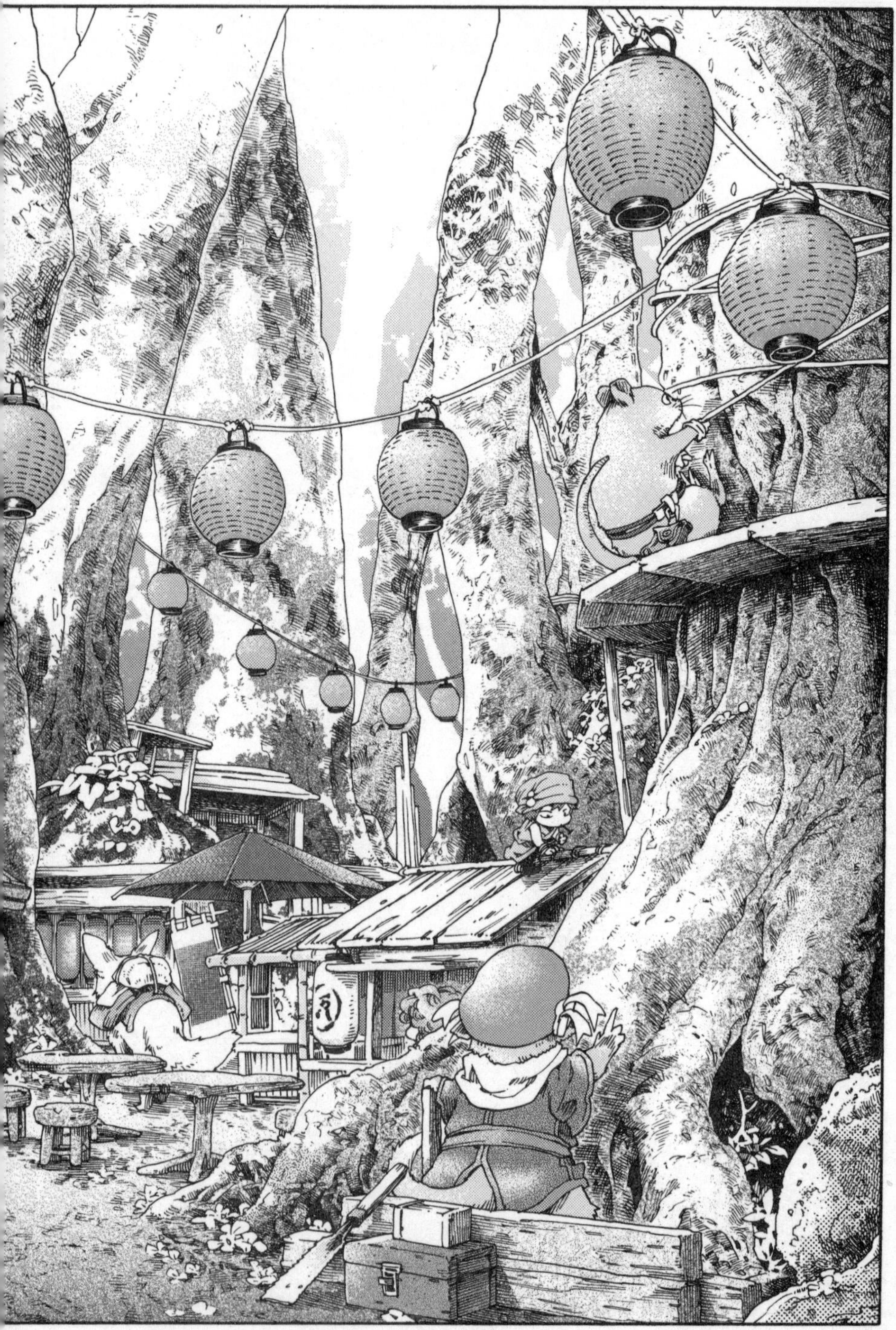

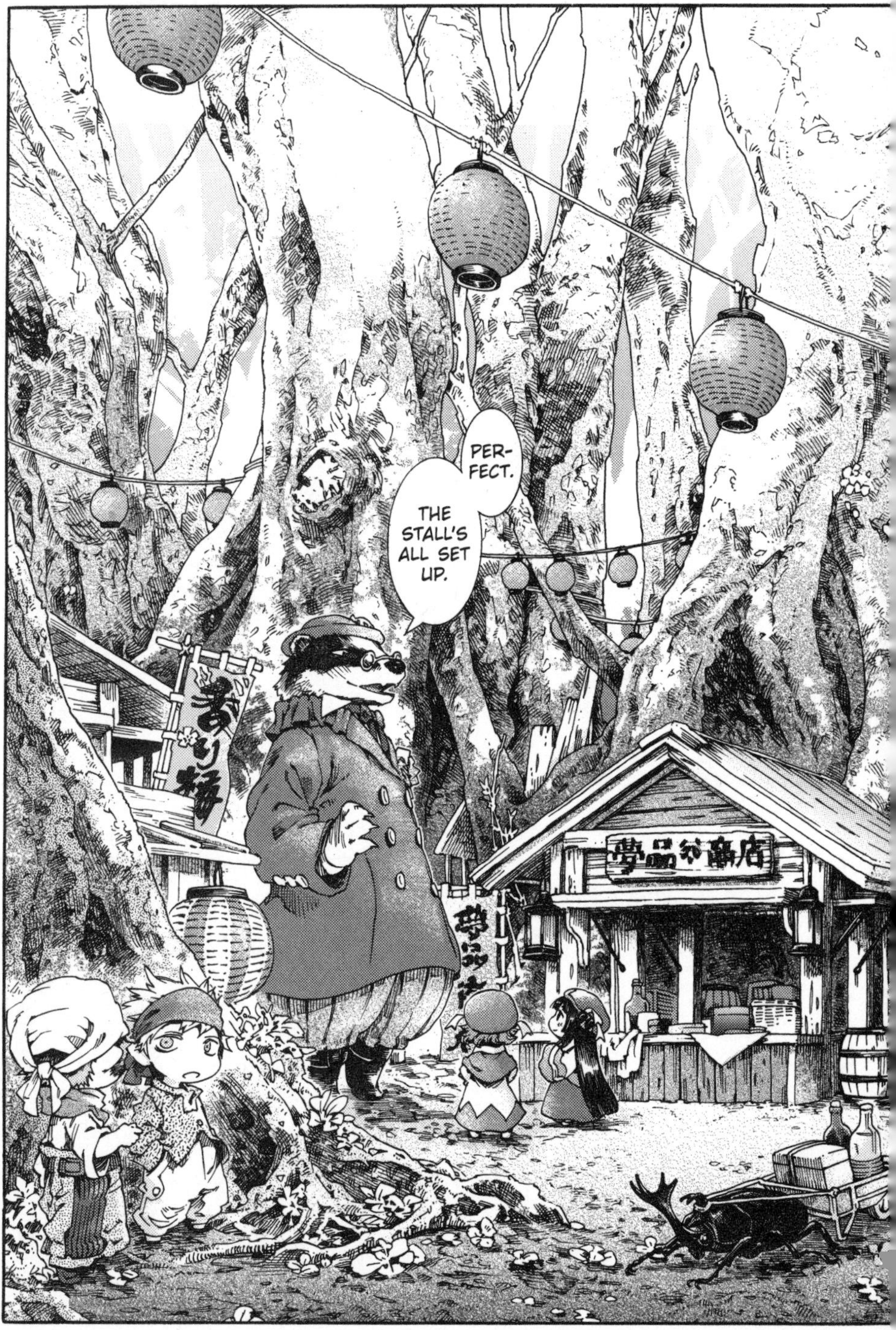
PER-FECT.
THE STALL'S ALL SET UP.

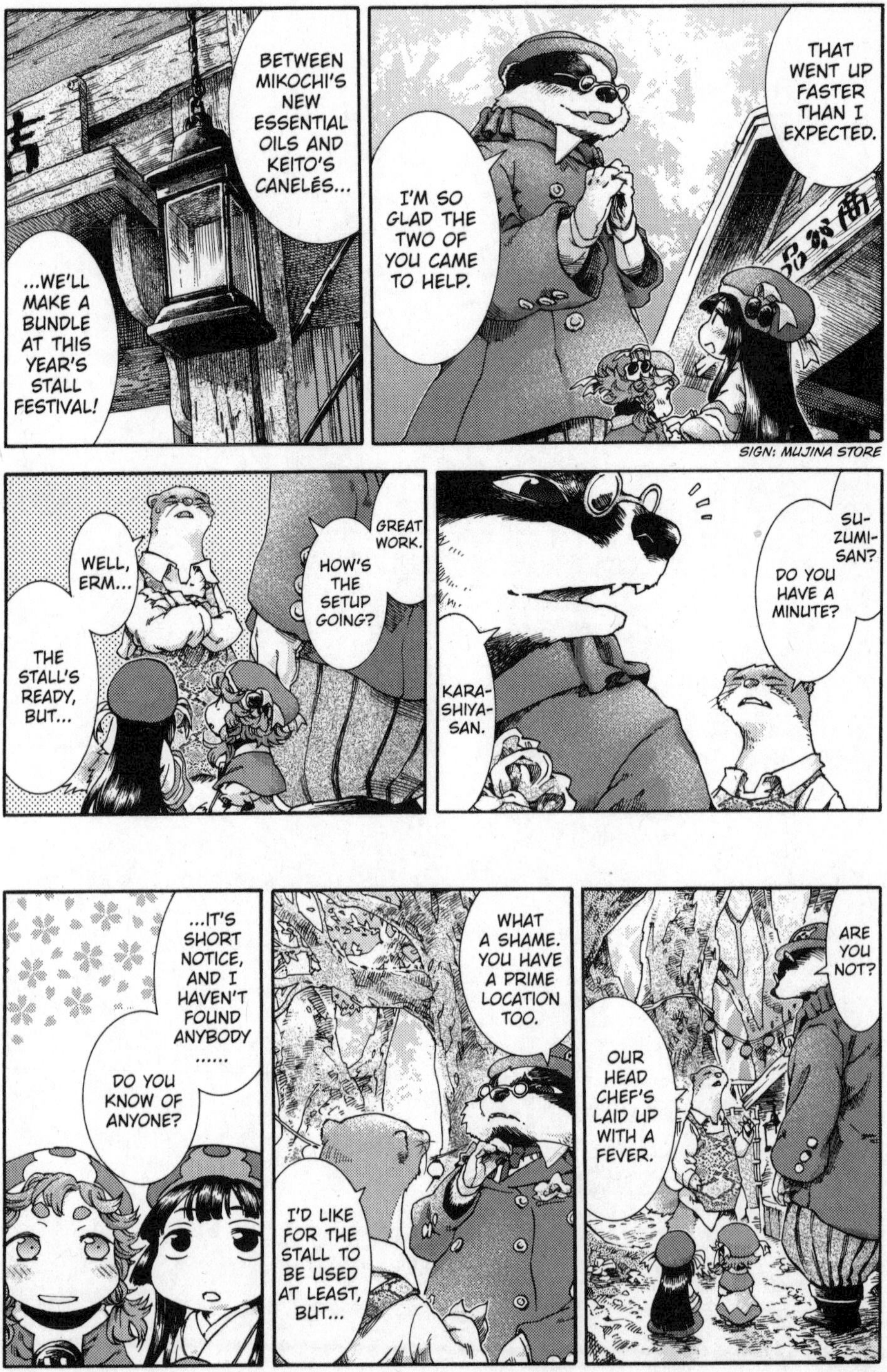
THAT WENT UP FASTER THAN I EXPECTED.
I'M SO GLAD THE TWO OF YOU CAME TO HELP.
BETWEEN MIKOCHI'S NEW ESSENTIAL OILS AND KEITO'S CANELÉS...
...WE'LL MAKE A BUNDLE AT THIS YEAR'S STALL FESTIVAL!
SIGN: MUJINA STORE
SU-ZUMI-SAN? DO YOU HAVE A MINUTE?
KARASHIYA-SAN.
GREAT WORK. HOW'S THE SETUP GOING?
WELL, ERM...
THE STALL'S READY, BUT...
ARE YOU NOT?
OUR HEAD CHEF'S LAID UP WITH A FEVER.
WHAT A SHAME. YOU HAVE A PRIME LOCATION TOO.
I'D LIKE FOR THE STALL TO BE USED AT LEAST, BUT...
...IT'S SHORT NOTICE, AND I HAVEN'T FOUND ANYBODY......
DO YOU KNOW OF ANYONE?

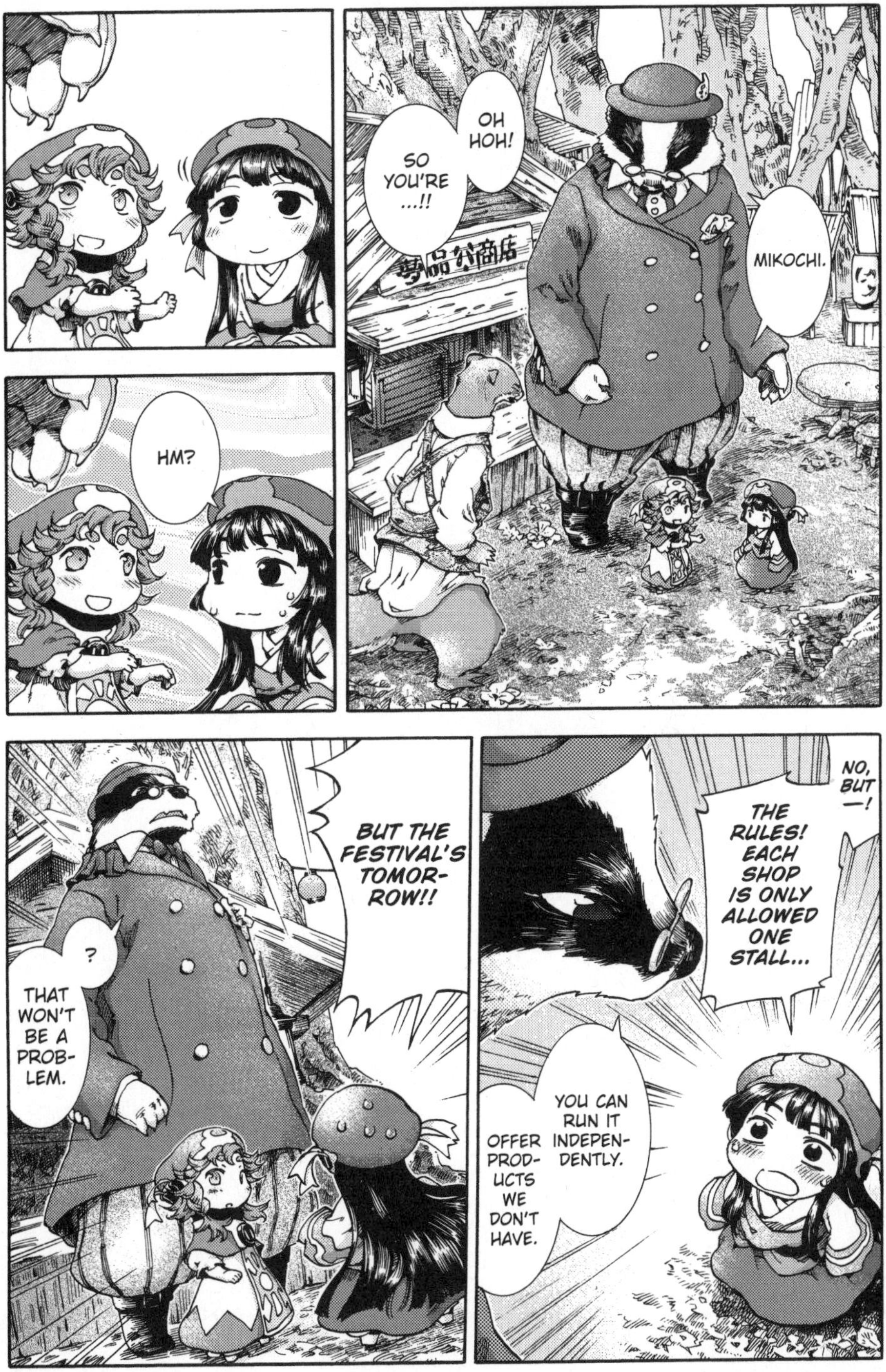
OH HOH!
SO YOU'RE ...!!
MIKOCHI.
HM?
NO, BUT—!
THE RULES! EACH SHOP IS ONLY ALLOWED ONE STALL...
YOU CAN RUN IT INDEPENDENTLY.
OFFER PRODUCTS WE DON'T HAVE.
BUT THE FESTIVAL'S TOMORROW!!
?
THAT WON'T BE A PROBLEM.

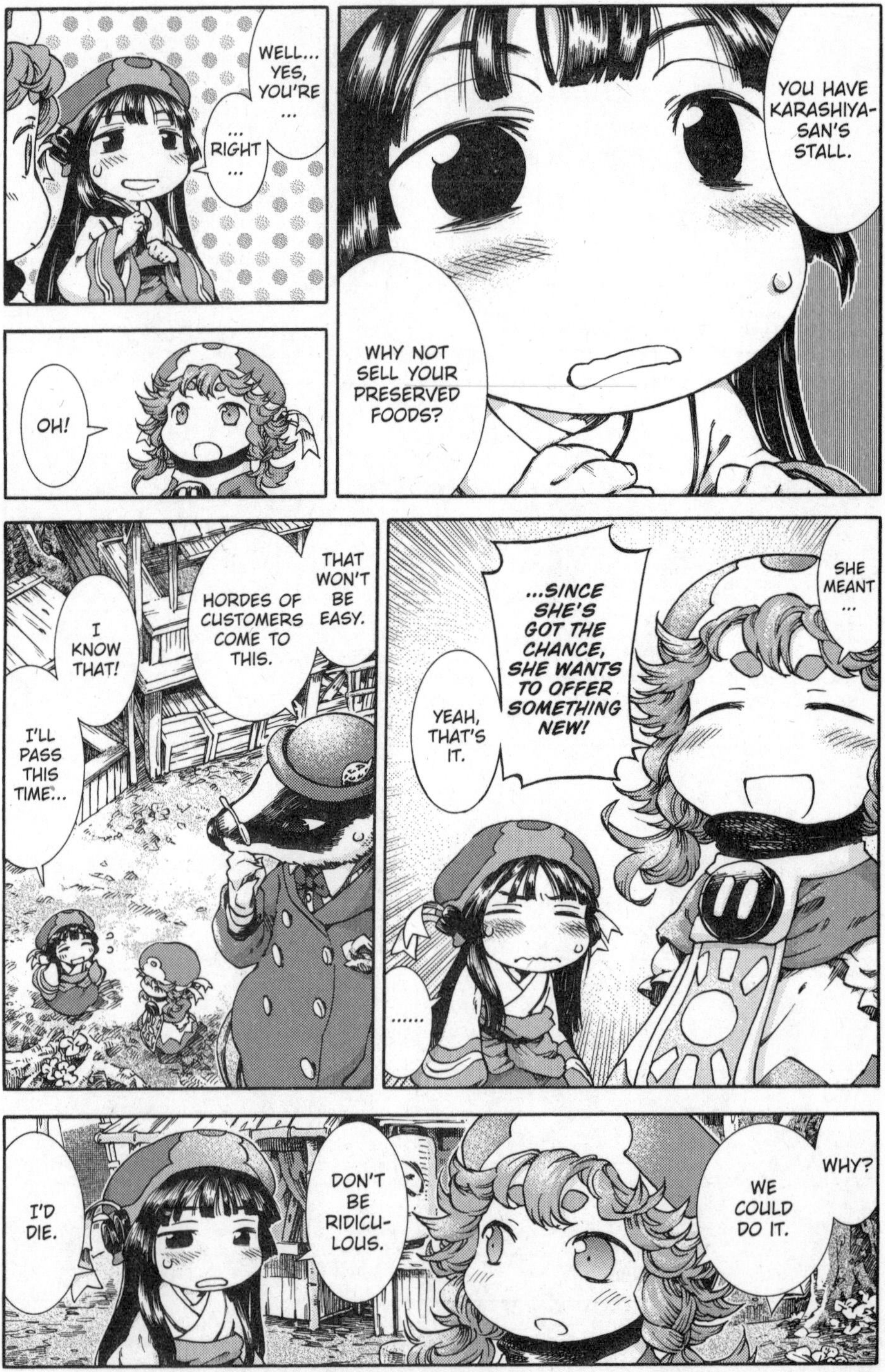
YOU HAVE KARASHIYA-SAN'S STALL.
WHY NOT SELL YOUR PRESERVED FOODS?
WELL... YES, YOU'RE ...
... RIGHT ...
OH!
SHE MEANT ...
...SINCE SHE'S GOT THE CHANCE, SHE WANTS TO OFFER SOMETHING NEW!
YEAH, THAT'S IT.
......
THAT WON'T BE EASY.
HORDES OF CUSTOMERS COME TO THIS.
I KNOW THAT!
I'LL PASS THIS TIME...
WHY?
WE COULD DO IT.
DON'T BE RIDICULOUS.
I'D DIE.

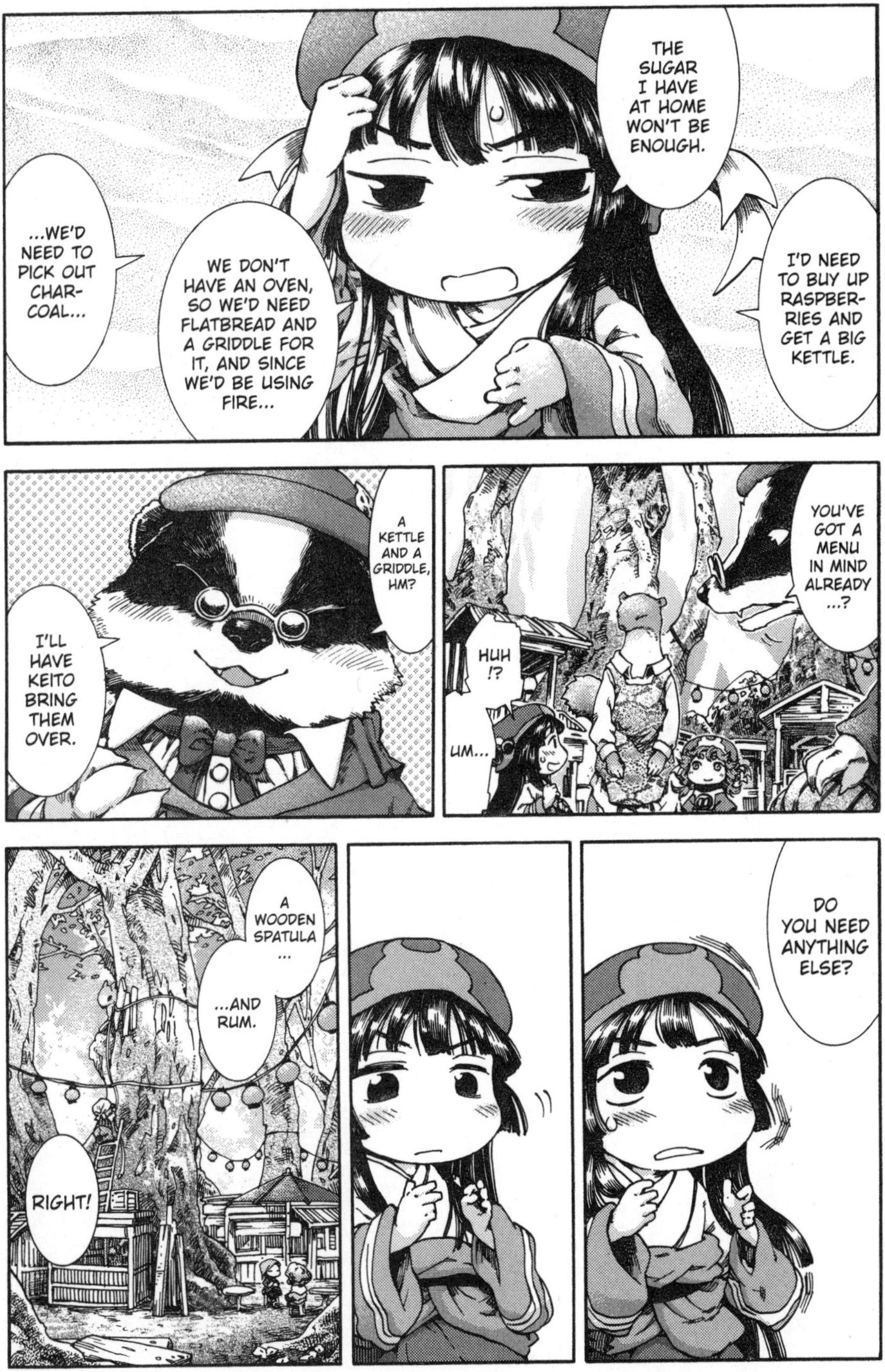
THE SUGAR I HAVE AT HOME WON'T BE ENOUGH.
I'D NEED TO BUY UP RASPBERRIES AND GET A BIG KETTLE.
WE DON'T HAVE AN OVEN, SO WE'D NEED FLATBREAD AND A GRIDDLE FOR IT, AND SINCE WE'D BE USING FIRE...
...WE'D NEED TO PICK OUT CHARCOAL...
YOU'VE GOT A MENU IN MIND ALREADY ...?
HUH !?
UM...
A KETTLE AND A GRIDDLE, HM?
I'LL HAVE KEITO BRING THEM OVER.
DO YOU NEED ANYTHING ELSE?
A WOODEN SPATULA ...
...AND RUM.
RIGHT!

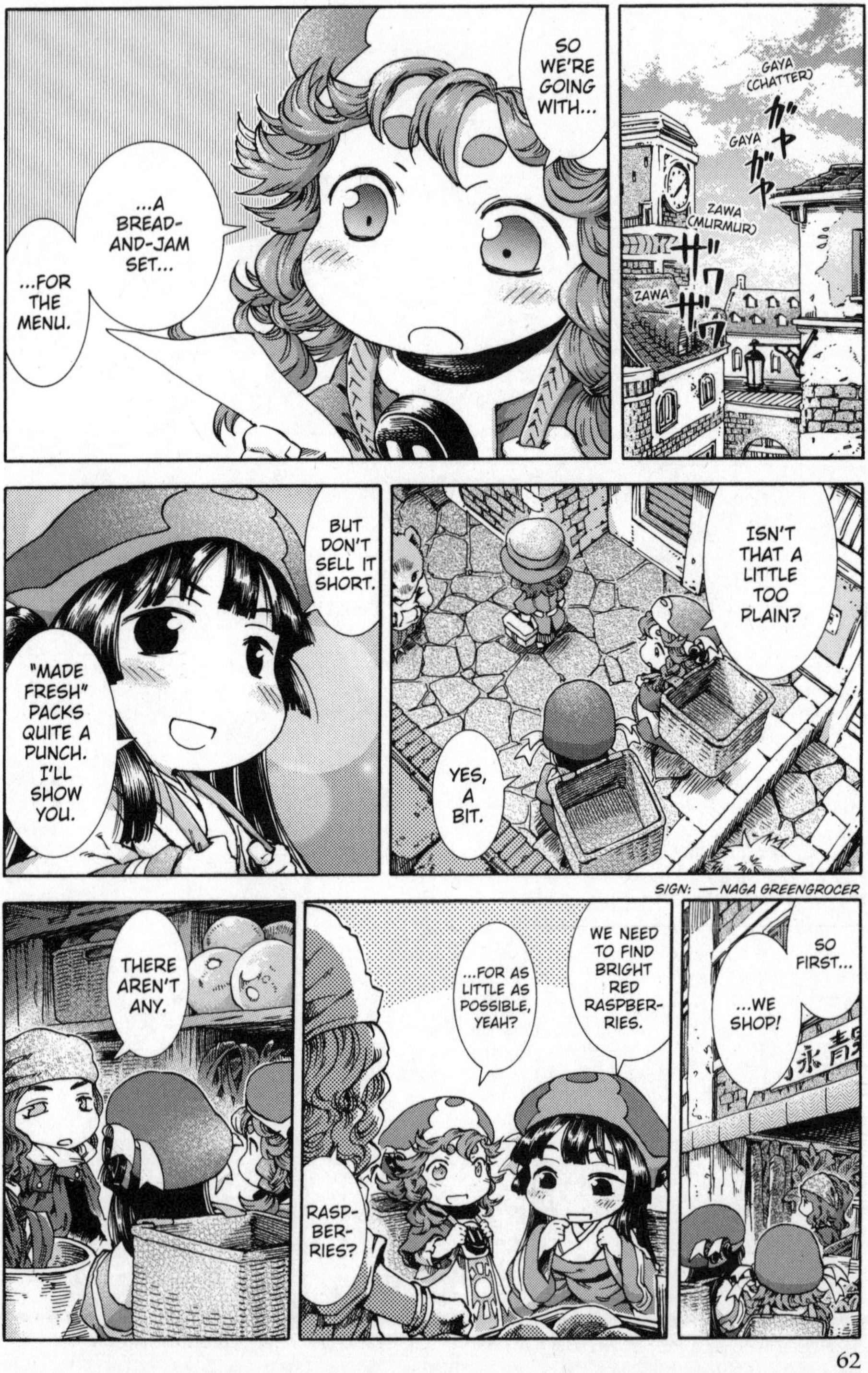
GAYA (CHATTER)
ガヤ
GAYA
ガヤ
ZAWA (MURMUR)
ザワ
ZAWA
ザワ
SO WE'RE GOING WITH...
...A BREAD-AND-JAM SET...
...FOR THE MENU.
ISN'T THAT A LITTLE TOO PLAIN?
YES, A BIT.
BUT DON'T SELL IT SHORT.
"MADE FRESH" PACKS QUITE A PUNCH. I'LL SHOW YOU.
SIGN: —NAGA GREENGROCER
SO FIRST...
...WE SHOP!
WE NEED TO FIND BRIGHT RED RASPBERRIES.
...FOR AS LITTLE AS POSSIBLE, YEAH?
RASPBERRIES?
THERE AREN'T ANY.

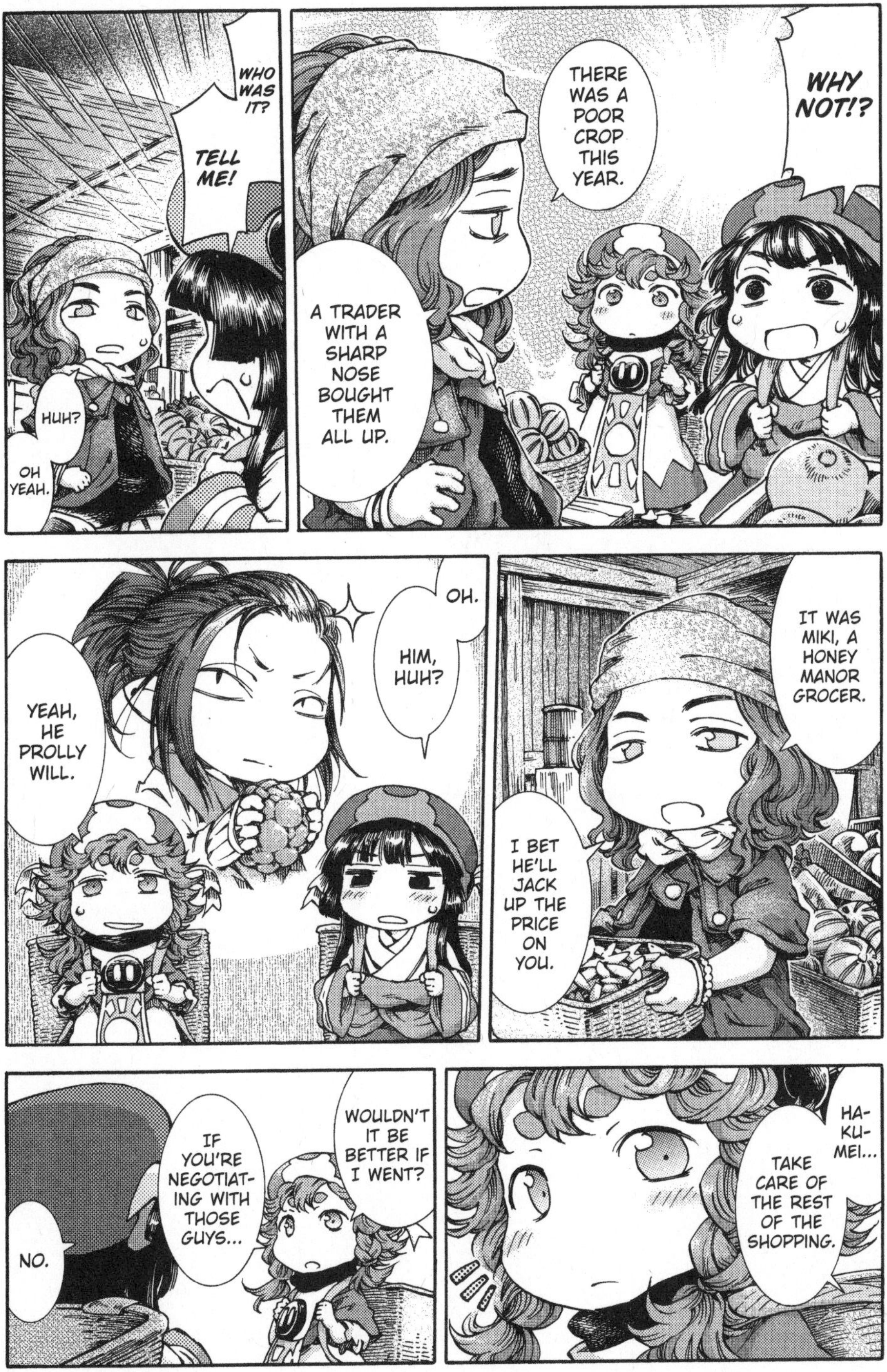
WHY NOT!?
THERE WAS A POOR CROP THIS YEAR.
A TRADER WITH A SHARP NOSE BOUGHT THEM ALL UP.
WHO WAS IT?
TELL ME!
HUH?
OH YEAH.
IT WAS MIKI, A HONEY MANOR GROCER.
I BET HE'LL JACK UP THE PRICE ON YOU.
OH.
HIM, HUH?
YEAH, HE PROLLY WILL.
HA-KU-MEI...
TAKE CARE OF THE REST OF THE SHOPPING.
WOULDN'T IT BE BETTER IF I WENT?
IF YOU'RE NEGOTIAT-ING WITH THOSE GUYS...
NO.

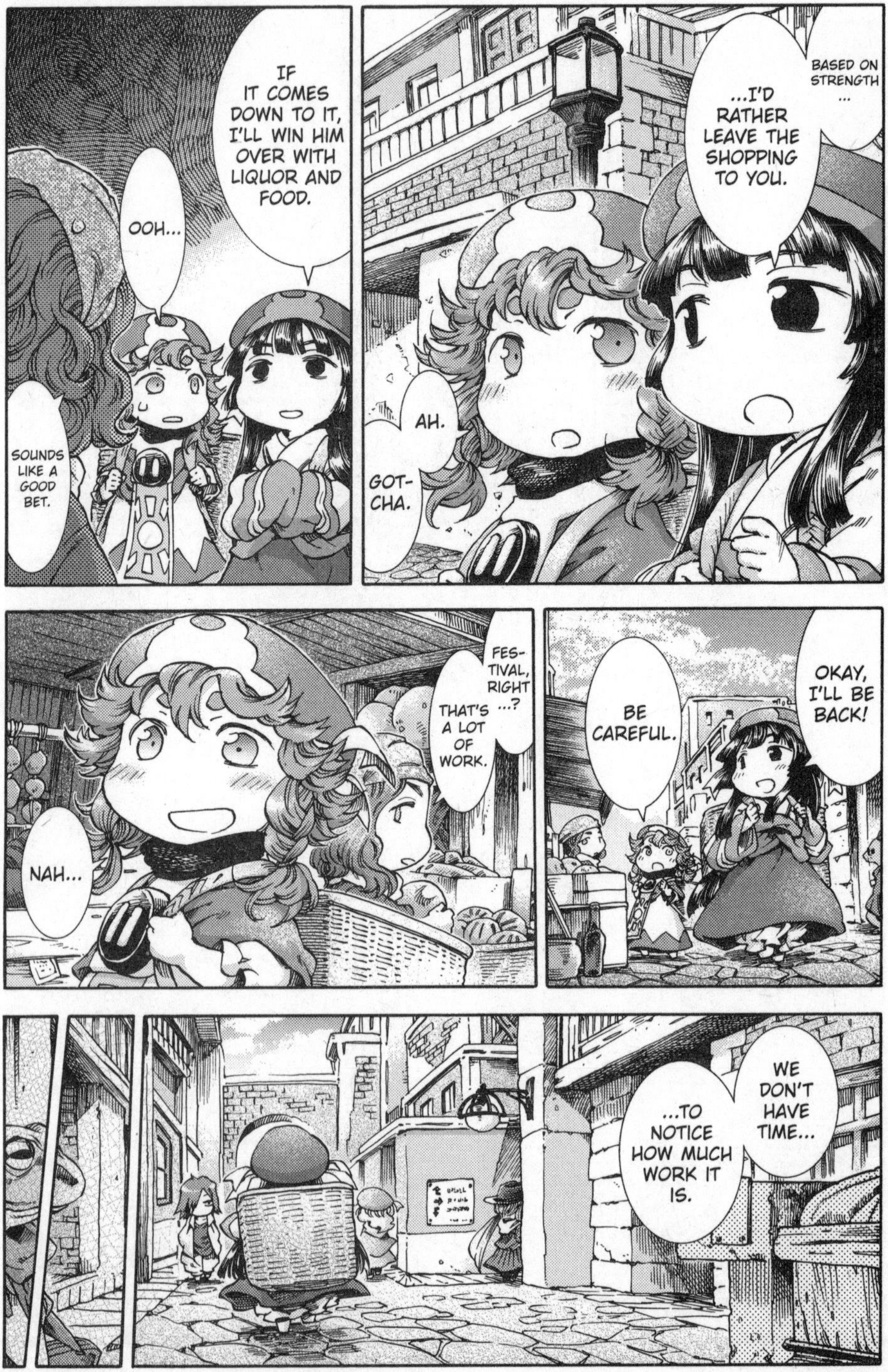
BASED ON STRENGTH...
...I'D RATHER LEAVE THE SHOPPING TO YOU.
AH.
GOT-CHA.
IF IT COMES DOWN TO IT, I'LL WIN HIM OVER WITH LIQUOR AND FOOD.
OOH...
SOUNDS LIKE A GOOD BET.
OKAY, I'LL BE BACK!
BE CAREFUL.
FES-TIVAL, RIGHT...?
THAT'S A LOT OF WORK.
NAH...
WE DON'T HAVE TIME...
...TO NOTICE HOW MUCH WORK IT IS.

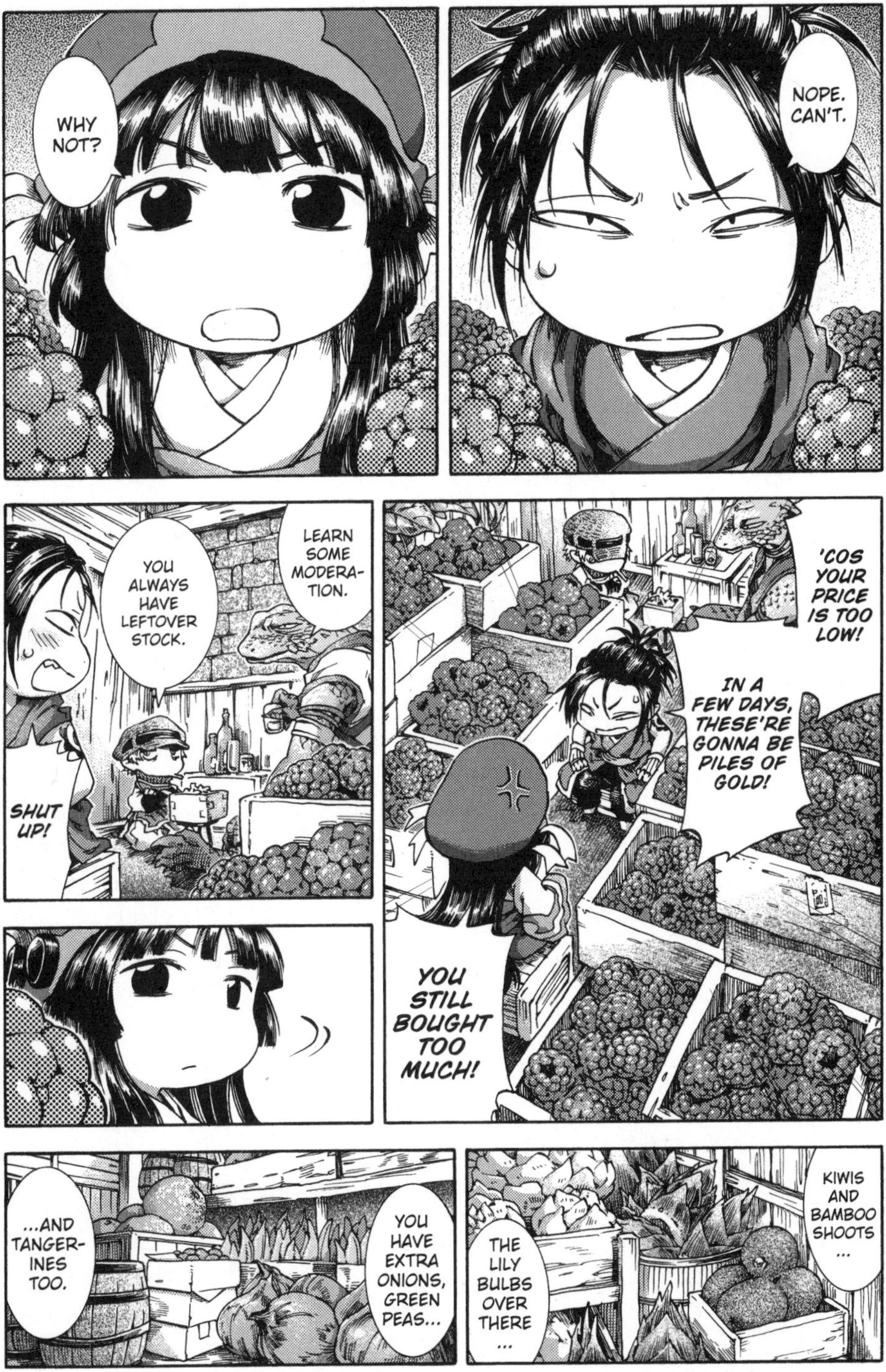
NOPE. CAN'T.
WHY NOT?
'COS YOUR PRICE IS TOO LOW!
IN A FEW DAYS, THESE'RE GONNA BE PILES OF GOLD!
YOU STILL BOUGHT TOO MUCH!
LEARN SOME MODERATION.
YOU ALWAYS HAVE LEFTOVER STOCK.
SHUT UP!
KIWIS AND BAMBOO SHOOTS...
THE LILY BULBS OVER THERE...
YOU HAVE EXTRA ONIONS, GREEN PEAS...
...AND TANGERINES TOO.

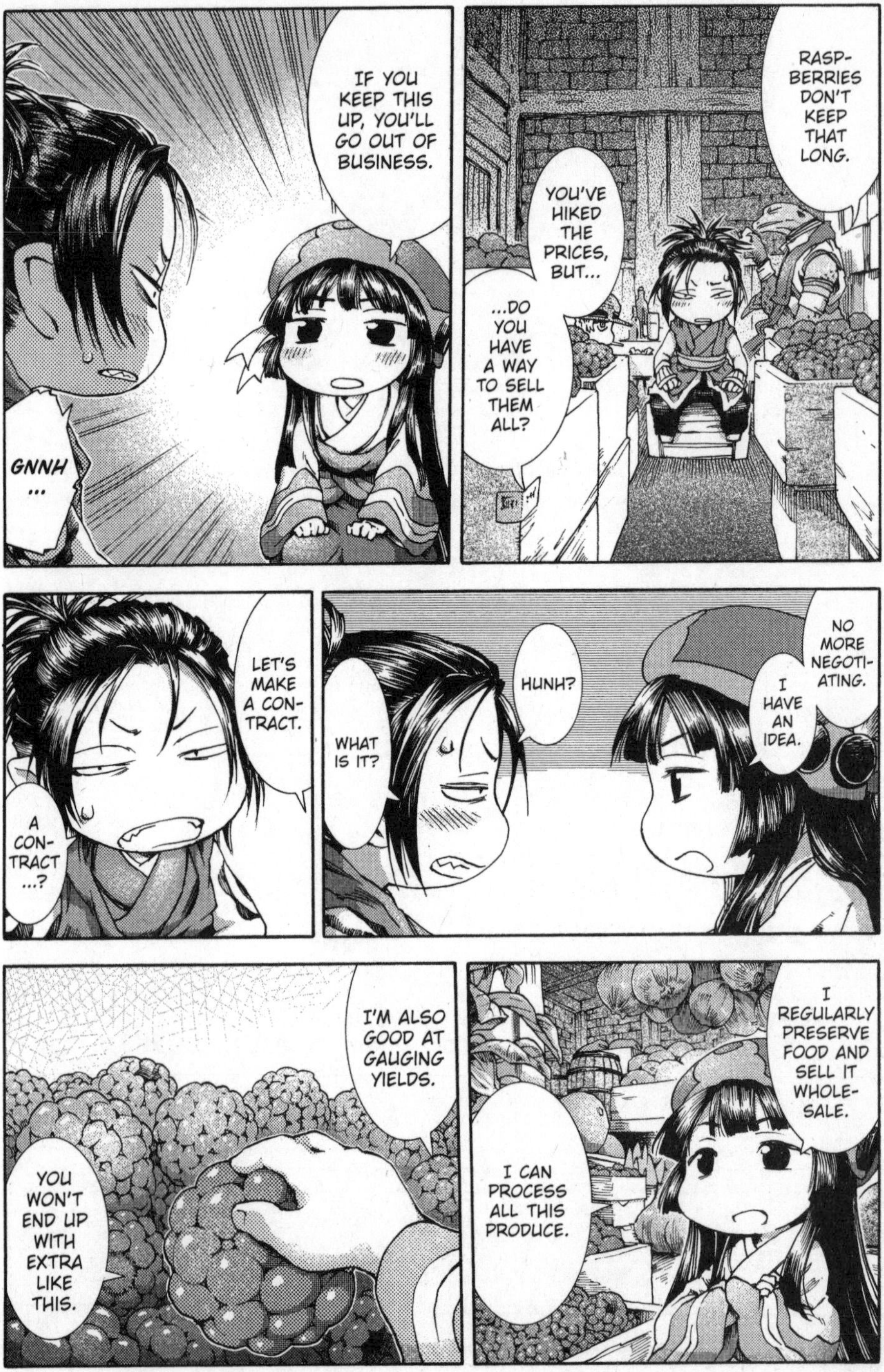
RASPBERRIES DON'T KEEP THAT LONG.
YOU'VE HIKED THE PRICES, BUT...
...DO YOU HAVE A WAY TO SELL THEM ALL?
IF YOU KEEP THIS UP, YOU'LL GO OUT OF BUSINESS.
GNNH...
NO MORE NEGOTIATING.
I HAVE AN IDEA.
HUNH?
WHAT IS IT?
LET'S MAKE A CONTRACT.
A CONTRACT...?
I REGULARLY PRESERVE FOOD AND SELL IT WHOLESALE.
I CAN PROCESS ALL THIS PRODUCE.
I'M ALSO GOOD AT GAUGING YIELDS.
YOU WON'T END UP WITH EXTRA LIKE THIS.

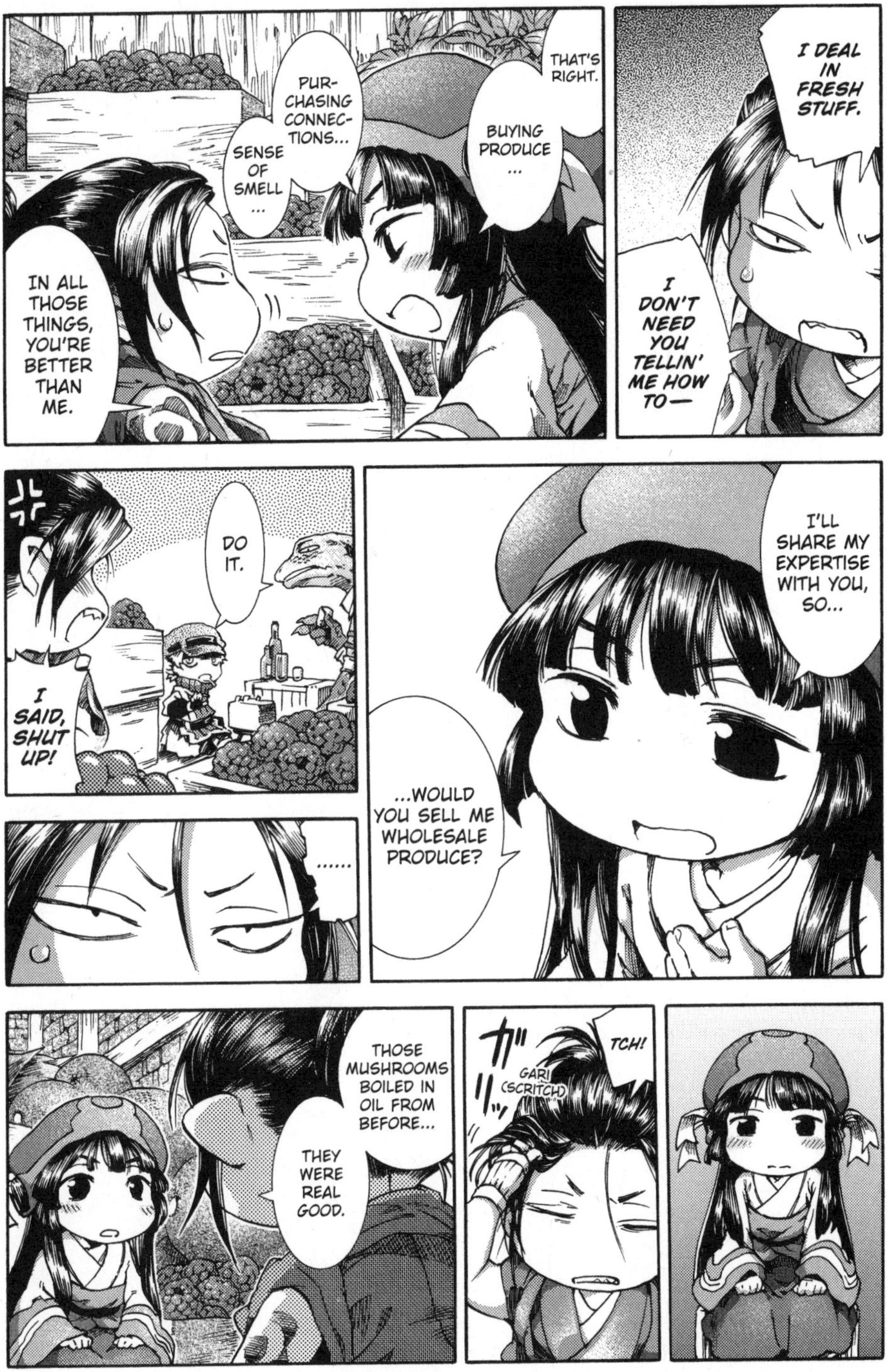
I DEAL IN FRESH STUFF.
I DON'T NEED YOU TELLIN' ME HOW TO—
THAT'S RIGHT.
BUYING PRODUCE ...
PUR-CHASING CONNEC-TIONS...
SENSE OF SMELL ...
IN ALL THOSE THINGS, YOU'RE BETTER THAN ME.
I'LL SHARE MY EXPERTISE WITH YOU, SO...
...WOULD YOU SELL ME WHOLESALE PRODUCE?
DO IT.
I SAID, SHUT UP!
......
TCH!
GARI (SCRITCH)
THOSE MUSHROOMS BOILED IN OIL FROM BEFORE...
THEY WERE REAL GOOD.

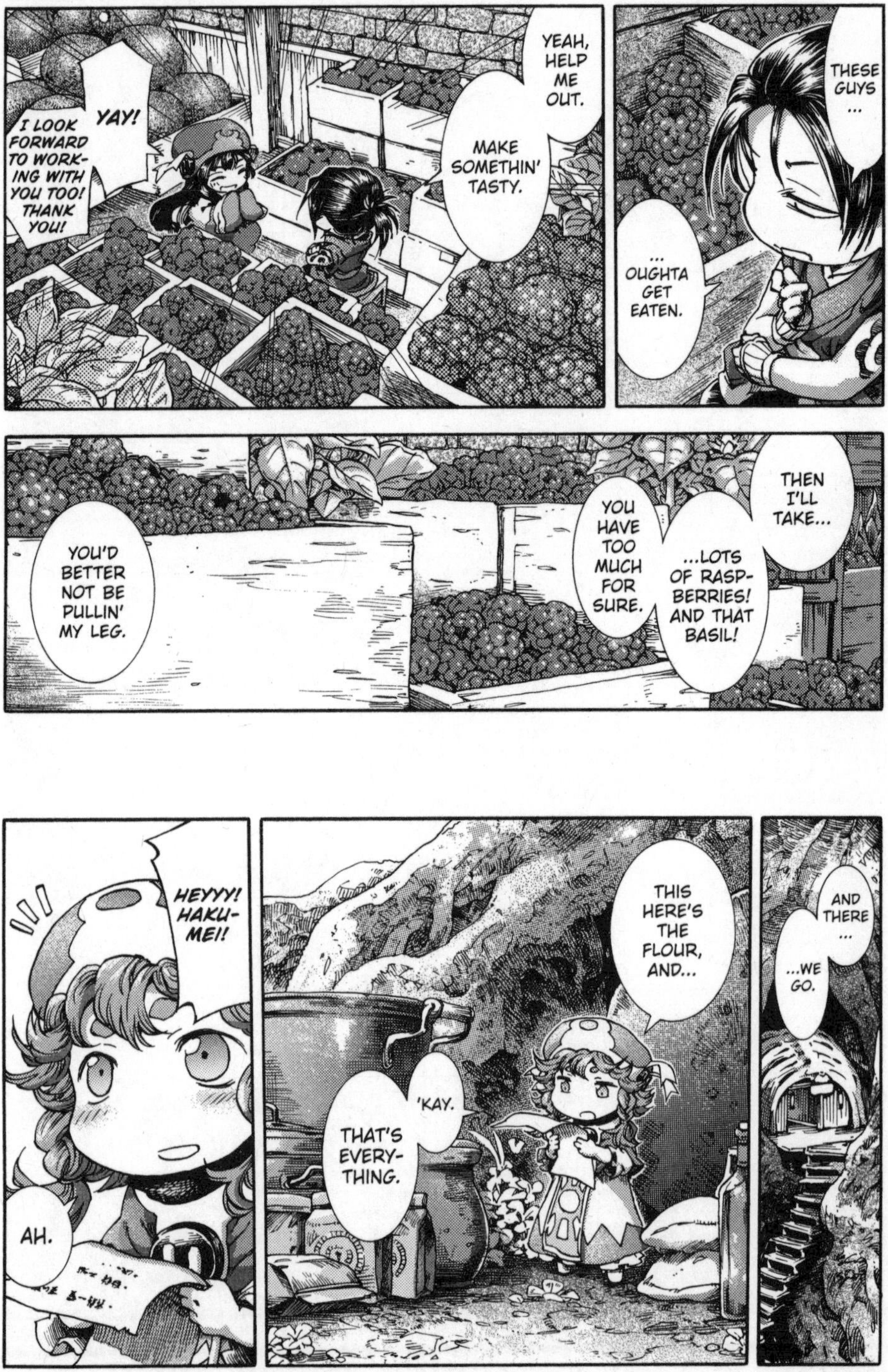
THESE GUYS ...
... OUGHTA GET EATEN.
YEAH, HELP ME OUT.
MAKE SOMETHIN' TASTY.
YAY!
I LOOK FORWARD TO WORKING WITH YOU TOO! THANK YOU!
THEN I'LL TAKE...
...LOTS OF RASPBERRIES! AND THAT BASIL!
YOU HAVE TOO MUCH FOR SURE.
YOU'D BETTER NOT BE PULLIN' MY LEG.
AND THERE ...
...WE GO.
THIS HERE'S THE FLOUR, AND...
'KAY.
THAT'S EVERYTHING.
HEYYY! HAKUMEI!
AH.

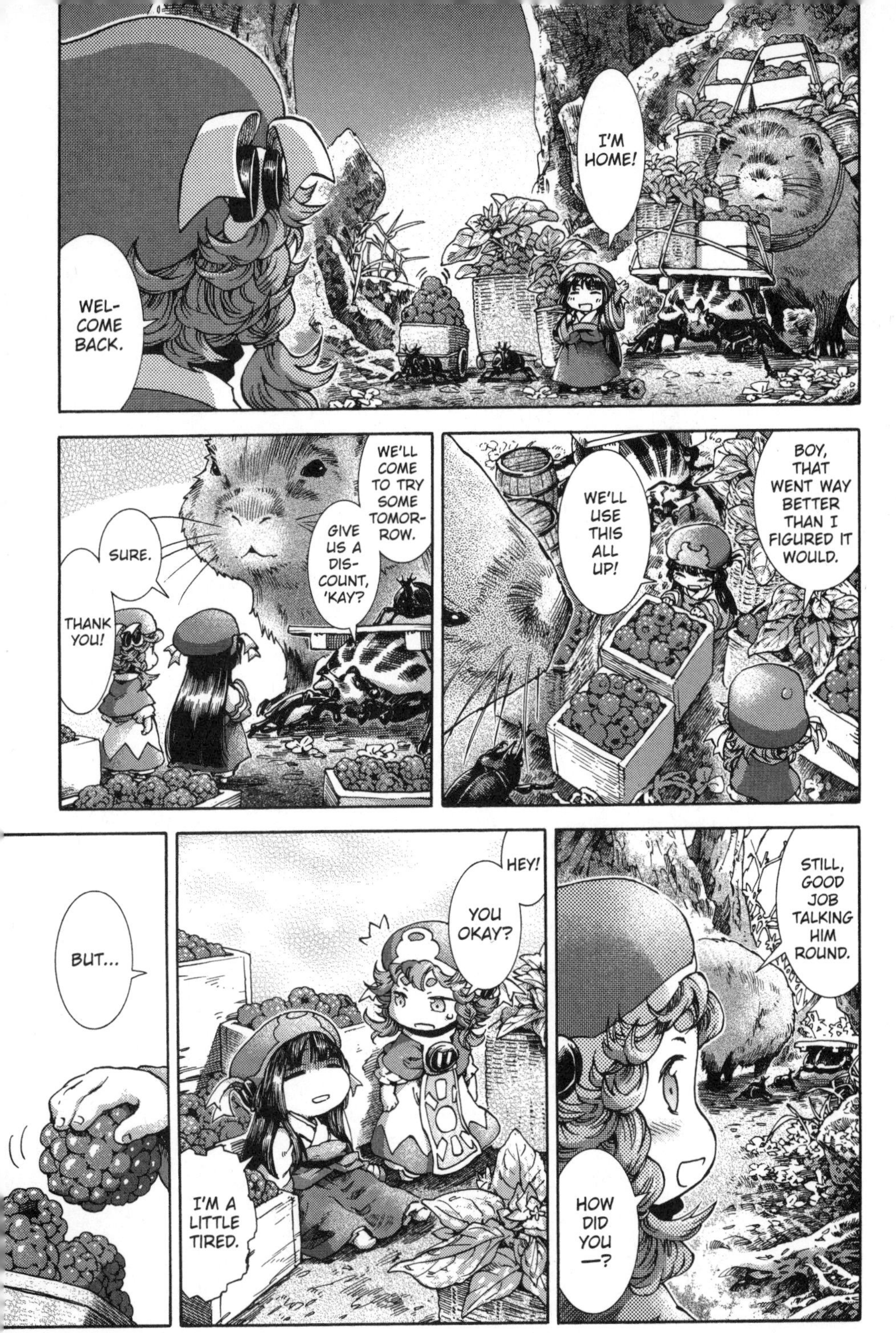
I'M HOME!
WEL-COME BACK.
BOY, THAT WENT WAY BETTER THAN I FIGURED IT WOULD.
WE'LL USE THIS ALL UP!
WE'LL COME TO TRY SOME TOMOR-ROW.
GIVE US A DIS-COUNT, 'KAY?
SURE.
THANK YOU!
STILL, GOOD JOB TALKING HIM ROUND.
HOW DID YOU—?
HEY!
YOU OKAY?
I'M A LITTLE TIRED.
BUT...

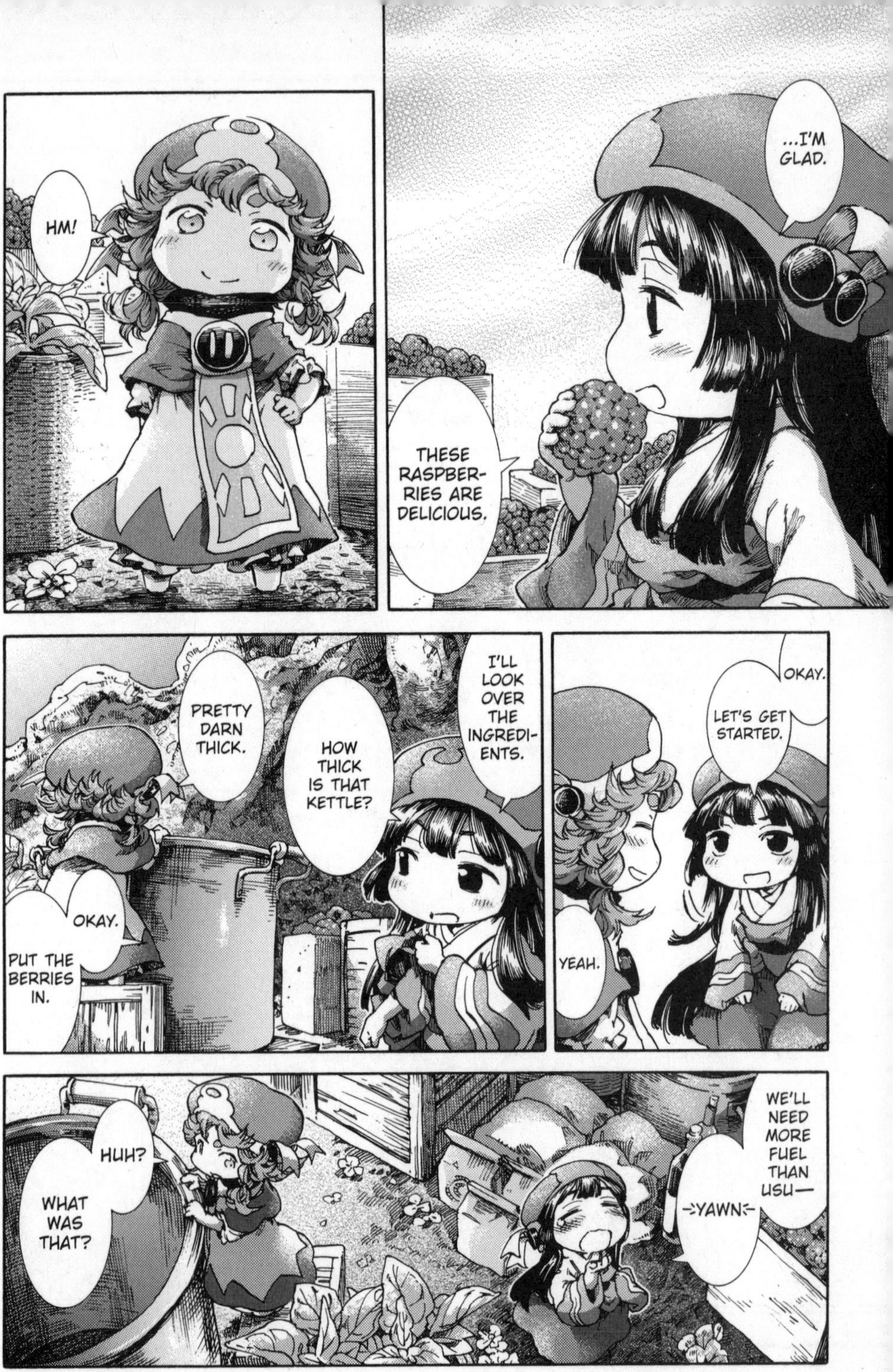
...I'M GLAD.
THESE RASPBERRIES ARE DELICIOUS.
HM!
OKAY.
LET'S GET STARTED.
YEAH.
I'LL LOOK OVER THE INGREDIENTS.
HOW THICK IS THAT KETTLE?
PRETTY DARN THICK.
OKAY.
PUT THE BERRIES IN.
WE'LL NEED MORE FUEL THAN USU—
~YAWN~
HUH?
WHAT WAS THAT?

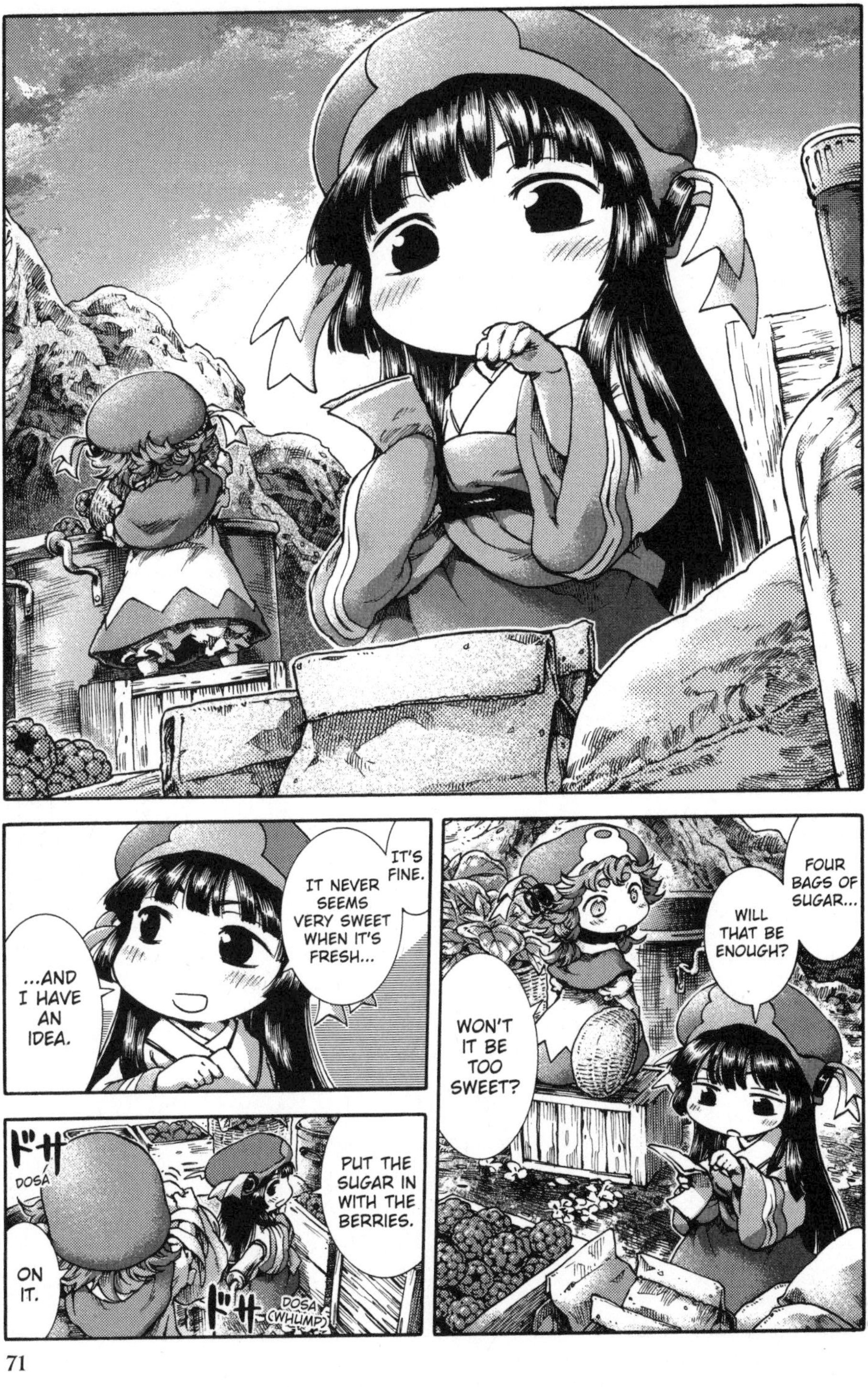
FOUR BAGS OF SUGAR...
WILL THAT BE ENOUGH?
WON'T IT BE TOO SWEET?
IT'S FINE.
IT NEVER SEEMS VERY SWEET WHEN IT'S FRESH...
...AND I HAVE AN IDEA.
PUT THE SUGAR IN WITH THE BERRIES.
ドサ
DOSA
ON IT.
ドサ
DOSA (WHLUMP)

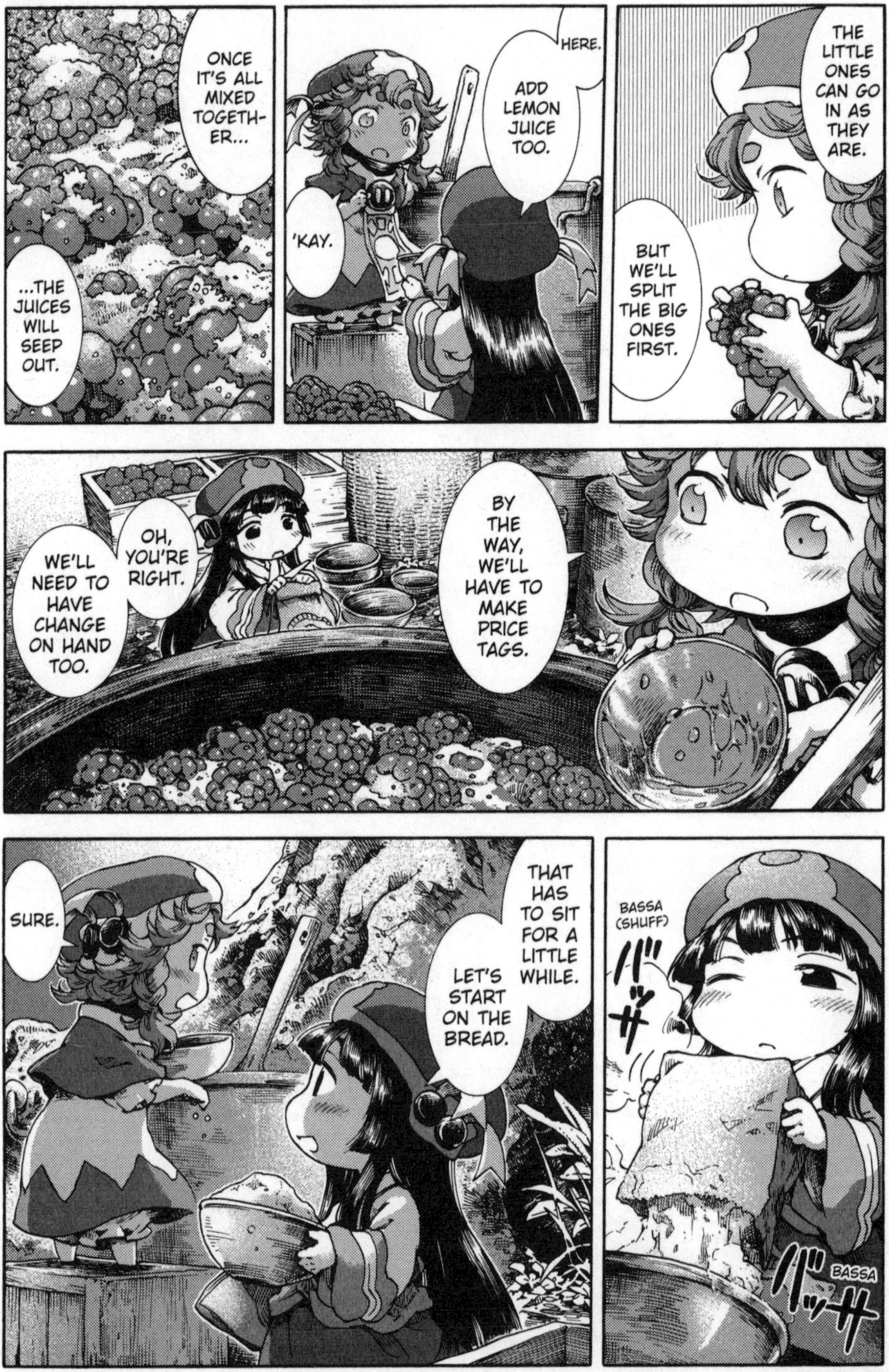
THE LITTLE ONES CAN GO IN AS THEY ARE.
BUT WE'LL SPLIT THE BIG ONES FIRST.
HERE.
ADD LEMON JUICE TOO.
'KAY.
ONCE IT'S ALL MIXED TOGETH-ER...
...THE JUICES WILL SEEP OUT.
BY THE WAY, WE'LL HAVE TO MAKE PRICE TAGS.
OH, YOU'RE RIGHT.
WE'LL NEED TO HAVE CHANGE ON HAND TOO.
バッサ
BASSA (SHUFF)
バッサ
BASSA
THAT HAS TO SIT FOR A LITTLE WHILE.
LET'S START ON THE BREAD.
SURE.

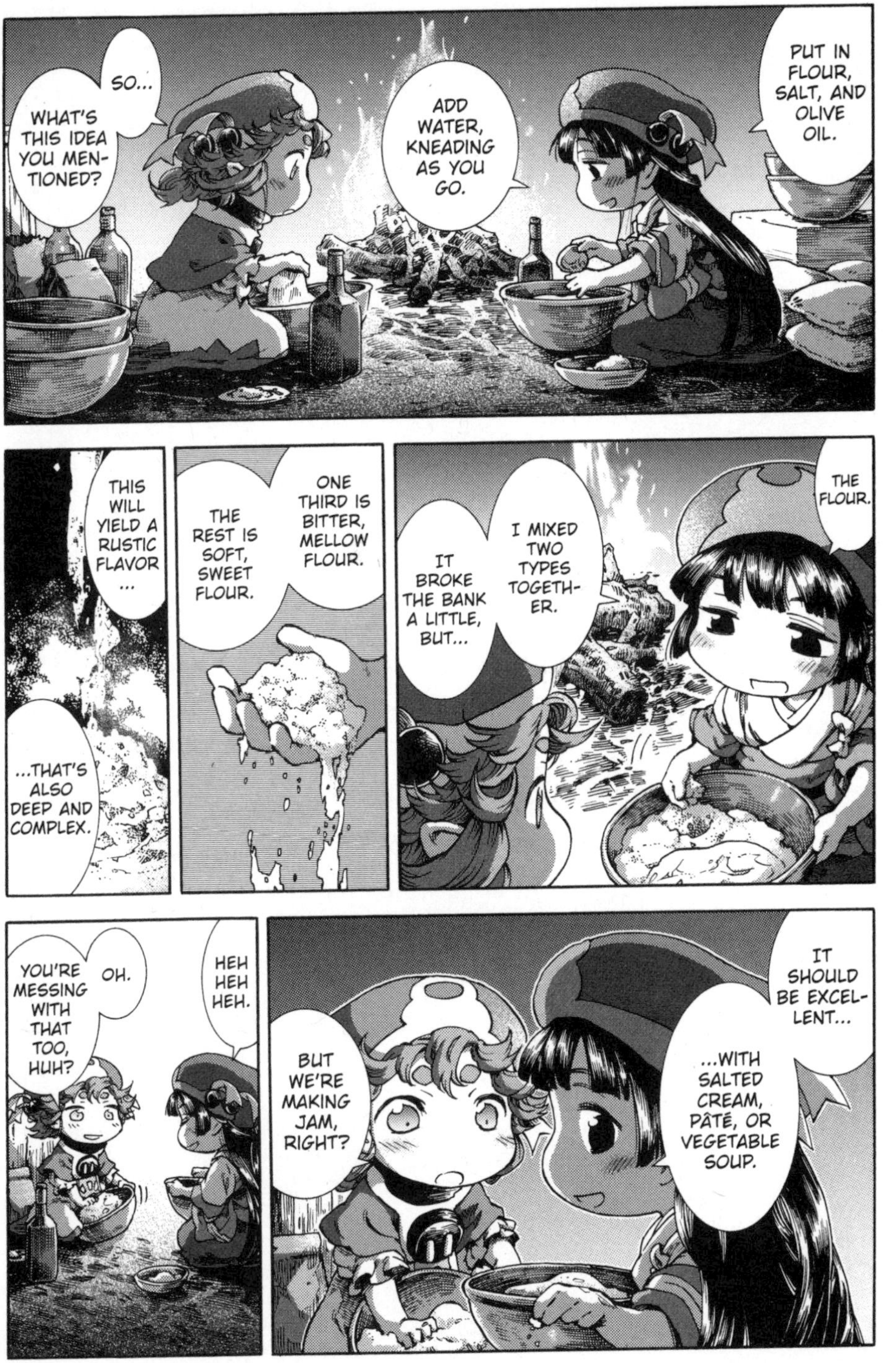
PUT IN FLOUR, SALT, AND OLIVE OIL.
ADD WATER, KNEADING AS YOU GO.
SO...
WHAT'S THIS IDEA YOU MENTIONED?
THE FLOUR.
I MIXED TWO TYPES TOGETHER.
IT BROKE THE BANK A LITTLE, BUT...
ONE THIRD IS BITTER, MELLOW FLOUR.
THE REST IS SOFT, SWEET FLOUR.
THIS WILL YIELD A RUSTIC FLAVOR...
...THAT'S ALSO DEEP AND COMPLEX.
IT SHOULD BE EXCELLENT...
...WITH SALTED CREAM, PÂTÉ, OR VEGETABLE SOUP.
BUT WE'RE MAKING JAM, RIGHT?
HEH HEH HEH.
OH.
YOU'RE MESSING WITH THAT TOO, HUH?

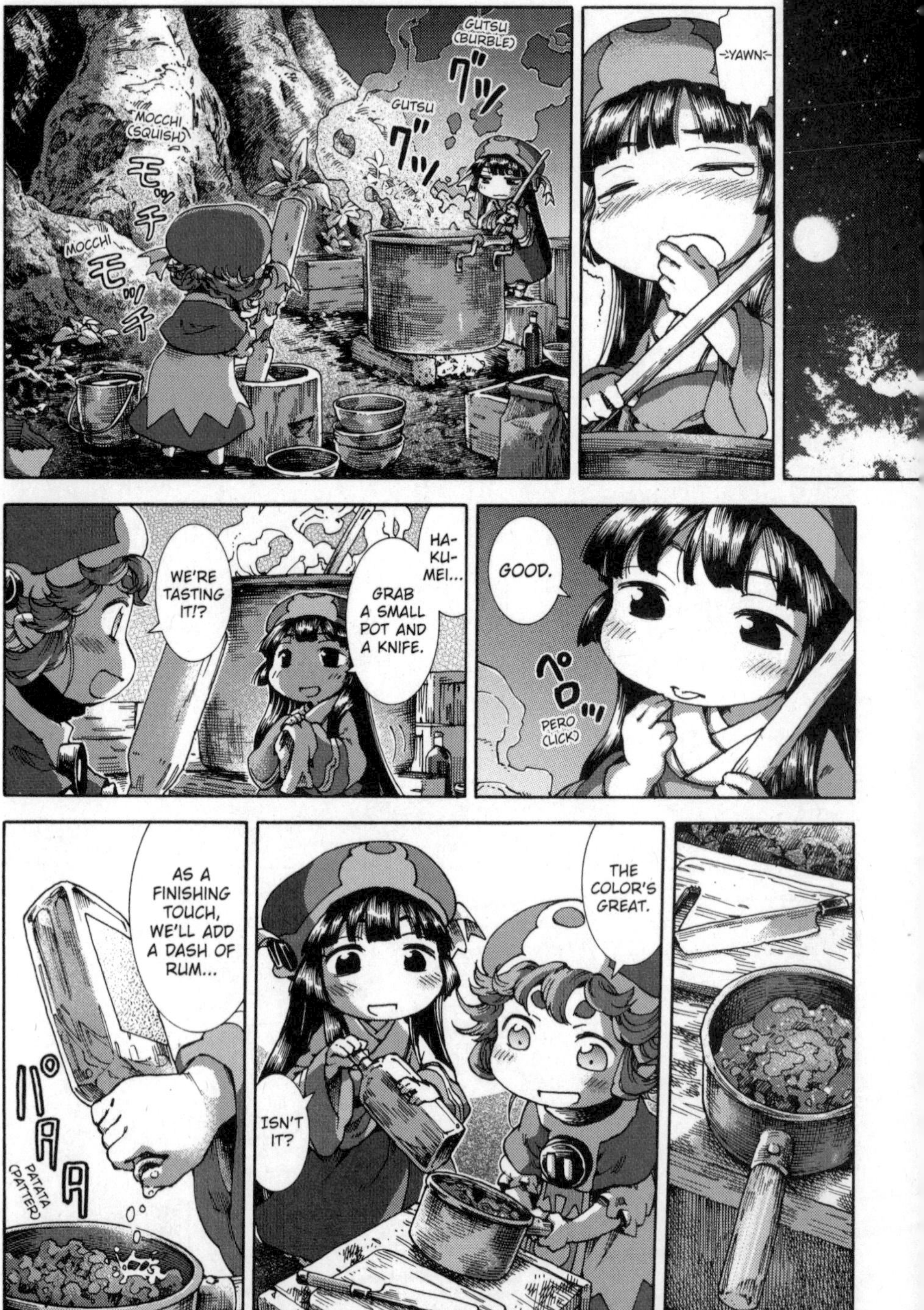
~YAWN~
GUTSU (BURBLE)
グツ
GUTSU
グツ
MOCCHI (SQUISH)
モッチ
MOCCHI
モッチ
GOOD.
ペロッ
PERO (LICK)
HAKU-MEI...
GRAB A SMALL POT AND A KNIFE.
WE'RE TASTING IT!?
THE COLOR'S GREAT.
ISN'T IT?
AS A FINISHING TOUCH, WE'LL ADD A DASH OF RUM...
パタタ
PATATA (PATTER)

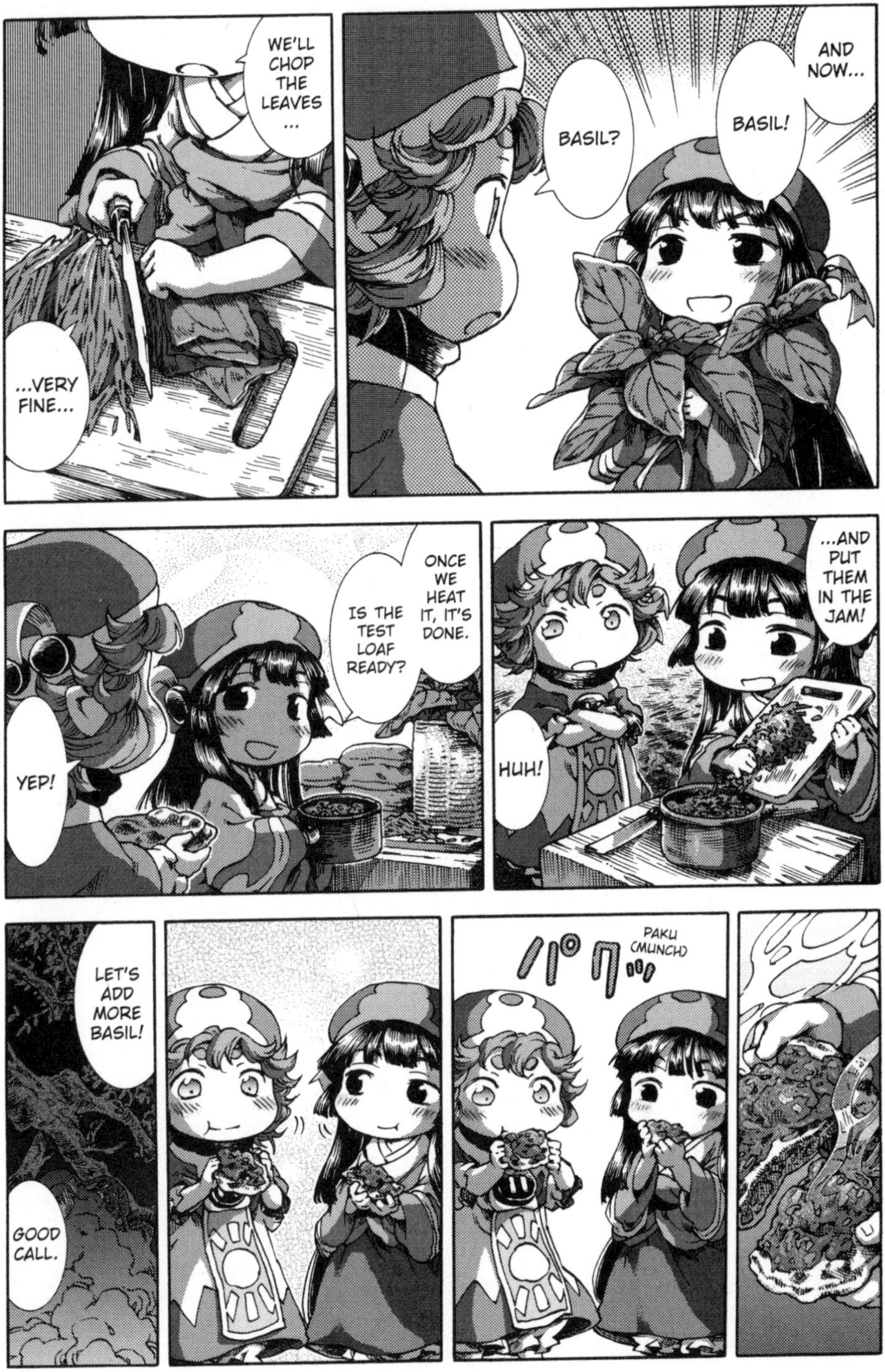
AND NOW...
BASIL!
BASIL?
WE'LL CHOP THE LEAVES ...
...VERY FINE...
...AND PUT THEM IN THE JAM!
HUH!
ONCE WE HEAT IT, IT'S DONE.
IS THE TEST LOAF READY?
YEP!
パクッ
PAKU (MUNCH)
LET'S ADD MORE BASIL!
GOOD CALL.

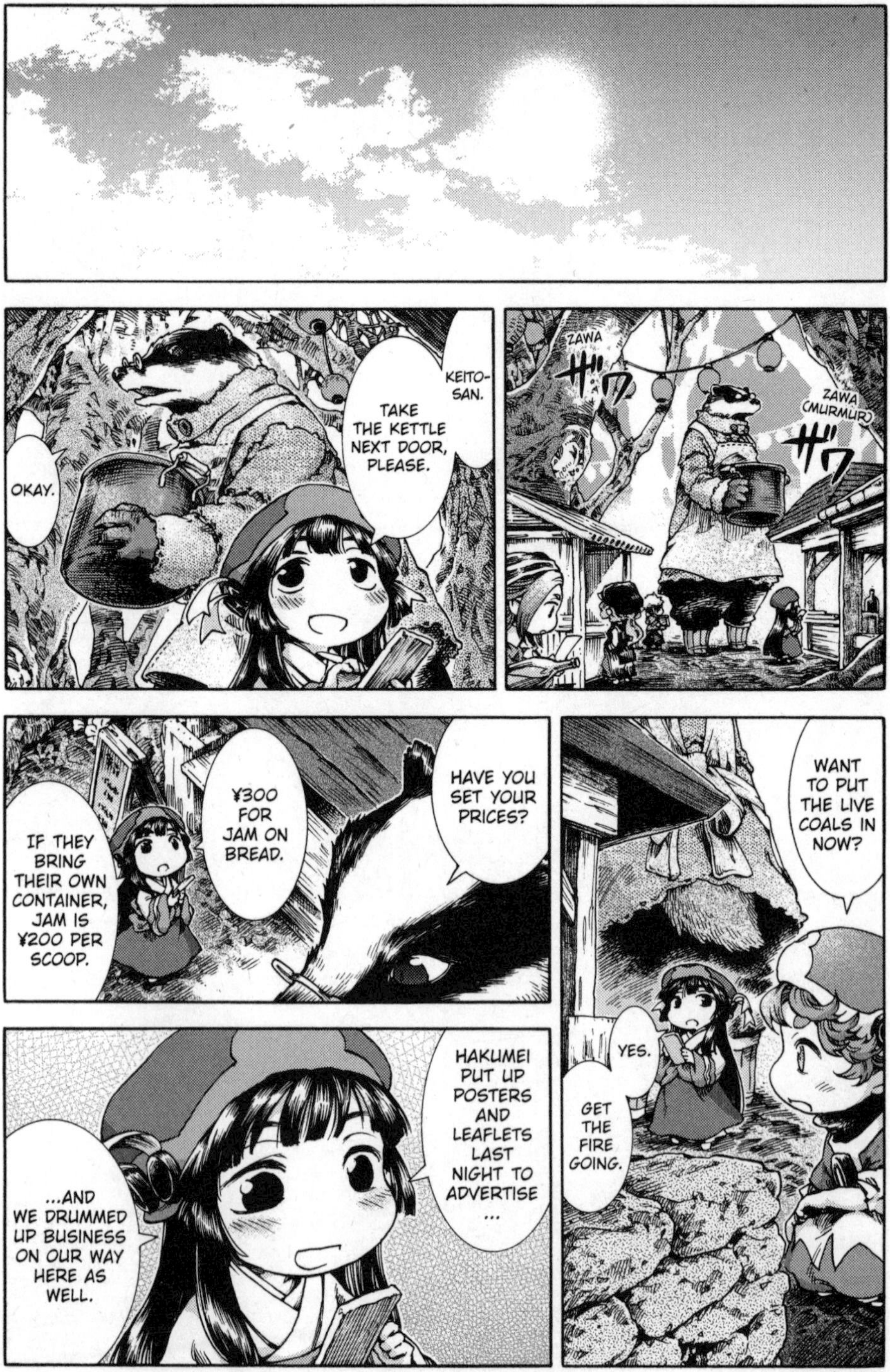
ZAWA (MURMUR)
ザワ
ZAWA
ザワ
KEITO-SAN.
TAKE THE KETTLE NEXT DOOR, PLEASE.
OKAY.
WANT TO PUT THE LIVE COALS IN NOW?
YES.
GET THE FIRE GOING.
HAVE YOU SET YOUR PRICES?
¥300 FOR JAM ON BREAD.
IF THEY BRING THEIR OWN CONTAINER, JAM IS ¥200 PER SCOOP.
HAKUMEI PUT UP POSTERS AND LEAFLETS LAST NIGHT TO ADVERTISE ...
...AND WE DRUMMED UP BUSINESS ON OUR WAY HERE AS WELL.

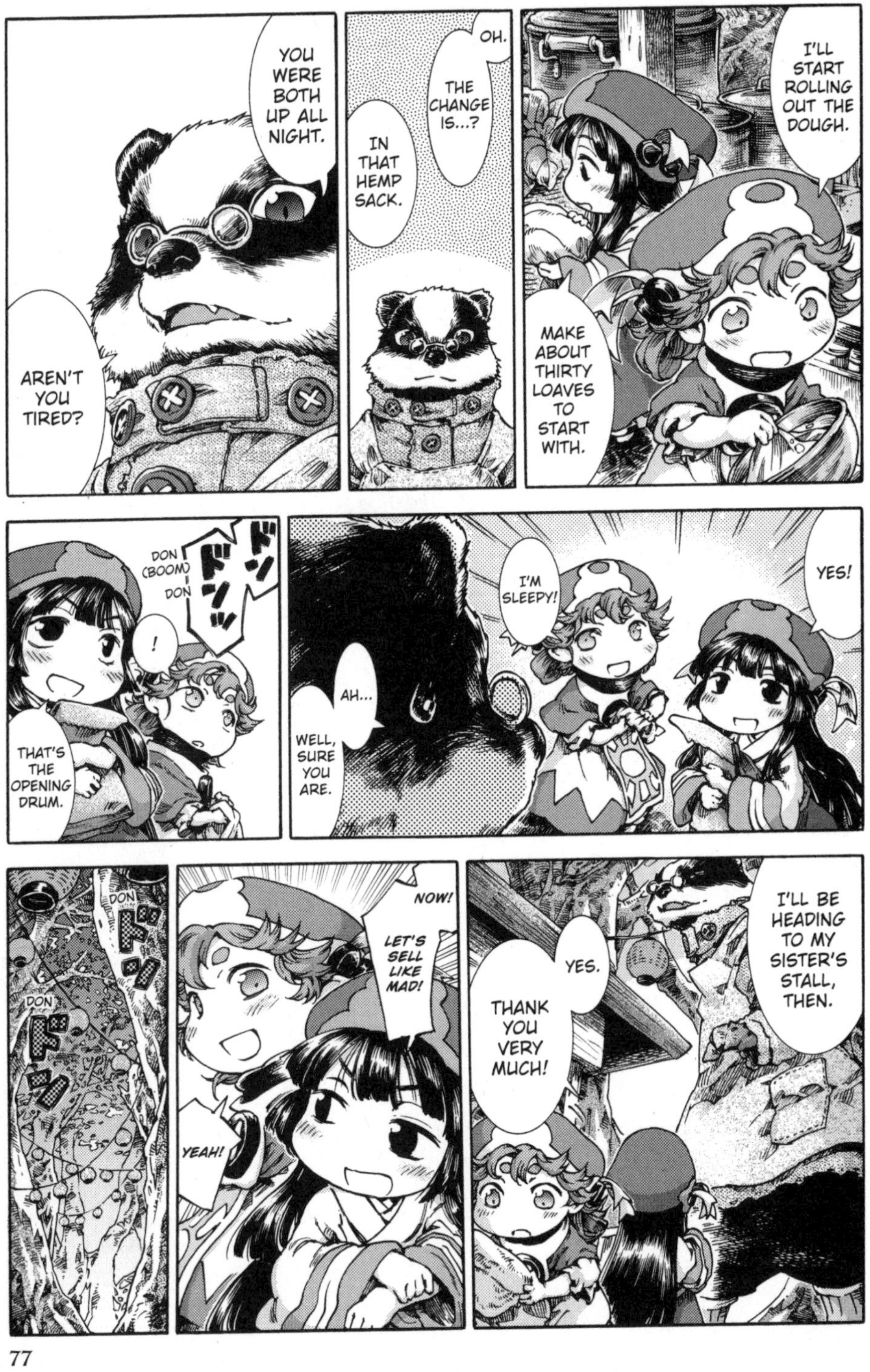
I'LL START ROLLING OUT THE DOUGH.
MAKE ABOUT THIRTY LOAVES TO START WITH.
OH.
THE CHANGE IS...?
IN THAT HEMP SACK.
YOU WERE BOTH UP ALL NIGHT.
AREN'T YOU TIRED?
YES!
I'M SLEEPY!
AH...
WELL, SURE YOU ARE.
DON (BOOM) DON
!
THAT'S THE OPENING DRUM.
I'LL BE HEADING TO MY SISTER'S STALL, THEN.
YES.
THANK YOU VERY MUCH!
NOW!
LET'S SELL LIKE MAD!
YEAH!
DON
DON

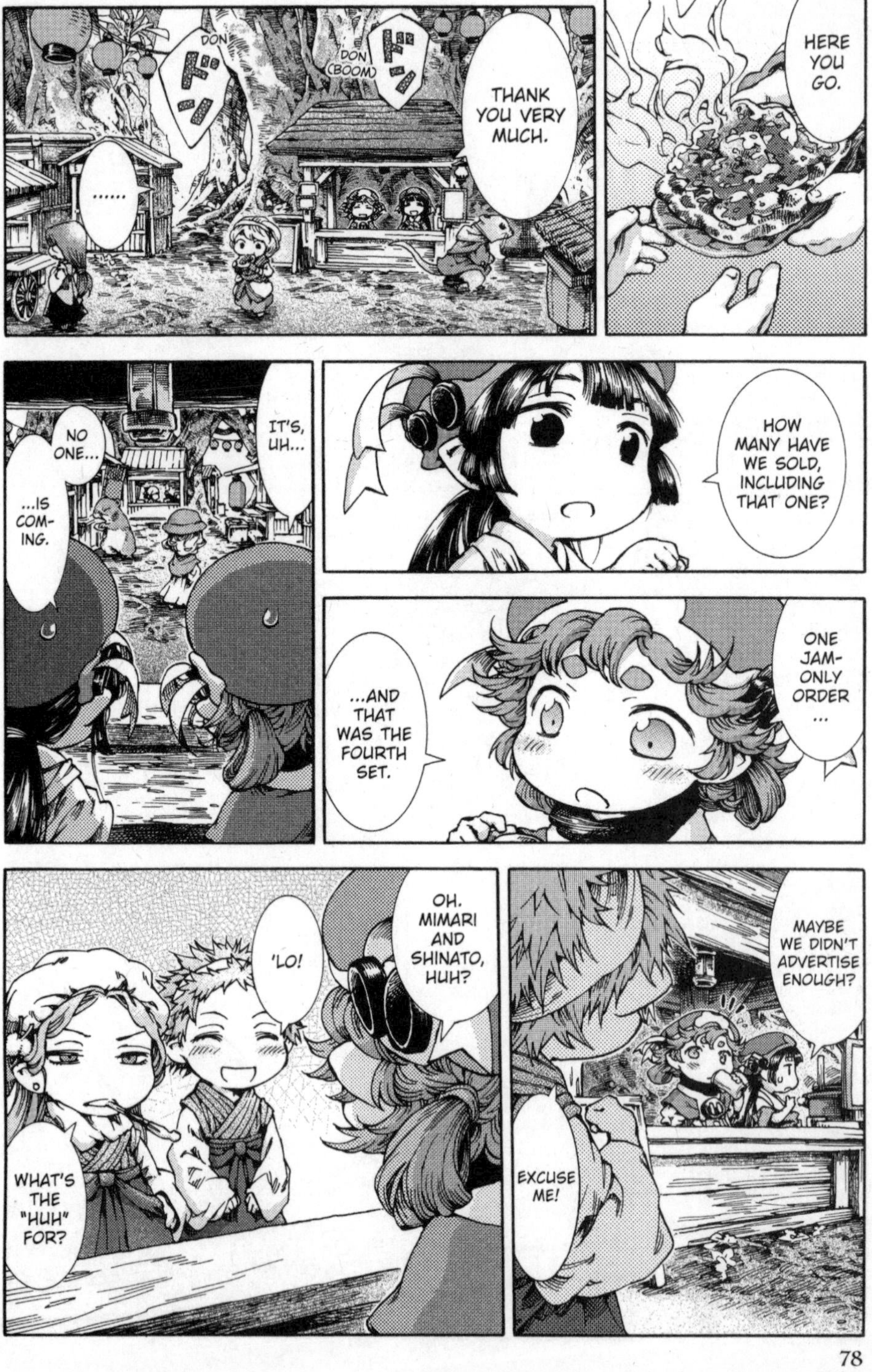
HERE YOU GO.
THANK YOU VERY MUCH.
DON
ドン
DON (BOOM)
ドン
......
HOW MANY HAVE WE SOLD, INCLUDING THAT ONE?
ONE JAM-ONLY ORDER ...
...AND THAT WAS THE FOURTH SET.
IT'S, UH...
NO ONE...
...IS COMING.
MAYBE WE DIDN'T ADVERTISE ENOUGH?
EXCUSE ME!
OH. MIMARI AND SHINATO, HUH?
'LO!
WHAT'S THE "HUH" FOR?

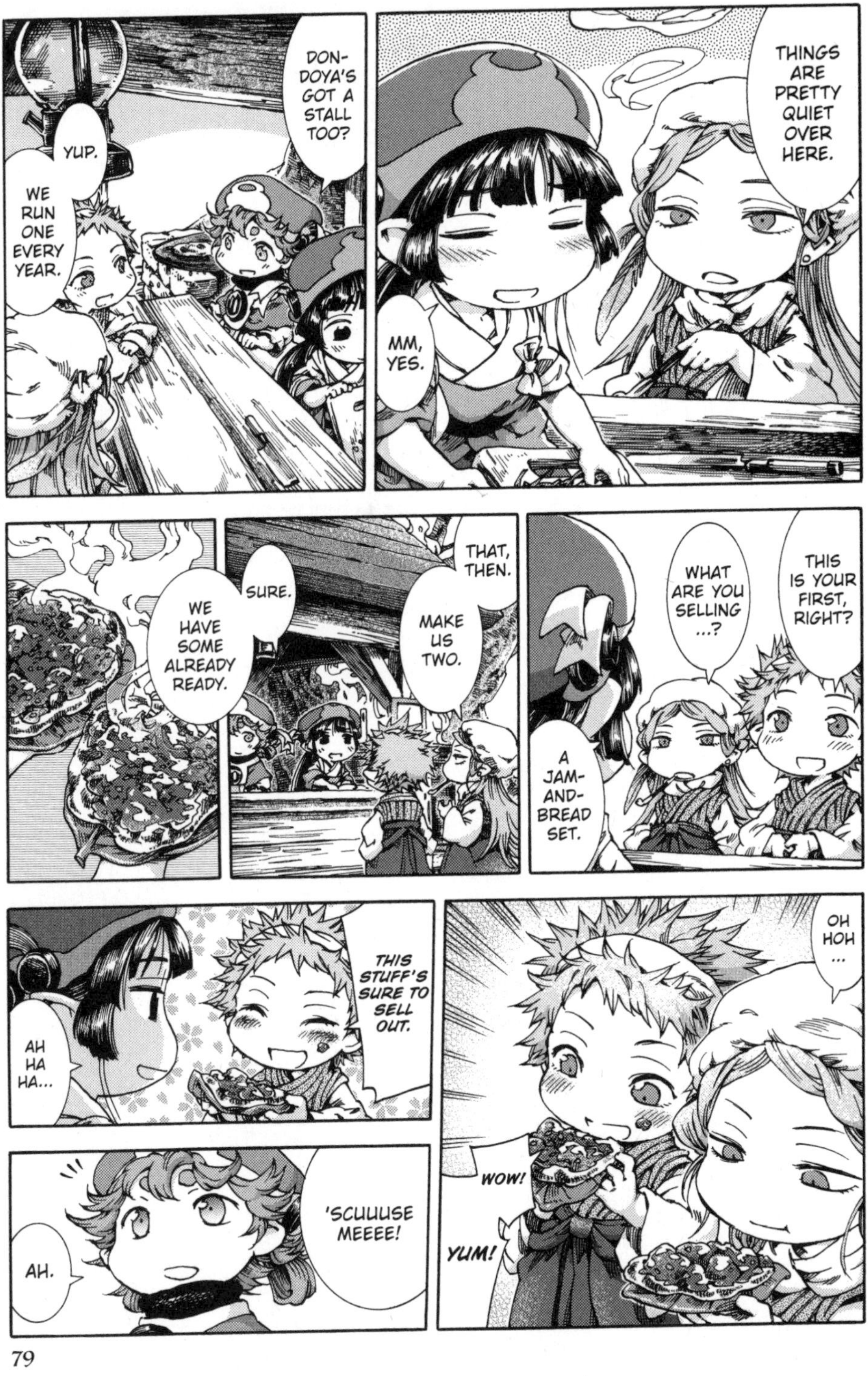
THINGS ARE PRETTY QUIET OVER HERE.
MM, YES.
DON-DOYA'S GOT A STALL TOO?
YUP.
WE RUN ONE EVERY YEAR.
THIS IS YOUR FIRST, RIGHT?
WHAT ARE YOU SELLING ...?
A JAM-AND-BREAD SET.
THAT, THEN.
MAKE US TWO.
SURE.
WE HAVE SOME ALREADY READY.
OH HOH ...
WOW!
YUM!
THIS STUFF'S SURE TO SELL OUT.
AH HA HA...
'SCUUUSE MEEEE!
AH.

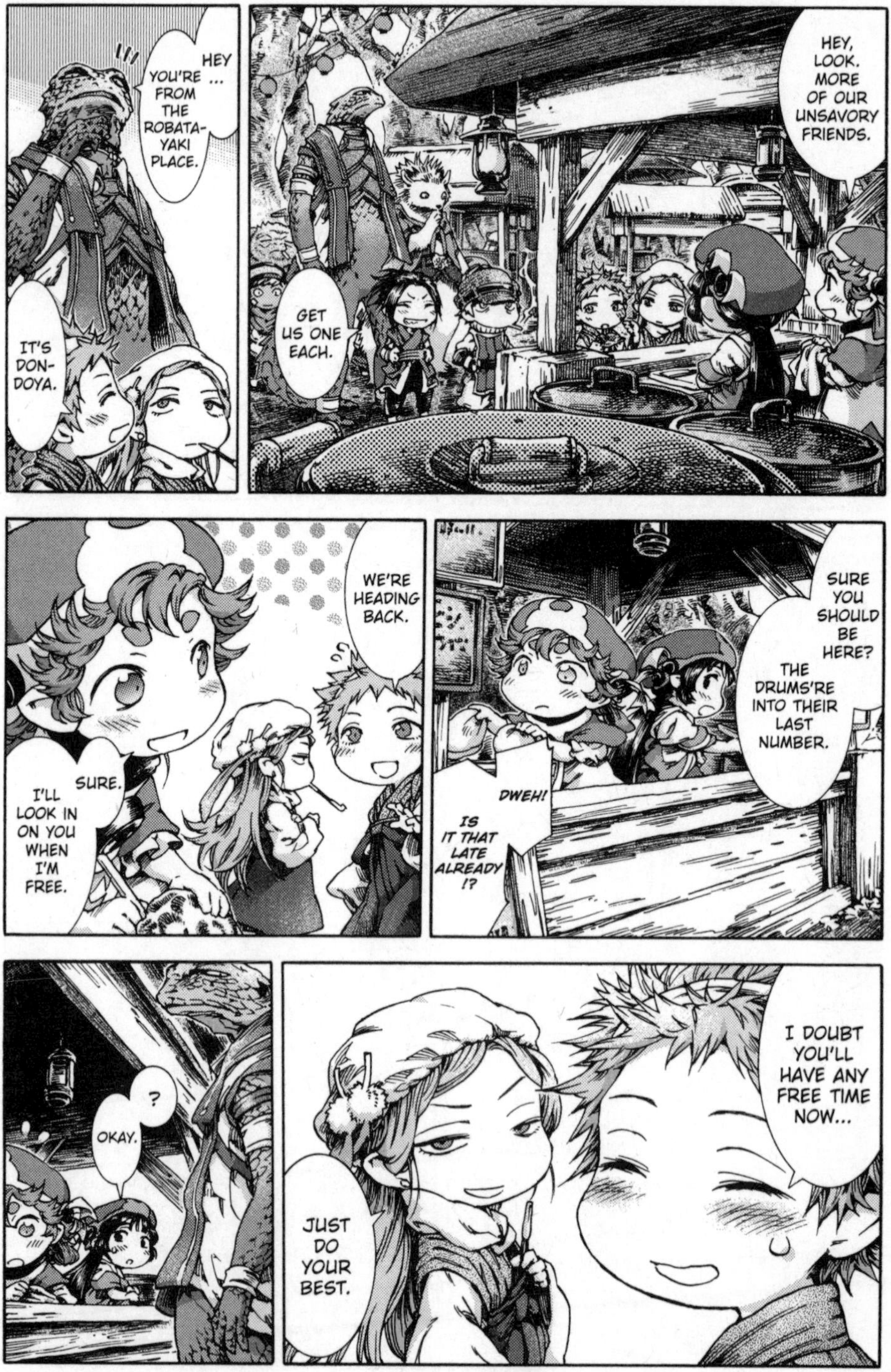
HEY, LOOK. MORE OF OUR UNSAVORY FRIENDS.
GET US ONE EACH.
HEY ... YOU'RE FROM THE ROBATA-YAKI PLACE.
IT'S DON-DOYA.
SURE YOU SHOULD BE HERE?
THE DRUMS'RE INTO THEIR LAST NUMBER.
DWEH!
IS IT THAT LATE ALREADY !?
WE'RE HEADING BACK.
SURE.
I'LL LOOK IN ON YOU WHEN I'M FREE.
I DOUBT YOU'LL HAVE ANY FREE TIME NOW...
JUST DO YOUR BEST.
?
OKAY.

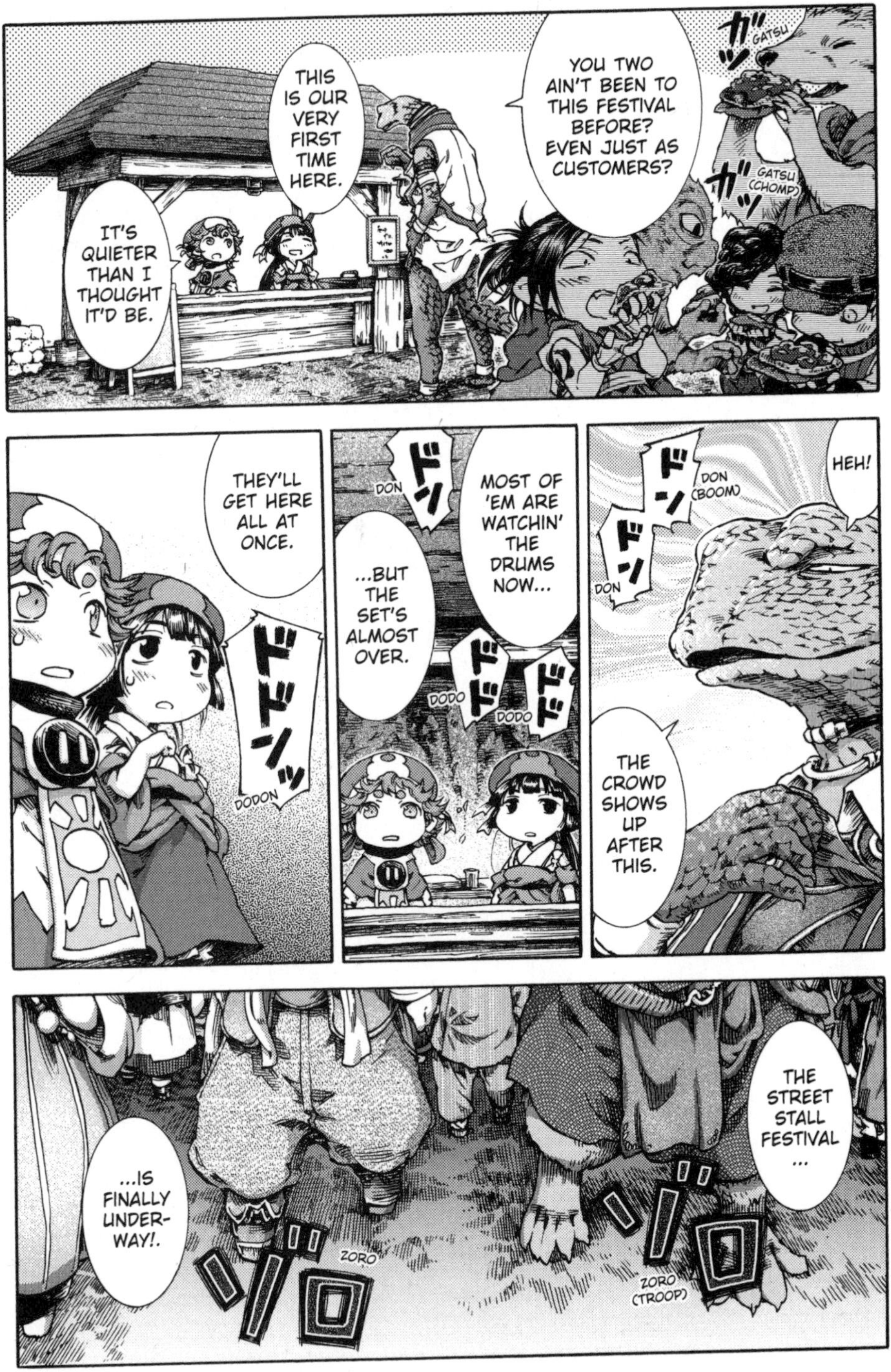
GATSU
GATSU (CHOMP)
YOU TWO AIN'T BEEN TO THIS FESTIVAL BEFORE? EVEN JUST AS CUSTOMERS?
THIS IS OUR VERY FIRST TIME HERE.
IT'S QUIETER THAN I THOUGHT IT'D BE.
HEH!
DON (BOOM)
DON
THE CROWD SHOWS UP AFTER THIS.
DON
MOST OF 'EM ARE WATCHIN' THE DRUMS NOW...
...BUT THE SET'S ALMOST OVER.
DODO
DODO
THEY'LL GET HERE ALL AT ONCE.
DODON
THE STREET STALL FESTIVAL...
ZORO (TROOP)
...IS FINALLY UNDER-WAY!.
ZORO

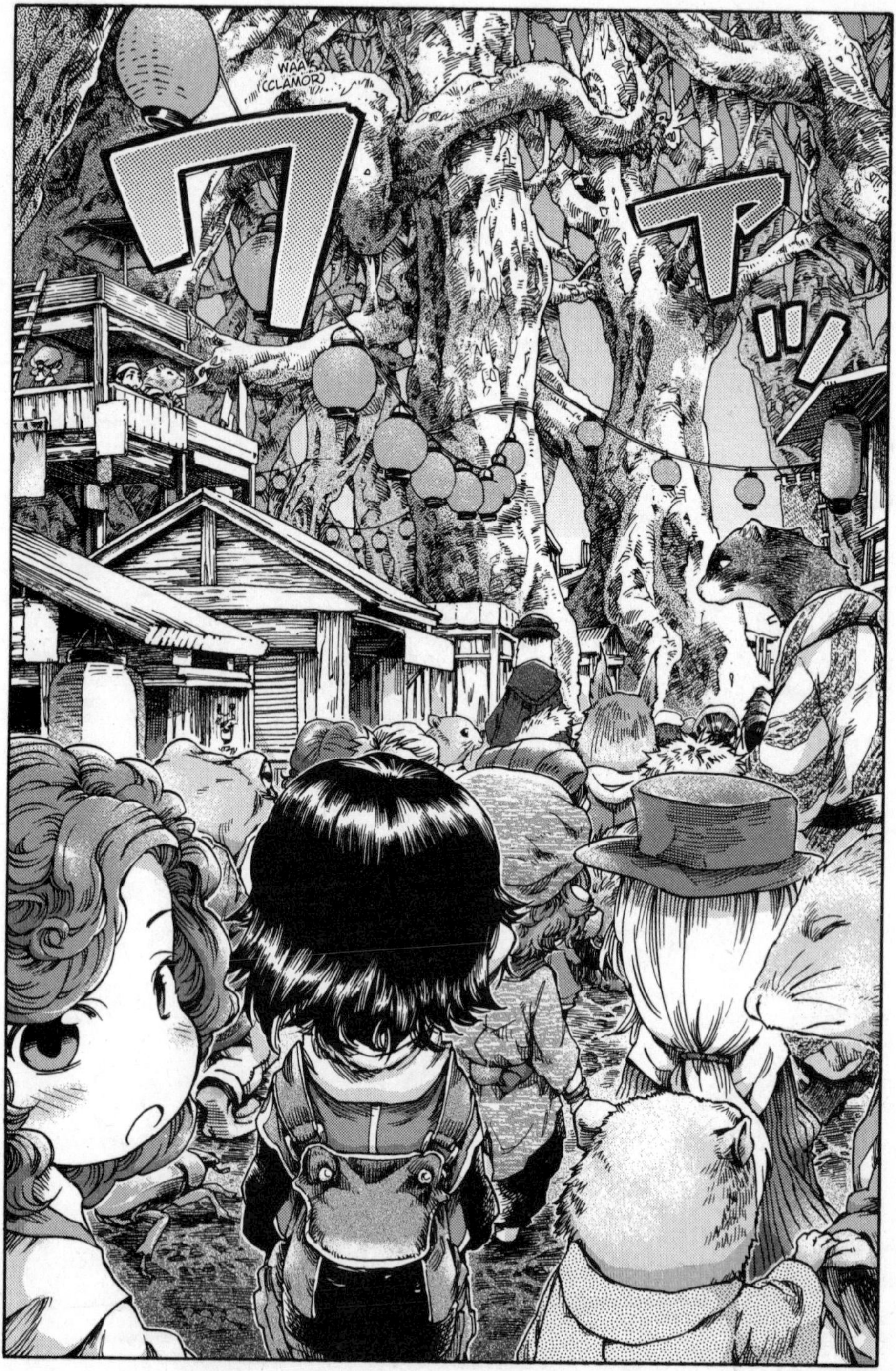
ワァッ
WAA (CLAMOR)

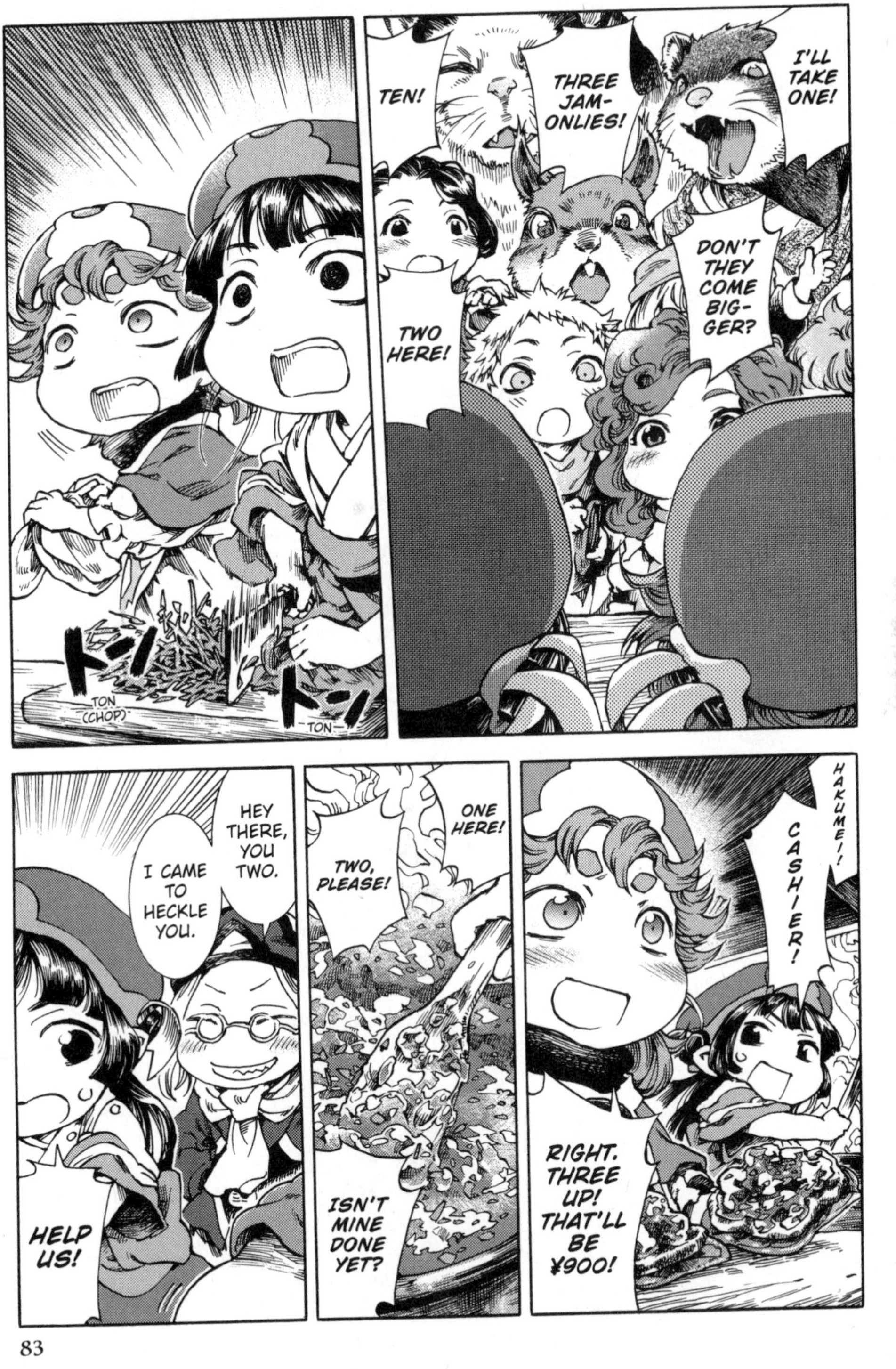
I'LL TAKE ONE!
THREE JAM-ONLIES!
TEN!
DON'T THEY COME BIGGER?
TWO HERE!
トーン
TON (CHOP)
トーン
TON
HAKUME!!
CASHIER!
RIGHT. THREE UP! THAT'LL BE ¥900!
ONE HERE!
TWO, PLEASE!
ISN'T MINE DONE YET?
HEY THERE, YOU TWO.
I CAME TO HECKLE YOU.
HELP US!

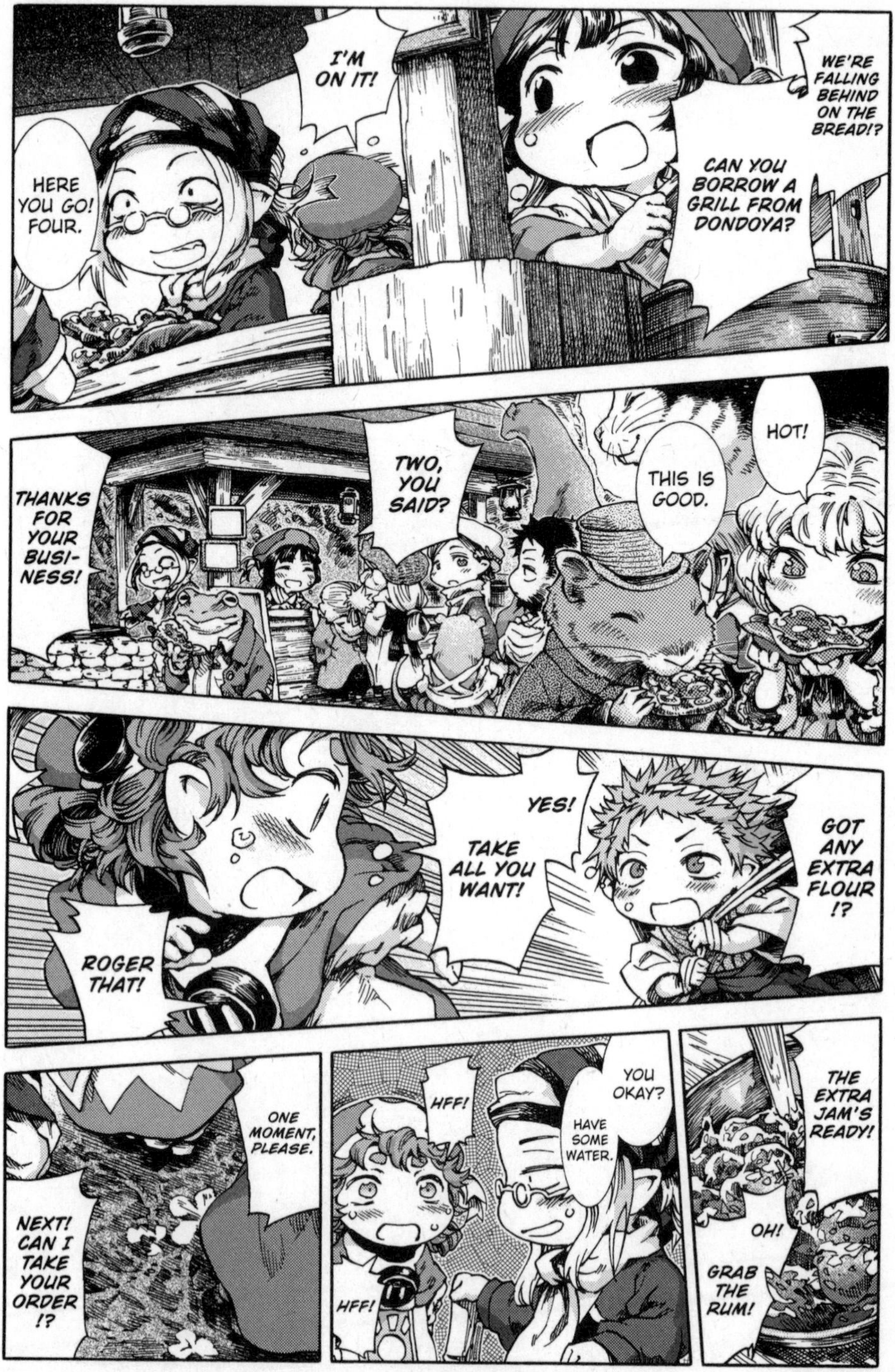
WE'RE FALLING BEHIND ON THE BREAD!?
CAN YOU BORROW A GRILL FROM DONDOYA?
I'M ON IT!
HERE YOU GO! FOUR.
HOT!
THIS IS GOOD.
TWO, YOU SAID?
THANKS FOR YOUR BUSI-NESS!
GOT ANY EXTRA FLOUR!?
YES!
TAKE ALL YOU WANT!
ROGER THAT!
THE EXTRA JAM'S READY!
OH! GRAB THE RUM!
YOU OKAY?
HAVE SOME WATER.
HFF!
HFF!
ONE MOMENT, PLEASE.
NEXT! CAN I TAKE YOUR ORDER!?

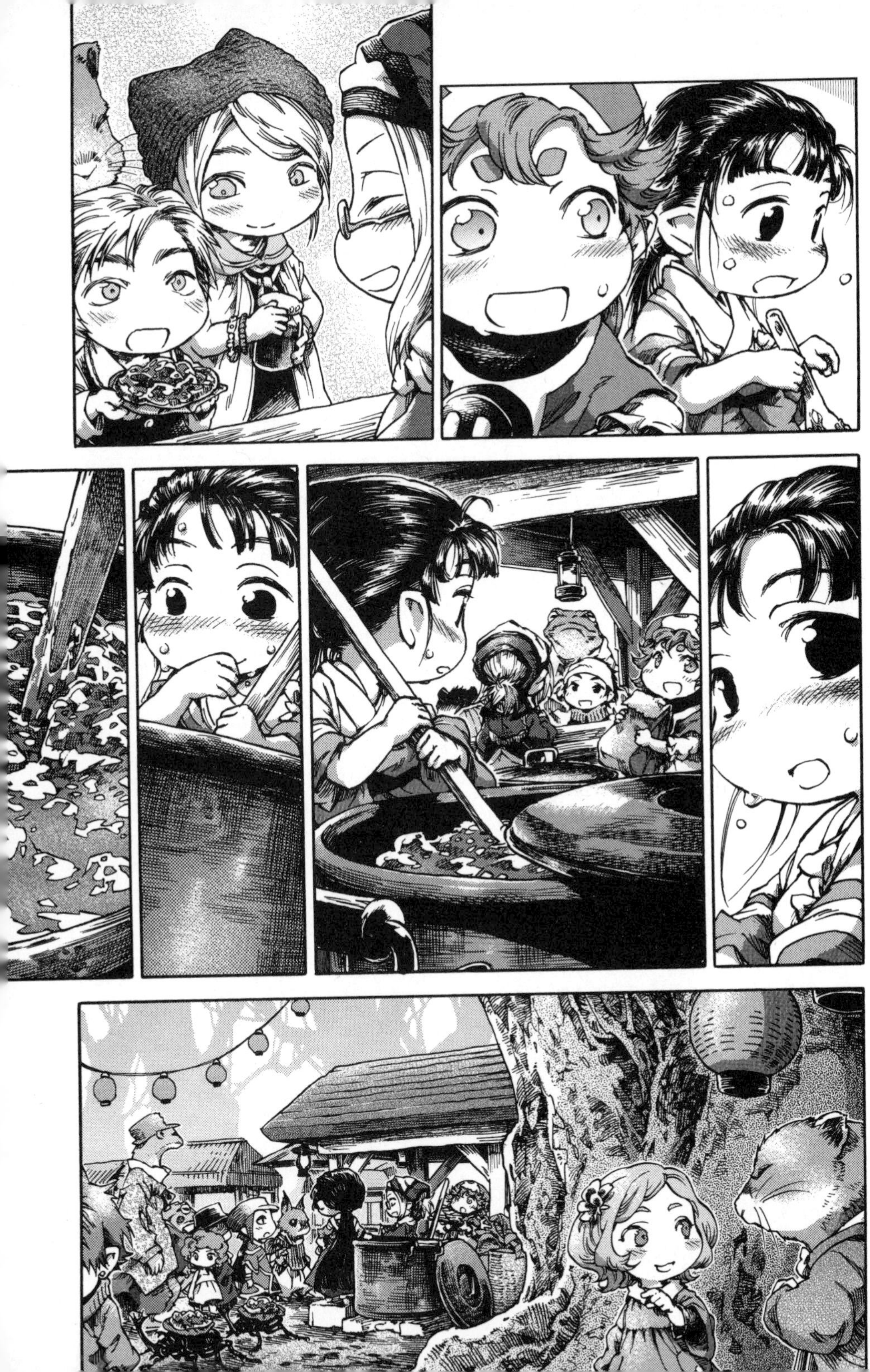

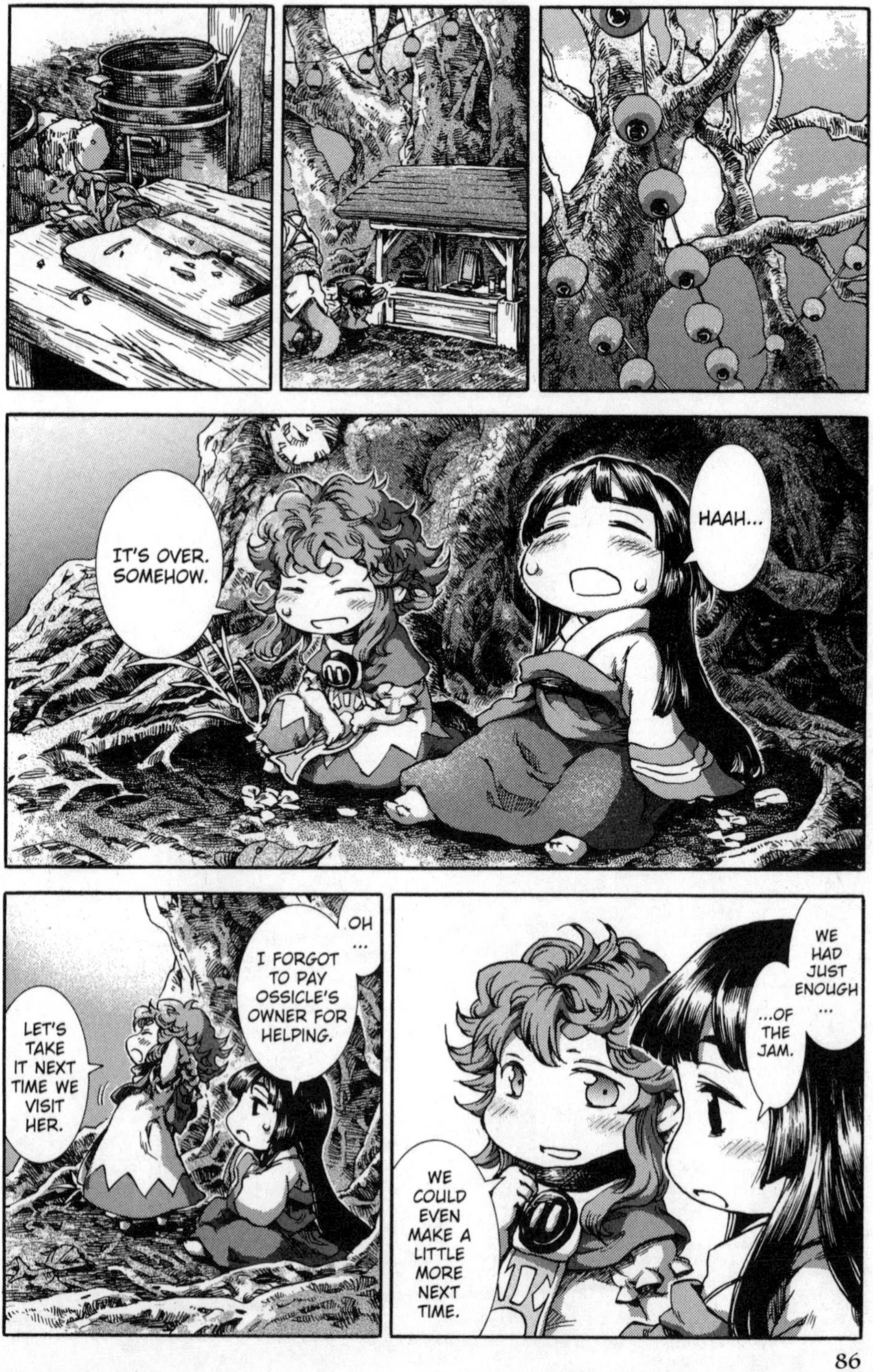
HAAH...
IT'S OVER. SOMEHOW.
WE HAD JUST ENOUGH ...
...OF THE JAM.
WE COULD EVEN MAKE A LITTLE MORE NEXT TIME.
OH ...
I FORGOT TO PAY OSSICLE'S OWNER FOR HELPING.
LET'S TAKE IT NEXT TIME WE VISIT HER.

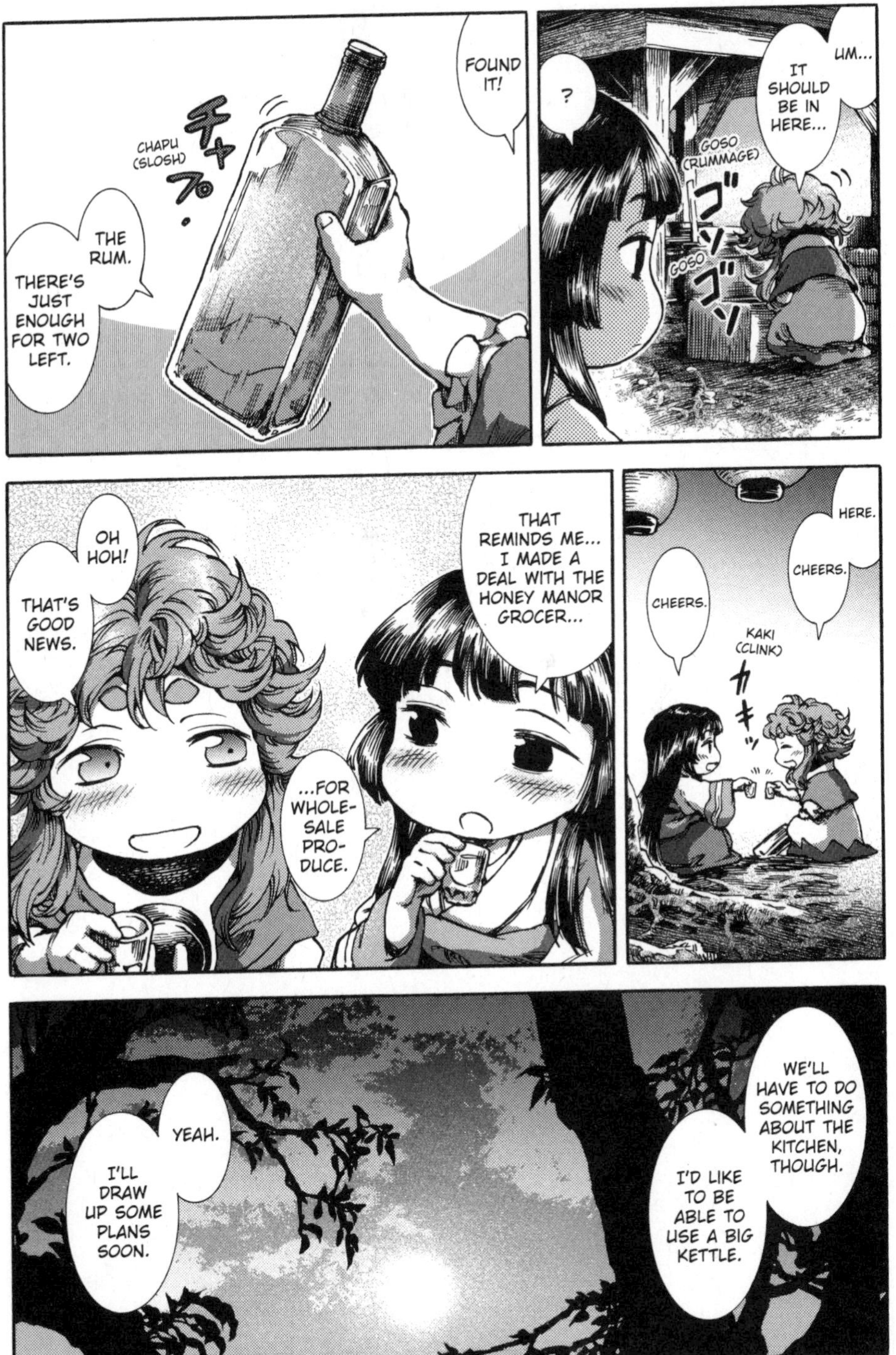
UM...
IT SHOULD BE IN HERE...
?
GOSO (RUMMAGE)
ゴソ
GOSO
ゴソ
FOUND IT!
CHAPU (SLOSH)
チャプ
THE RUM.
THERE'S JUST ENOUGH FOR TWO LEFT.
HERE.
CHEERS.
CHEERS.
KAKI (CLINK)
カキッ
THAT REMINDS ME... I MADE A DEAL WITH THE HONEY MANOR GROCER...
...FOR WHOLE-SALE PRO-DUCE.
OH HOH!
THAT'S GOOD NEWS.
WE'LL HAVE TO DO SOMETHING ABOUT THE KITCHEN, THOUGH.
I'D LIKE TO BE ABLE TO USE A BIG KETTLE.
YEAH.
I'LL DRAW UP SOME PLANS SOON.

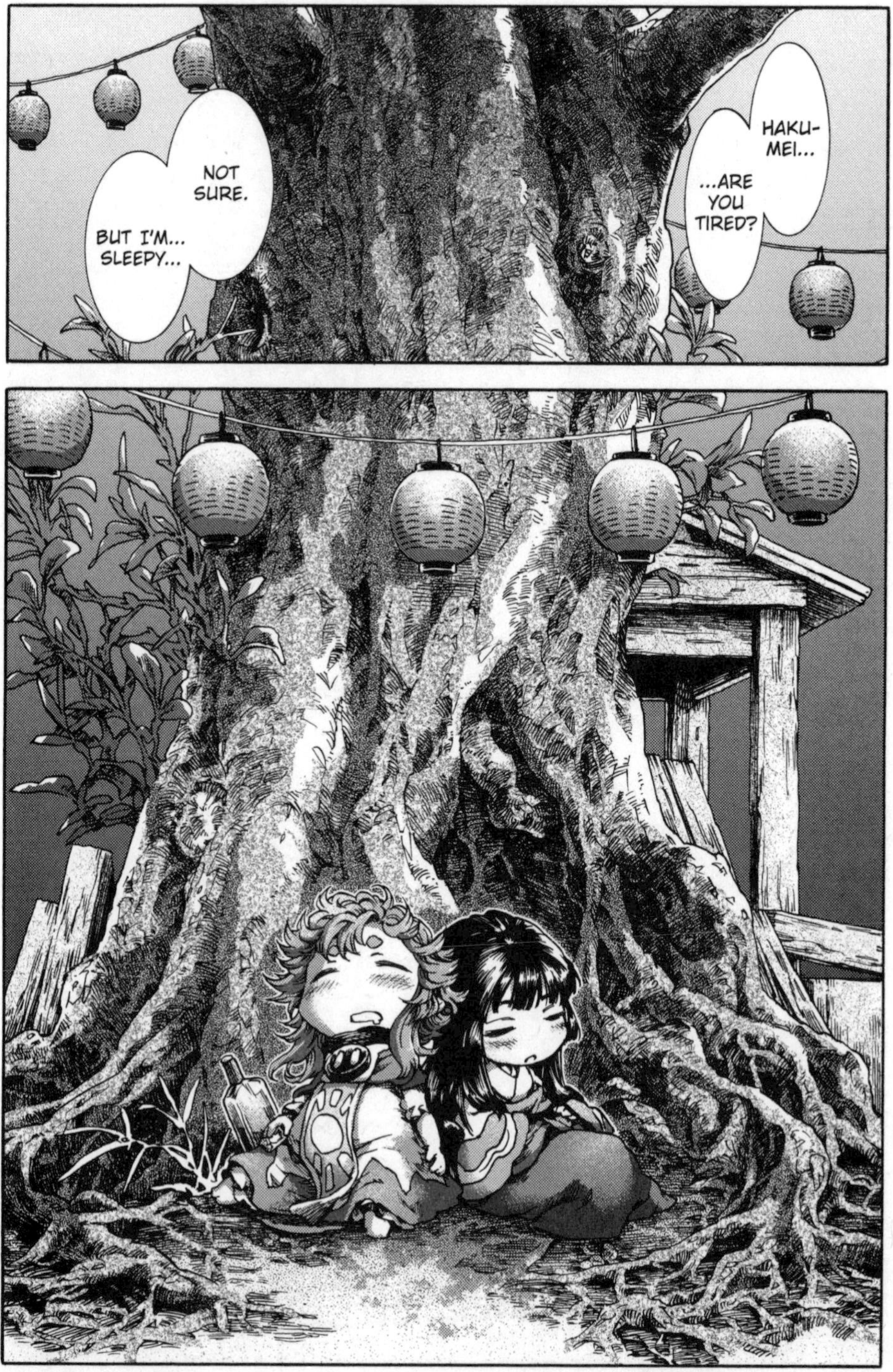
HAKU-MEI...
...ARE YOU TIRED?
NOT SURE.
BUT I'M... SLEEPY...

•*Column*• Underfoot Steps 22 / Miki the Greengrocer

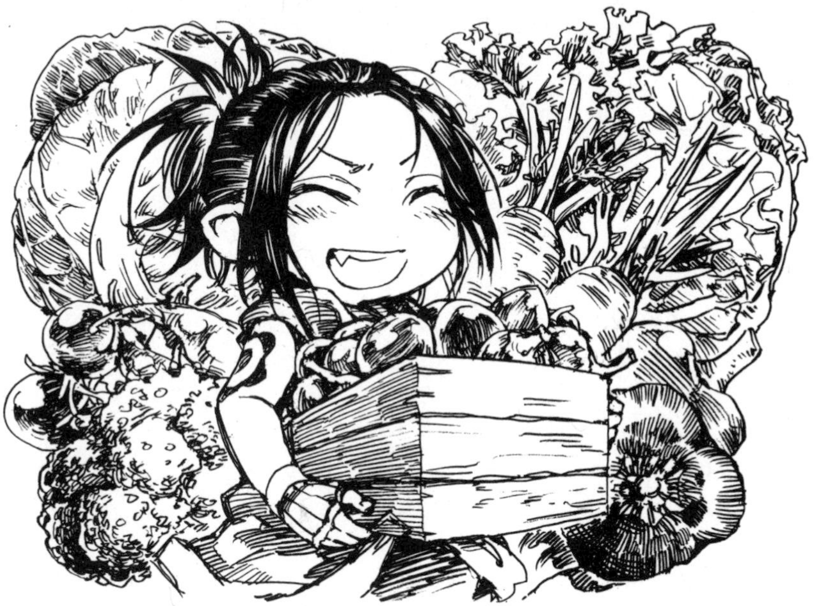

Greengrocer Miki is a shop within Honey Manor. Miki, its owner, is an excellent stockist, and his merchandise is consistently very flavorful and fresh. He stocks an abundant array not only of seasonal produce, but also of rare, sought-after varieties.

However, due to poor advertising, a bad location, and aggressive pricing (except for the very small percentage he sells wholesale to restaurants), nearly all of his produce remains unsold.

As a result, Greengrocer Miki has a remarkably bad reputation among those in the business. His passion for produce is true, so it's hoped that he'll drastically reform his management policy.

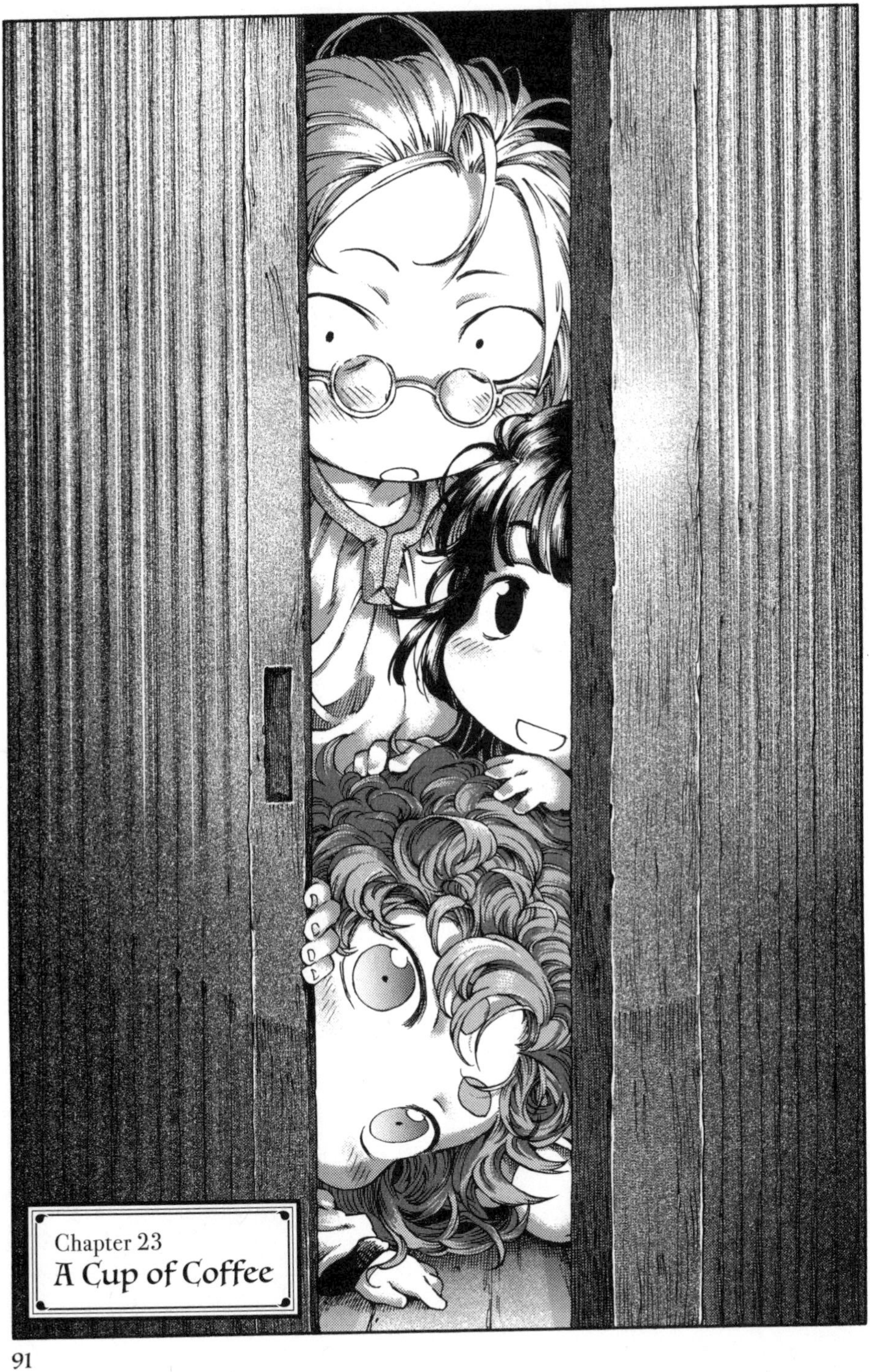
Chapter 23
A Cup of Coffee

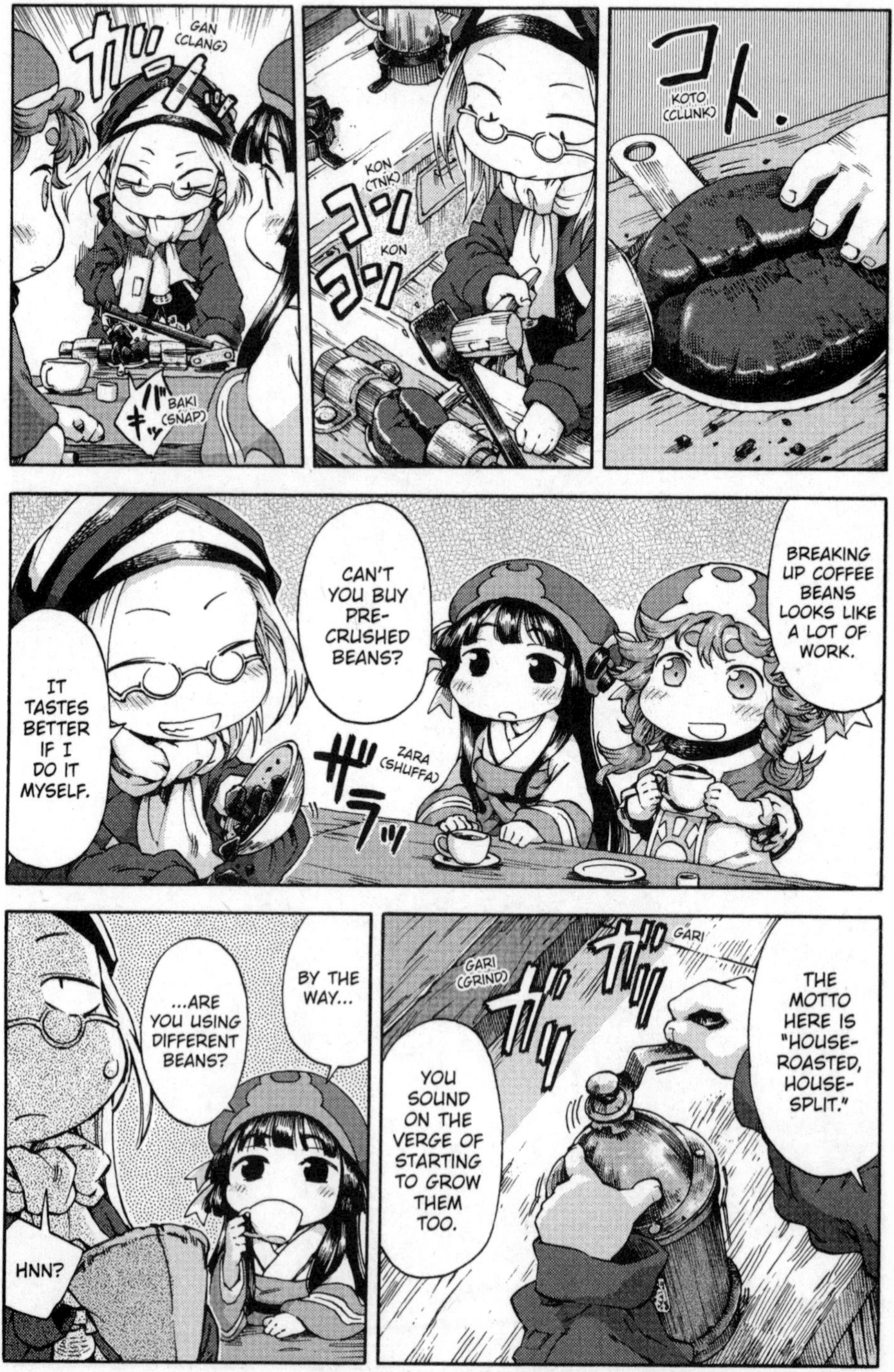

KOTO (CLUNK)
KON (TNK)
KON
GAN (CLANG)
BAKI (SNAP)
BREAKING UP COFFEE BEANS LOOKS LIKE A LOT OF WORK.
CAN'T YOU BUY PRE-CRUSHED BEANS?
ZARA (SHUFFA)
IT TASTES BETTER IF I DO IT MYSELF.
GARI
GARI (GRIND)
THE MOTTO HERE IS "HOUSE-ROASTED, HOUSE-SPLIT."
YOU SOUND ON THE VERGE OF STARTING TO GROW THEM TOO.
BY THE WAY...
...ARE YOU USING DIFFERENT BEANS?
HNN?

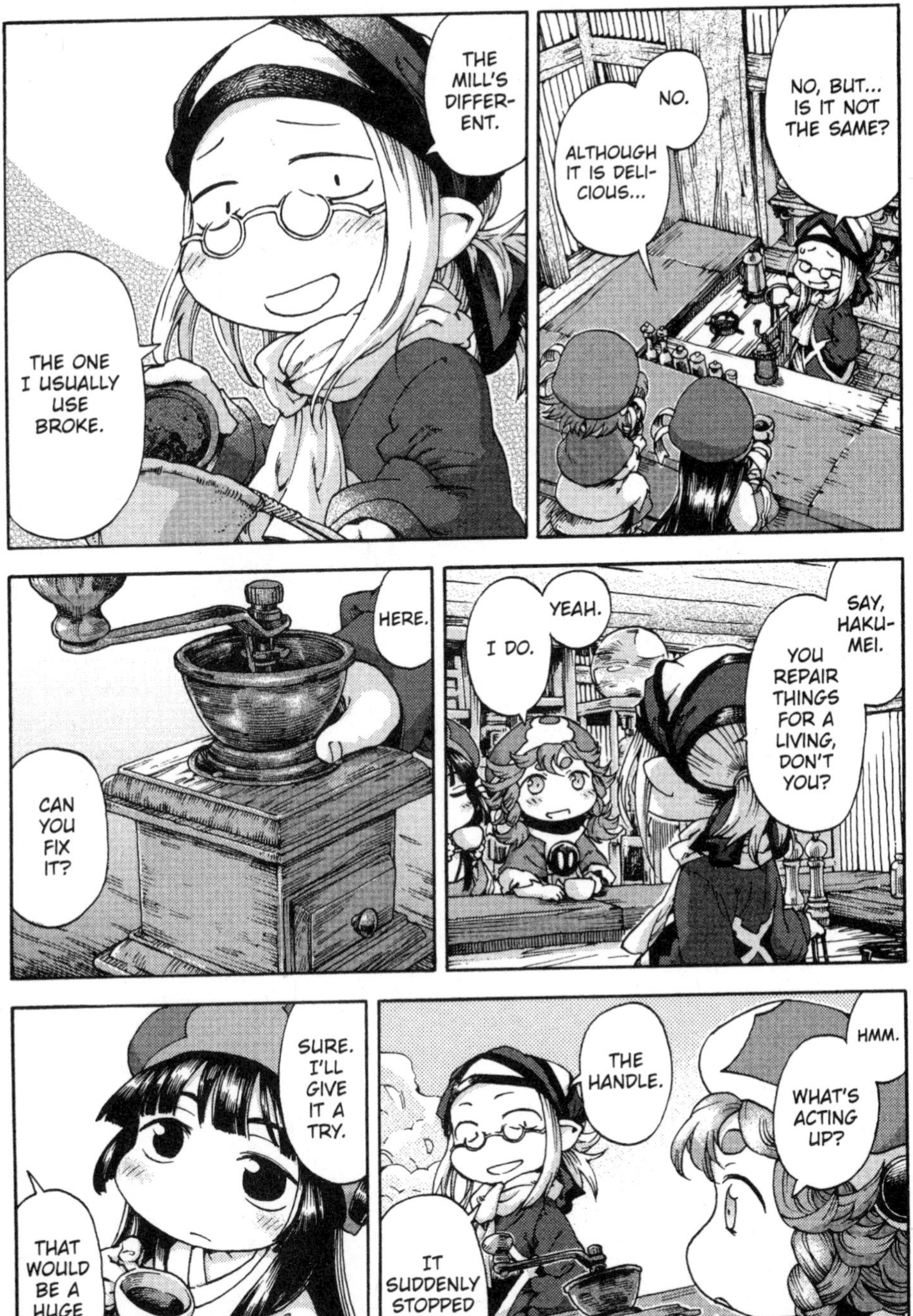
NO, BUT... IS IT NOT THE SAME?
NO.
ALTHOUGH IT IS DELICIOUS...
THE MILL'S DIFFERENT.
THE ONE I USUALLY USE BROKE.
SAY, HAKUMEI.
YOU REPAIR THINGS FOR A LIVING, DON'T YOU?
YEAH.
I DO.
HERE.
CAN YOU FIX IT?
HMM.
WHAT'S ACTING UP?
THE HANDLE.
IT SUDDENLY STOPPED TURNING.
SURE. I'LL GIVE IT A TRY.
THAT WOULD BE A HUGE HELP.

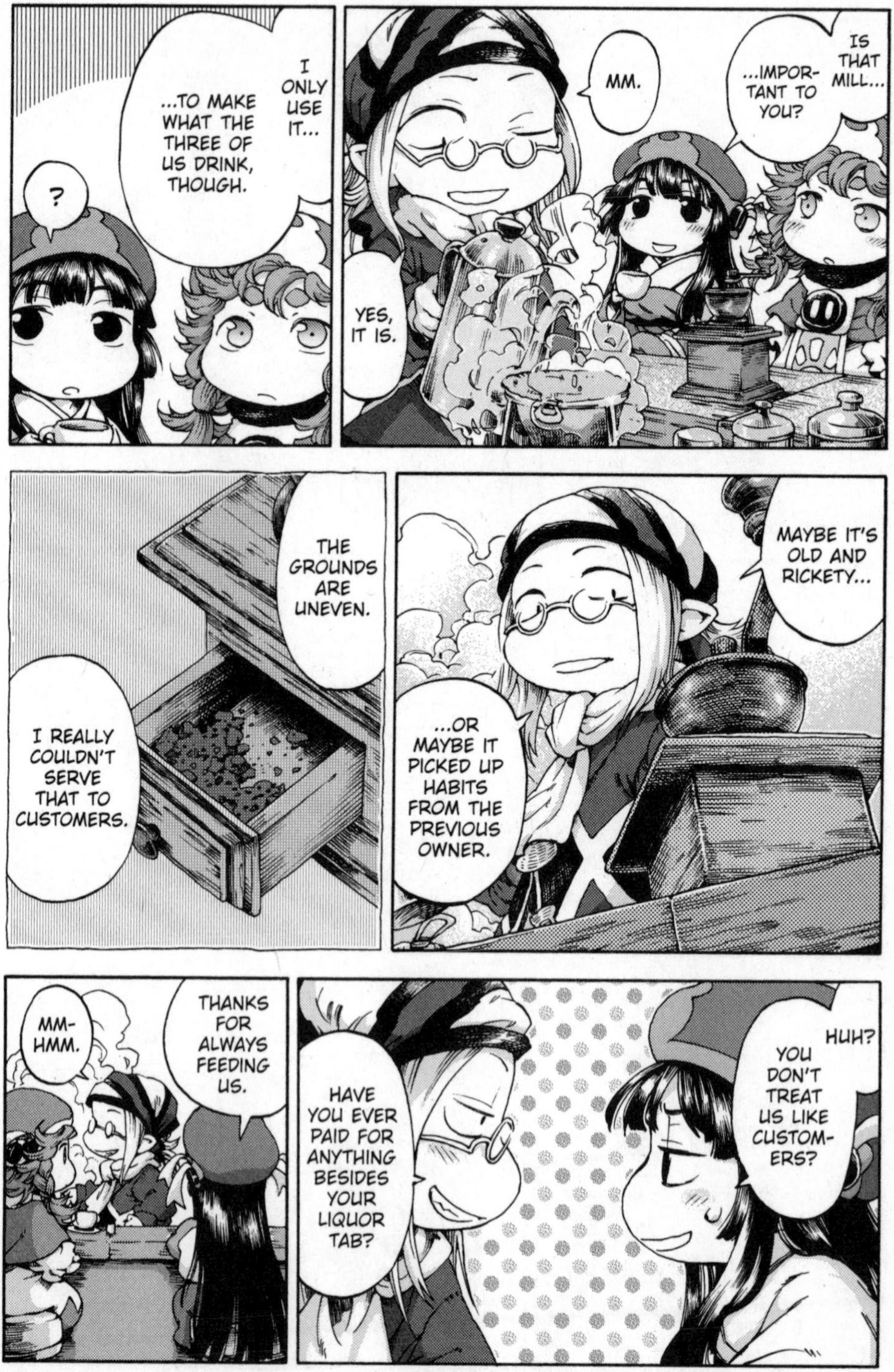
IS THAT MILL...
...IMPORTANT TO YOU?
MM.
YES, IT IS.
I ONLY USE IT...
...TO MAKE WHAT THE THREE OF US DRINK, THOUGH.
?
MAYBE IT'S OLD AND RICKETY...
...OR MAYBE IT PICKED UP HABITS FROM THE PREVIOUS OWNER.
THE GROUNDS ARE UNEVEN.
I REALLY COULDN'T SERVE THAT TO CUSTOMERS.
HUH?
YOU DON'T TREAT US LIKE CUSTOMERS?
HAVE YOU EVER PAID FOR ANYTHING BESIDES YOUR LIQUOR TAB?
THANKS FOR ALWAYS FEEDING US.
MM-HMM.

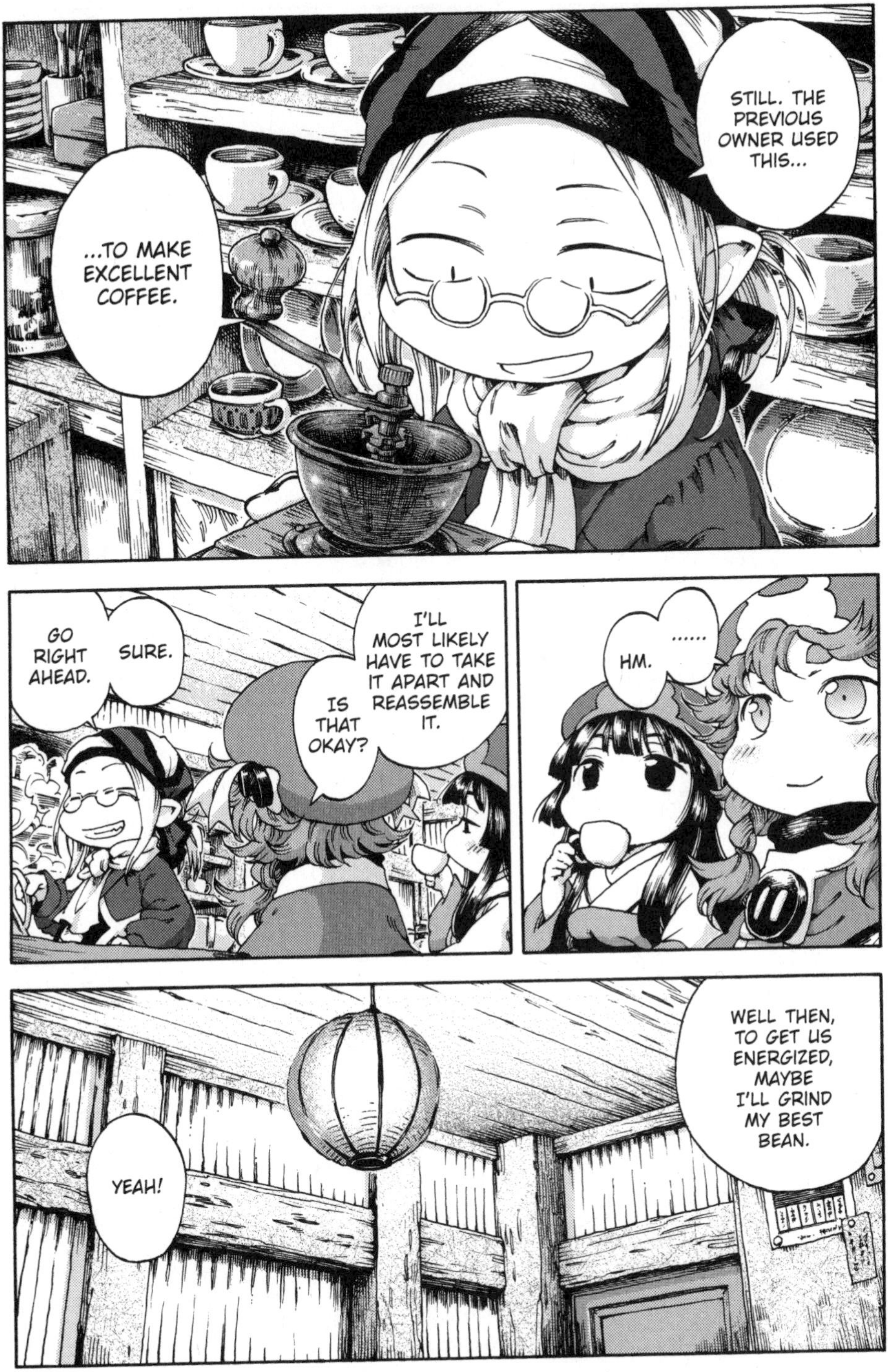
STILL. THE PREVIOUS OWNER USED THIS...
...TO MAKE EXCELLENT COFFEE.
......
HM.
I'LL MOST LIKELY HAVE TO TAKE IT APART AND REASSEMBLE IT.
IS THAT OKAY?
SURE.
GO RIGHT AHEAD.
WELL THEN, TO GET US ENERGIZED, MAYBE I'LL GRIND MY BEST BEAN.
YEAH!

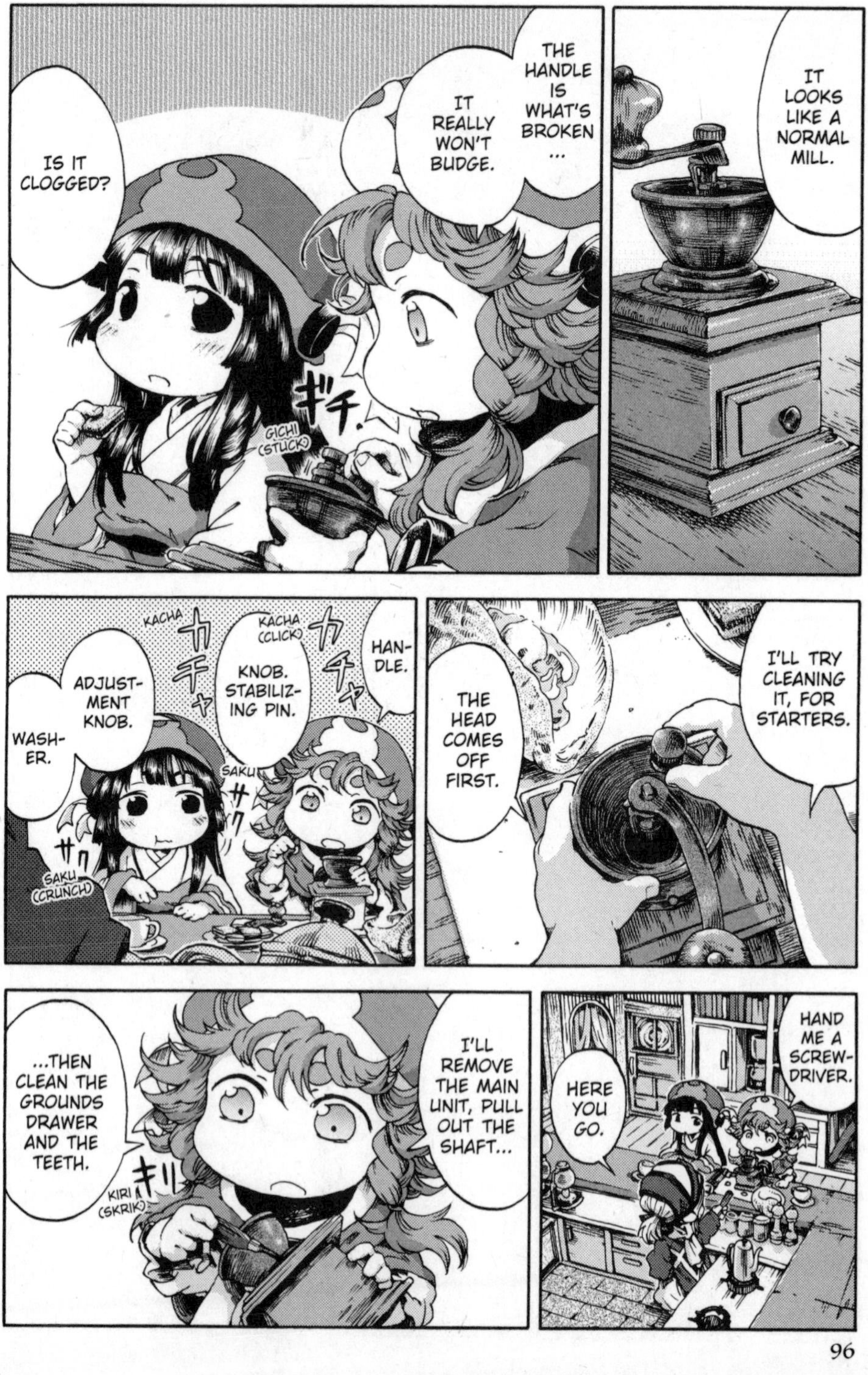
IT LOOKS LIKE A NORMAL MILL.
THE HANDLE IS WHAT'S BROKEN ...
IT REALLY WON'T BUDGE.
GICHI (STUCK)
IS IT CLOGGED?
I'LL TRY CLEANING IT, FOR STARTERS.
THE HEAD COMES OFF FIRST.
HANDLE.
KACHA (CLICK)
KNOB. STABILIZING PIN.
KACHA
ADJUSTMENT KNOB.
WASHER.
SAKU
SAKU (CRUNCH)
HAND ME A SCREWDRIVER.
HERE YOU GO.
I'LL REMOVE THE MAIN UNIT, PULL OUT THE SHAFT...
KIRI (SKRIK)
...THEN CLEAN THE GROUNDS DRAWER AND THE TEETH.

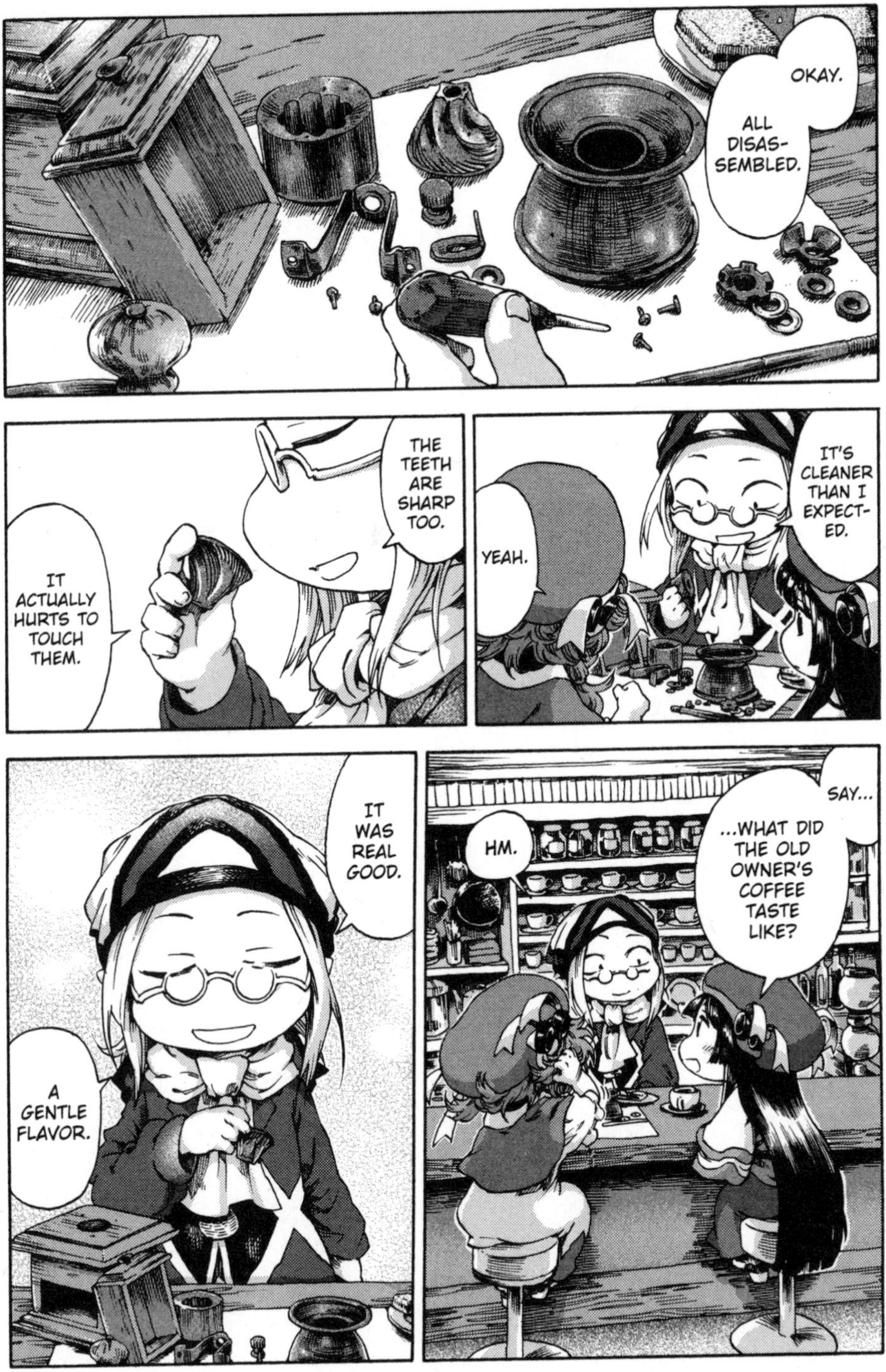
OKAY.
ALL DISAS-SEMBLED.
IT'S CLEANER THAN I EXPECT-ED.
YEAH.
THE TEETH ARE SHARP TOO.
IT ACTUALLY HURTS TO TOUCH THEM.
SAY...
...WHAT DID THE OLD OWNER'S COFFEE TASTE LIKE?
HM.
IT WAS REAL GOOD.
A GENTLE FLAVOR.

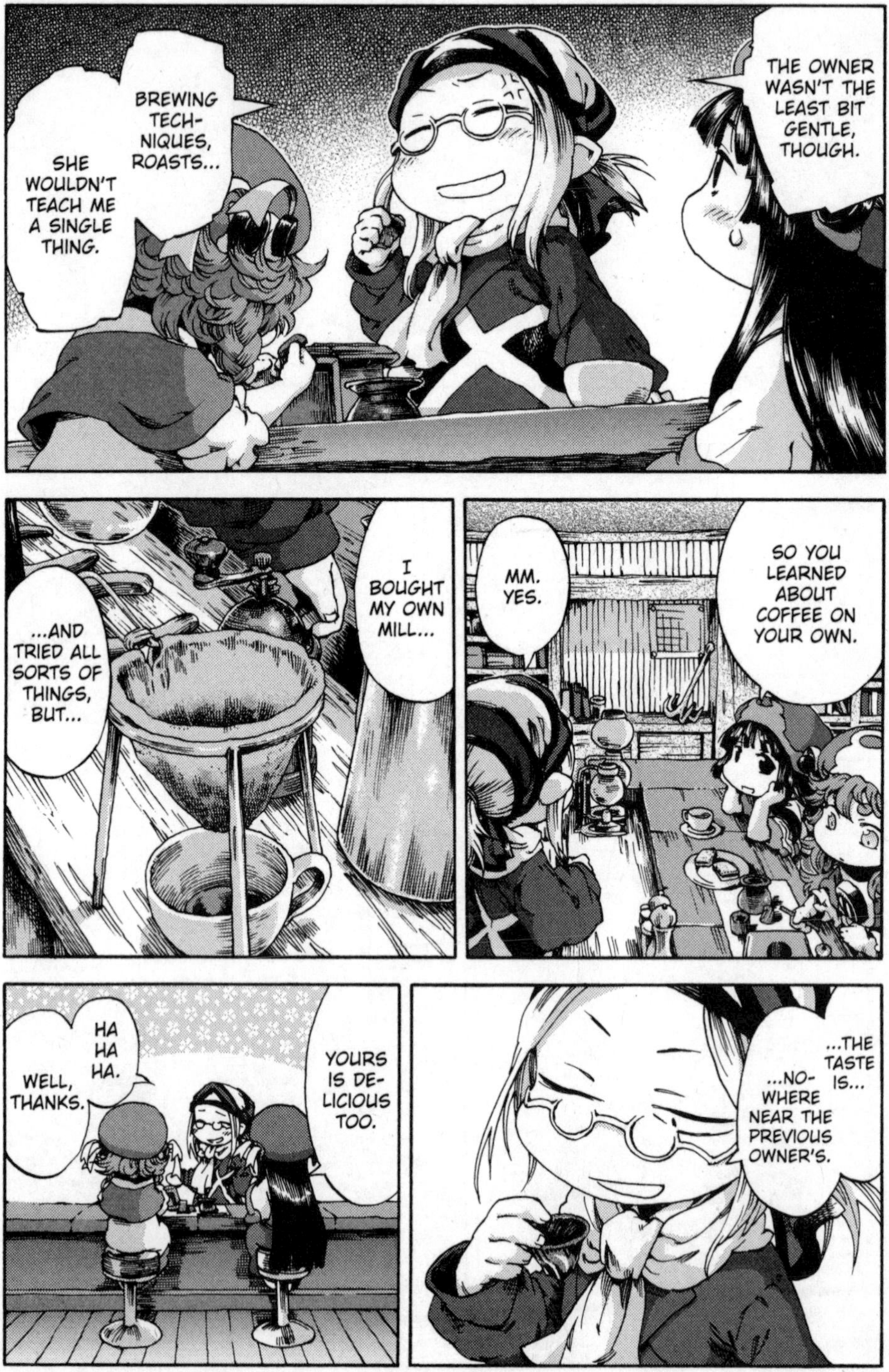
THE OWNER WASN'T THE LEAST BIT GENTLE, THOUGH.
BREWING TECH-NIQUES, ROASTS...
SHE WOULDN'T TEACH ME A SINGLE THING.
SO YOU LEARNED ABOUT COFFEE ON YOUR OWN.
MM. YES.
I BOUGHT MY OWN MILL...
...AND TRIED ALL SORTS OF THINGS, BUT...
...THE TASTE IS...
...NO-WHERE NEAR THE PREVIOUS OWNER'S.
YOURS IS DE-LICIOUS TOO.
HA HA HA.
WELL, THANKS.

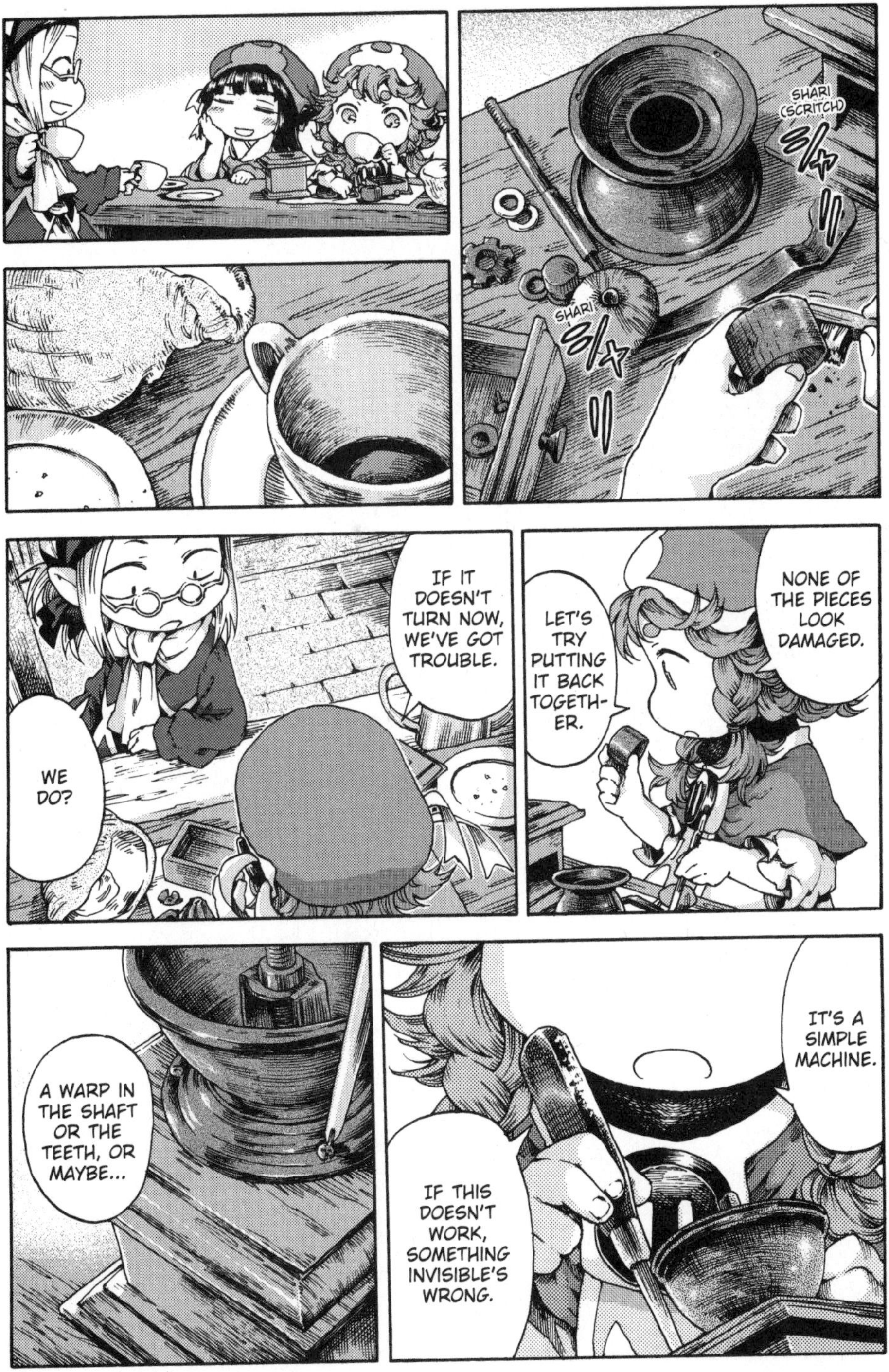
SHARI (SCRITCH)
SHARI
NONE OF THE PIECES LOOK DAMAGED.
LET'S TRY PUTTING IT BACK TOGETH-ER.
IF IT DOESN'T TURN NOW, WE'VE GOT TROUBLE.
WE DO?
IT'S A SIMPLE MACHINE.
IF THIS DOESN'T WORK, SOMETHING INVISIBLE'S WRONG.
A WARP IN THE SHAFT OR THE TEETH, OR MAYBE...

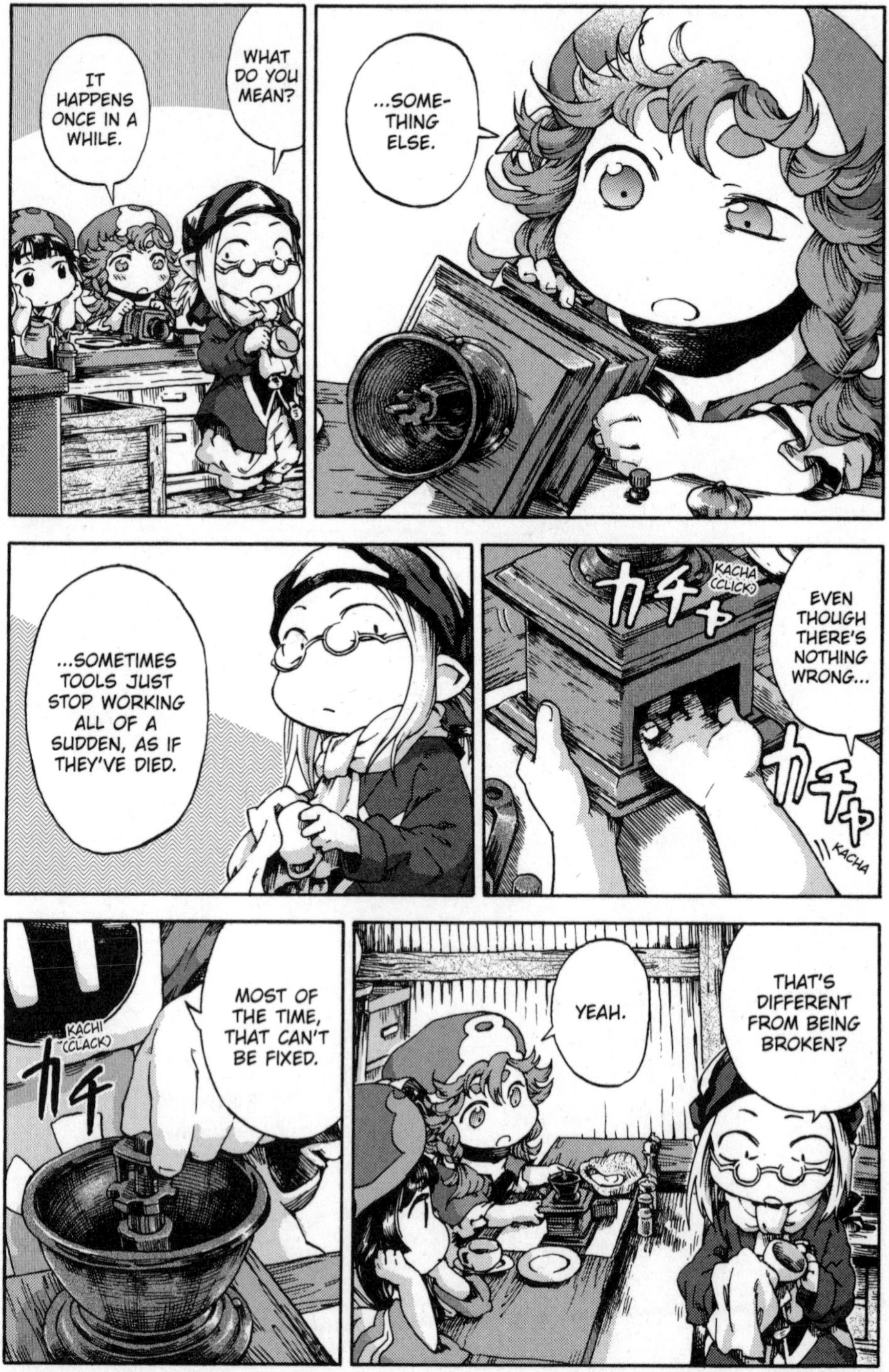
...SOME-THING ELSE.
WHAT DO YOU MEAN?
IT HAPPENS ONCE IN A WHILE.
KACHA (CLICK)
カチャ
EVEN THOUGH THERE'S NOTHING WRONG...
カチャ
KACHA
...SOMETIMES TOOLS JUST STOP WORKING ALL OF A SUDDEN, AS IF THEY'VE DIED.
THAT'S DIFFERENT FROM BEING BROKEN?
YEAH.
MOST OF THE TIME, THAT CAN'T BE FIXED.
KACHI (CLACK)
カチ

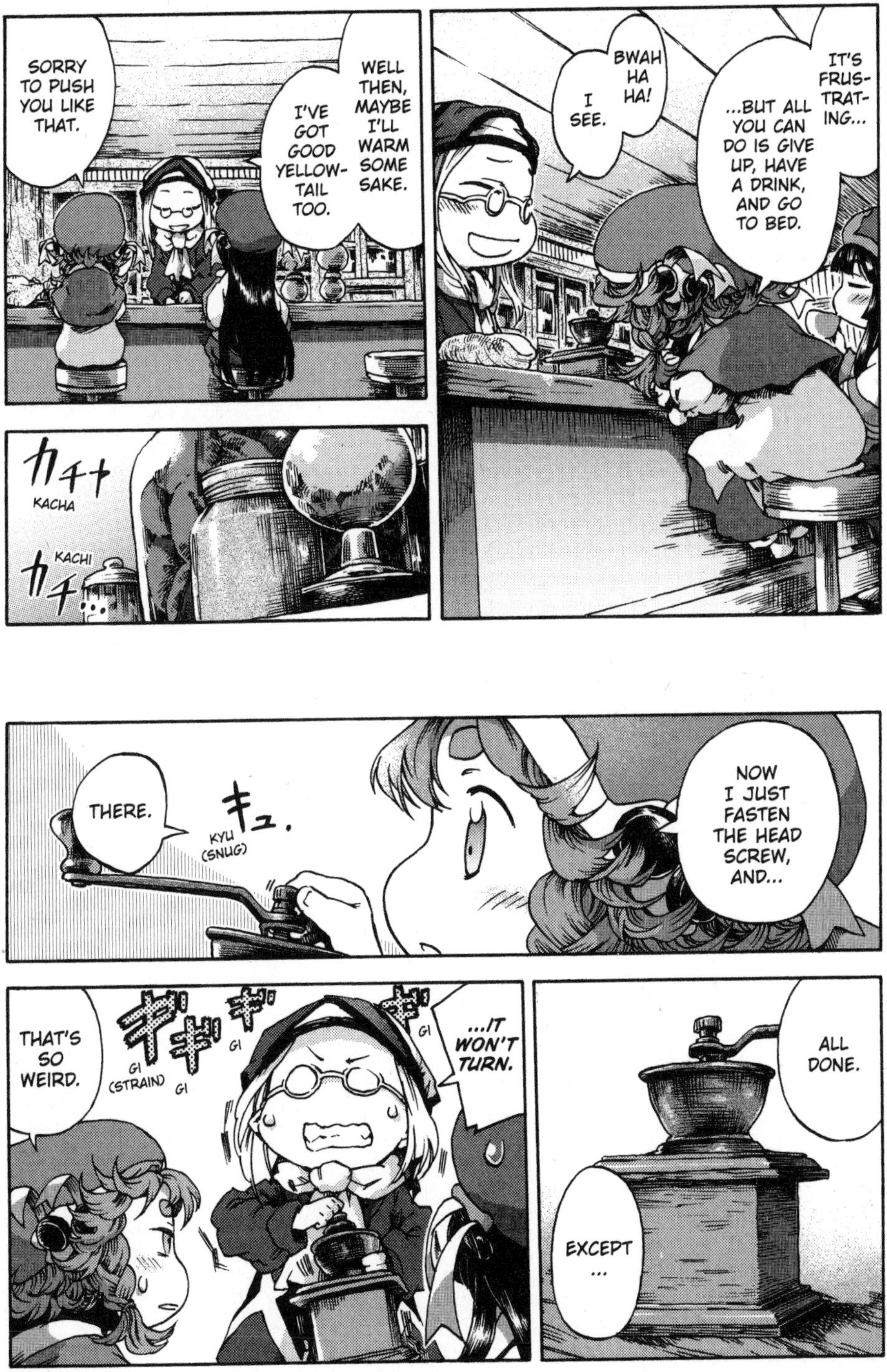
IT'S FRUSTRATING...
...BUT ALL YOU CAN DO IS GIVE UP, HAVE A DRINK, AND GO TO BED.
BWAH HA HA!
I SEE.
WELL THEN, MAYBE I'LL WARM SOME SAKE.
I'VE GOT GOOD YELLOWTAIL TOO.
SORRY TO PUSH YOU LIKE THAT.
カチャ
KACHA
KACHI
カチ
NOW I JUST FASTEN THE HEAD SCREW, AND...
キュ.
KYU (SNUG)
THERE.
ALL DONE.
EXCEPT...
...IT WON'T TURN.
ギギギギ
GI
GI
GI (STRAIN)
GI
THAT'S SO WEIRD.

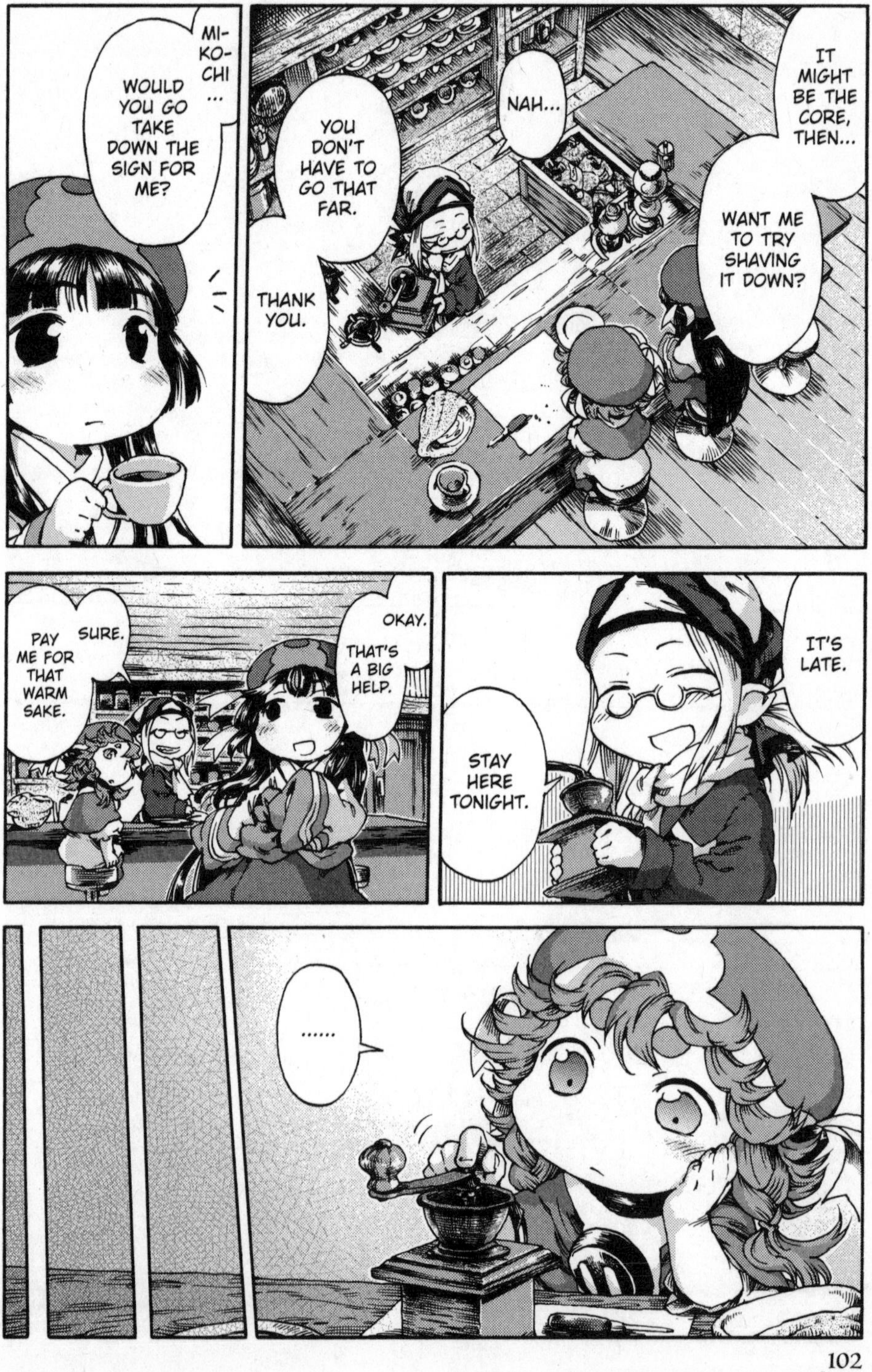
IT MIGHT BE THE CORE, THEN...
WANT ME TO TRY SHAVING IT DOWN?
NAH...
YOU DON'T HAVE TO GO THAT FAR.
THANK YOU.
MI-KO-CHI ...
WOULD YOU GO TAKE DOWN THE SIGN FOR ME?
IT'S LATE.
STAY HERE TONIGHT.
OKAY.
THAT'S A BIG HELP.
SURE.
PAY ME FOR THAT WARM SAKE.
......

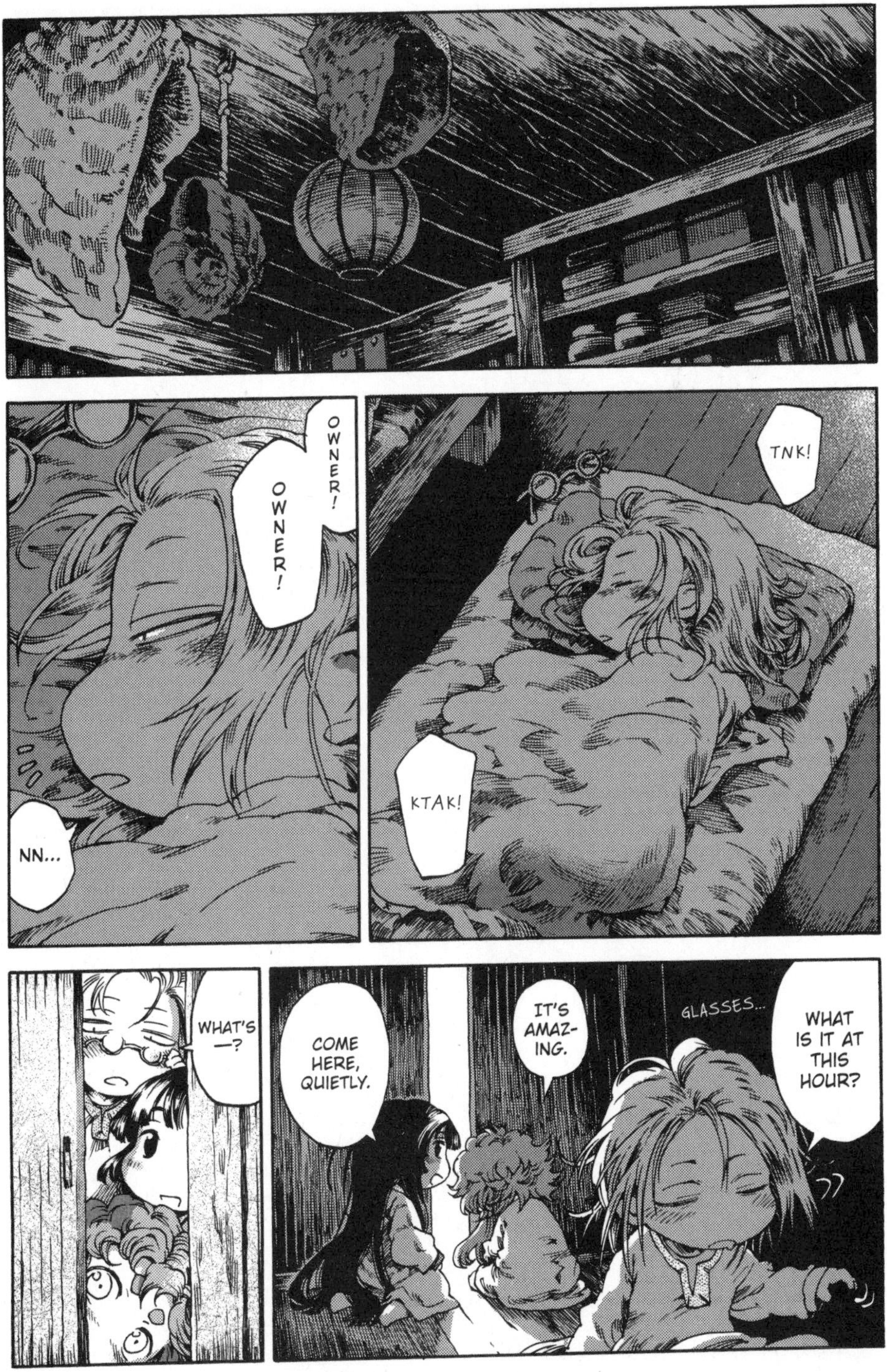
TNK!
KTAK!
OWNER! OWNER!
NN...
WHAT IS IT AT THIS HOUR?
GLASSES...
IT'S AMAZ-ING.
COME HERE, QUIETLY.
WHAT'S—?

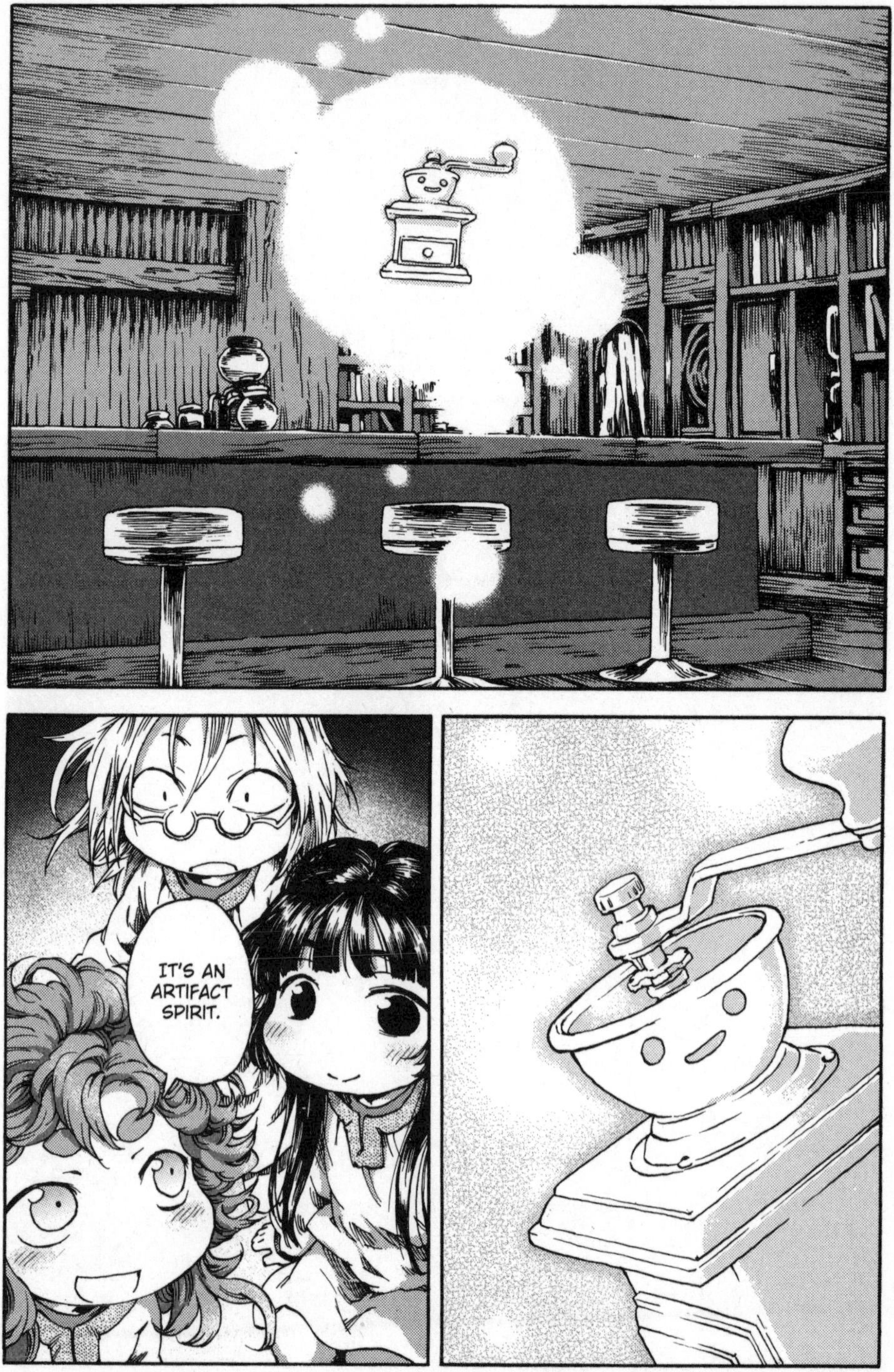
IT'S AN ARTIFACT SPIRIT.

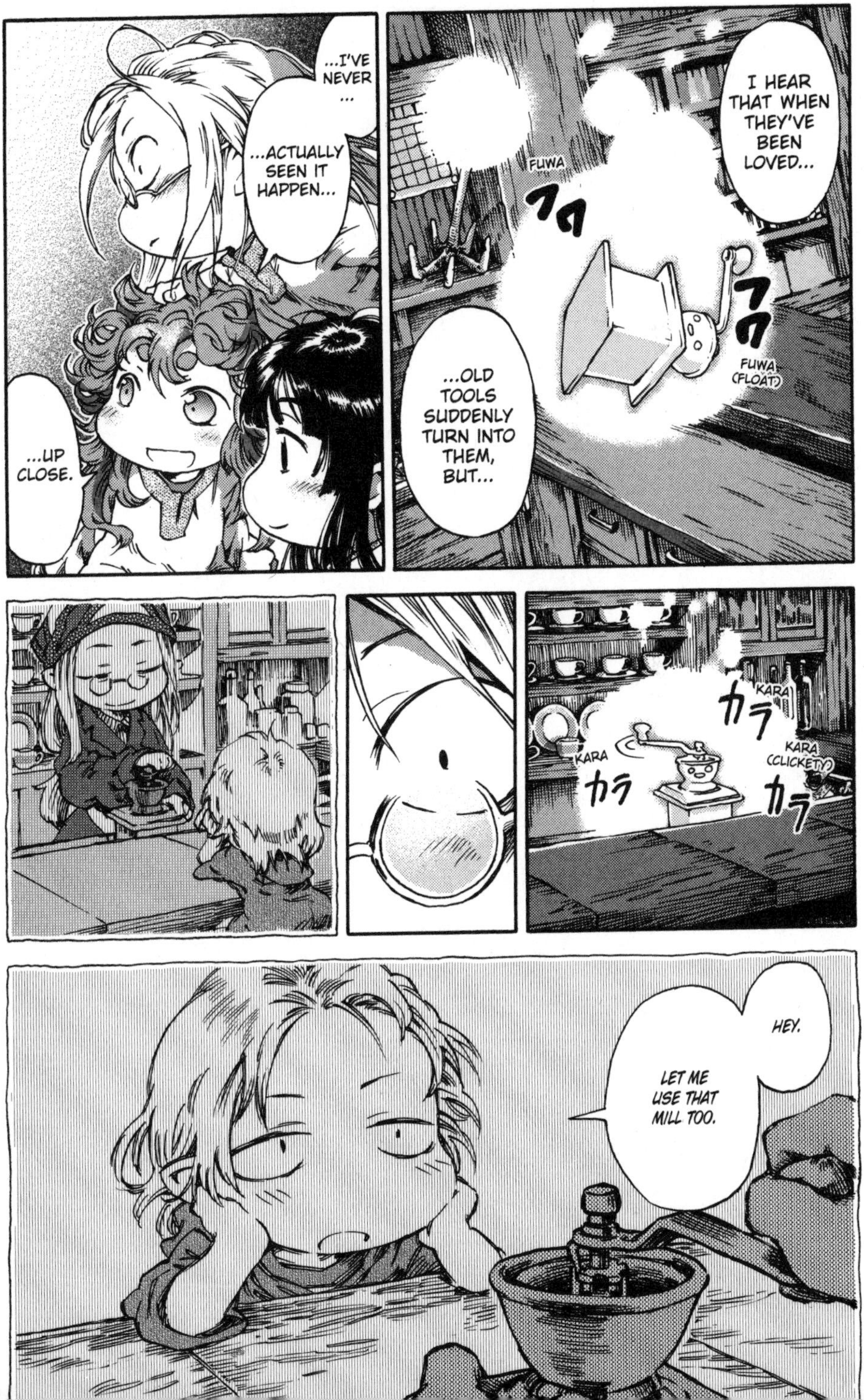
I HEAR THAT WHEN THEY'VE BEEN LOVED...
FUWA
フワ
...OLD TOOLS SUDDENLY TURN INTO THEM, BUT...
フワ
FUWA (FLOAT)
...I'VE NEVER...
...ACTUALLY SEEN IT HAPPEN...
...UP CLOSE.
KARA
カラ
KARA (CLICKETY)
カラ
KARA
カラ
HEY.
LET ME USE THAT MILL TOO.

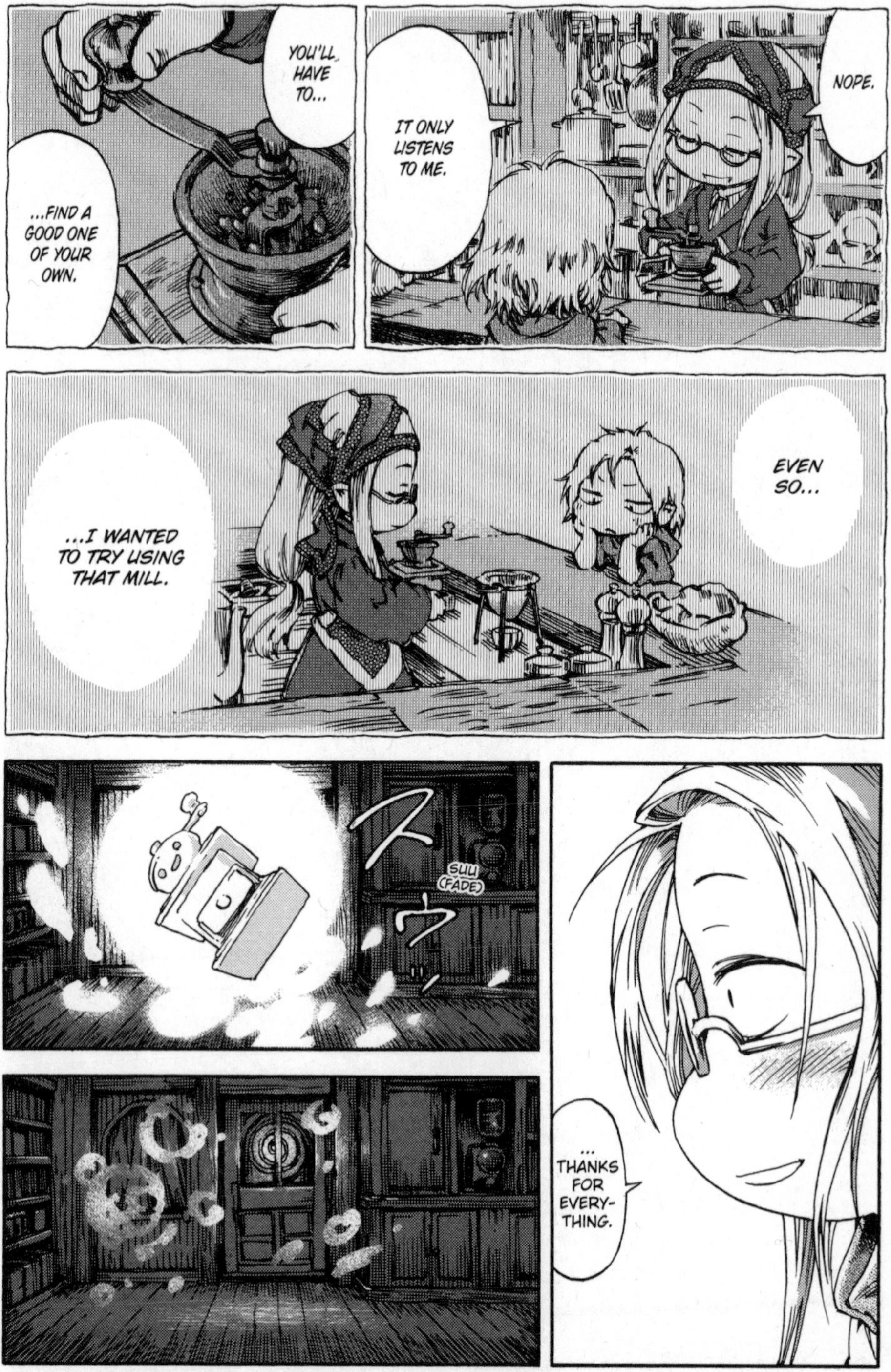

NOPE.
IT ONLY LISTENS TO ME.
YOU'LL HAVE TO...
...FIND A GOOD ONE OF YOUR OWN.
EVEN SO...
...I WANTED TO TRY USING THAT MILL.
...THANKS FOR EVERY-THING.
SUU (FADE)

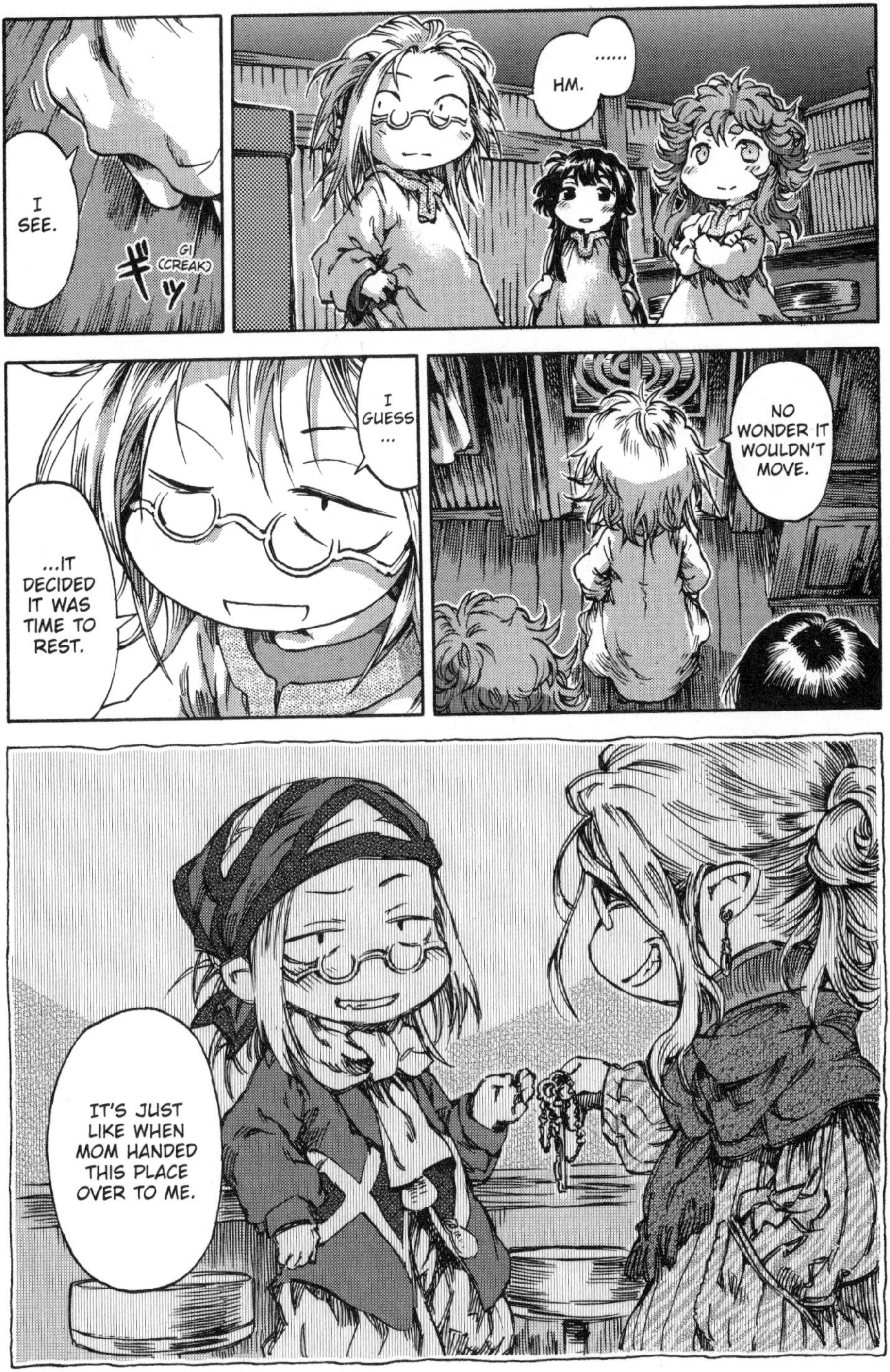
......
HM.
I SEE.
ギッ
GI (CREAK)
NO WONDER IT WOULDN'T MOVE.
I GUESS...
...IT DECIDED IT WAS TIME TO REST.
IT'S JUST LIKE WHEN MOM HANDED THIS PLACE OVER TO ME.

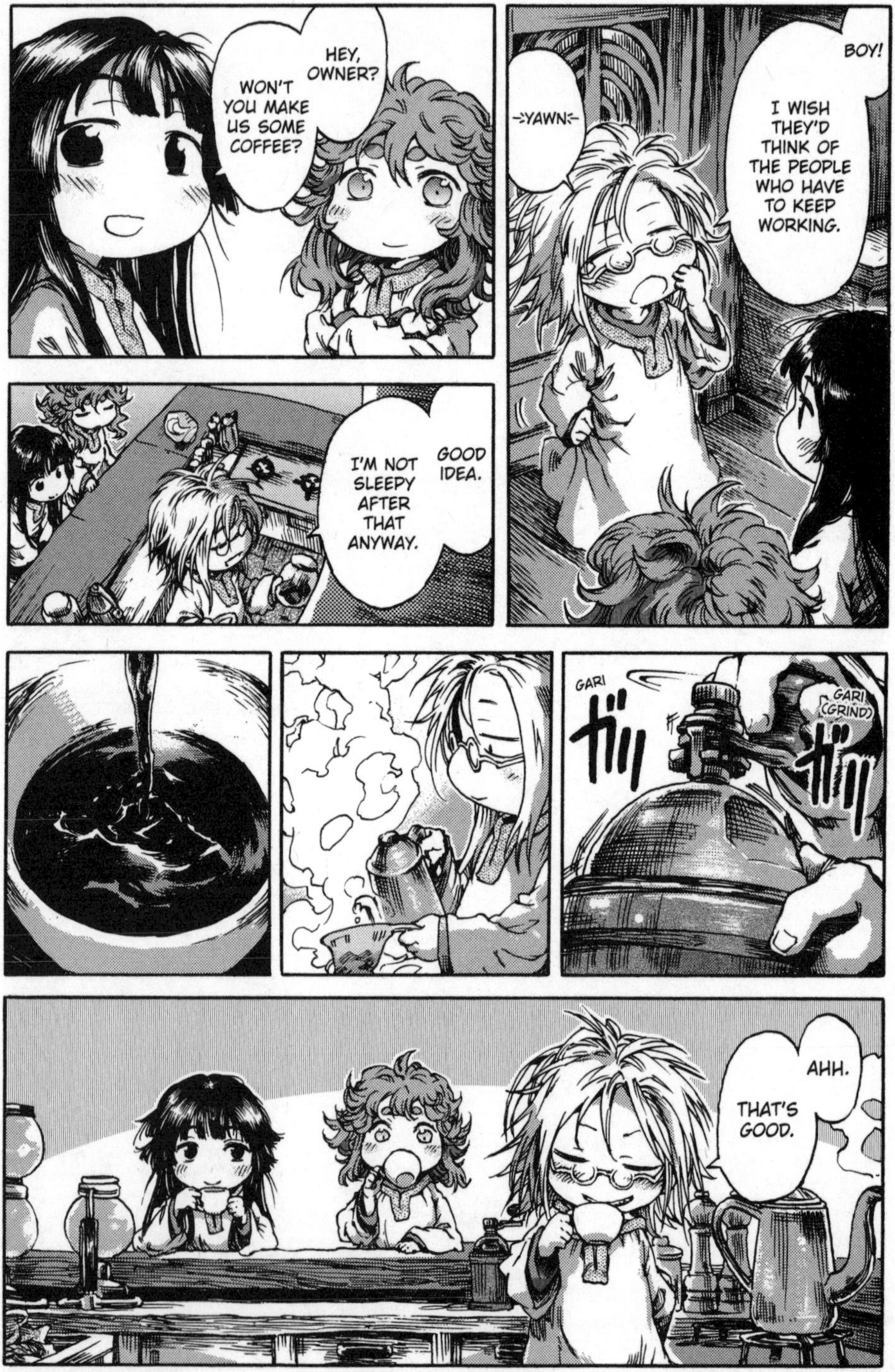
BOY!
I WISH THEY'D THINK OF THE PEOPLE WHO HAVE TO KEEP WORKING.
-YAWN-
HEY, OWNER?
WON'T YOU MAKE US SOME COFFEE?
GOOD IDEA.
I'M NOT SLEEPY AFTER THAT ANYWAY.
GARI (GRIND)
ガリ
GARI
ガリ
AHH.
THAT'S GOOD.

How are you? Doing well? I'm doing so well it's liable to kill me. Right now, I'm steadily making my way north. In the town I left yesterday, there was nothing but snow.

Still, the bean seller was impressive, and even in that cold place, I got to drink good coffee. When I asked the café owner where they got their beans, they said they had them flown up by bird-mounted courier from an island that's much farther south than Arabi even. The beans were very acidic and fragrant, but they yielded a wonderfully mellow brew. I won't tell you where they were from. I'm enclosing a couple, so hunt them down yourself.

From here, I'll head to the northernmost tip of the continent, then board the first ship I find. I hope I land somewhere warm next. ...Although, as long as it has coffee, anywhere will do.

About the shop...Well, don't work too hard. Keep the place up and running if you can manage it.

—Mother

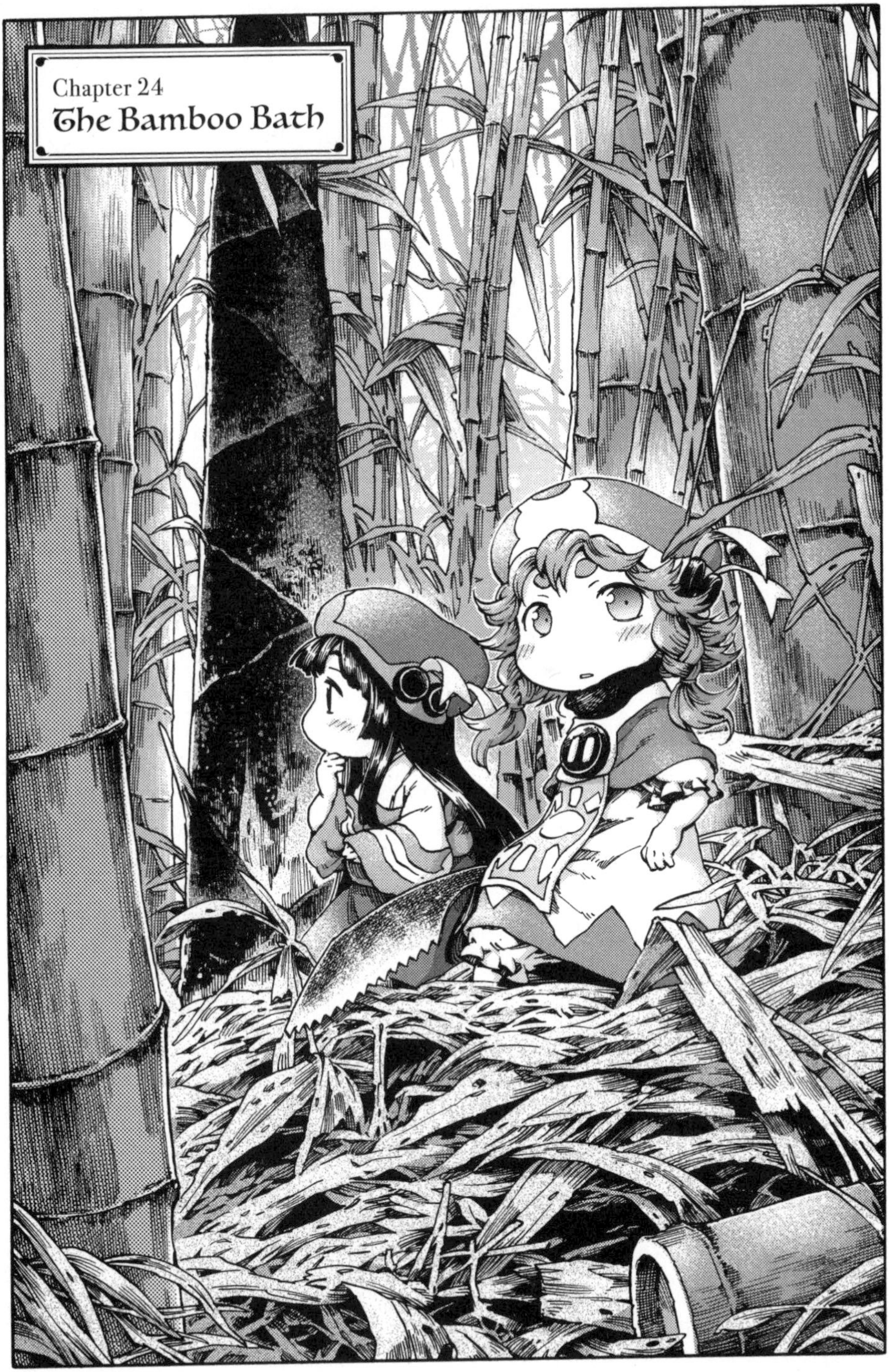
Chapter 24
The Bamboo Bath

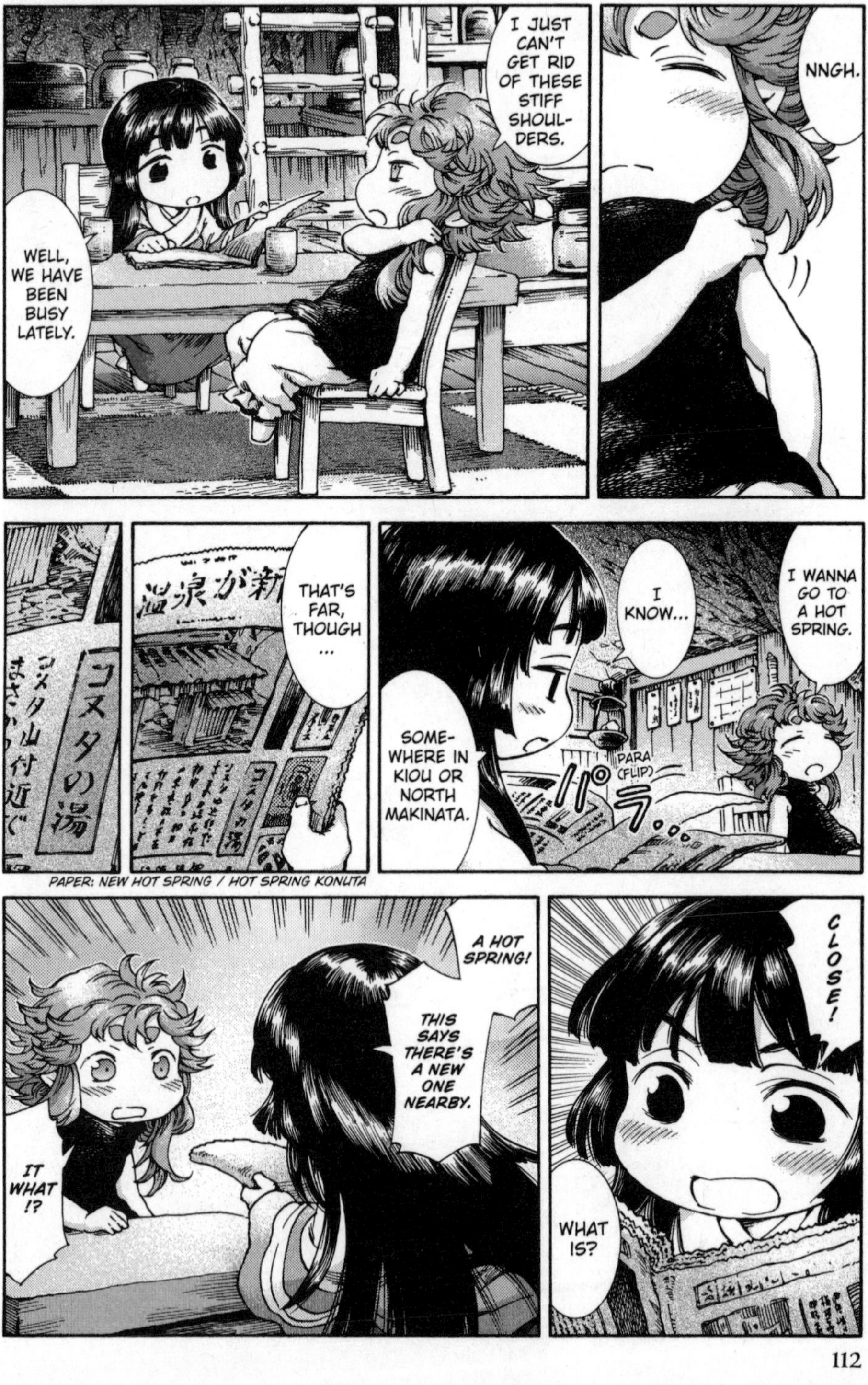
NNGH.
I JUST CAN'T GET RID OF THESE STIFF SHOULDERS.
WELL, WE HAVE BEEN BUSY LATELY.
I WANNA GO TO A HOT SPRING.
I KNOW...
SOME-WHERE IN KIOU OR NORTH MAKINATA.
PARA (FLIP)
THAT'S FAR, THOUGH...
温泉が新
コヌタの湯
PAPER: NEW HOT SPRING / HOT SPRING KONUTA
CLOSE!
WHAT IS?
A HOT SPRING!
THIS SAYS THERE'S A NEW ONE NEARBY.
IT WHAT!?

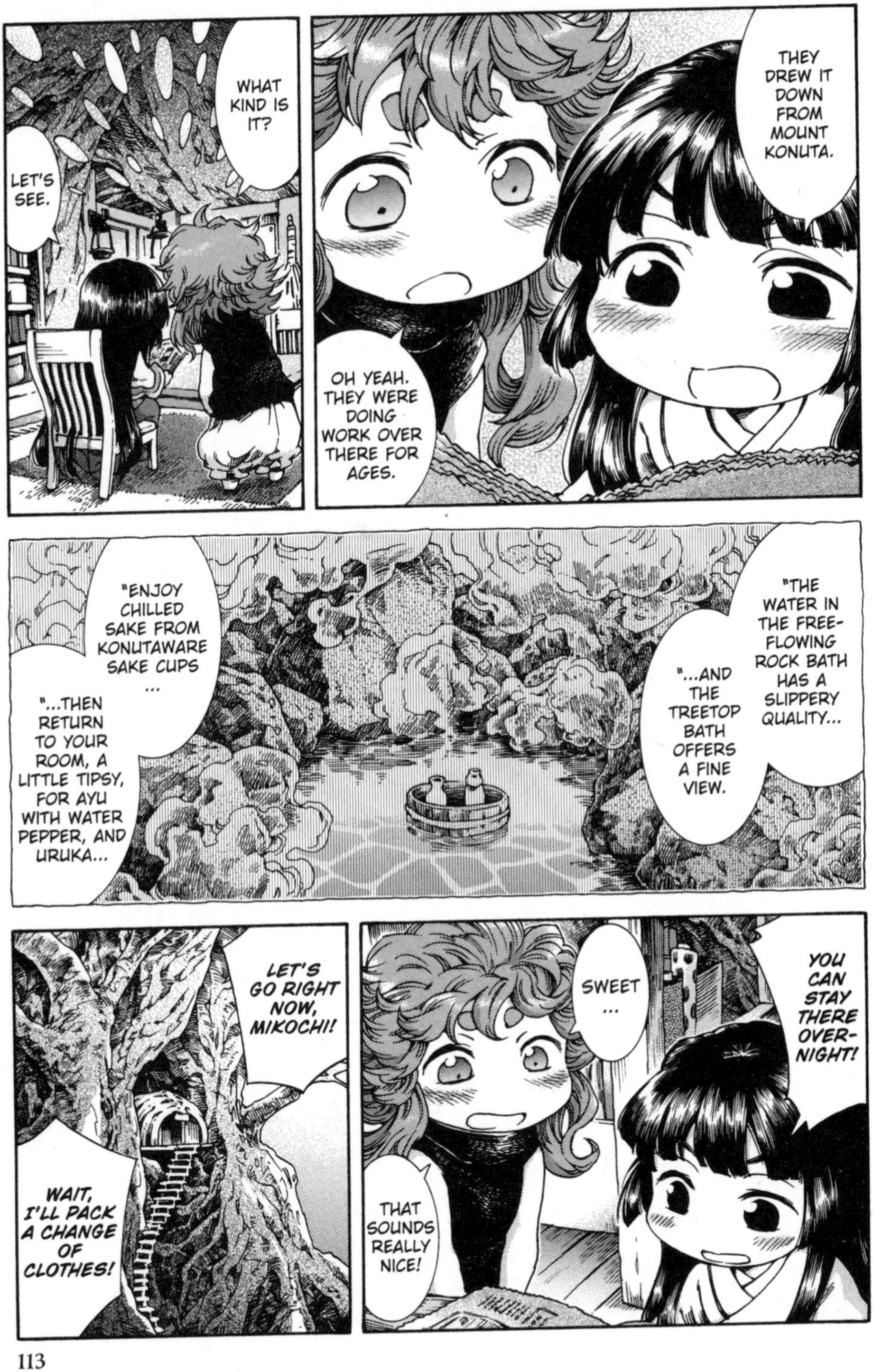

THEY DREW IT DOWN FROM MOUNT KONUTA.
OH YEAH. THEY WERE DOING WORK OVER THERE FOR AGES.
WHAT KIND IS IT?
LET'S SEE.
"THE WATER IN THE FREE-FLOWING ROCK BATH HAS A SLIPPERY QUALITY...
"...AND THE TREETOP BATH OFFERS A FINE VIEW.
"ENJOY CHILLED SAKE FROM KONUTAWARE SAKE CUPS ...
"...THEN RETURN TO YOUR ROOM, A LITTLE TIPSY, FOR AYU WITH WATER PEPPER, AND URUKA...
YOU CAN STAY THERE OVER-NIGHT!
SWEET ...
THAT SOUNDS REALLY NICE!
LET'S GO RIGHT NOW, MIKOCHI!
WAIT, I'LL PACK A CHANGE OF CLOTHES!

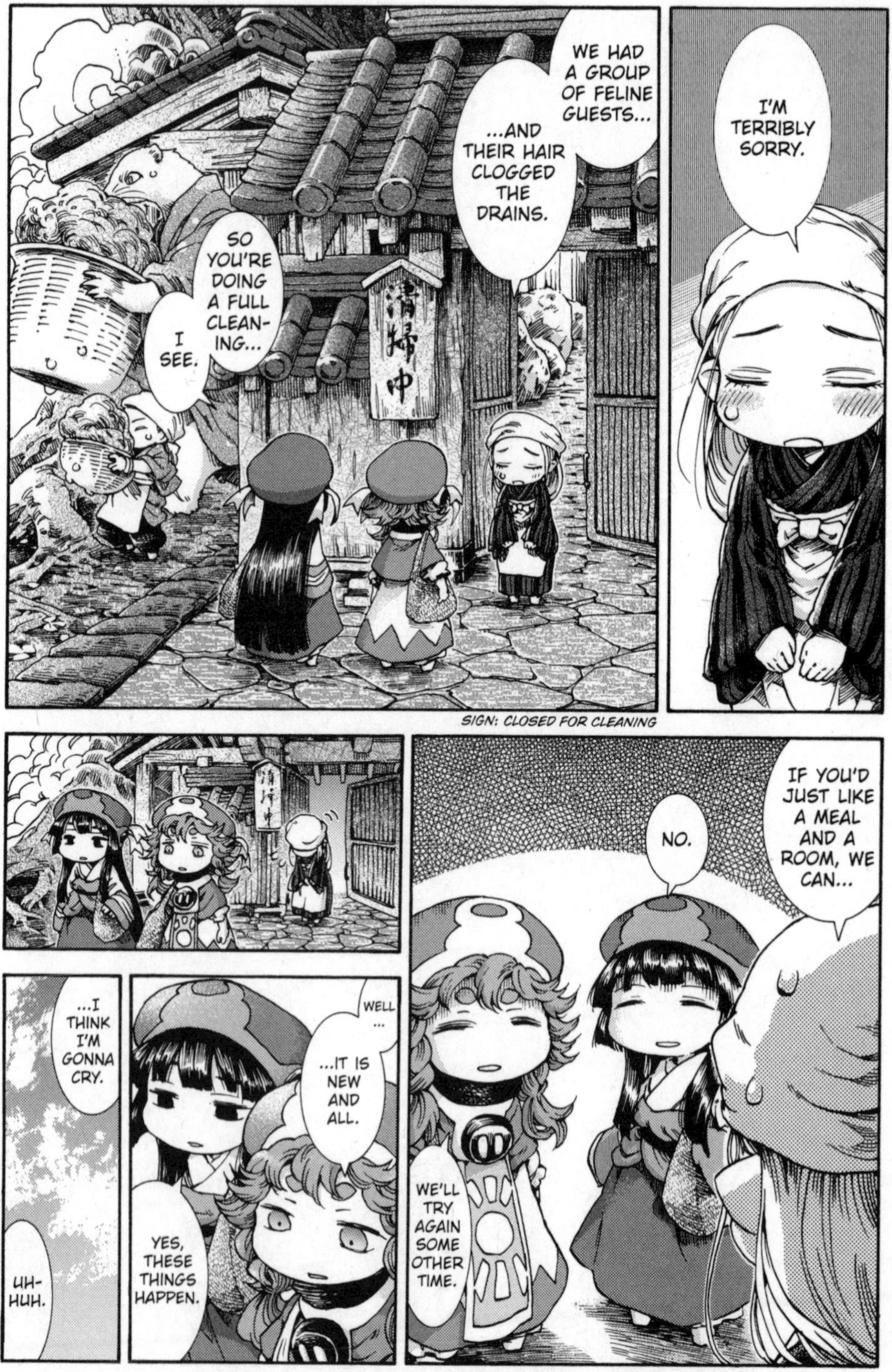
I'M TERRIBLY SORRY.
WE HAD A GROUP OF FELINE GUESTS...
...AND THEIR HAIR CLOGGED THE DRAINS.
SO YOU'RE DOING A FULL CLEAN-ING...
I SEE.
SIGN: CLOSED FOR CLEANING
IF YOU'D JUST LIKE A MEAL AND A ROOM, WE CAN...
NO.
WE'LL TRY AGAIN SOME OTHER TIME.
WELL ...
...IT IS NEW AND ALL.
YES, THESE THINGS HAPPEN.
...I THINK I'M GONNA CRY.
UH-HUH.

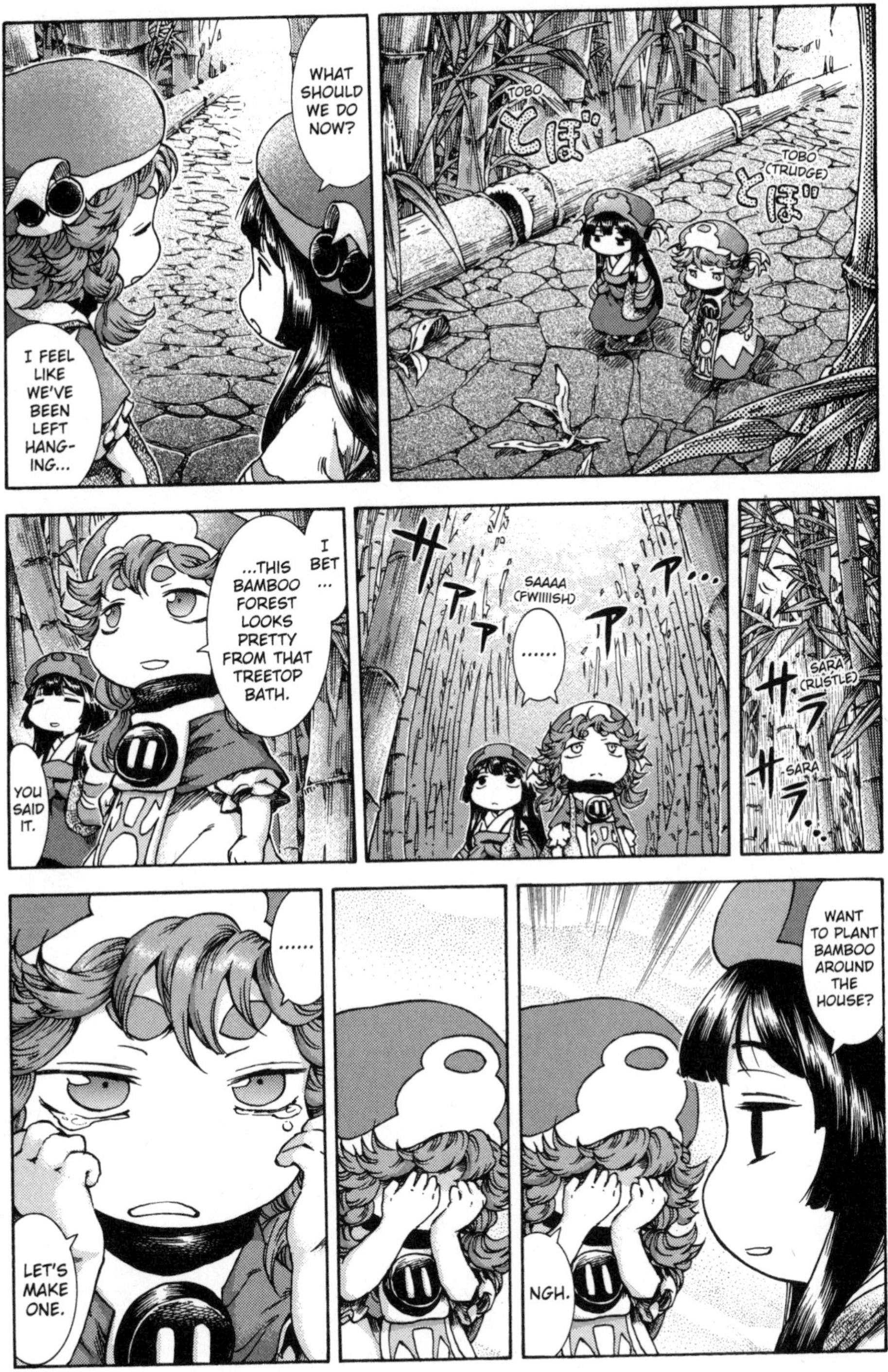

TOBO
とぼ
TOBO (TRUDGE)
とぼ
WHAT SHOULD WE DO NOW?
I FEEL LIKE WE'VE BEEN LEFT HANG-ING...
SARA (RUSTLE)
サラ
SARA
サラ...
SAAAA (FWIIIISH)
サアアアア...
......
I BET...
...THIS BAMBOO FOREST LOOKS PRETTY FROM THAT TREETOP BATH.
YOU SAID IT.
WANT TO PLANT BAMBOO AROUND THE HOUSE?
NGH.
......
LET'S MAKE ONE.

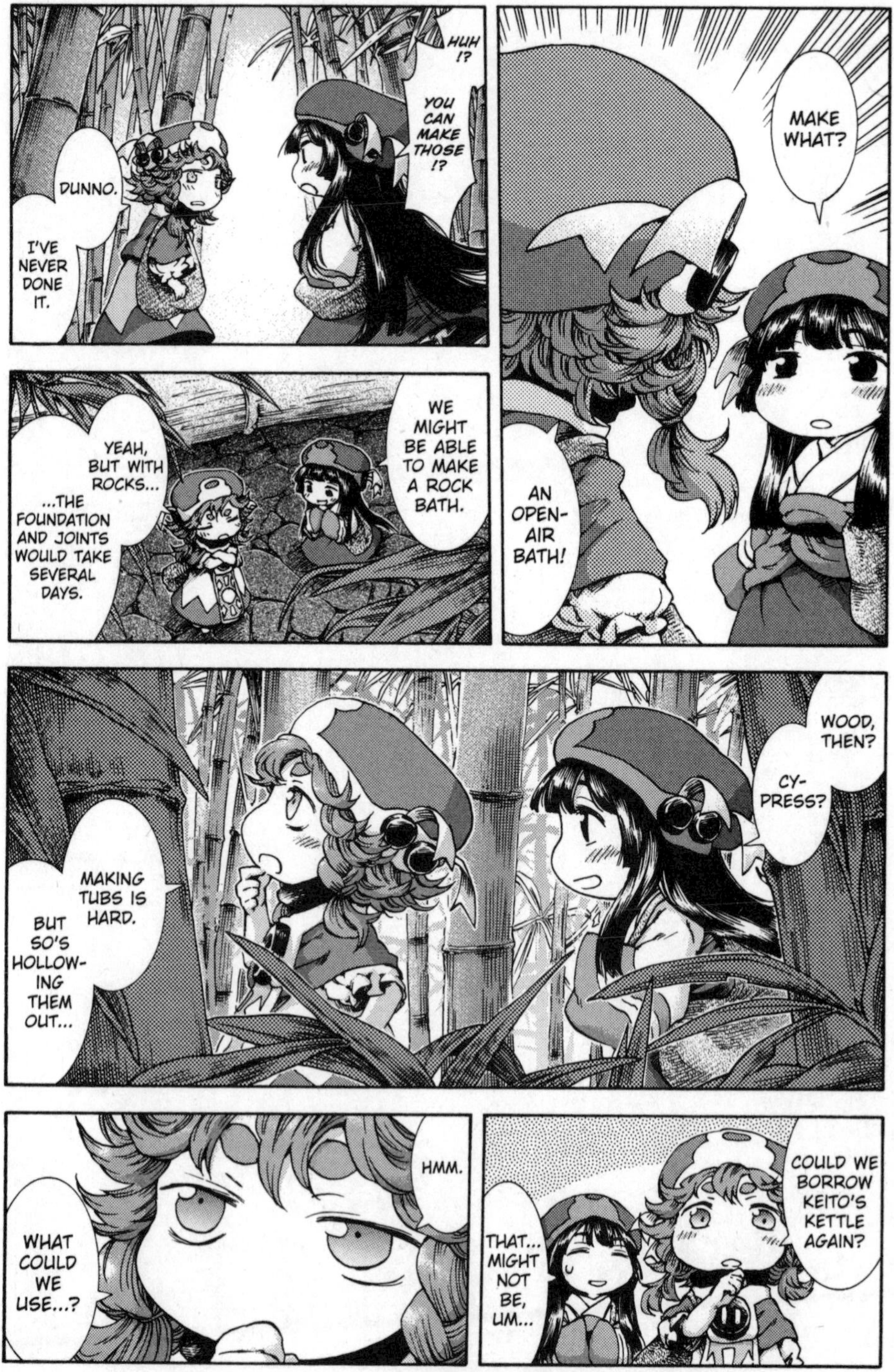
MAKE WHAT?
AN OPEN-AIR BATH!
HUH!?
YOU CAN MAKE THOSE!?
DUNNO.
I'VE NEVER DONE IT.
WE MIGHT BE ABLE TO MAKE A ROCK BATH.
YEAH, BUT WITH ROCKS...
...THE FOUNDATION AND JOINTS WOULD TAKE SEVERAL DAYS.
WOOD, THEN?
CY-PRESS?
MAKING TUBS IS HARD.
BUT SO'S HOLLOWING THEM OUT...
COULD WE BORROW KEITO'S KETTLE AGAIN?
THAT... MIGHT NOT BE, UM...
HMM.
WHAT COULD WE USE...?

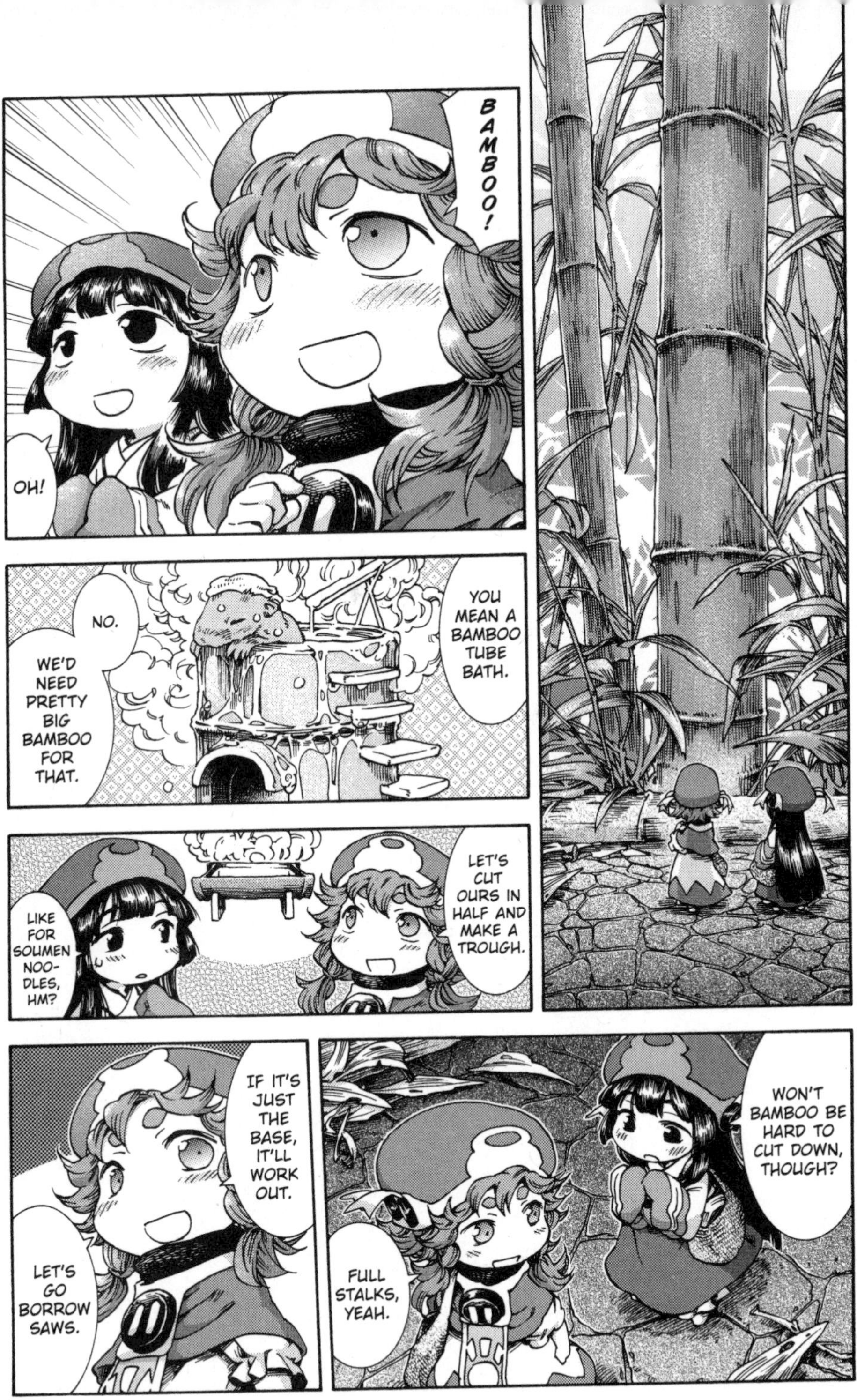
BAMBOO!
OH!
YOU MEAN A BAMBOO TUBE BATH.
NO.
WE'D NEED PRETTY BIG BAMBOO FOR THAT.
LET'S CUT OURS IN HALF AND MAKE A TROUGH.
LIKE FOR SOUMEN NOO-DLES, HM?
WON'T BAMBOO BE HARD TO CUT DOWN, THOUGH?
FULL STALKS, YEAH.
IF IT'S JUST THE BASE, IT'LL WORK OUT.
LET'S GO BORROW SAWS.

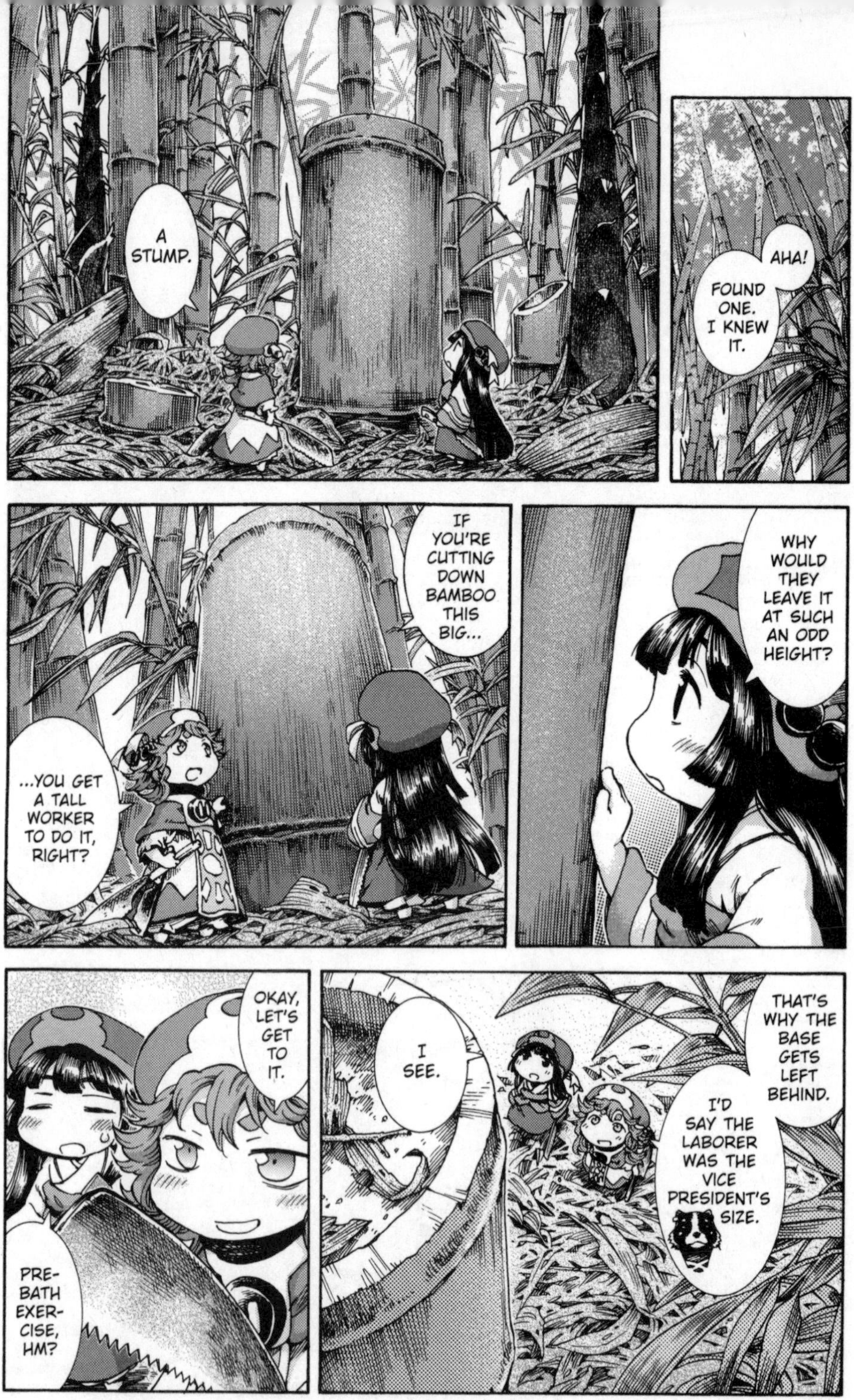
AHA!
FOUND ONE. I KNEW IT.
A STUMP.
WHY WOULD THEY LEAVE IT AT SUCH AN ODD HEIGHT?
IF YOU'RE CUTTING DOWN BAMBOO THIS BIG...
...YOU GET A TALL WORKER TO DO IT, RIGHT?
THAT'S WHY THE BASE GETS LEFT BEHIND.
I'D SAY THE LABORER WAS THE VICE PRESIDENT'S SIZE.
I SEE.
OKAY, LET'S GET TO IT.
PRE-BATH EXERCISE, HM?

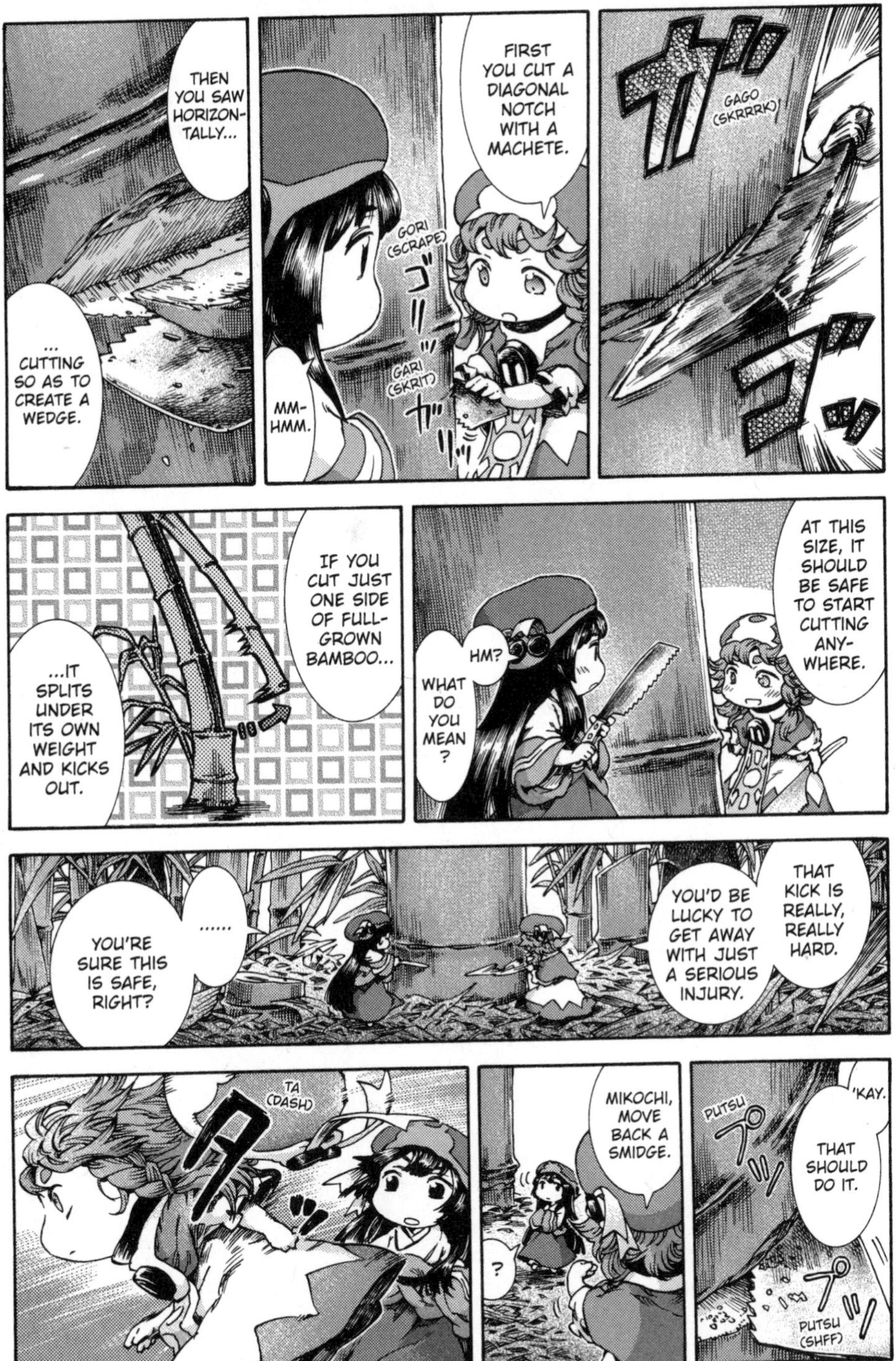
GAGO (SKRRRK)
FIRST YOU CUT A DIAGONAL NOTCH WITH A MACHETE.
GORI (SCRAPE)
GARI (SKRIT)
MM-HMM.
THEN YOU SAW HORIZONTALLY...
...CUTTING SO AS TO CREATE A WEDGE.
AT THIS SIZE, IT SHOULD BE SAFE TO START CUTTING ANYWHERE.
HM?
WHAT DO YOU MEAN?
IF YOU CUT JUST ONE SIDE OF FULL-GROWN BAMBOO...
...IT SPLITS UNDER ITS OWN WEIGHT AND KICKS OUT.
THAT KICK IS REALLY, REALLY HARD.
YOU'D BE LUCKY TO GET AWAY WITH JUST A SERIOUS INJURY.
......
YOU'RE SURE THIS IS SAFE, RIGHT?
'KAY.
PUTSU
THAT SHOULD DO IT.
PUTSU (SHFF)
MIKOCHI, MOVE BACK A SMIDGE.
?
TA (DASH)

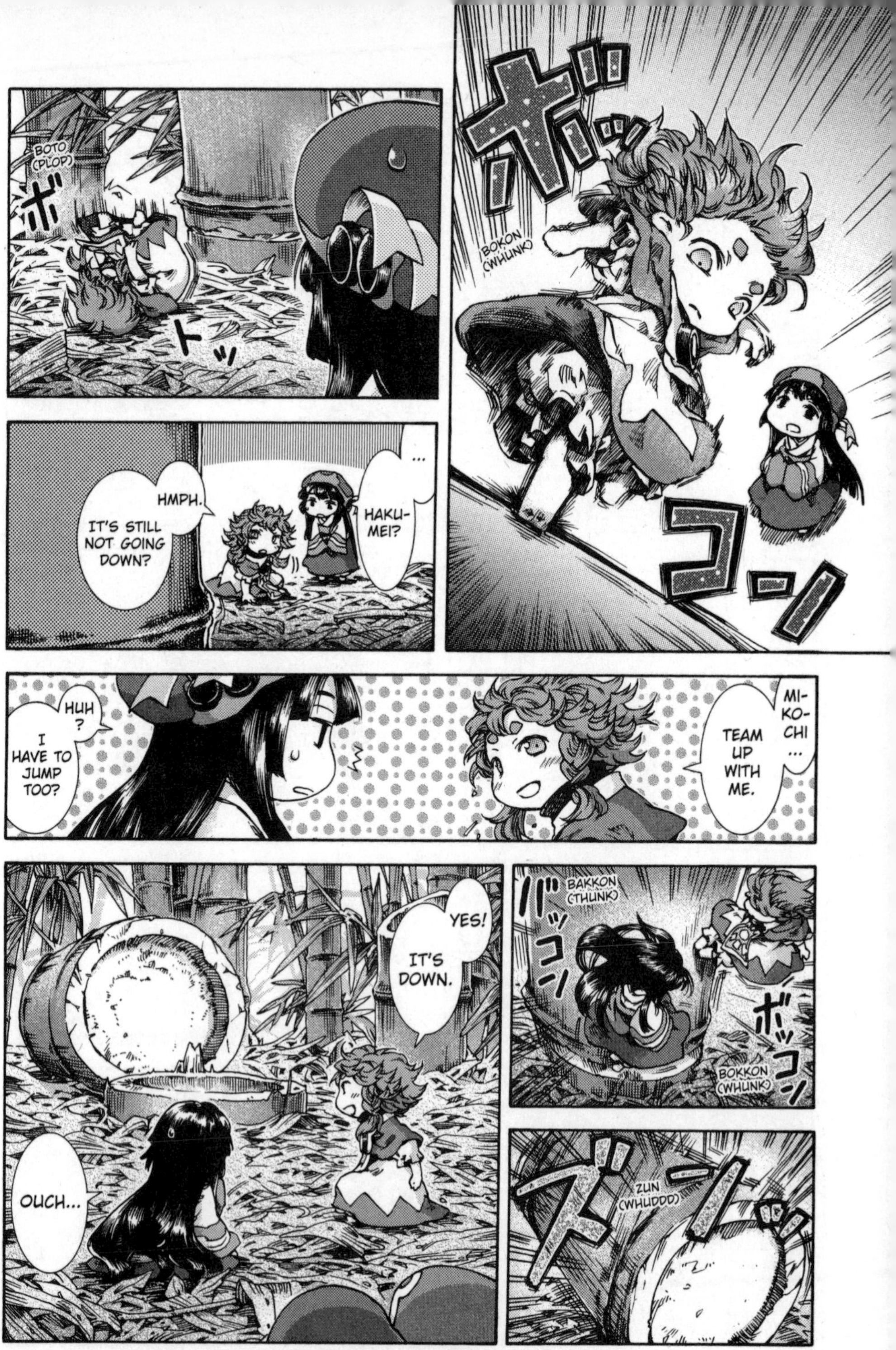
BOKON (WHUNK)
BOTO (PLOP)
...
HAKU-MEI?
HMPH.
IT'S STILL NOT GOING DOWN?
MI-KO-CHI...
TEAM UP WITH ME.
HUH?
I HAVE TO JUMP TOO?
BAKKON (THUNK)
BOKKON (WHUNK)
ZUN (WHUDDD)
YES!
IT'S DOWN.
OUCH...

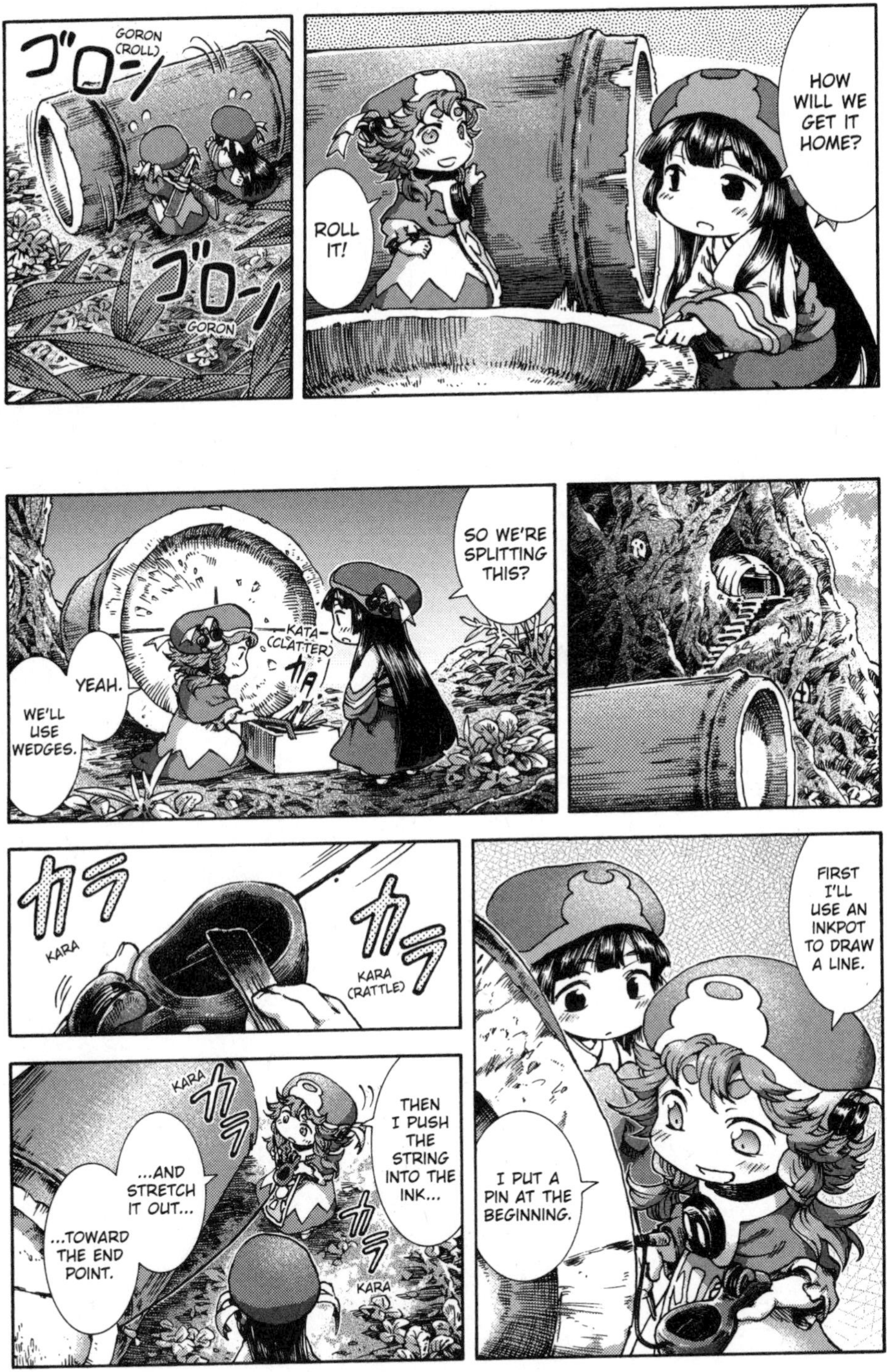
HOW WILL WE GET IT HOME?
ROLL IT!
ゴローン
GORON (ROLL)
ゴローン
GORON
SO WE'RE SPLITTING THIS?
YEAH.
WE'LL USE WEDGES.
KATA (CLATTER)
カタ
FIRST I'LL USE AN INKPOT TO DRAW A LINE.
I PUT A PIN AT THE BEGINNING.
カラ
KARA (RATTLE)
カラ
KARA
THEN I PUSH THE STRING INTO THE INK...
カラ
KARA
...AND STRETCH IT OUT...
...TOWARD THE END POINT.
カラ
KARA

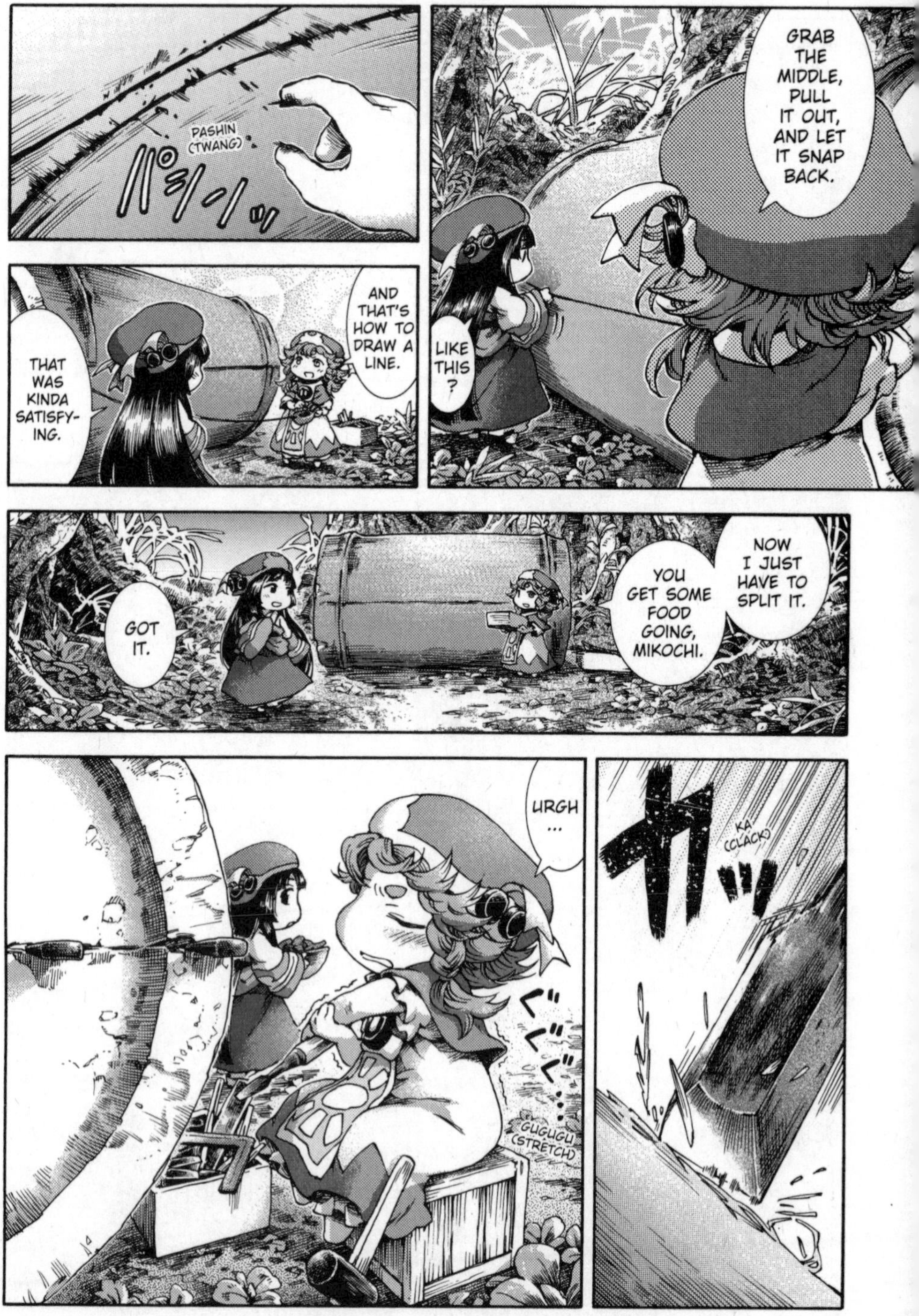
GRAB THE MIDDLE, PULL IT OUT, AND LET IT SNAP BACK.
LIKE THIS?
PASHIN (TWANG)
AND THAT'S HOW TO DRAW A LINE.
THAT WAS KINDA SATISFY-ING.
NOW I JUST HAVE TO SPLIT IT.
YOU GET SOME FOOD GOING, MIKOCHI.
GOT IT.
KA (CLACK)
URGH...
GUGUGU (STRETCH)

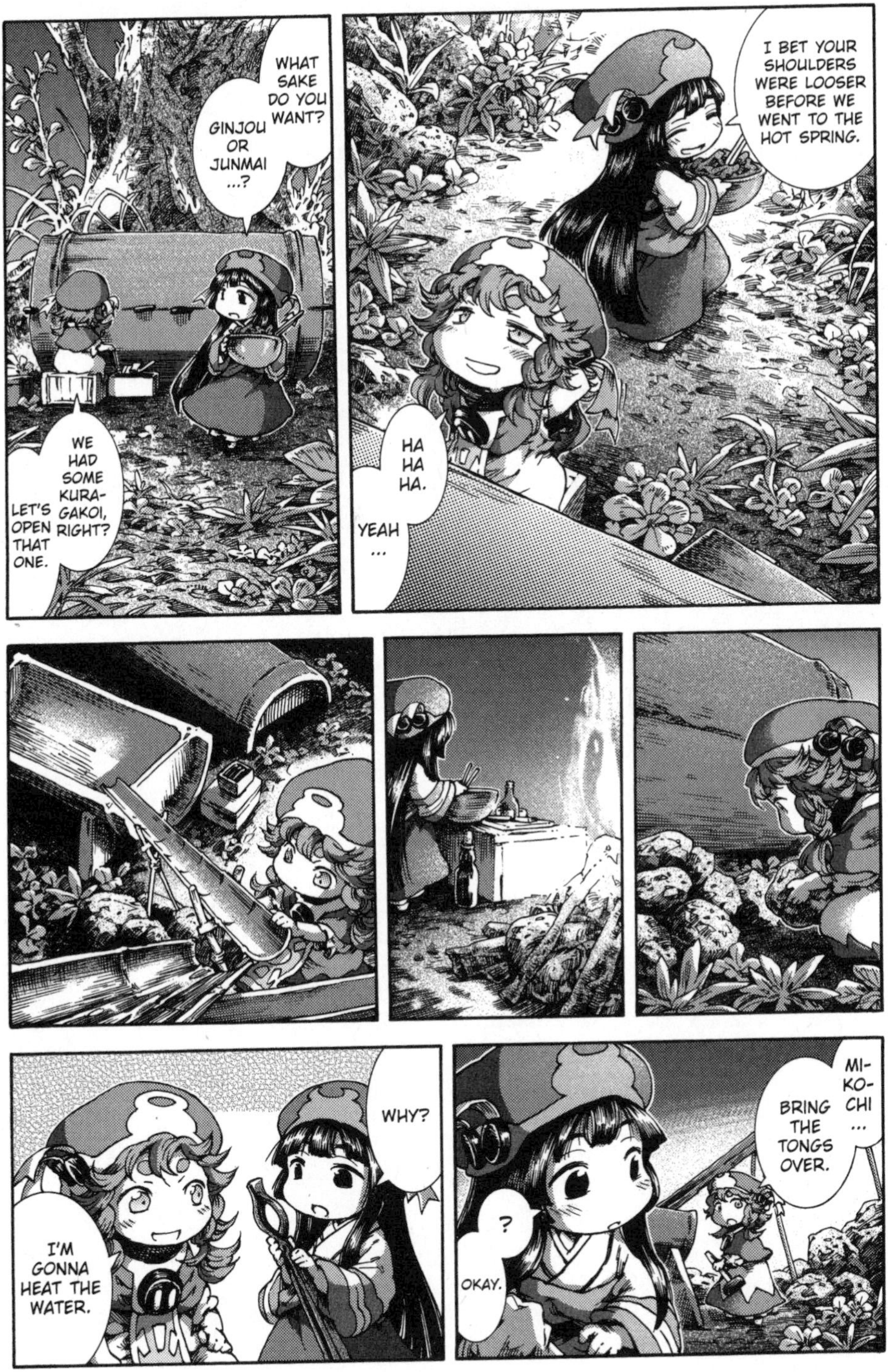
I BET YOUR SHOULDERS WERE LOOSER BEFORE WE WENT TO THE HOT SPRING.
HA HA HA.
YEAH ...
WHAT SAKE DO YOU WANT?
GINJOU OR JUNMAI ...?
WE HAD SOME KURA-GAKOI, RIGHT?
LET'S OPEN THAT ONE.
MIKO-CHI ...
BRING THE TONGS OVER.
?
OKAY.
WHY?
I'M GONNA HEAT THE WATER.

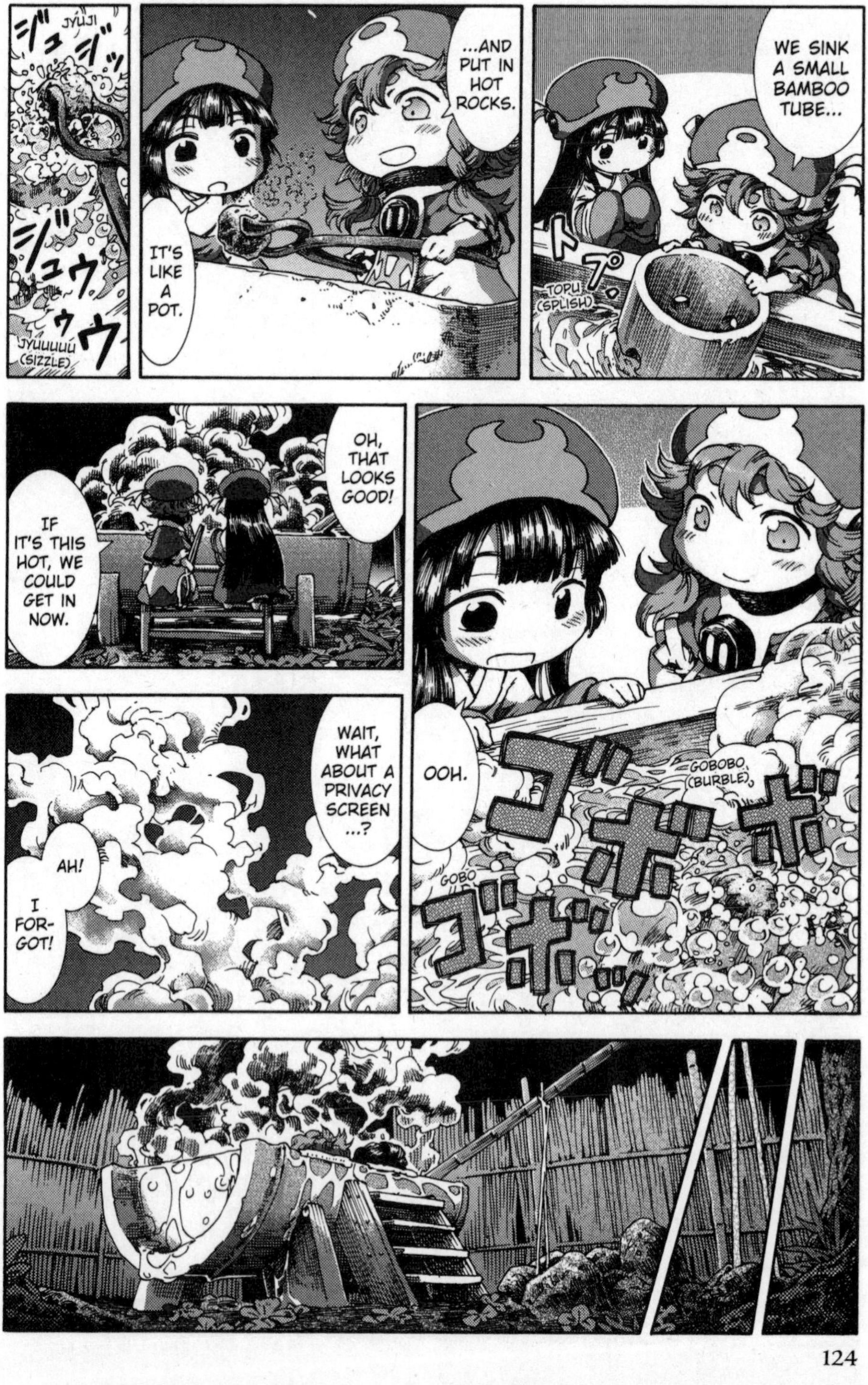
WE SINK A SMALL BAMBOO TUBE...
TOPU (SPLISH)
...AND PUT IN HOT ROCKS.
IT'S LIKE A POT.
JYUJI
JYUUUUU (SIZZLE)
OOH.
GOBOBO (BURBLE)
GOBO
OH, THAT LOOKS GOOD!
IF IT'S THIS HOT, WE COULD GET IN NOW.
WAIT, WHAT ABOUT A PRIVACY SCREEN ...?
AH!
I FOR-GOT!

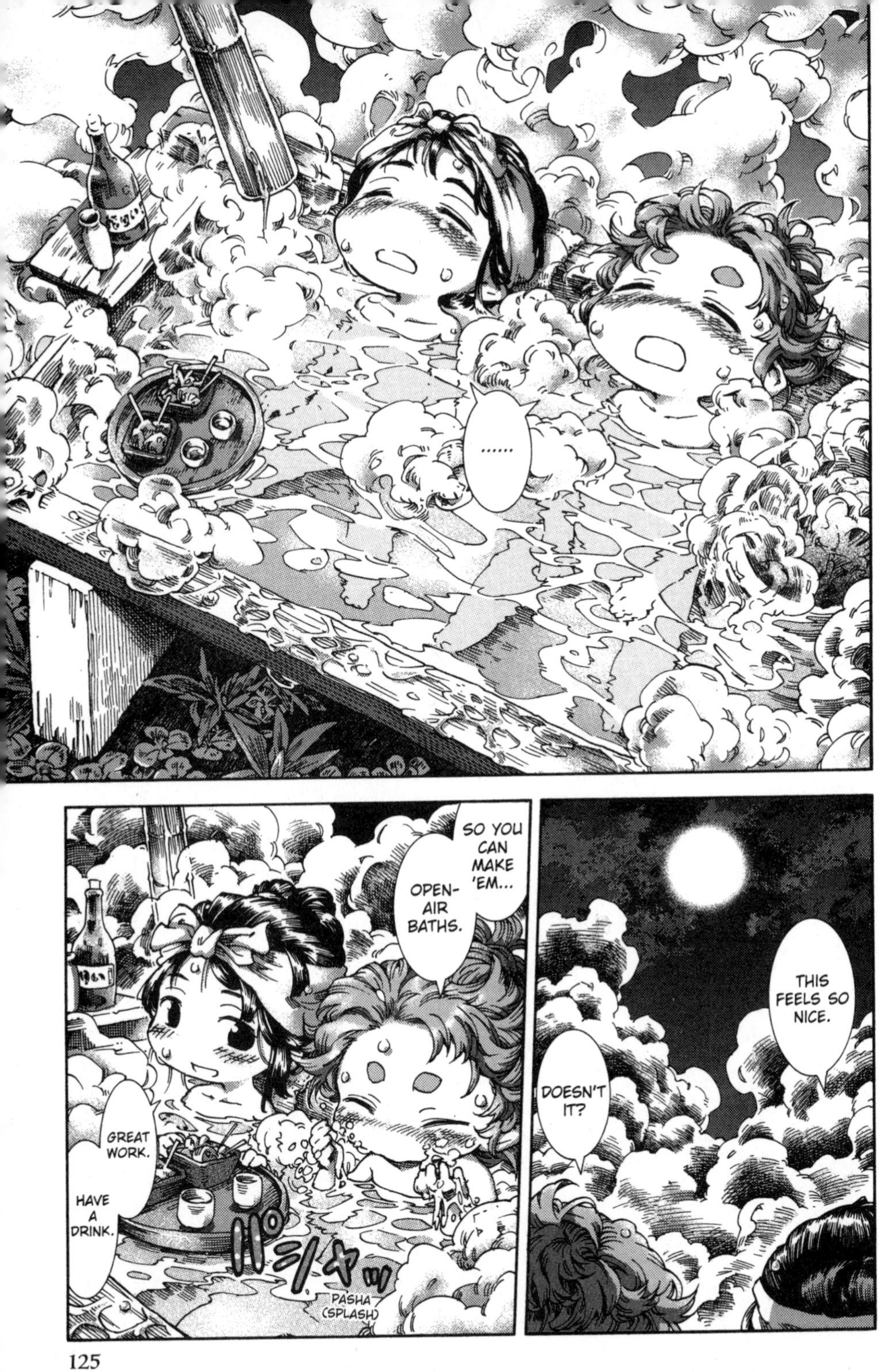
......
THIS FEELS SO NICE.
DOESN'T IT?
SO YOU CAN MAKE 'EM...
OPEN-AIR BATHS.
GREAT WORK.
HAVE A DRINK.
パシャッ
PASHA (SPLASH)

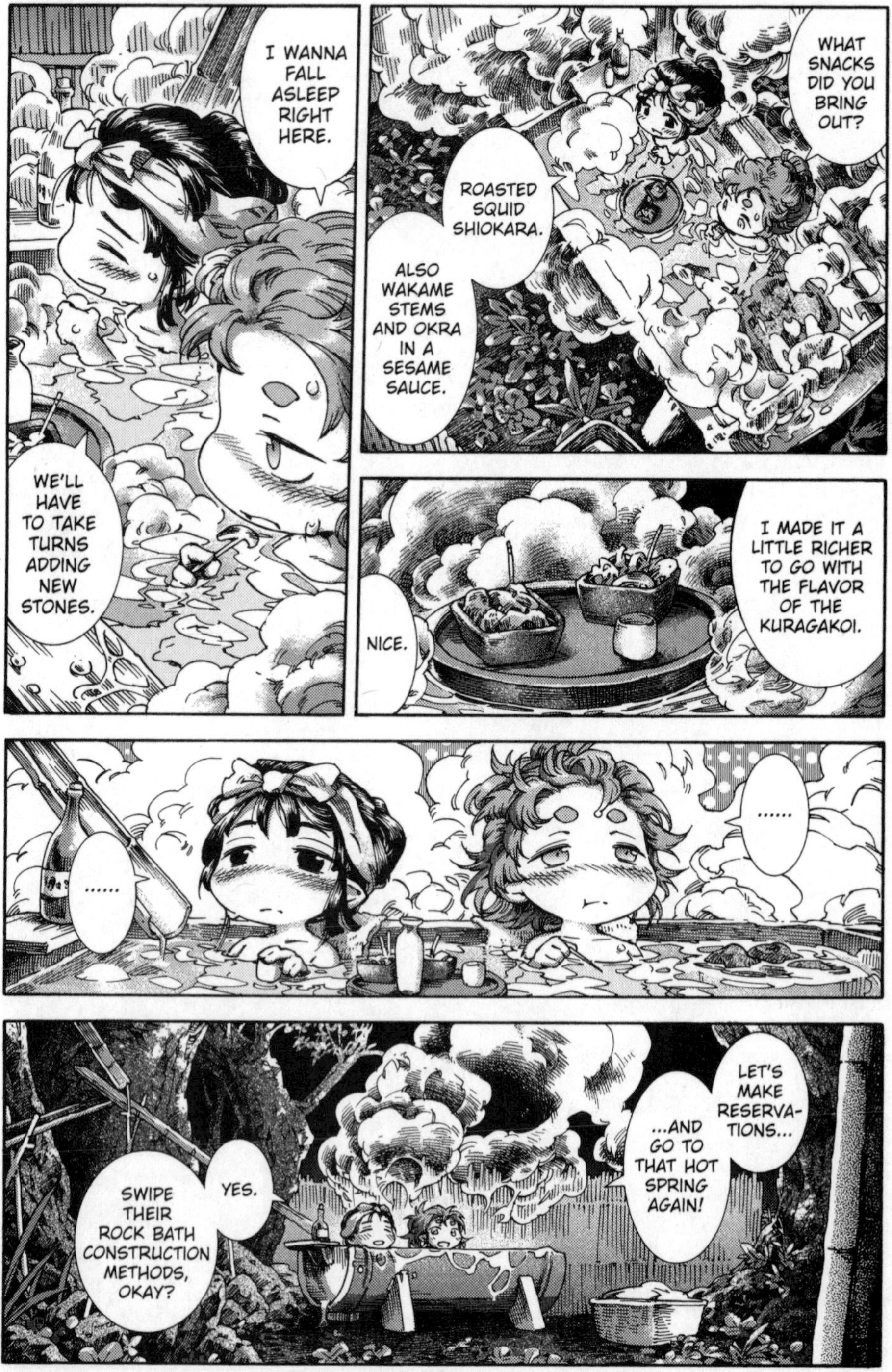
WHAT SNACKS DID YOU BRING OUT?
ROASTED SQUID SHIOKARA.
ALSO WAKAME STEMS AND OKRA IN A SESAME SAUCE.
I MADE IT A LITTLE RICHER TO GO WITH THE FLAVOR OF THE KURAGAKOI.
NICE.
I WANNA FALL ASLEEP RIGHT HERE.
WE'LL HAVE TO TAKE TURNS ADDING NEW STONES.
......
......
LET'S MAKE RESERVATIONS...
...AND GO TO THAT HOT SPRING AGAIN!
YES.
SWIPE THEIR ROCK BATH CONSTRUCTION METHODS, OKAY?

Konutaware is a type of pottery made in the kilns around western Makinata. After the opening of the Arabi sea route, large volumes of porcelain were imported, and the competition put all the kilns out of business. However, in recent years, other industries have begun providing support and getting involved, and a once closely guarded book of pottery methods has been made public. As a result, the industry has made a comeback.

The rustic, thick, practical pieces, which are made from the rough porcelain clay excavated around Konuta and then dipped in a dark-brown iron glaze, are known as Black Konuta. After the revival, people began to manufacture pieces in which a glossy white glaze was poured over the iron glaze. Because many of these pieces have a bluish cast to them, they're known as Blue Konuta. The pieces used at Hot Spring Konuta fall into this category.

Even now, only one kiln fires Black Konuta pottery, and it's extremely difficult to obtain new pieces. As a rule, the only type of Konutaware in circulation outside Makinata is Blue Konuta.

Chapter 25
Daikon Radish and Pipe

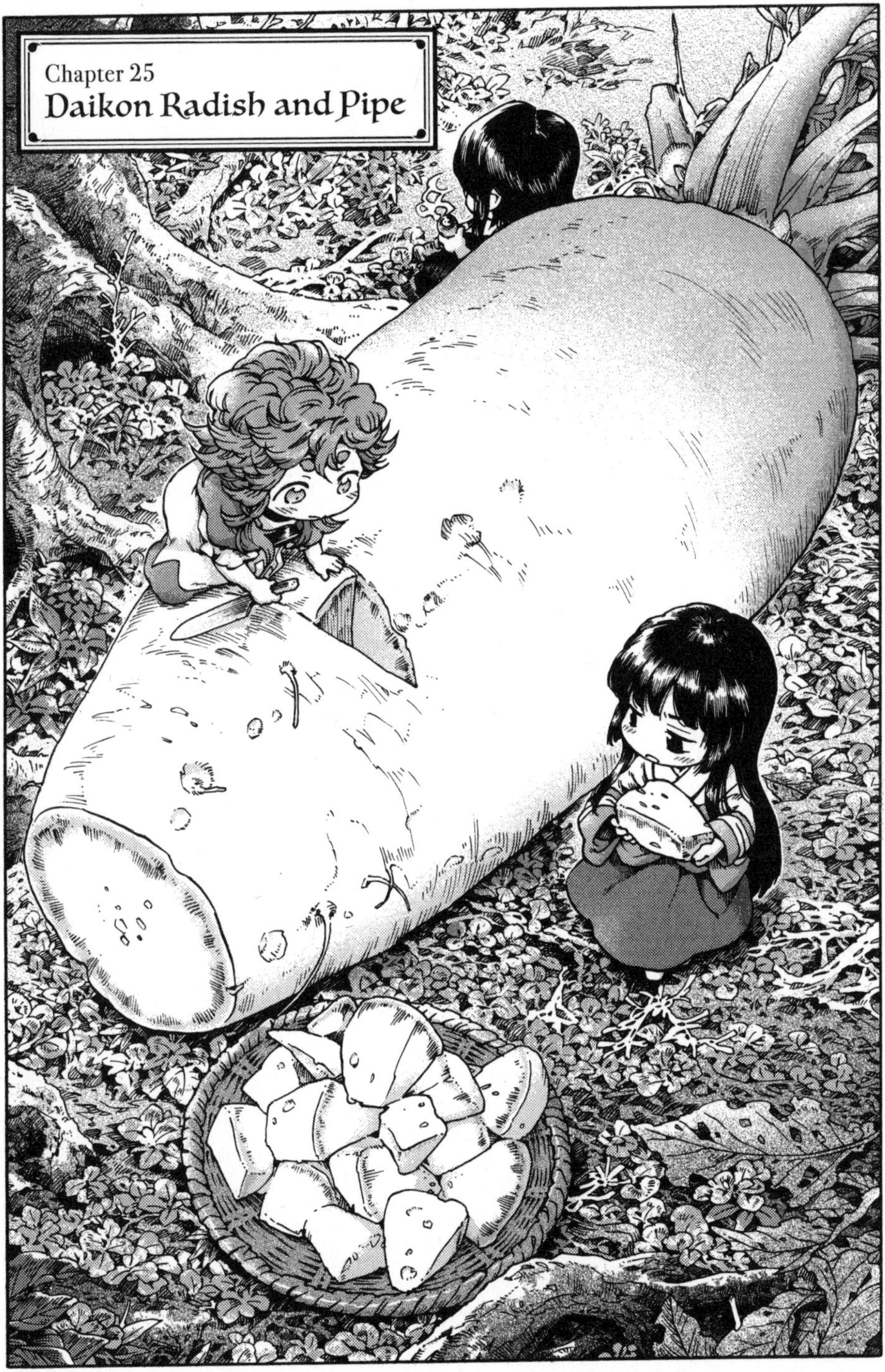

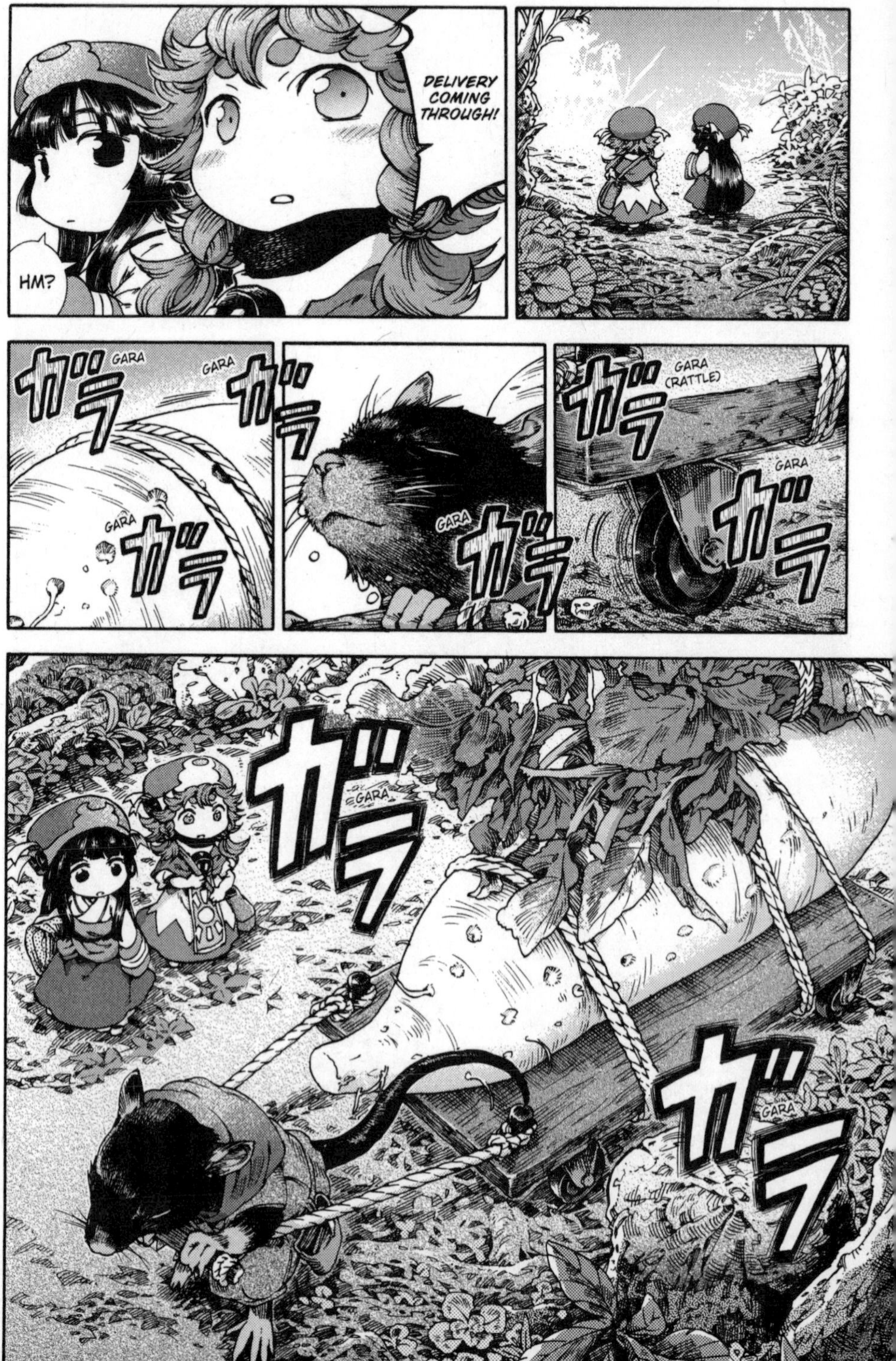
DELIVERY COMING THROUGH!
HM?
ガラ
GARA (RATTLE)
GARA
ガラ
GARA
ガラ
GARA
ガラ
ガラ
GARA
GARA
ガラ
ガラ
GARA
GARA
ガラ

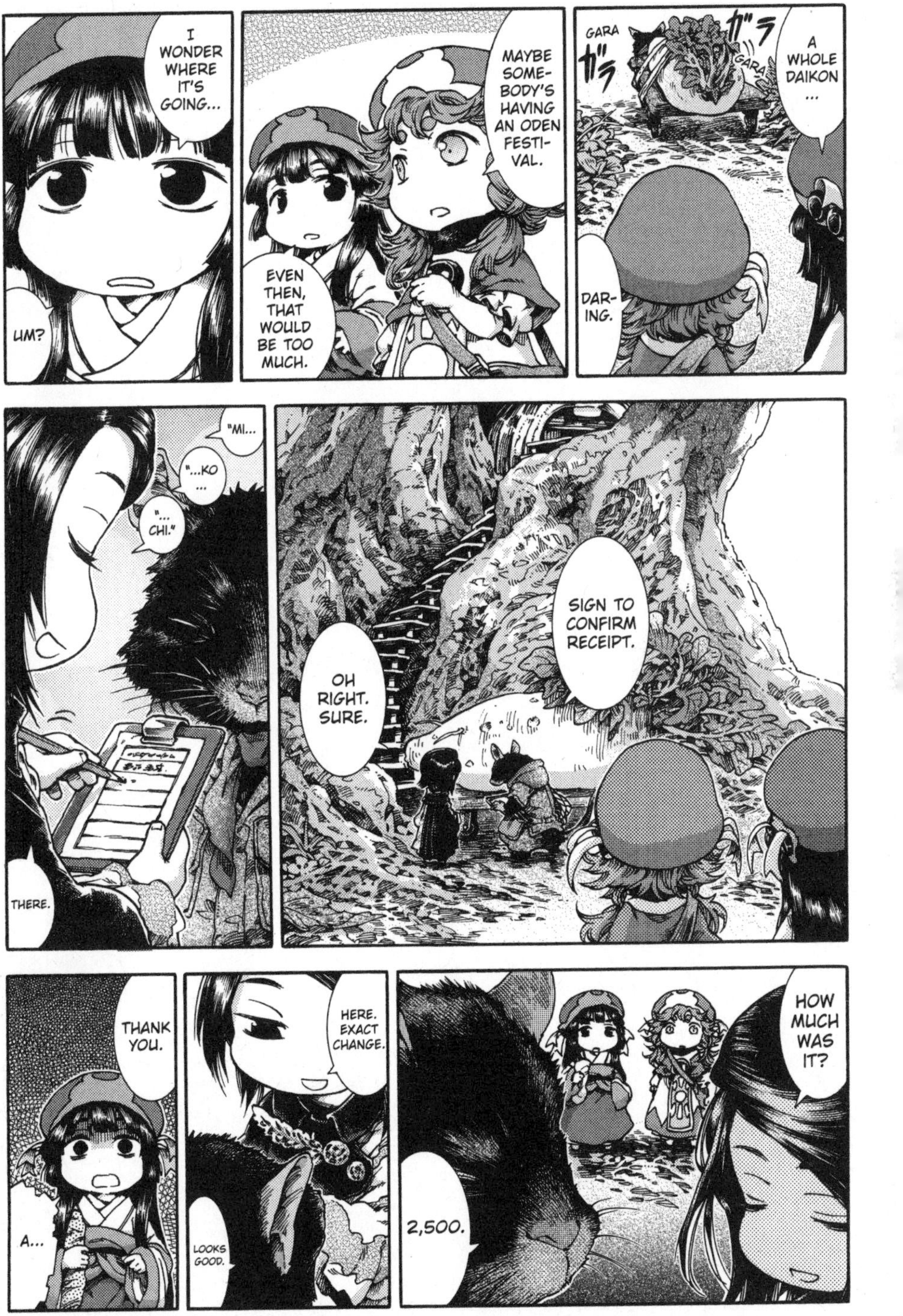
A WHOLE DAIKON...
GARA
ガラ
GARA
ガラ
DAR-ING.
MAYBE SOME-BODY'S HAVING AN ODEN FESTI-VAL.
EVEN THEN, THAT WOULD BE TOO MUCH.
I WONDER WHERE IT'S GOING...
UM?
SIGN TO CONFIRM RECEIPT.
OH RIGHT. SURE.
"MI...
"...KO ...
"... CHI."
THERE.
HOW MUCH WAS IT?
2,500.
HERE. EXACT CHANGE.
LOOKS GOOD.
THANK YOU.
A...

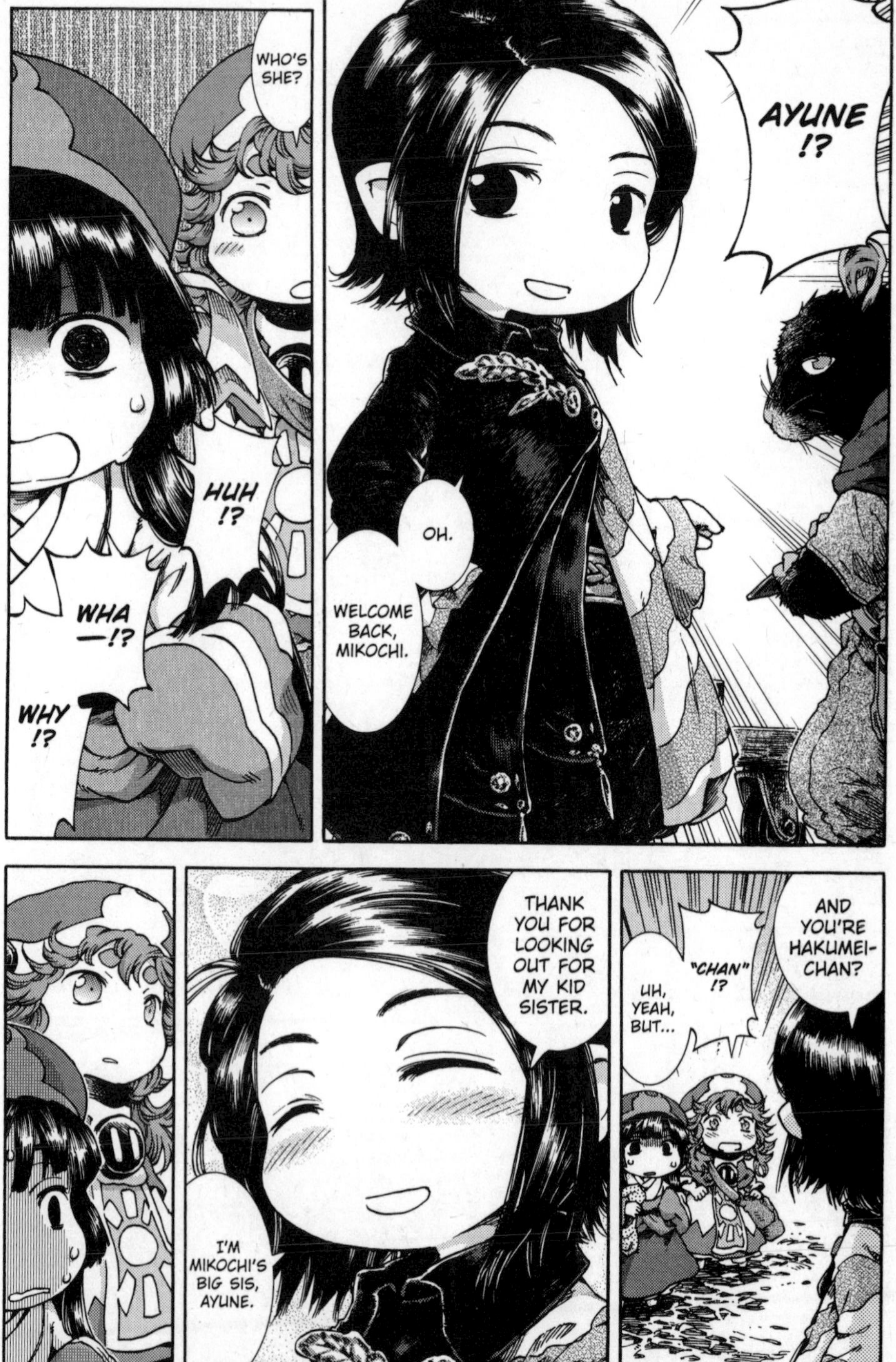
AYUNE !?
OH.
WELCOME BACK, MIKOCHI.
WHO'S SHE?
HUH !?
WHA —!?
WHY !?
AND YOU'RE HAKUMEI-CHAN?
"CHAN" !?
UH, YEAH, BUT...
THANK YOU FOR LOOKING OUT FOR MY KID SISTER.
I'M MIKOCHI'S BIG SIS, AYUNE.

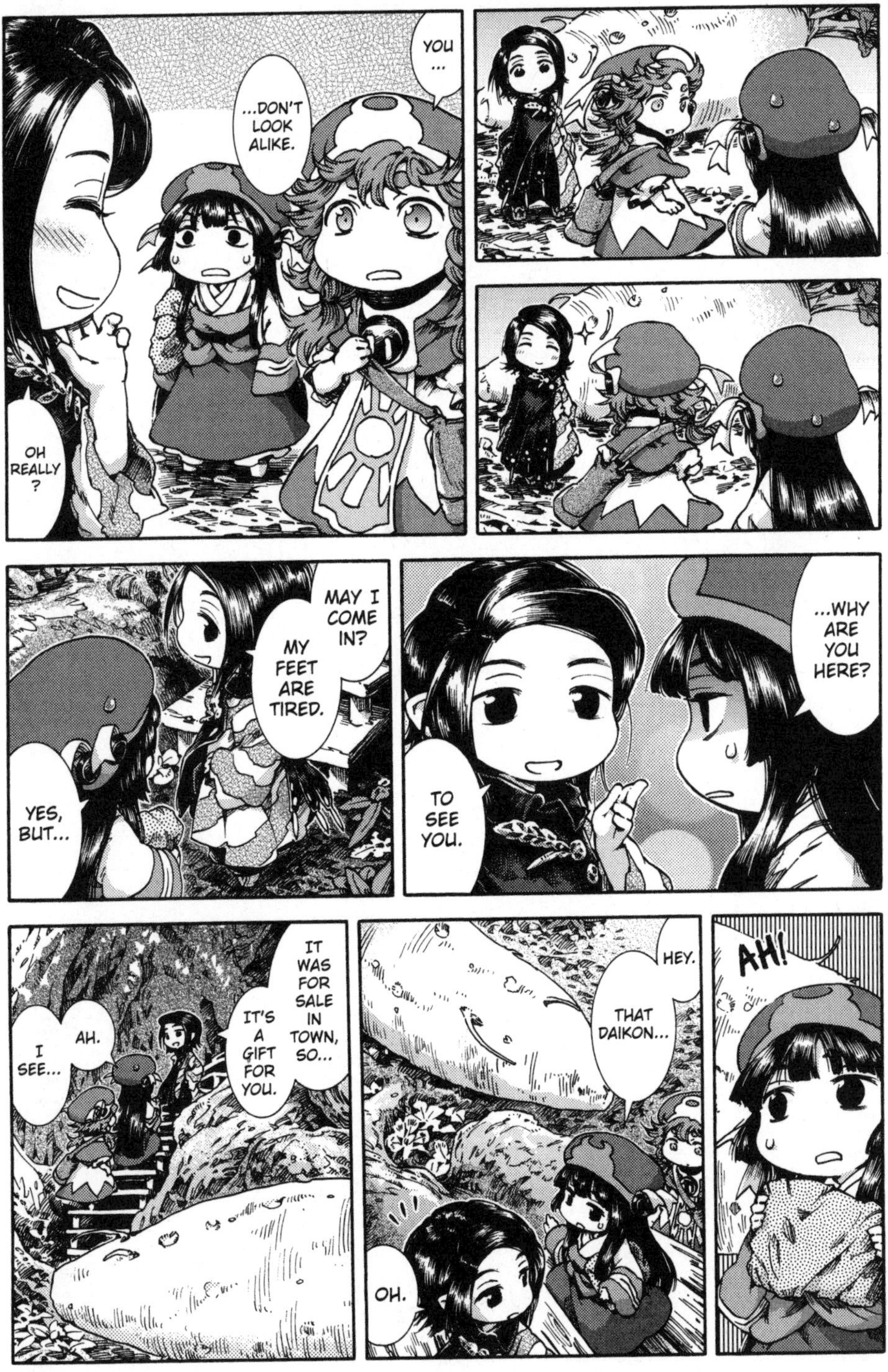
YOU ...
...DON'T LOOK ALIKE.
OH REALLY ?
...WHY ARE YOU HERE?
TO SEE YOU.
MAY I COME IN?
MY FEET ARE TIRED.
YES, BUT...
AH!
HEY.
THAT DAIKON...
OH.
IT WAS FOR SALE IN TOWN, SO...
IT'S A GIFT FOR YOU.
AH.
I SEE...

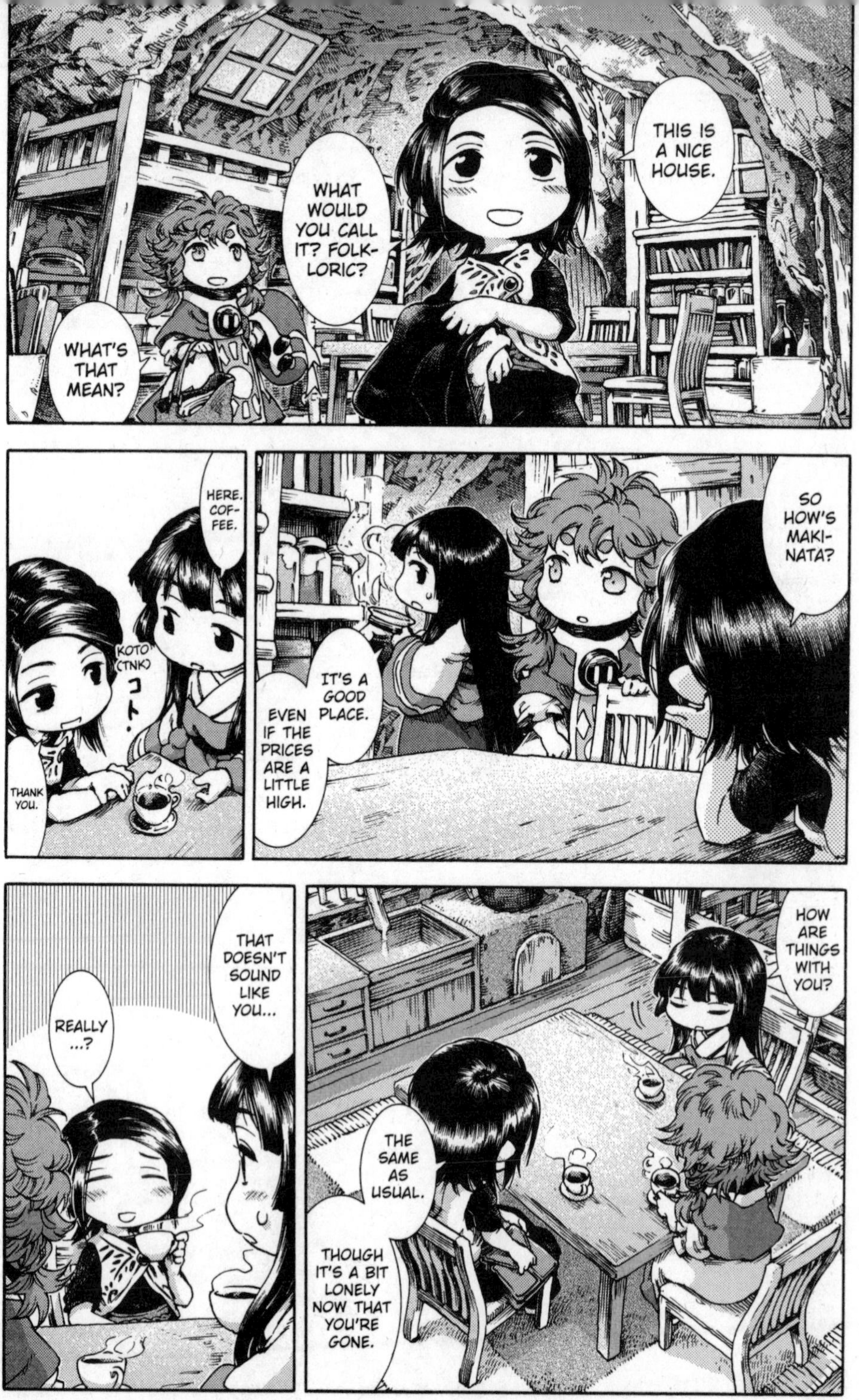
THIS IS A NICE HOUSE.
WHAT WOULD YOU CALL IT? FOLK-LORIC?
WHAT'S THAT MEAN?
SO HOW'S MAKI-NATA?
IT'S A GOOD PLACE.
EVEN IF THE PRICES ARE A LITTLE HIGH.
HERE. COF-FEE.
KOTO (TNK)
コト・
THANK YOU.
HOW ARE THINGS WITH YOU?
THE SAME AS USUAL.
THOUGH IT'S A BIT LONELY NOW THAT YOU'RE GONE.
THAT DOESN'T SOUND LIKE YOU...
REALLY ...?

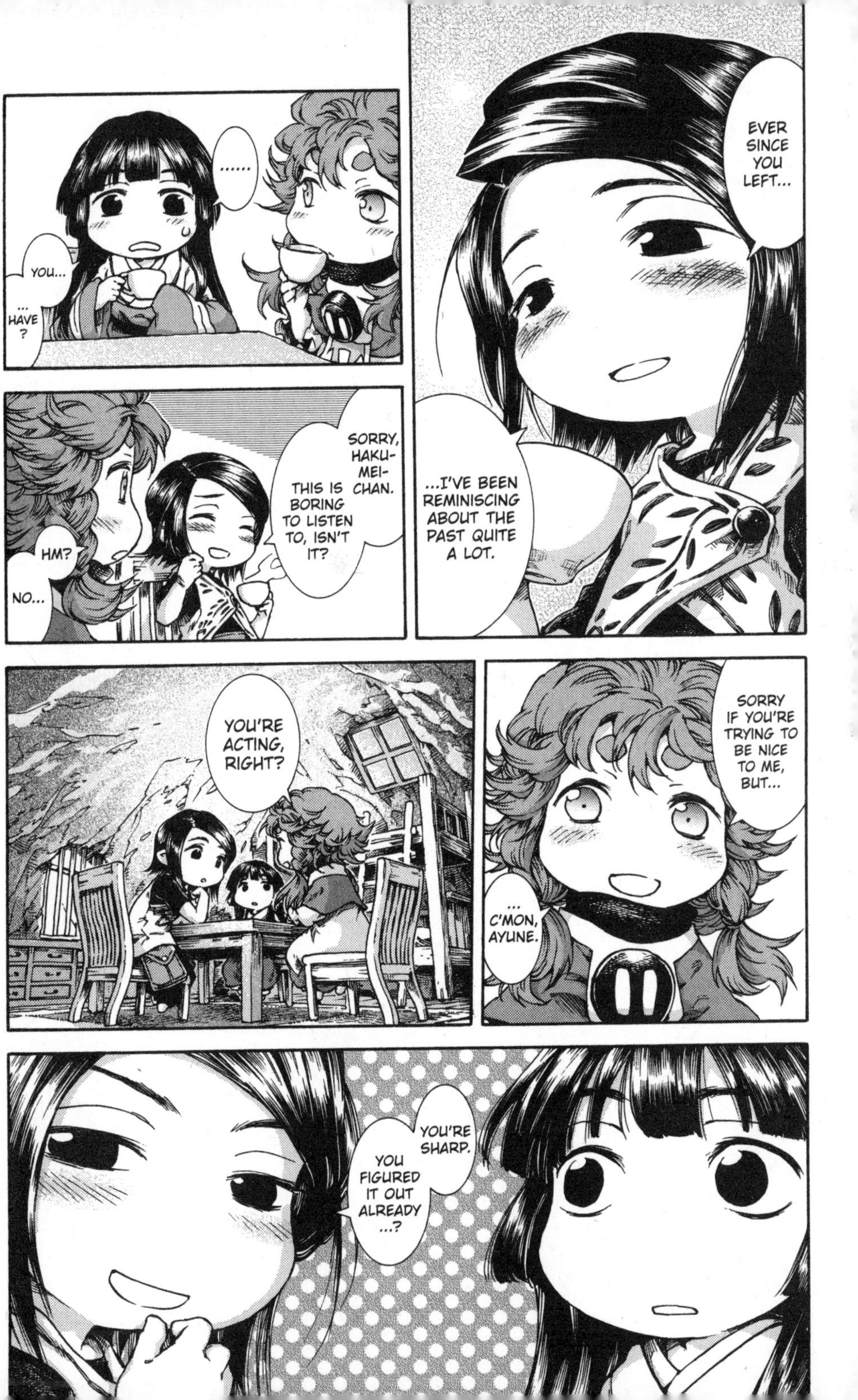
EVER SINCE YOU LEFT...
...I'VE BEEN REMINISCING ABOUT THE PAST QUITE A LOT.
......
YOU...
...HAVE?
SORRY, HAKU-MEI-CHAN.
THIS IS BORING TO LISTEN TO, ISN'T IT?
HM?
NO...
SORRY IF YOU'RE TRYING TO BE NICE TO ME, BUT...
...C'MON, AYUNE.
YOU'RE ACTING, RIGHT?
YOU'RE SHARP.
YOU FIGURED IT OUT ALREADY...?

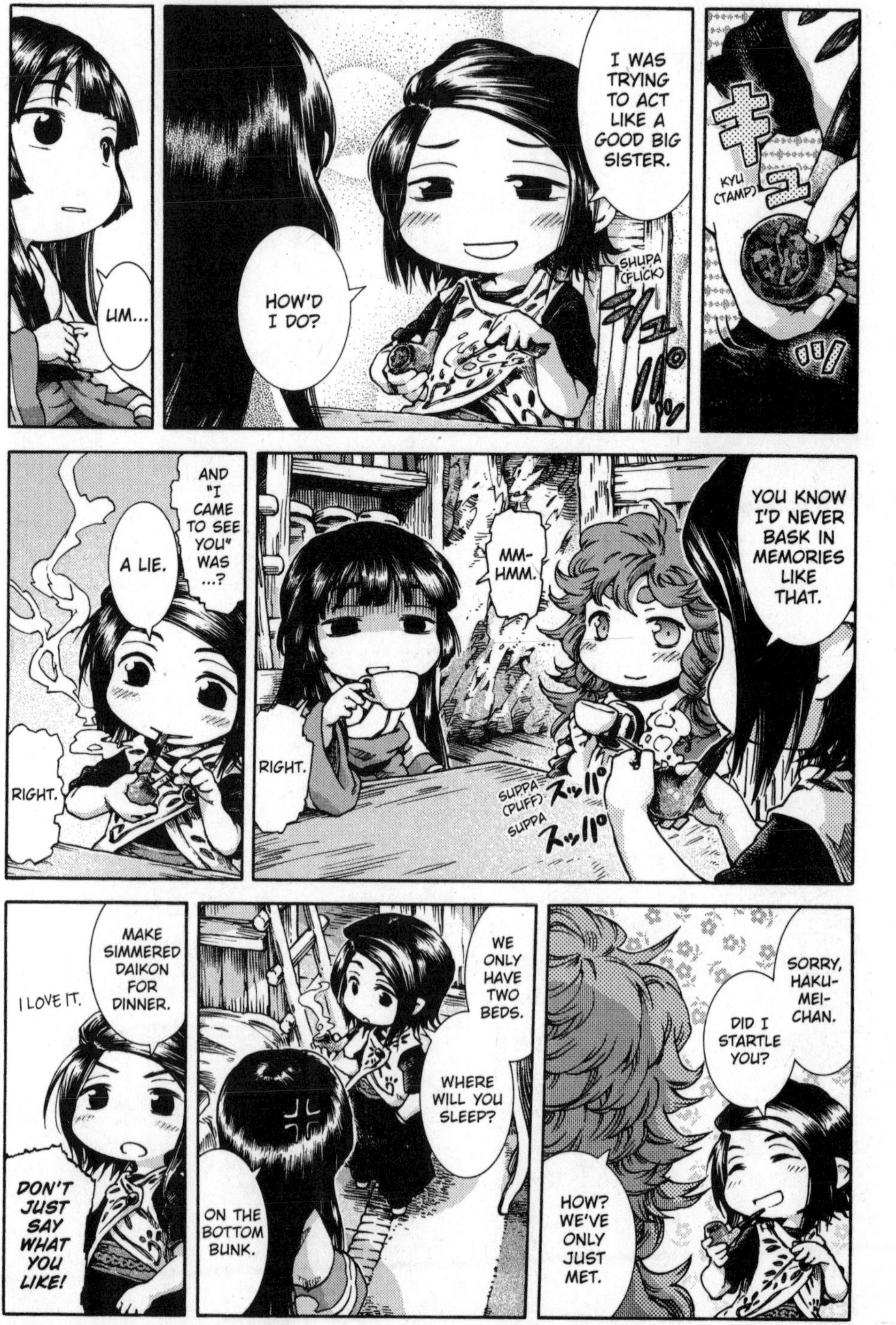
KYU (TAMP)
I WAS TRYING TO ACT LIKE A GOOD BIG SISTER.
SHUPA (FLICK)
HOW'D I DO?
UM...
YOU KNOW I'D NEVER BASK IN MEMORIES LIKE THAT.
MM-HMM.
SUPPA (PUFF)
SUPPA
RIGHT.
AND "I CAME TO SEE YOU" WAS ...?
A LIE.
RIGHT.
SORRY, HAKU-MEI-CHAN.
DID I STARTLE YOU?
HOW? WE'VE ONLY JUST MET.
WE ONLY HAVE TWO BEDS.
WHERE WILL YOU SLEEP?
ON THE BOTTOM BUNK.
MAKE SIMMERED DAIKON FOR DINNER.
I LOVE IT.
DON'T JUST SAY WHAT YOU LIKE!

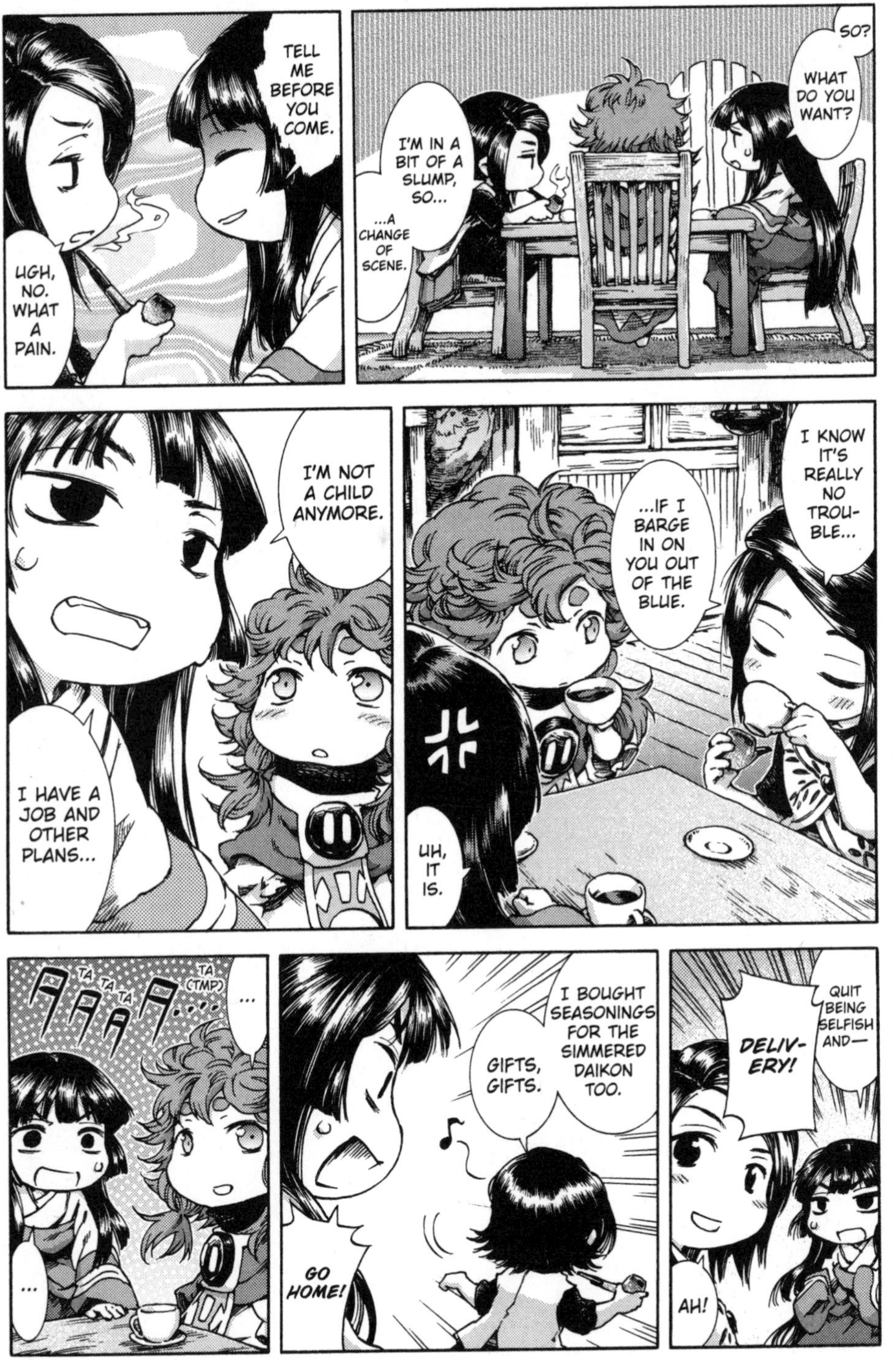
SO?
WHAT DO YOU WANT?
I'M IN A BIT OF A SLUMP, SO...
...A CHANGE OF SCENE.
TELL ME BEFORE YOU COME.
UGH, NO. WHAT A PAIN.
I KNOW IT'S REALLY NO TROUBLE...
...IF I BARGE IN ON YOU OUT OF THE BLUE.
UH, IT IS.
I'M NOT A CHILD ANYMORE.
I HAVE A JOB AND OTHER PLANS...
QUIT BEING SELFISH AND—
DELIVERY!
AH!
I BOUGHT SEASONINGS FOR THE SIMMERED DAIKON TOO.
GIFTS, GIFTS.
GO HOME!
TA TA TA TA (TMP)
...
...

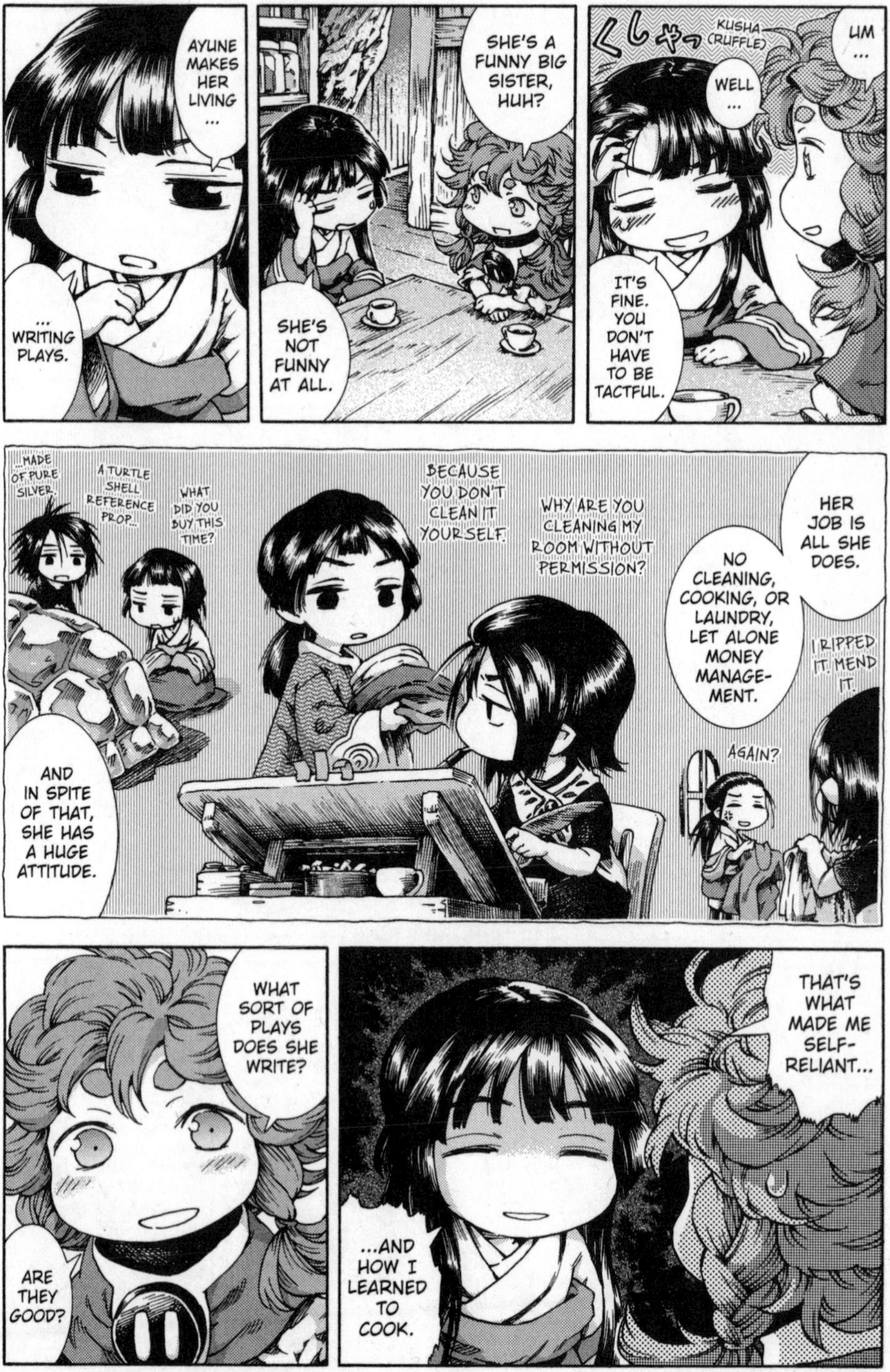

くしゃっ
KUSHA (RUFFLE)
UM ...
WELL ...
IT'S FINE. YOU DON'T HAVE TO BE TACTFUL.
SHE'S A FUNNY BIG SISTER, HUH?
SHE'S NOT FUNNY AT ALL.
AYUNE MAKES HER LIVING ...
... WRITING PLAYS.
HER JOB IS ALL SHE DOES.
I RIPPED IT. MEND IT.
NO CLEANING, COOKING, OR LAUNDRY, LET ALONE MONEY MANAGEMENT.
AGAIN?
WHY ARE YOU CLEANING MY ROOM WITHOUT PERMISSION?
BECAUSE YOU DON'T CLEAN IT YOURSELF.
WHAT DID YOU BUY THIS TIME?
A TURTLE SHELL REFERENCE PROP...
...MADE OF PURE SILVER.
AND IN SPITE OF THAT, SHE HAS A HUGE ATTITUDE.
THAT'S WHAT MADE ME SELF-RELIANT...
...AND HOW I LEARNED TO COOK.
WHAT SORT OF PLAYS DOES SHE WRITE?
ARE THEY GOOD?

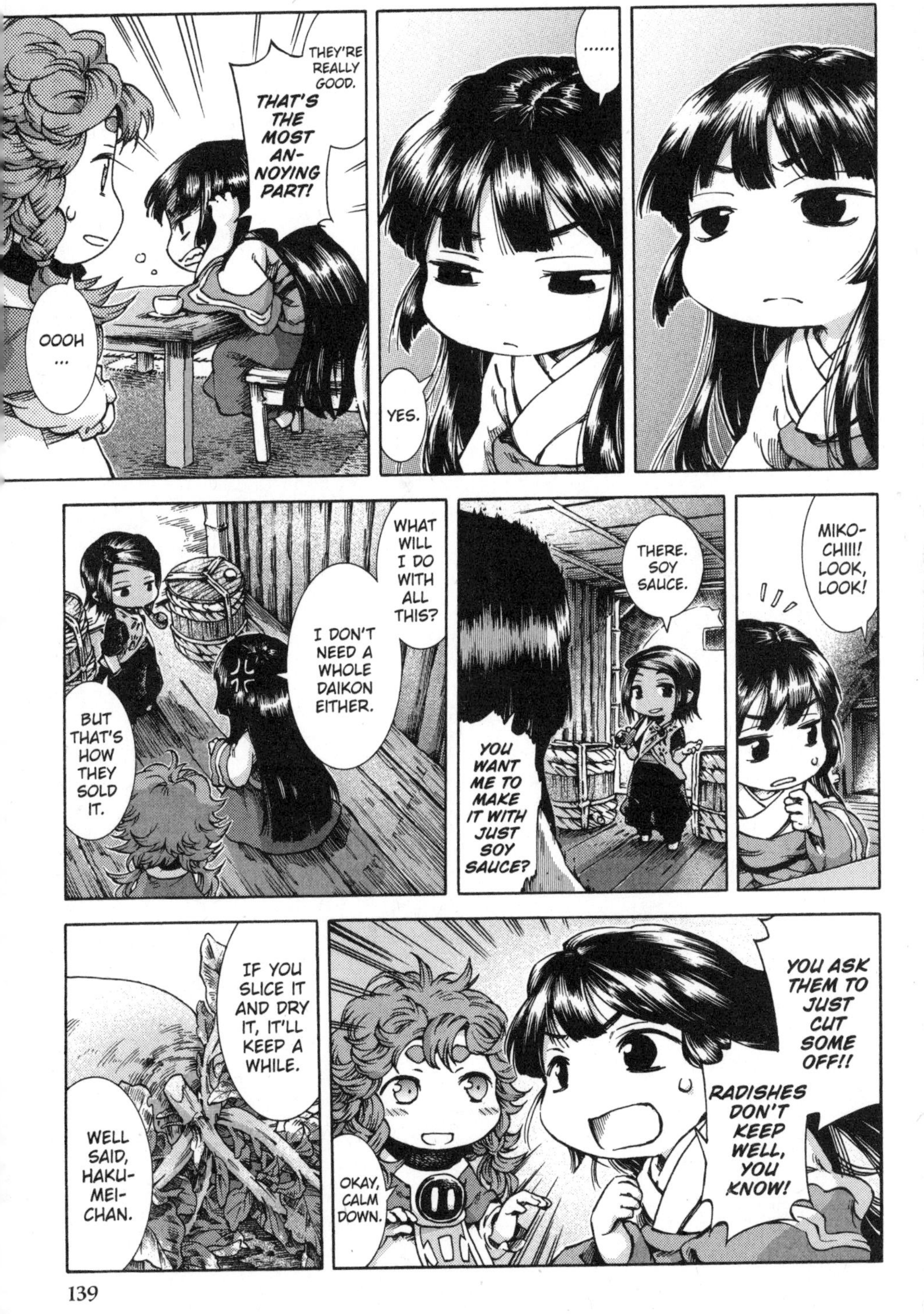
......
YES.
THEY'RE REALLY GOOD.
THAT'S THE MOST AN-NOYING PART!
OOOH ...
MIKO-CHIII! LOOK, LOOK!
THERE. SOY SAUCE.
YOU WANT ME TO MAKE IT WITH JUST SOY SAUCE?
WHAT WILL I DO WITH ALL THIS?
I DON'T NEED A WHOLE DAIKON EITHER.
BUT THAT'S HOW THEY SOLD IT.
YOU ASK THEM TO JUST CUT SOME OFF!!
RADISHES DON'T KEEP WELL, YOU KNOW!
OKAY, CALM DOWN.
IF YOU SLICE IT AND DRY IT, IT'LL KEEP A WHILE.
WELL SAID, HAKU-MEI-CHAN.

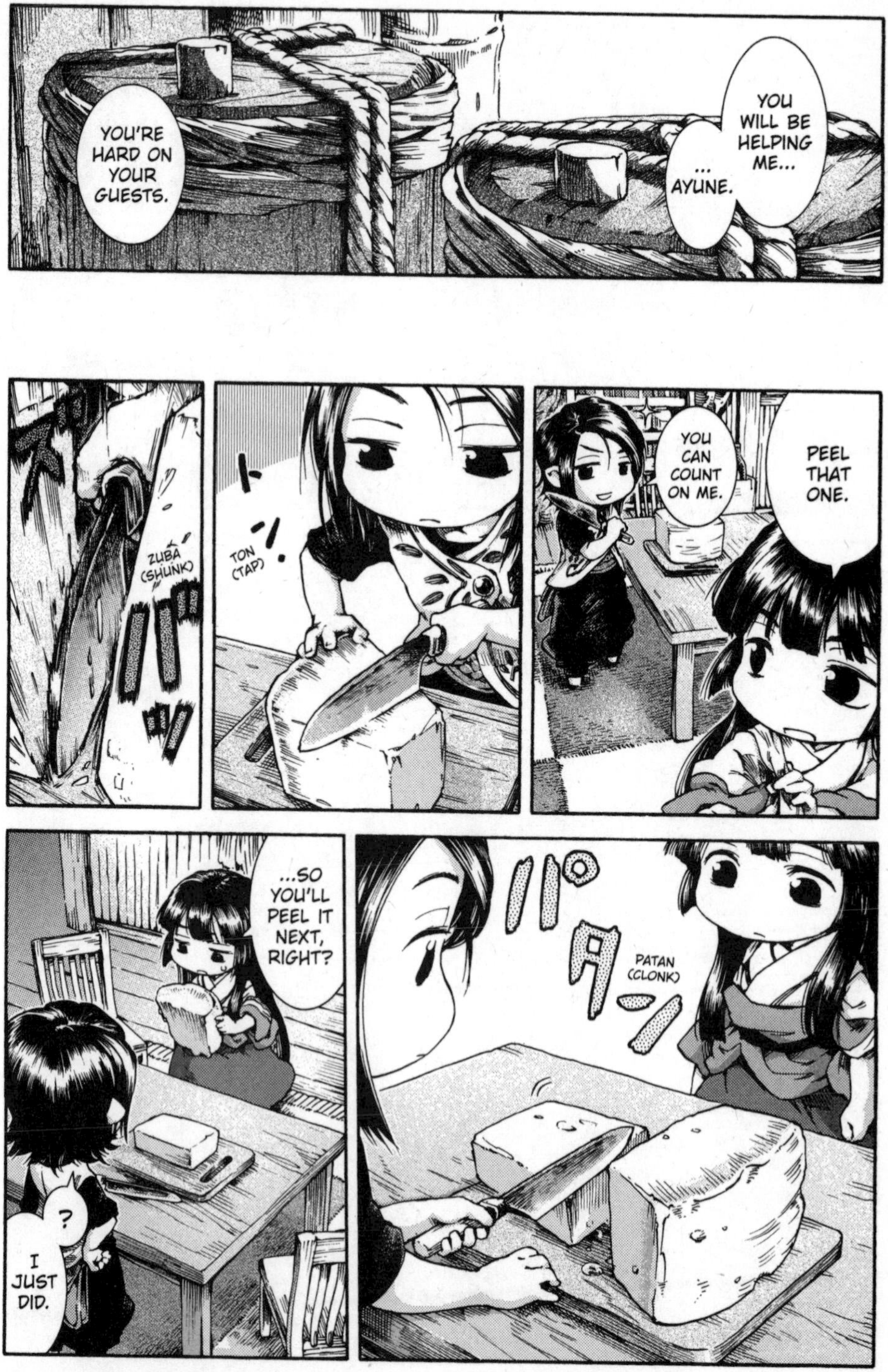
YOU WILL BE HELPING ME...
... AYUNE.
YOU'RE HARD ON YOUR GUESTS.
PEEL THAT ONE.
YOU CAN COUNT ON ME.
TON (TAP)
ZUBA (SHUNK)
PATAN (CLONK)
...SO YOU'LL PEEL IT NEXT, RIGHT?
?
I JUST DID.

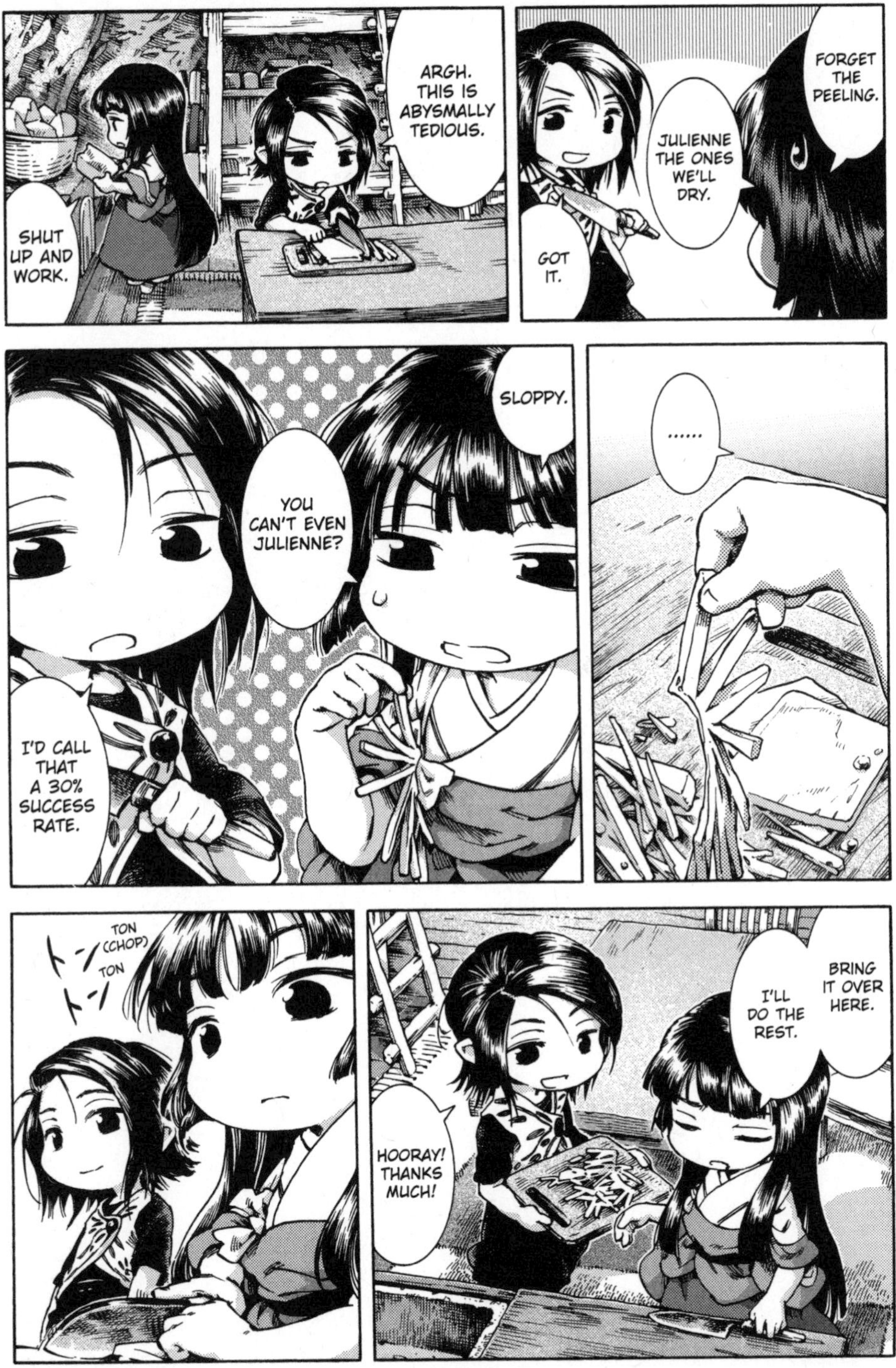
FORGET THE PEELING.
JULIENNE THE ONES WE'LL DRY.
GOT IT.
ARGH. THIS IS ABYSMALLY TEDIOUS.
SHUT UP AND WORK.
......
SLOPPY.
YOU CAN'T EVEN JULIENNE?
I'D CALL THAT A 30% SUCCESS RATE.
BRING IT OVER HERE.
I'LL DO THE REST.
HOORAY! THANKS MUCH!
TON (CHOP) TON

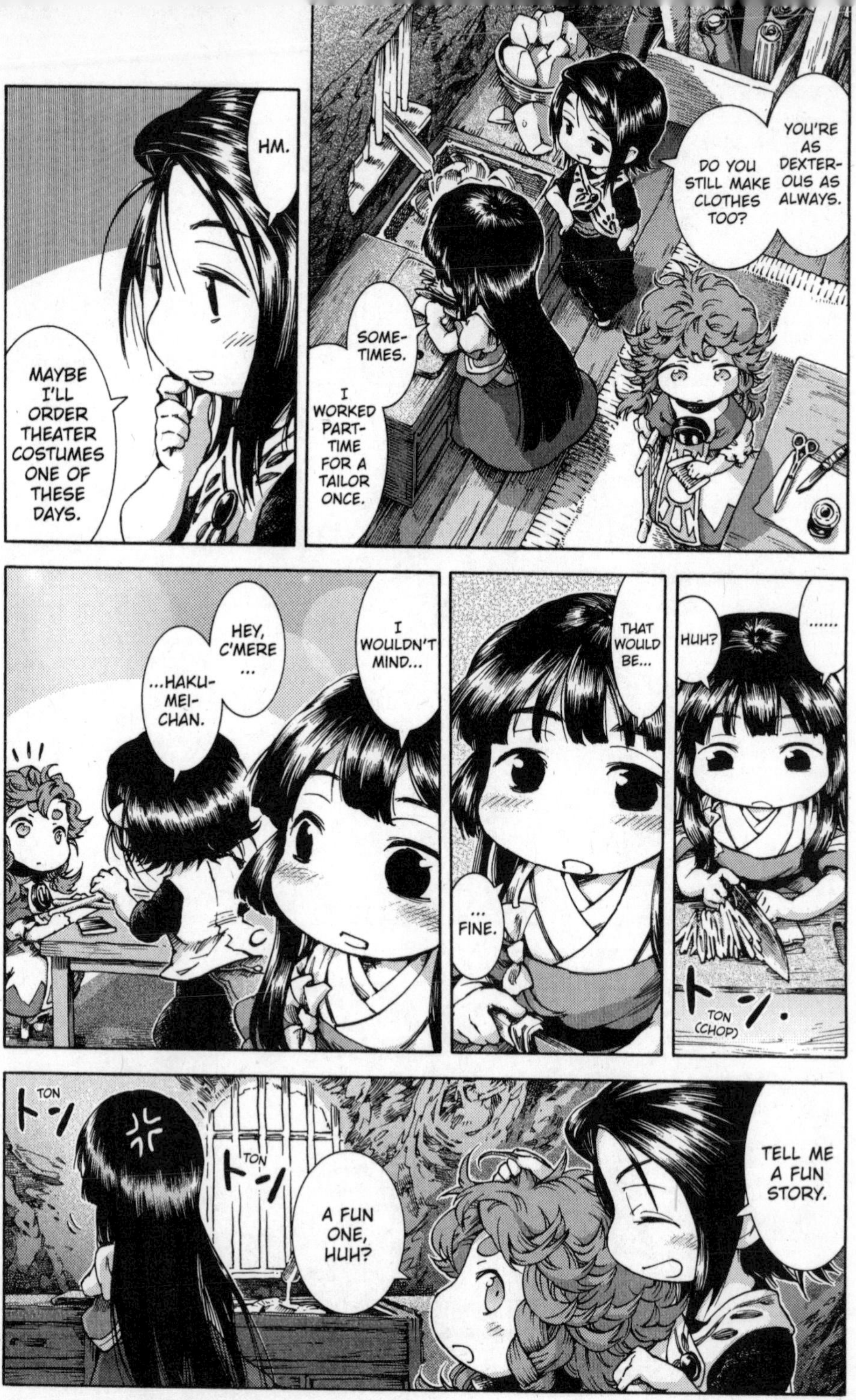
YOU'RE AS DEXTEROUS AS ALWAYS.
DO YOU STILL MAKE CLOTHES TOO?
SOMETIMES.
I WORKED PART-TIME FOR A TAILOR ONCE.
HM.
MAYBE I'LL ORDER THEATER COSTUMES ONE OF THESE DAYS.
......
HUH?
TON (CHOP)
THAT WOULD BE...
...FINE.
I WOULDN'T MIND...
HEY, C'MERE ...
...HAKUMEI-CHAN.
TELL ME A FUN STORY.
A FUN ONE, HUH?
TON
TON

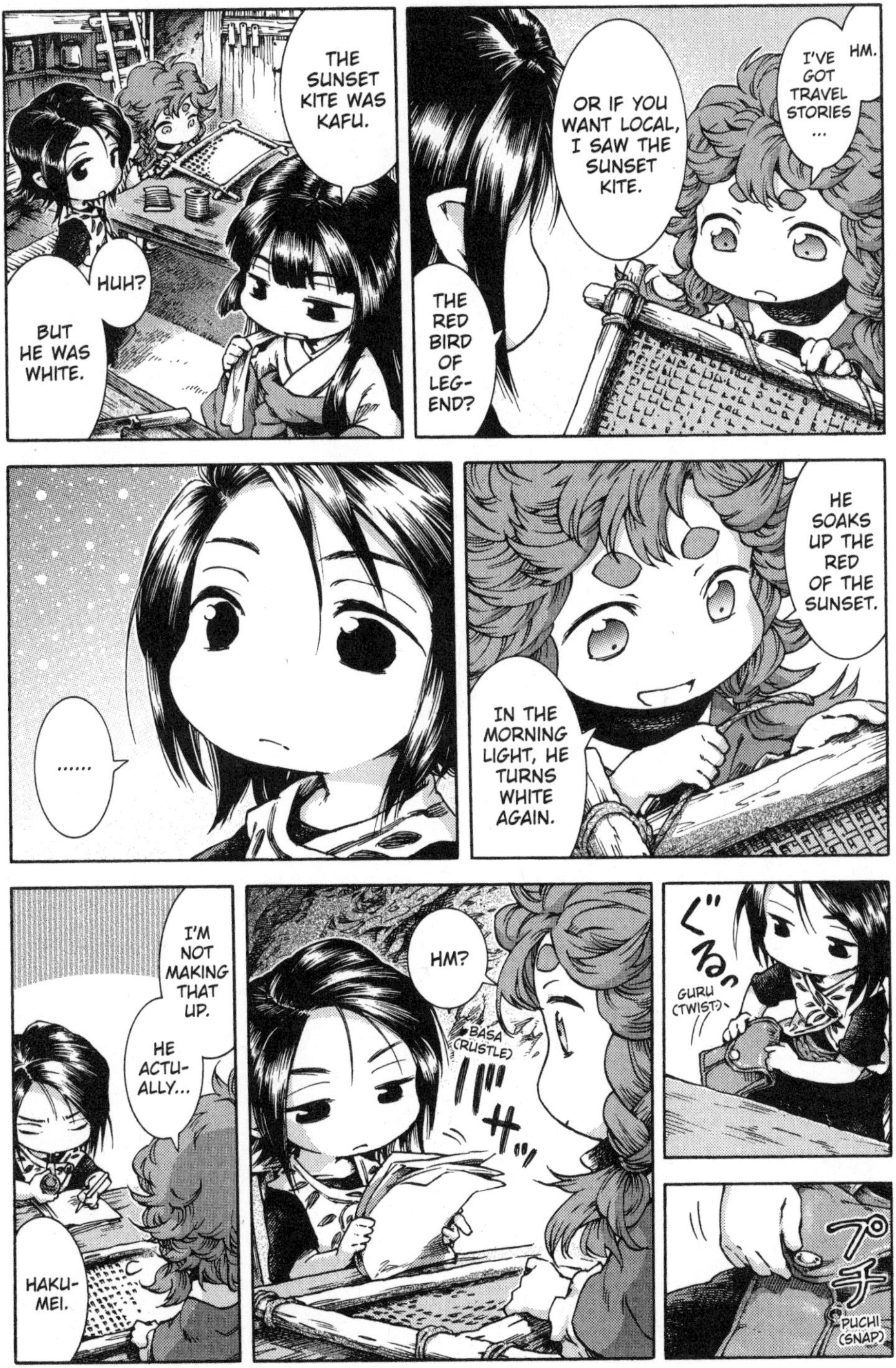
HM.
I'VE GOT TRAVEL STORIES ...
OR IF YOU WANT LOCAL, I SAW THE SUNSET KITE.
THE RED BIRD OF LEGEND?
THE SUNSET KITE WAS KAFU.
HUH?
BUT HE WAS WHITE.
HE SOAKS UP THE RED OF THE SUNSET.
IN THE MORNING LIGHT, HE TURNS WHITE AGAIN.
......
ぐるっ
GURU (TWIST)
プチ
PUCHI (SNAP)
HM?
バサッ
BASA (RUSTLE)
I'M NOT MAKING THAT UP.
HE ACTUALLY...
HAKUMEI.

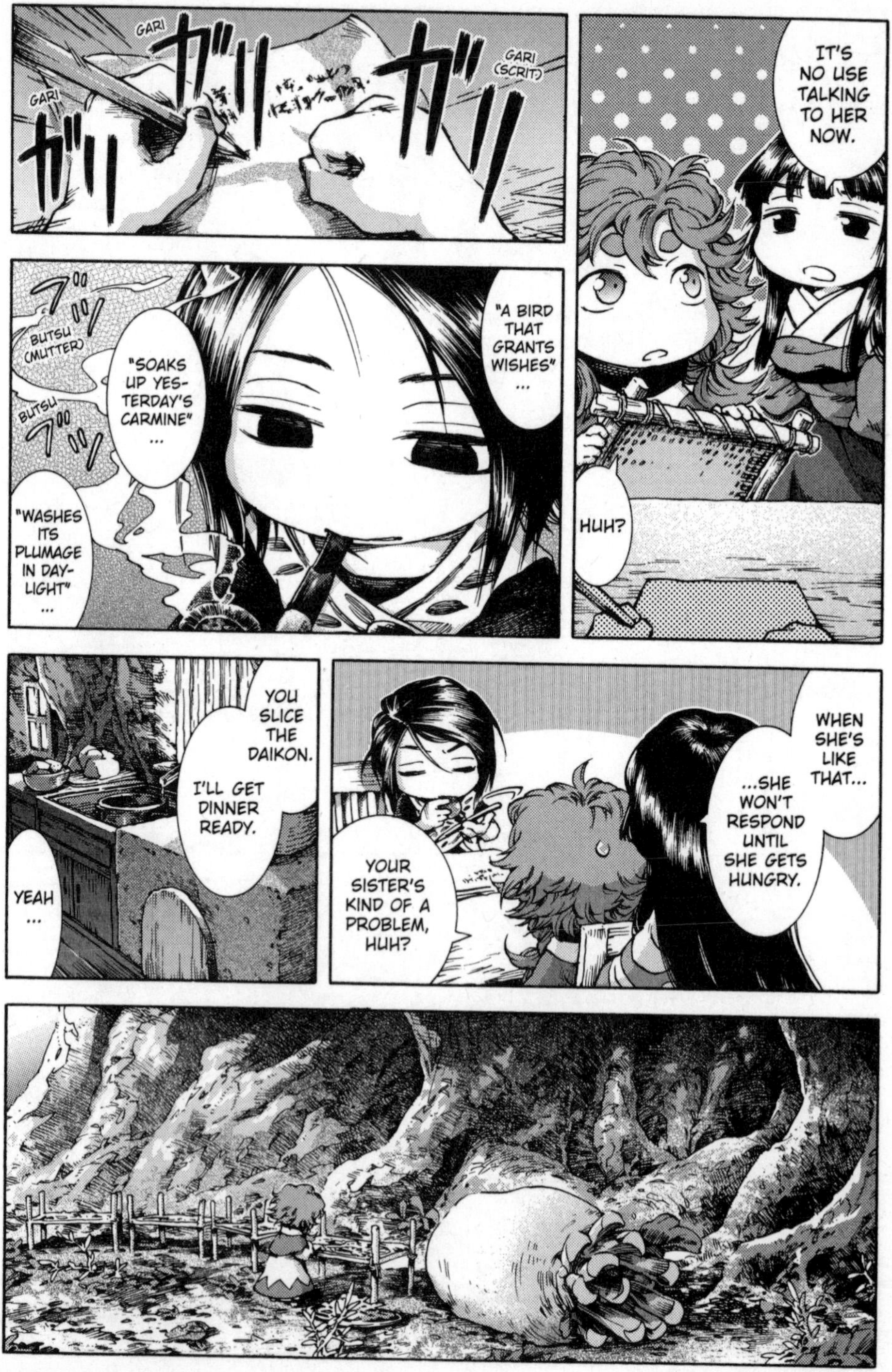
IT'S NO USE TALKING TO HER NOW.
HUH?
GARI
GARI
GARI (SCRIT)
"A BIRD THAT GRANTS WISHES" ...
"SOAKS UP YESTERDAY'S CARMINE" ...
BUTSU (MUTTER)
BUTSU
"WASHES ITS PLUMAGE IN DAYLIGHT" ...
WHEN SHE'S LIKE THAT...
...SHE WON'T RESPOND UNTIL SHE GETS HUNGRY.
YOUR SISTER'S KIND OF A PROBLEM, HUH?
YOU SLICE THE DAIKON.
I'LL GET DINNER READY.
YEAH ...

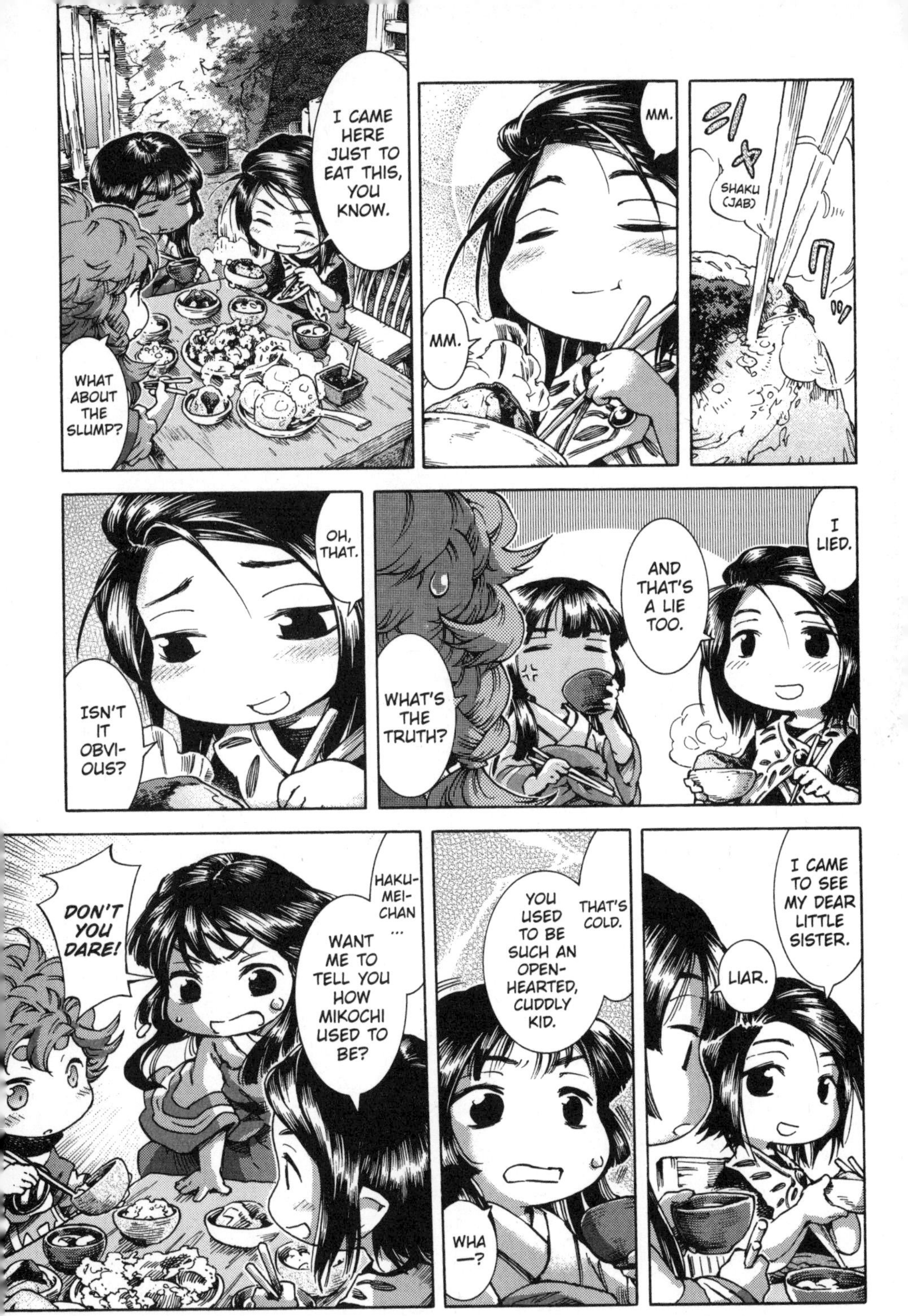
SHAKU (JAB)
MM.
MM.
I CAME HERE JUST TO EAT THIS, YOU KNOW.
WHAT ABOUT THE SLUMP?
I LIED.
AND THAT'S A LIE TOO.
WHAT'S THE TRUTH?
OH, THAT.
ISN'T IT OBVIOUS?
I CAME TO SEE MY DEAR LITTLE SISTER.
LIAR.
THAT'S COLD.
YOU USED TO BE SUCH AN OPEN-HEARTED, CUDDLY KID.
WHA—?
HAKU-MEI-CHAN...
WANT ME TO TELL YOU HOW MIKOCHI USED TO BE?
DON'T YOU DARE!

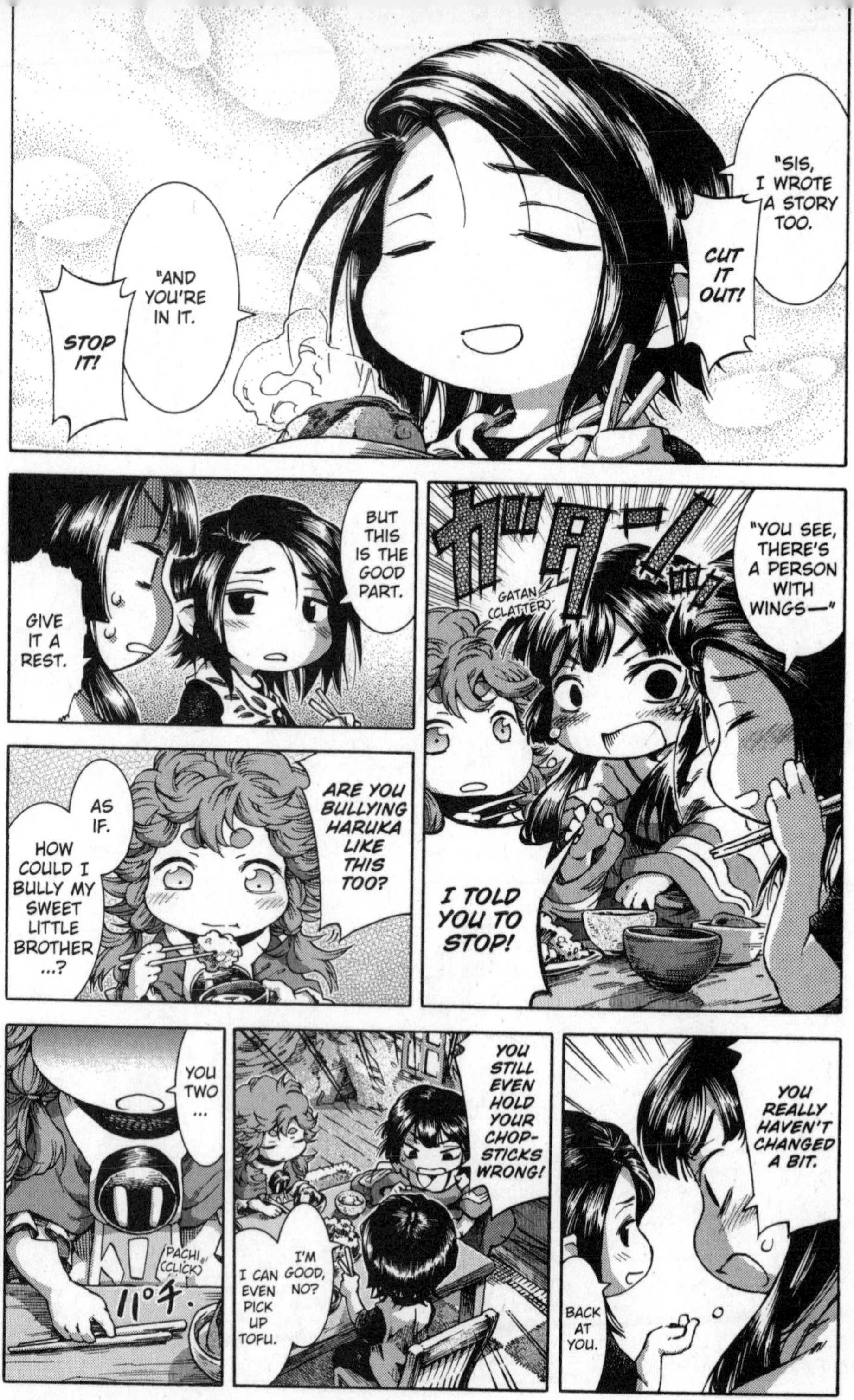
"SIS, I WROTE A STORY TOO.
CUT IT OUT!
"AND YOU'RE IN IT.
STOP IT!
"YOU SEE, THERE'S A PERSON WITH WINGS—"
GATAN (CLATTER)
I TOLD YOU TO STOP!
BUT THIS IS THE GOOD PART.
GIVE IT A REST.
ARE YOU BULLYING HARUKA LIKE THIS TOO?
AS IF. HOW COULD I BULLY MY SWEET LITTLE BROTHER ...?
YOU REALLY HAVEN'T CHANGED A BIT.
BACK AT YOU.
YOU STILL EVEN HOLD YOUR CHOPSTICKS WRONG!
I'M GOOD, NO? I CAN EVEN PICK UP TOFU.
YOU TWO ...
パチ.
PACHI (CLICK)

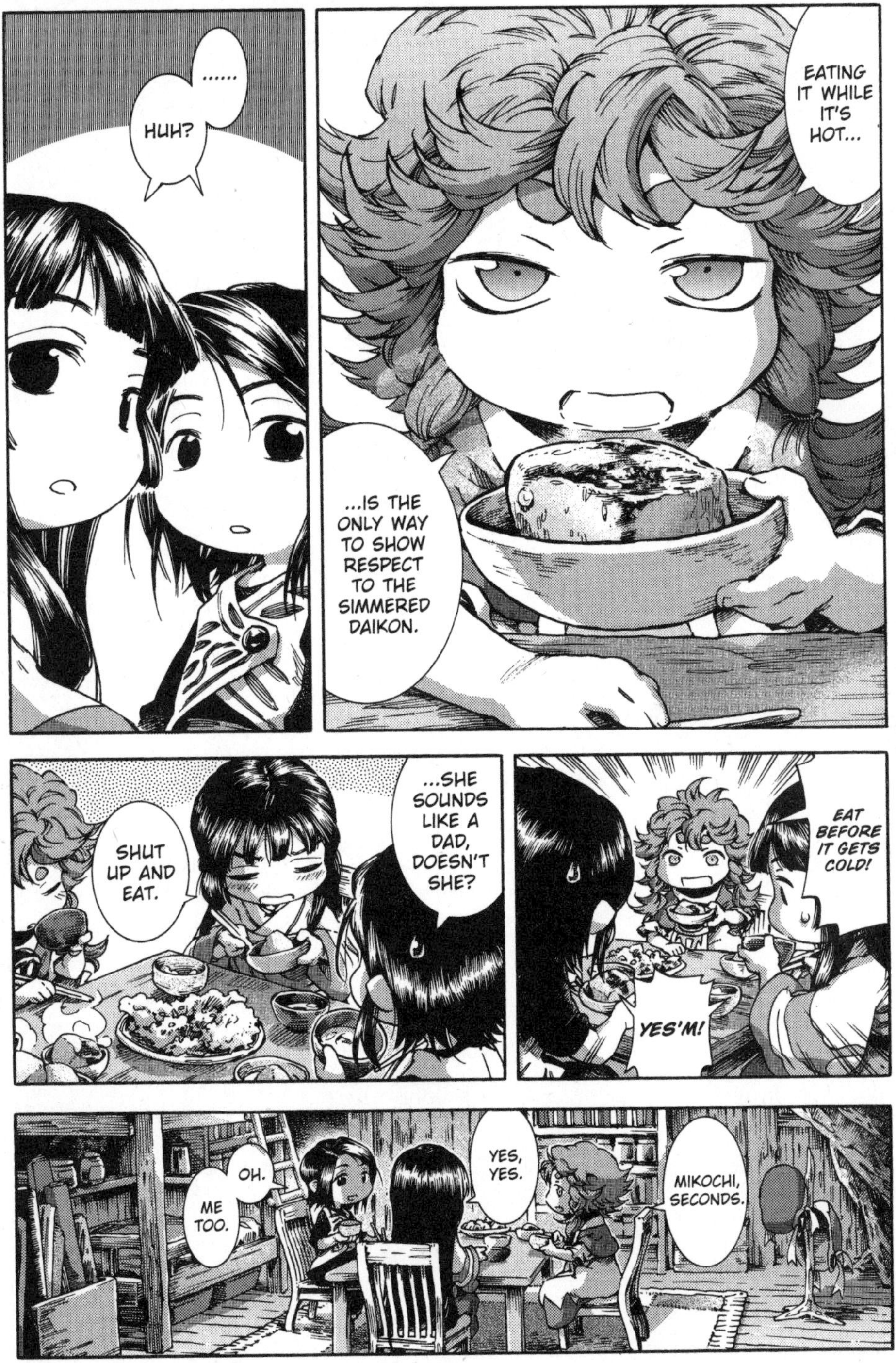
EATING IT WHILE IT'S HOT...
...IS THE ONLY WAY TO SHOW RESPECT TO THE SIMMERED DAIKON.
......
HUH?
EAT BEFORE IT GETS COLD!
YES'M!
...SHE SOUNDS LIKE A DAD, DOESN'T SHE?
SHUT UP AND EAT.
MIKOCHI, SECONDS.
YES, YES.
OH.
ME TOO.

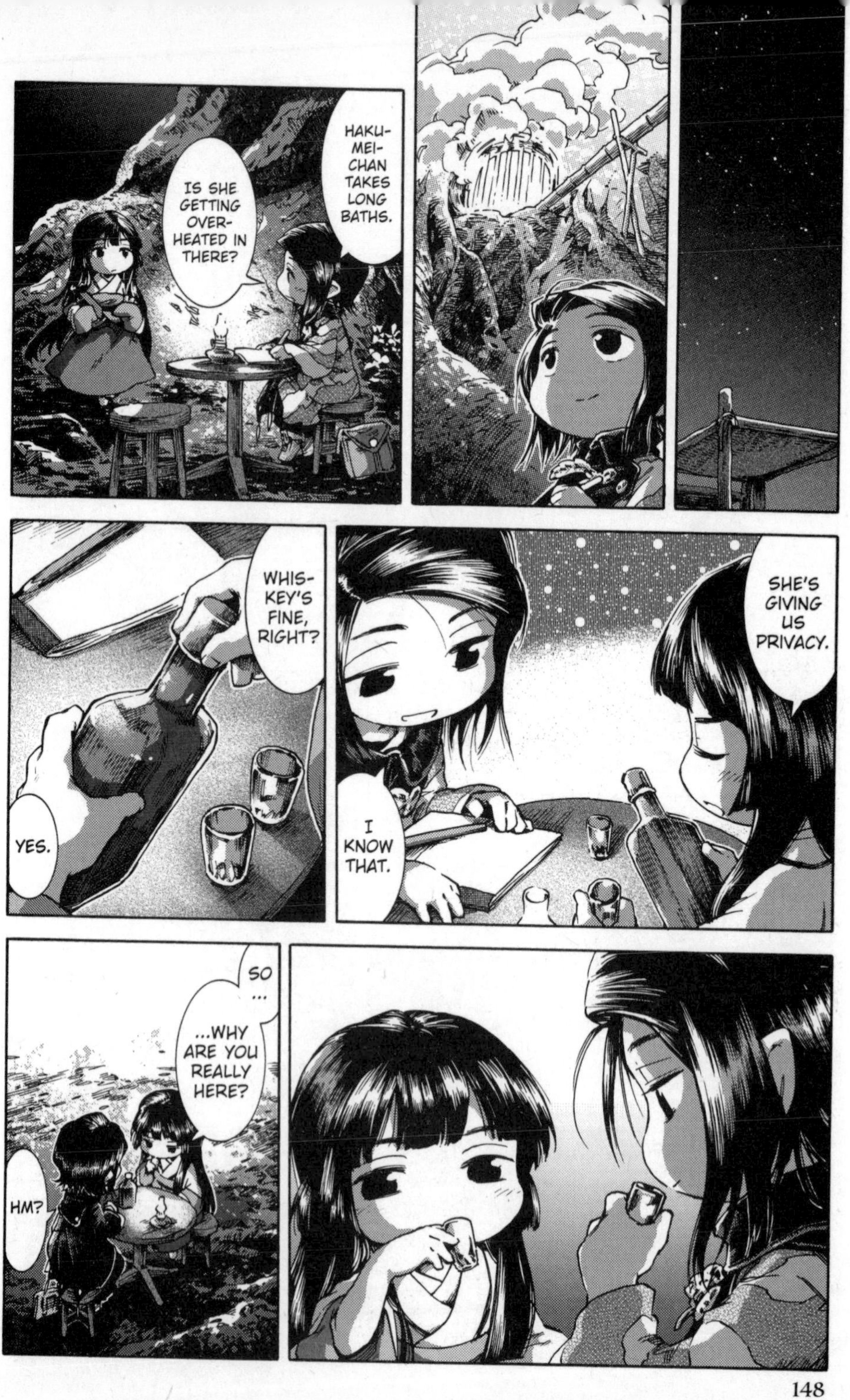
HAKU-MEI-CHAN TAKES LONG BATHS.
IS SHE GETTING OVER-HEATED IN THERE?
SHE'S GIVING US PRIVACY.
I KNOW THAT.
WHIS-KEY'S FINE, RIGHT?
YES.
SO ...
...WHY ARE YOU REALLY HERE?
HM?

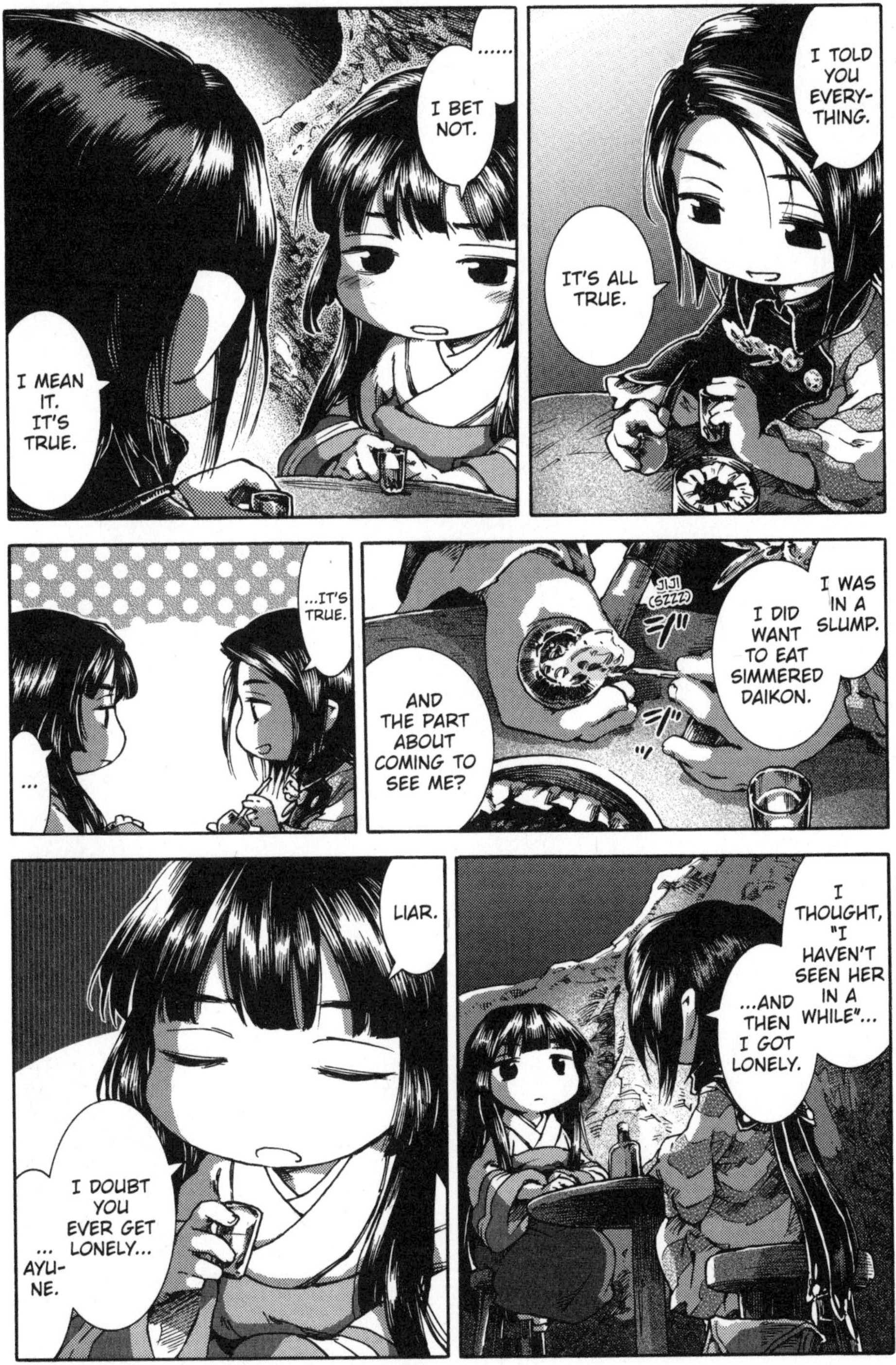
I TOLD YOU EVERY-THING.
IT'S ALL TRUE.
......
I BET NOT.
I MEAN IT. IT'S TRUE.
I WAS IN A SLUMP.
JIJI (SZZZ)
I DID WANT TO EAT SIMMERED DAIKON.
AND THE PART ABOUT COMING TO SEE ME?
...IT'S TRUE.
...
I THOUGHT, "I HAVEN'T SEEN HER IN A WHILE"...
...AND THEN I GOT LONELY.
LIAR.
I DOUBT YOU EVER GET LONELY... ...AYU-NE.

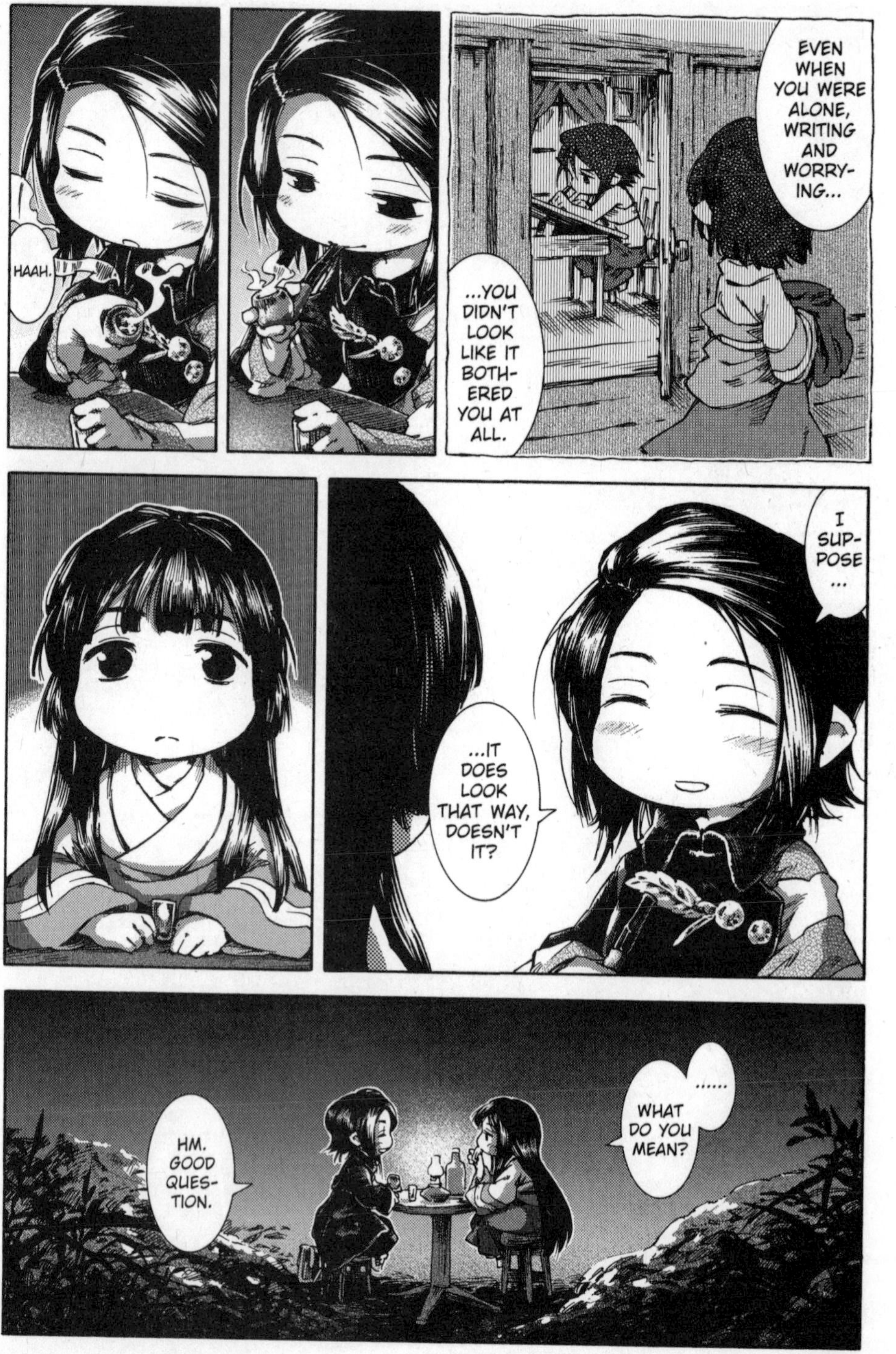
EVEN WHEN YOU WERE ALONE, WRITING AND WORRY-ING...
...YOU DIDN'T LOOK LIKE IT BOTH-ERED YOU AT ALL.
HAAH.
I SUP-POSE...
...IT DOES LOOK THAT WAY, DOESN'T IT?
......
WHAT DO YOU MEAN?
HM. GOOD QUES-TION.

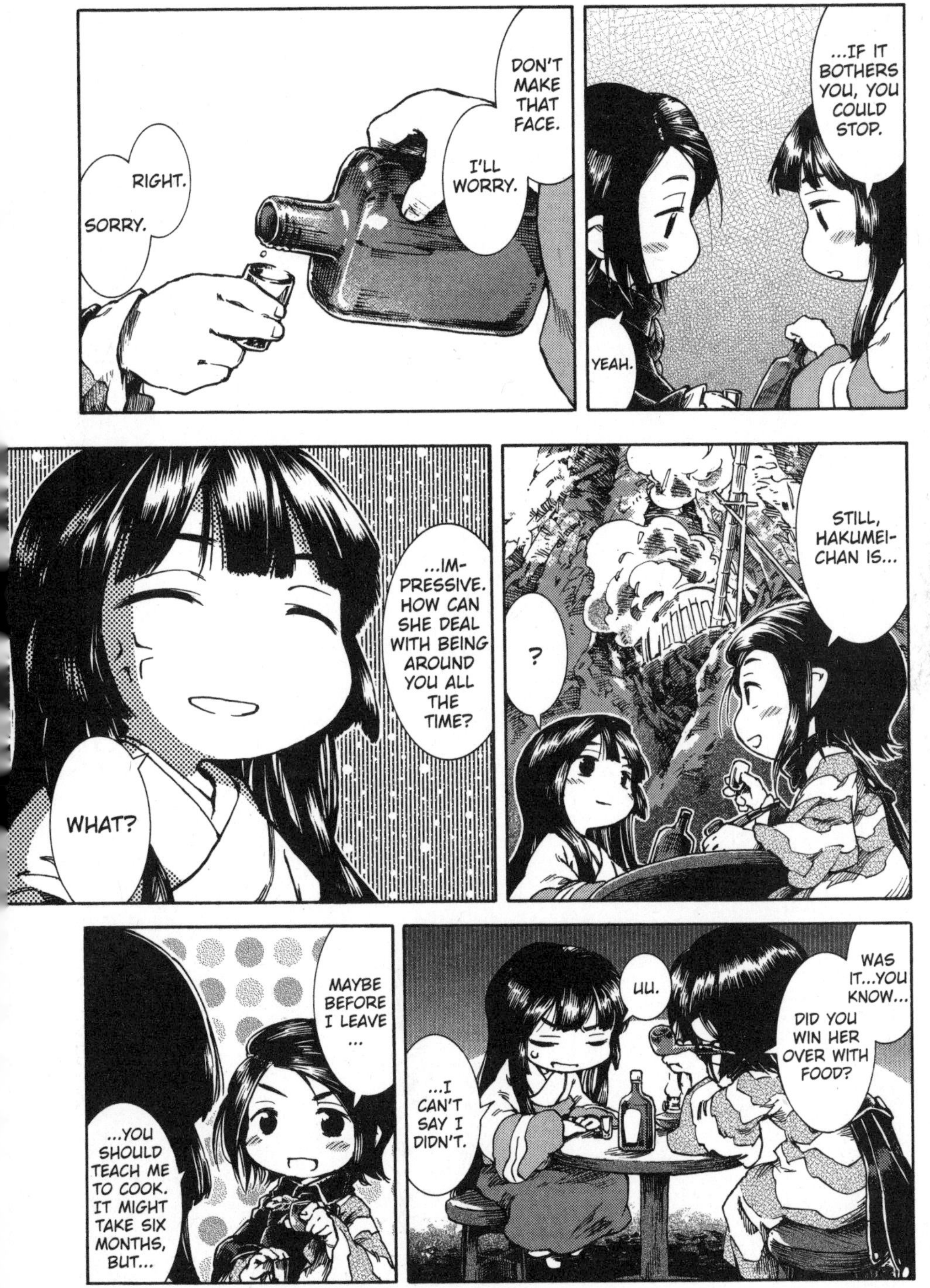
...IF IT BOTHERS YOU, YOU COULD STOP.
YEAH.
DON'T MAKE THAT FACE.
I'LL WORRY.
RIGHT.
SORRY.
STILL, HAKUMEI-CHAN IS...
?
...IM-PRESSIVE. HOW CAN SHE DEAL WITH BEING AROUND YOU ALL THE TIME?
WHAT?
WAS IT...YOU KNOW...
DID YOU WIN HER OVER WITH FOOD?
UU.
...I CAN'T SAY I DIDN'T.
MAYBE BEFORE I LEAVE ...
...YOU SHOULD TEACH ME TO COOK. IT MIGHT TAKE SIX MONTHS, BUT...

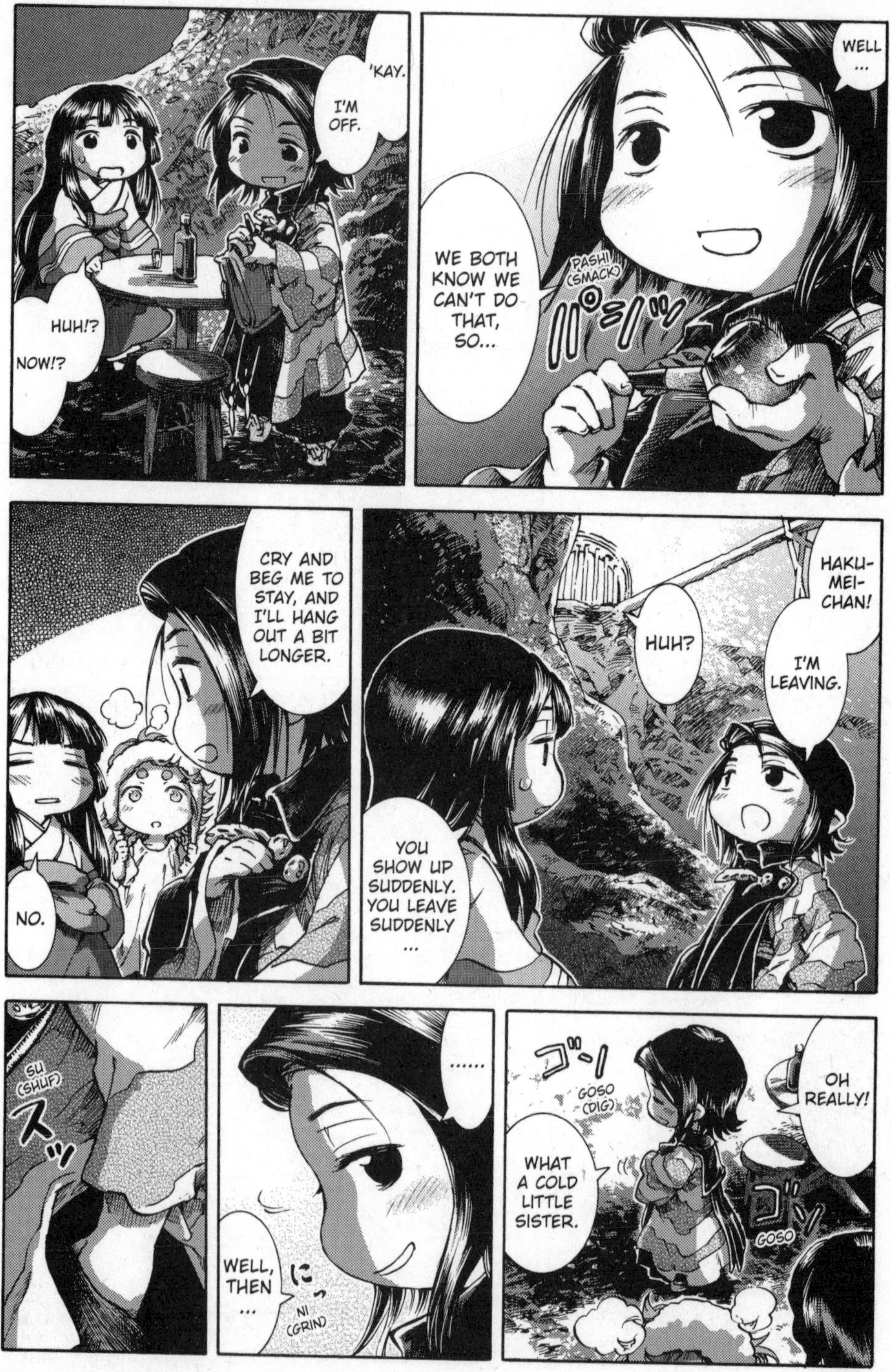
WELL ...
WE BOTH KNOW WE CAN'T DO THAT, SO...
PASHI (SMACK)
'KAY.
I'M OFF.
HUH!?
NOW!?
HAKU-MEI-CHAN!
I'M LEAVING.
HUH?
YOU SHOW UP SUDDENLY. YOU LEAVE SUDDENLY ...
CRY AND BEG ME TO STAY, AND I'LL HANG OUT A BIT LONGER.
NO.
OH REALLY!
GOSO (DIG)
WHAT A COLD LITTLE SISTER.
GOSO
......
WELL, THEN ...
NI (GRIN)
SU (SHUF)

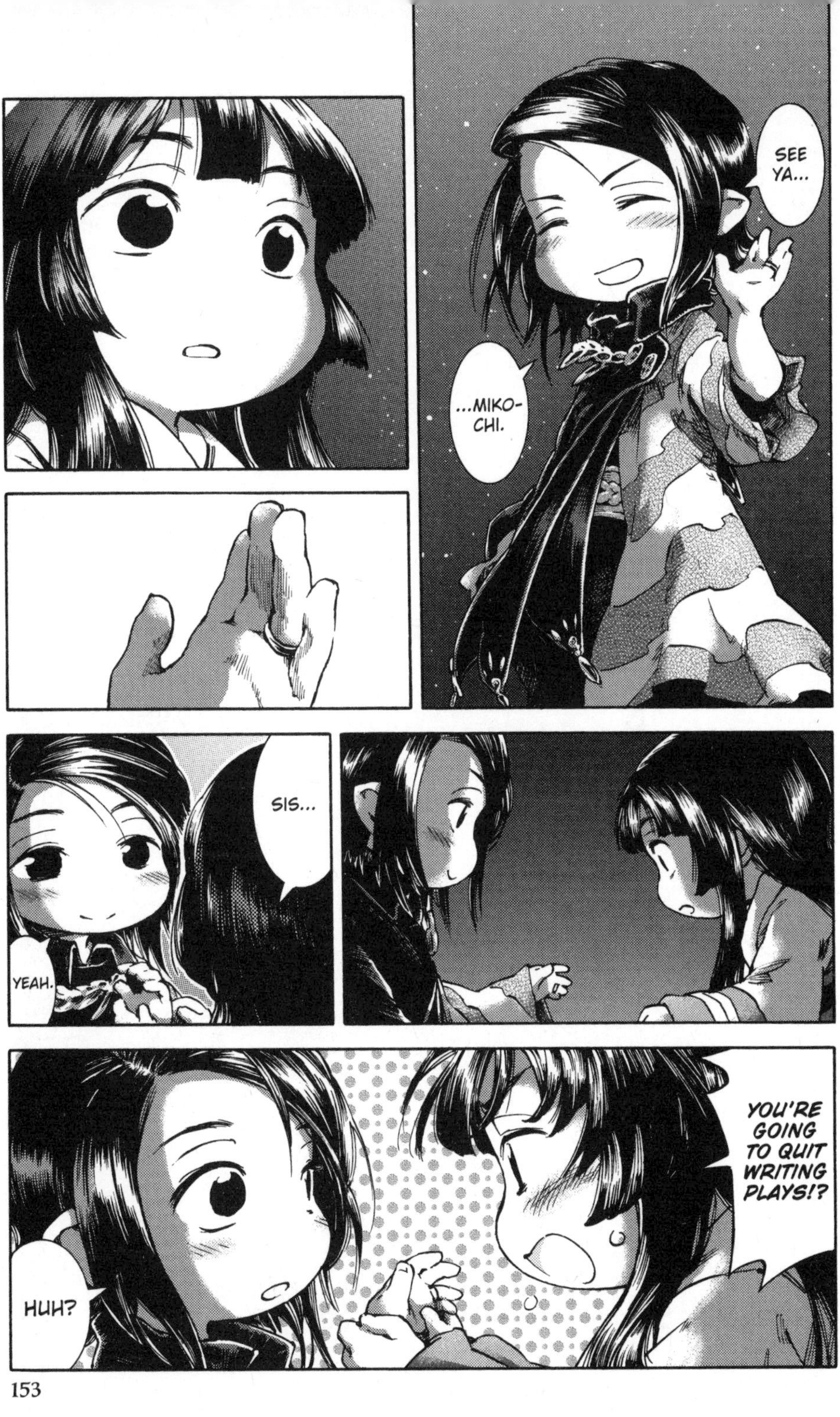
SEE YA...
...MIKO-CHI.
SIS...
YEAH.
YOU'RE GOING TO QUIT WRITING PLAYS!?
HUH?

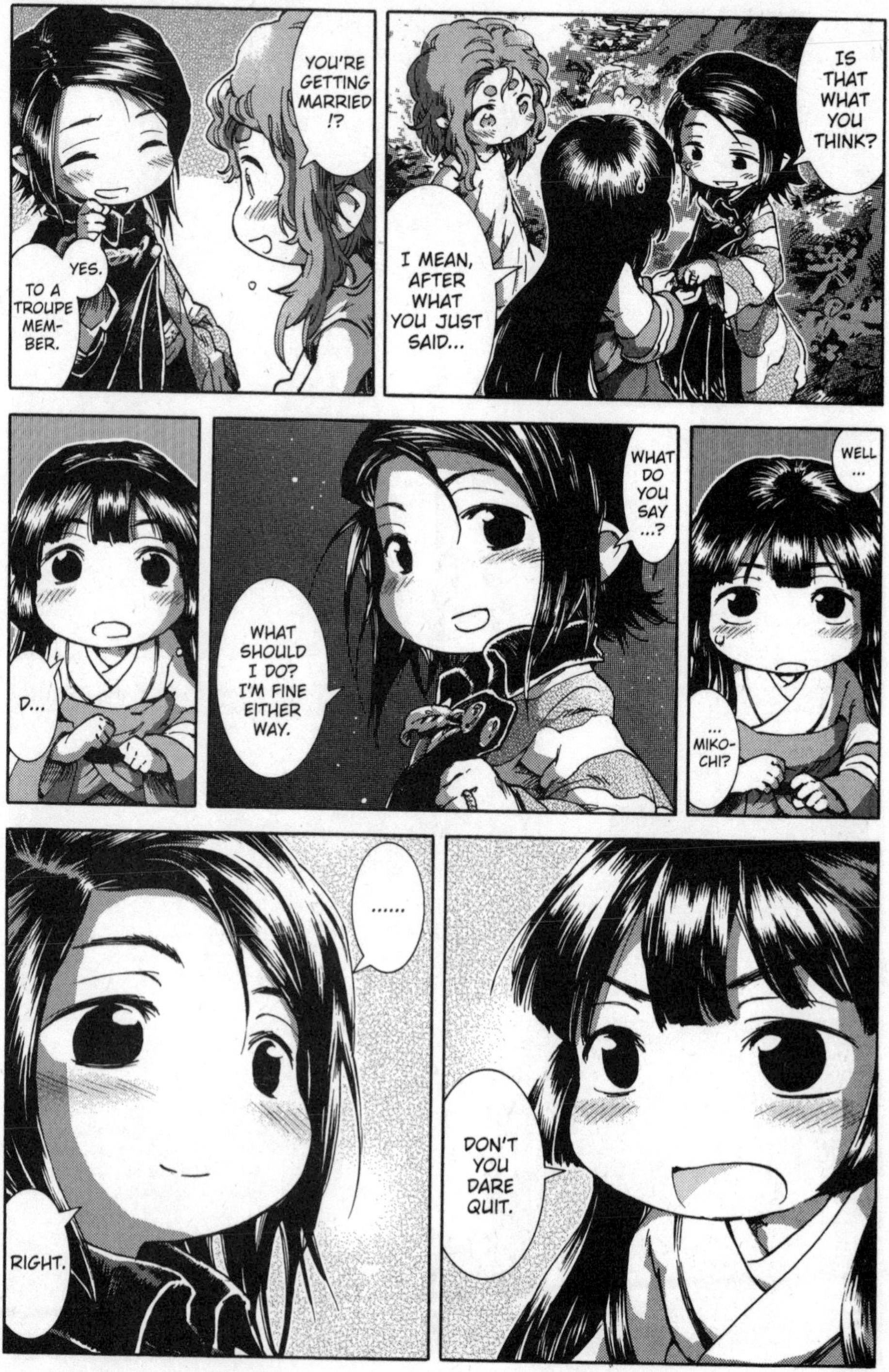
IS THAT WHAT YOU THINK?
I MEAN, AFTER WHAT YOU JUST SAID...
YOU'RE GETTING MARRIED!?
YES. TO A TROUPE MEMBER.
WELL...
...MIKO-CHI?
WHAT DO YOU SAY...?
WHAT SHOULD I DO? I'M FINE EITHER WAY.
D...
DON'T YOU DARE QUIT.
......
RIGHT.

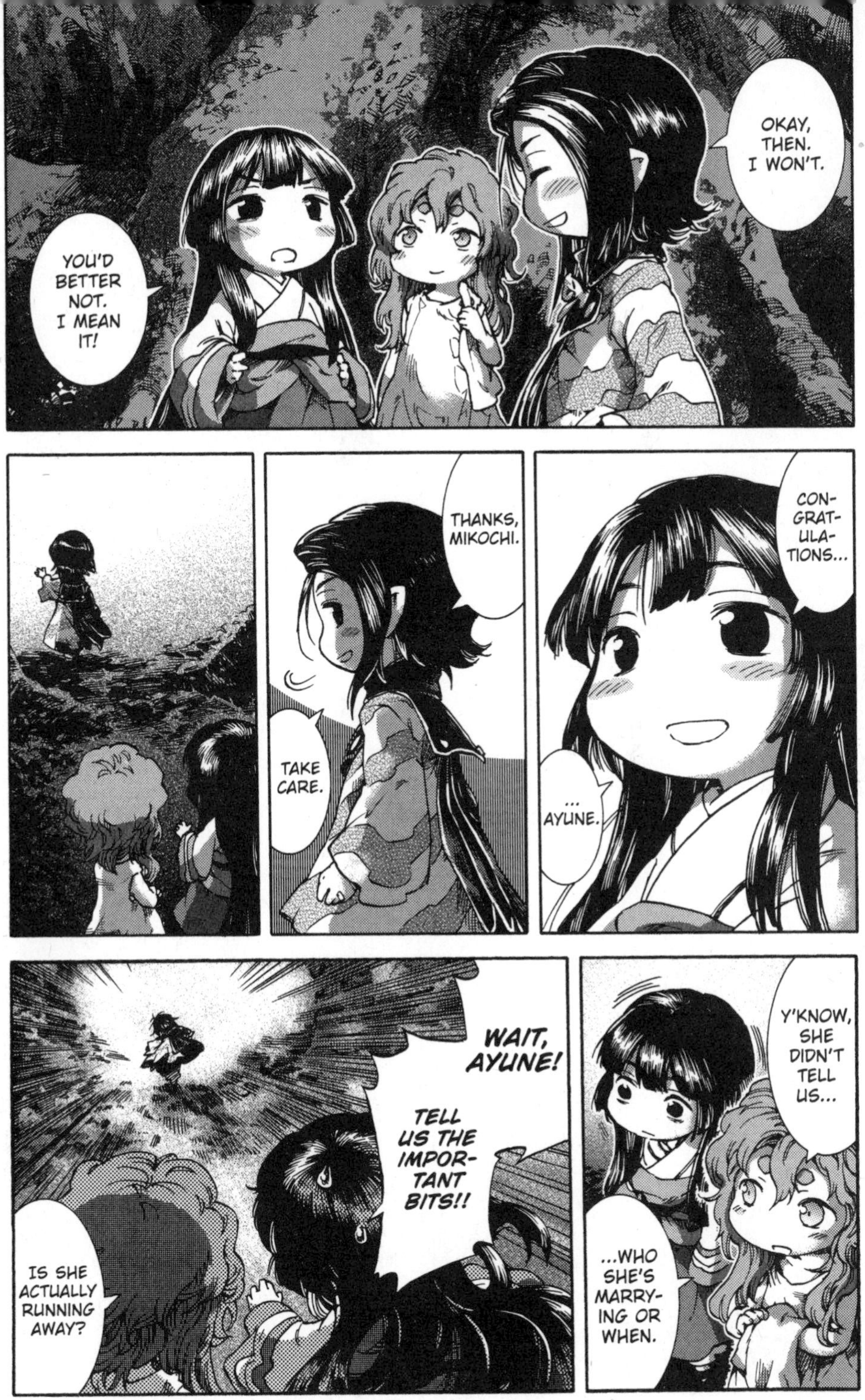
OKAY, THEN. I WON'T.
YOU'D BETTER NOT. I MEAN IT!
CON-GRAT-ULA-TIONS...
... AYUNE.
THANKS, MIKOCHI.
TAKE CARE.
Y'KNOW, SHE DIDN'T TELL US...
...WHO SHE'S MARRY-ING OR WHEN.
WAIT, AYUNE!
TELL US THE IMPOR-TANT BITS!!
IS SHE ACTUALLY RUNNING AWAY?

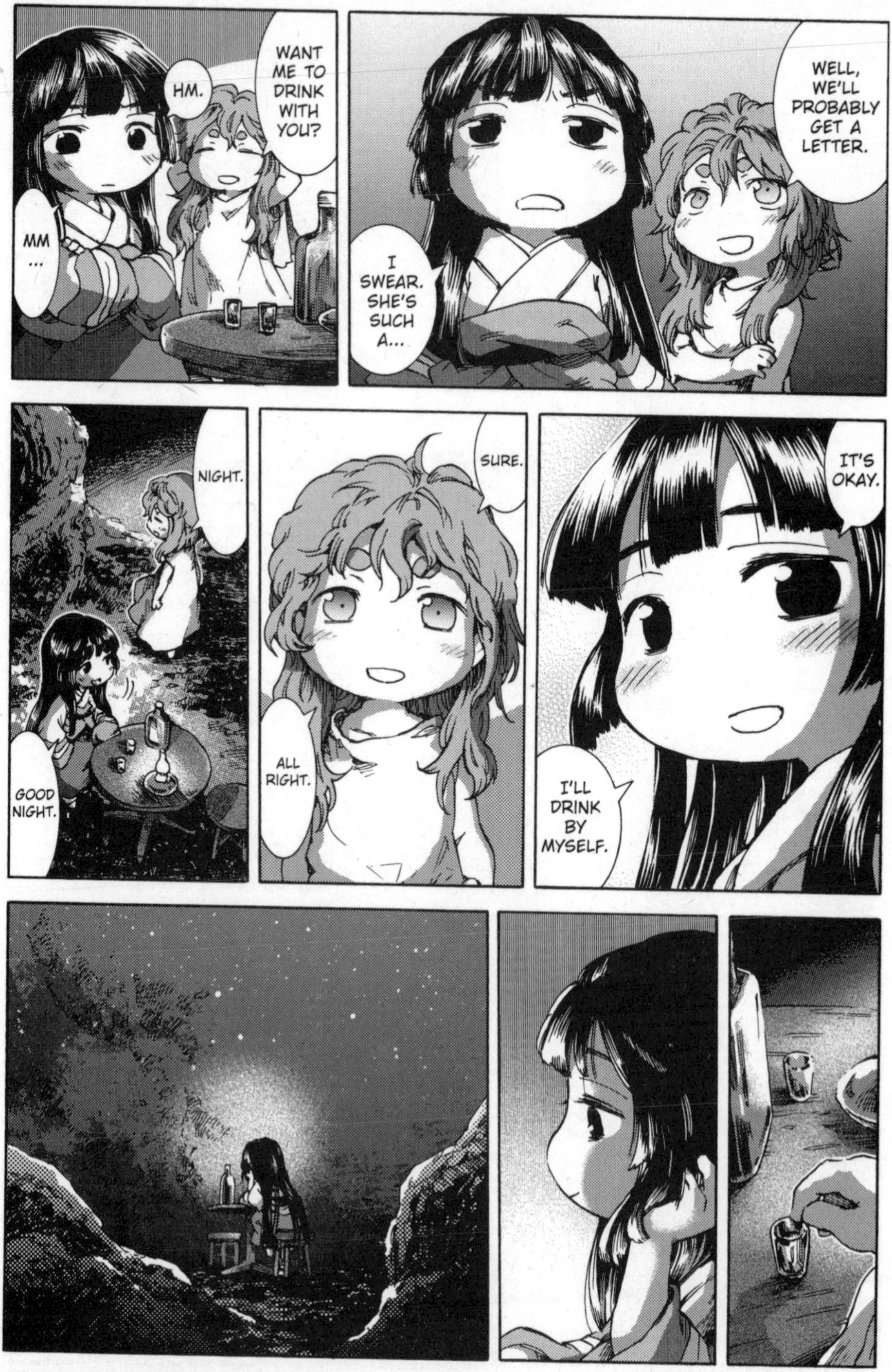
WELL, WE'LL PROBABLY GET A LETTER.
I SWEAR. SHE'S SUCH A...
WANT ME TO DRINK WITH YOU?
HM.
MM ...
IT'S OKAY.
I'LL DRINK BY MYSELF.
SURE.
ALL RIGHT.
NIGHT.
GOOD NIGHT.

•*Column*• Underfoot Steps 25 / Theater Tonpu Presents: *Recumbent Tobacco Smoke*

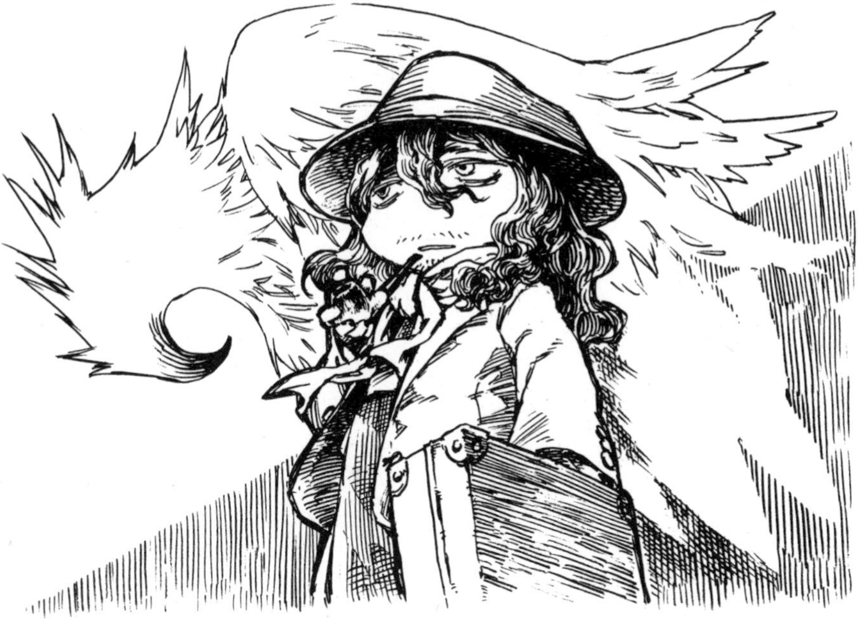

The town of Makinata—surrounded by majestic mountains and peppered with ruins, time flows peacefully in this place.

Aobane, a wandering painter, has taken up long-term lodgings here.

He's suffering from a chronic ailment and from mental exhaustion due to his slump, and this town, which is full of hard workers, is definitely not a comfortable place for him.

He spends his days running an empty brush over pictures he has already painted.

He's lost both his goal and his means of achieving it.

Around the time his days and nights begin to blur together, he hears an intriguing story from the innkeeper.

Kafu, a bird that can grant wishes, has been sighted.

Forcing his out-of-shape body into motion, he heads into the grim mountains, taking nothing but his amber-colored pipe and a day's worth of bread...

Theater Tonpu Presents: *Recumbent Tobacco Smoke*
March 2 to March 16 at the Hao Great Tree Performance Hall
Writer/Producer: Ayune

Chapter 26

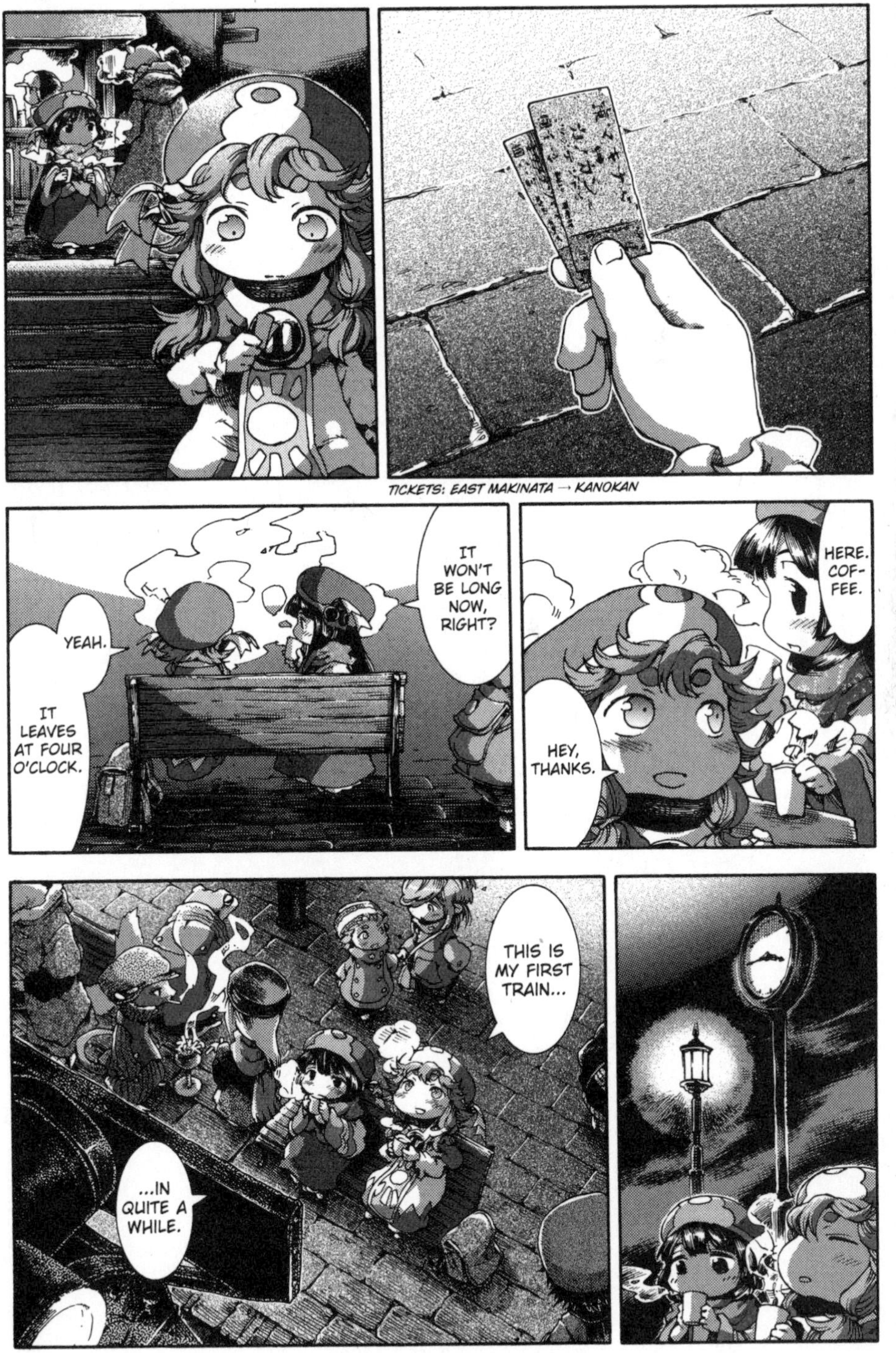
TICKETS: EAST MAKINATA → KANOKAN
HERE. COF-FEE.
HEY, THANKS.
IT WON'T BE LONG NOW, RIGHT?
YEAH.
IT LEAVES AT FOUR O'CLOCK.
THIS IS MY FIRST TRAIN...
...IN QUITE A WHILE.

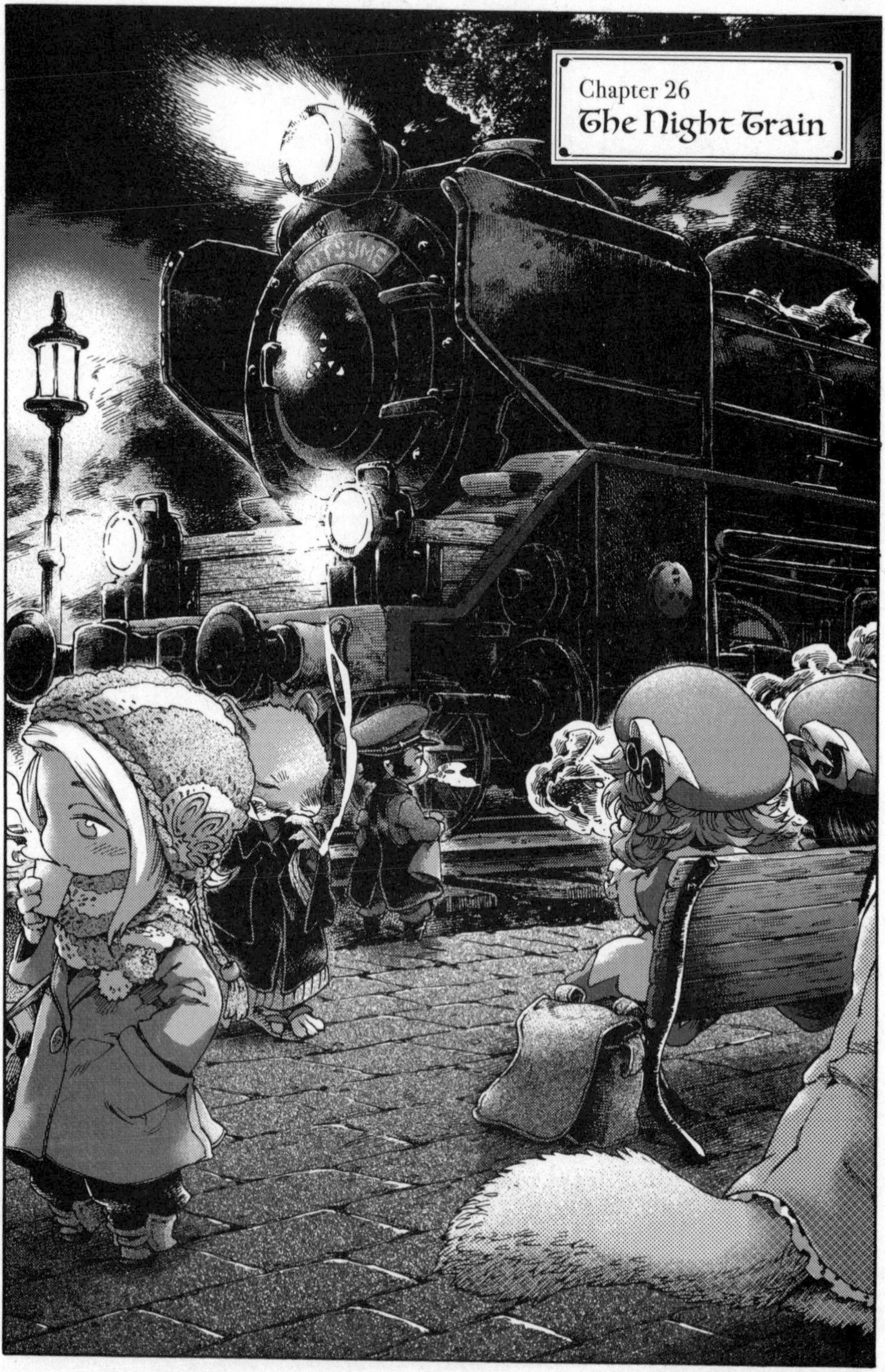
Chapter 26
The Night Train

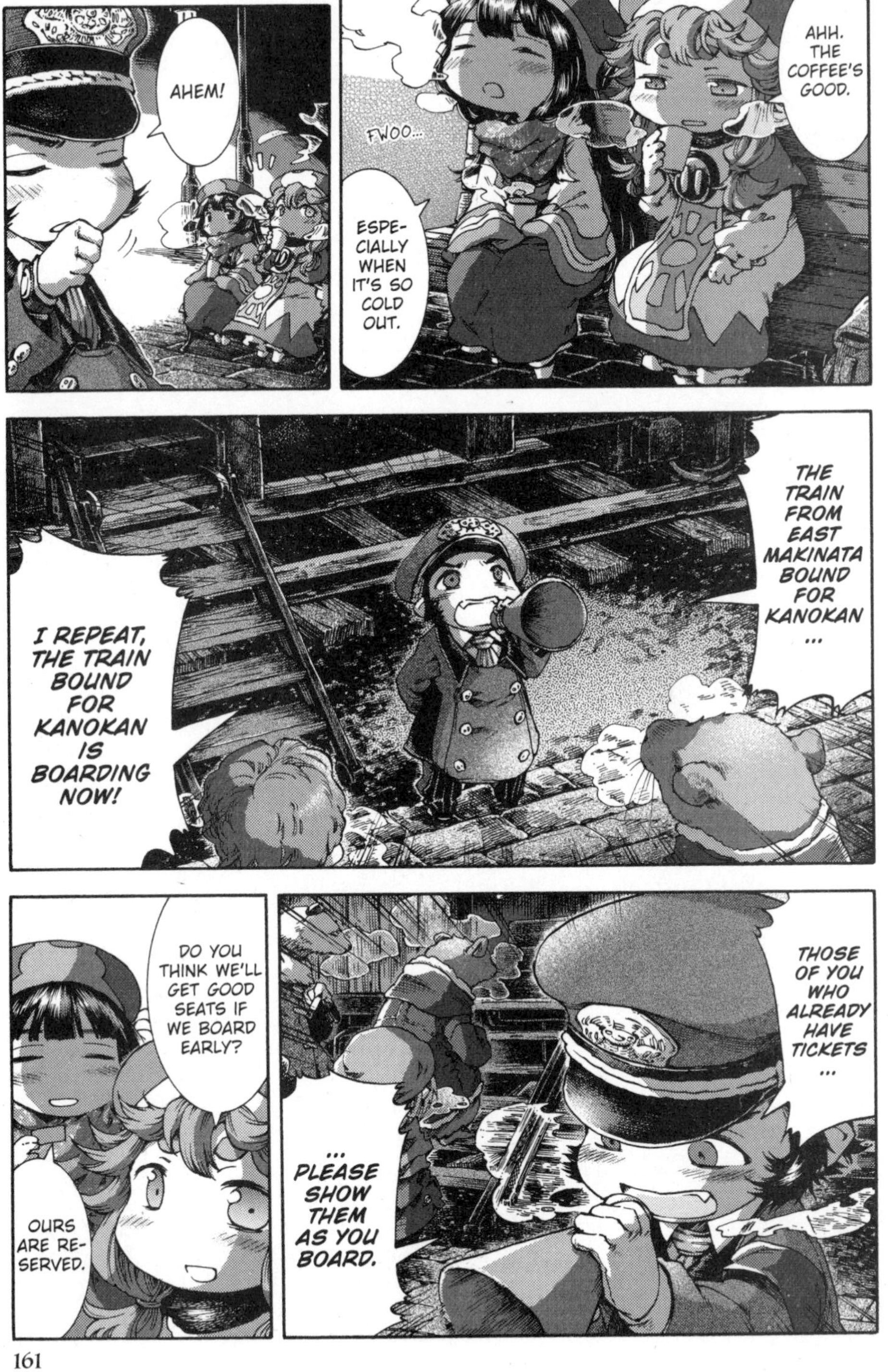
AHH. THE COFFEE'S GOOD.
FWOO...
ESPE-CIALLY WHEN IT'S SO COLD OUT.
AHEM!
THE TRAIN FROM EAST MAKINATA BOUND FOR KANOKAN...
I REPEAT, THE TRAIN BOUND FOR KANOKAN IS BOARDING NOW!
THOSE OF YOU WHO ALREADY HAVE TICKETS...
...PLEASE SHOW THEM AS YOU BOARD.
DO YOU THINK WE'LL GET GOOD SEATS IF WE BOARD EARLY?
OURS ARE RE-SERVED.

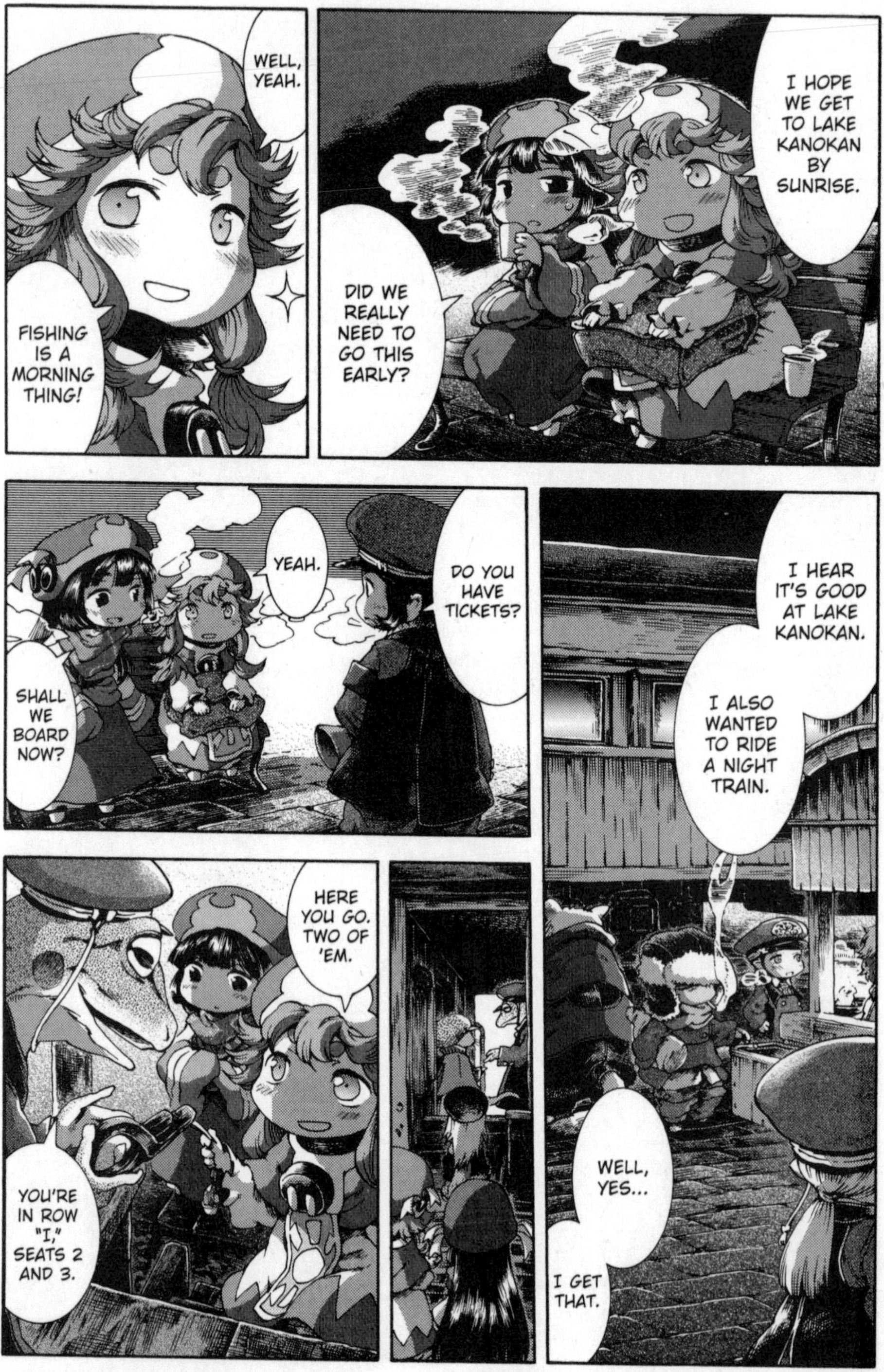
I HOPE WE GET TO LAKE KANOKAN BY SUNRISE.
DID WE REALLY NEED TO GO THIS EARLY?
WELL, YEAH.
FISHING IS A MORNING THING!
I HEAR IT'S GOOD AT LAKE KANOKAN.
I ALSO WANTED TO RIDE A NIGHT TRAIN.
WELL, YES...
I GET THAT.
DO YOU HAVE TICKETS?
YEAH.
SHALL WE BOARD NOW?
HERE YOU GO. TWO OF 'EM.
YOU'RE IN ROW "I," SEATS 2 AND 3.

WANT TO PUT OUR LUGGAGE UP?
I THINK ROW "S" IS IN THE NEXT CAR.
MOOOOM! I WANT SOME TEA, PLEASE!
NO, WE'RE LEAVING NOW.
HM.
THIS IS IT.
ROW "I"...
...2 AND...
...3.
......

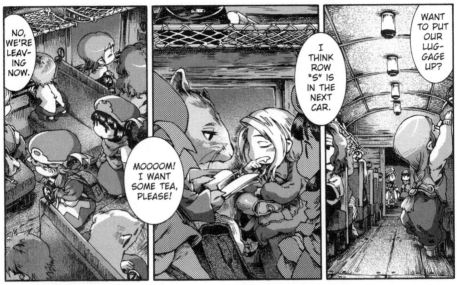

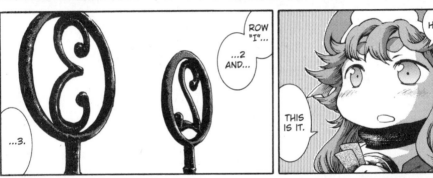

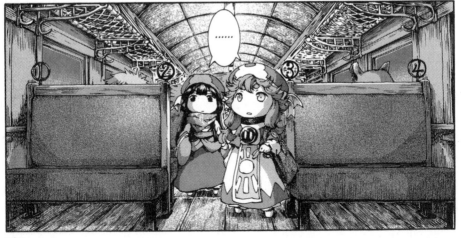

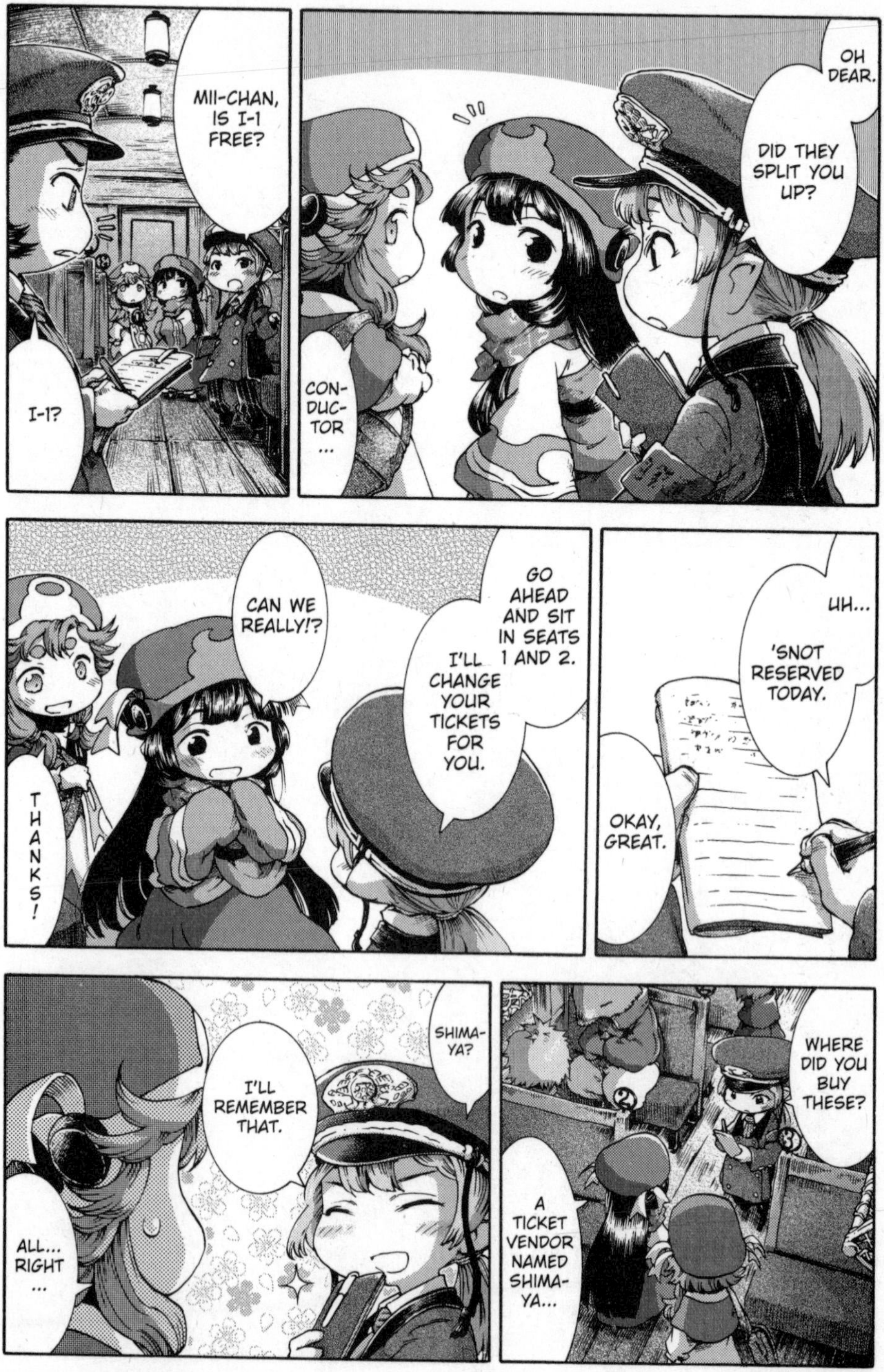
OH DEAR.
DID THEY SPLIT YOU UP?
CON-DUCTOR...
MII-CHAN, IS I-1 FREE?
I-1?
UH...
'SNOT RESERVED TODAY.
OKAY, GREAT.
GO AHEAD AND SIT IN SEATS 1 AND 2.
I'LL CHANGE YOUR TICKETS FOR YOU.
CAN WE REALLY!?
THANKS!
WHERE DID YOU BUY THESE?
A TICKET VENDOR NAMED SHIMA-YA...
SHIMA-YA?
I'LL REMEMBER THAT.
ALL... RIGHT...

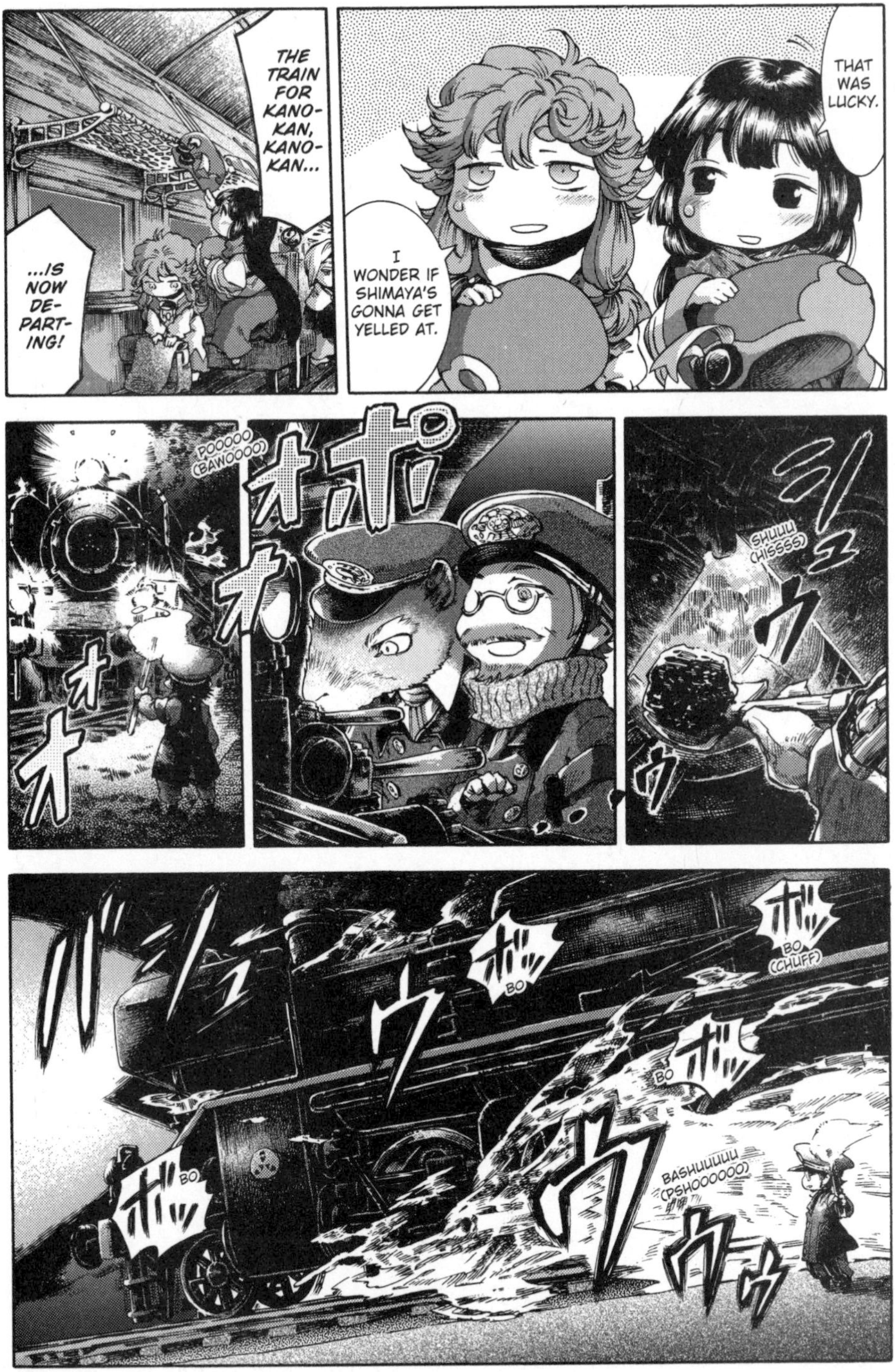
THAT WAS LUCKY.
I WONDER IF SHIMAYA'S GONNA GET YELLED AT.
THE TRAIN FOR KANO-KAN, KANO-KAN...
...IS NOW DE-PARTING!
SHUUU (HISSSS)
POOOOO (BAWOOOO)
BO (CHUFF)
BO
BO
BASHUUUUU (PSHOOOOOO)
BO

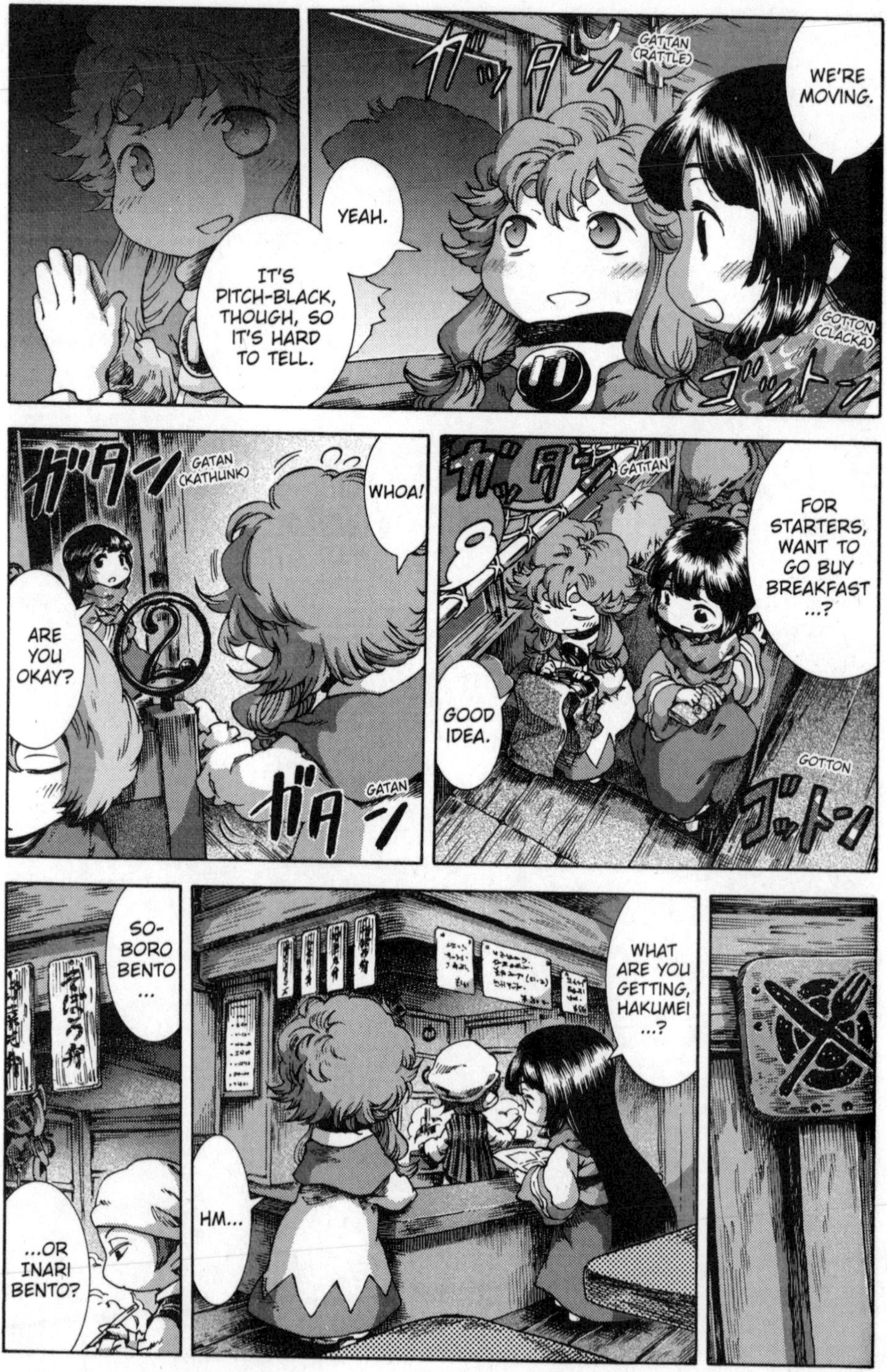
WE'RE MOVING.
GATTAN (RATTLE)
YEAH.
IT'S PITCH-BLACK, THOUGH, SO IT'S HARD TO TELL.
GOTTON (CLACKA)
GATTAN
FOR STARTERS, WANT TO GO BUY BREAKFAST ...?
GOOD IDEA.
GOTTON
GATAN (KATHUNK)
WHOA!
ARE YOU OKAY?
GATAN
WHAT ARE YOU GETTING, HAKUMEI ...?
HM...
SO-BORO BENTO ...
...OR INARI BENTO?

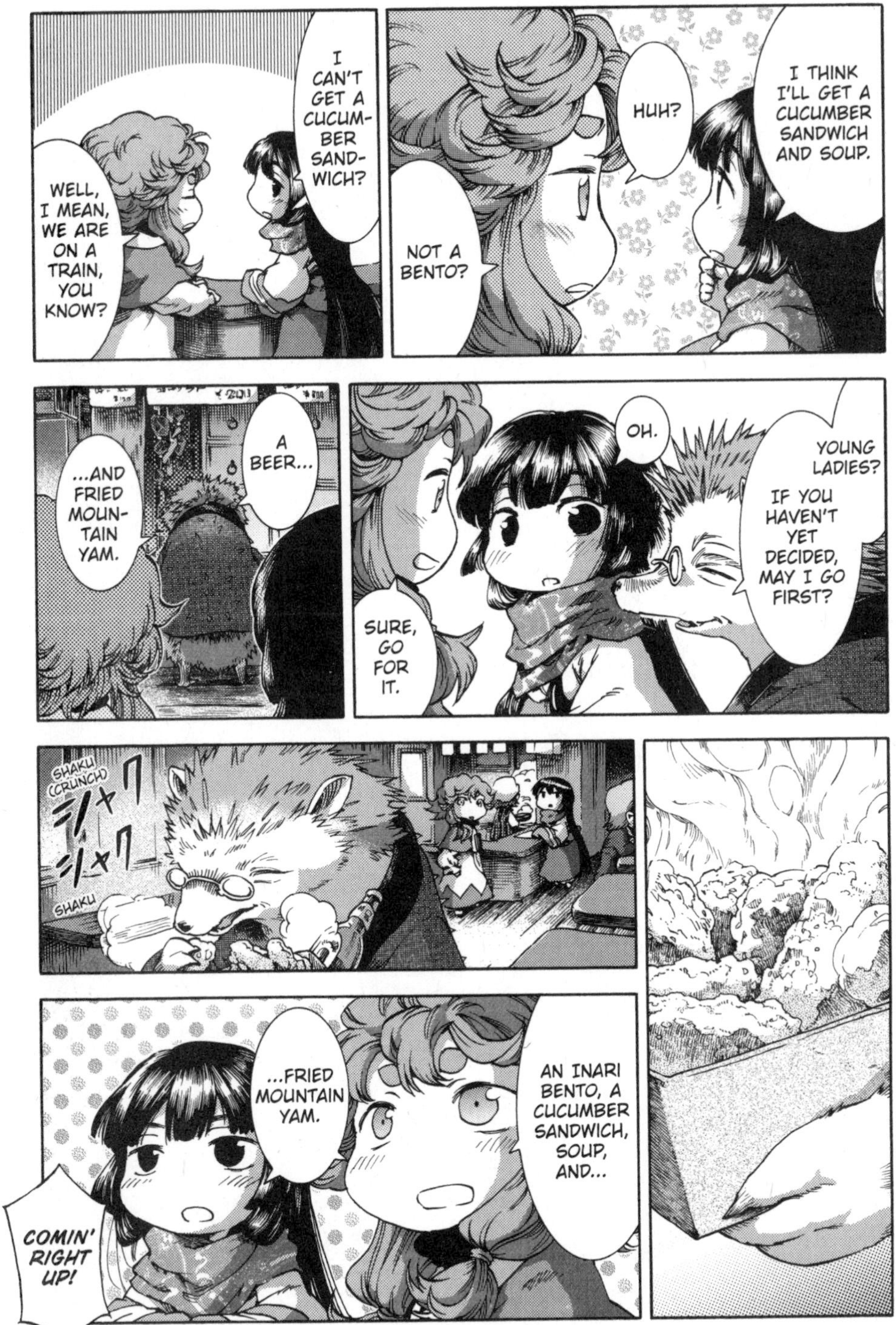
I THINK I'LL GET A CUCUMBER SANDWICH AND SOUP.
HUH?
NOT A BENTO?
I CAN'T GET A CUCUMBER SANDWICH?
WELL, I MEAN, WE ARE ON A TRAIN, YOU KNOW?
YOUNG LADIES?
IF YOU HAVEN'T YET DECIDED, MAY I GO FIRST?
OH.
SURE, GO FOR IT.
A BEER...
...AND FRIED MOUNTAIN YAM.
SHAKU (CRUNCH)
SHAKU
AN INARI BENTO, A CUCUMBER SANDWICH, SOUP, AND...
...FRIED MOUNTAIN YAM.
COMIN' RIGHT UP!

LET'S TRADE... ONE PIECE EACH.

SURE.

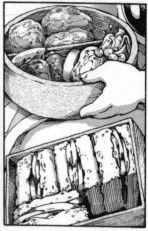

DID YOU SEE SOMETHING?

I YEAH. CAUGHT A GLIMPSE OF A RIVER.

HM?

SHU

SHU

SHU (PUFF)

SHU

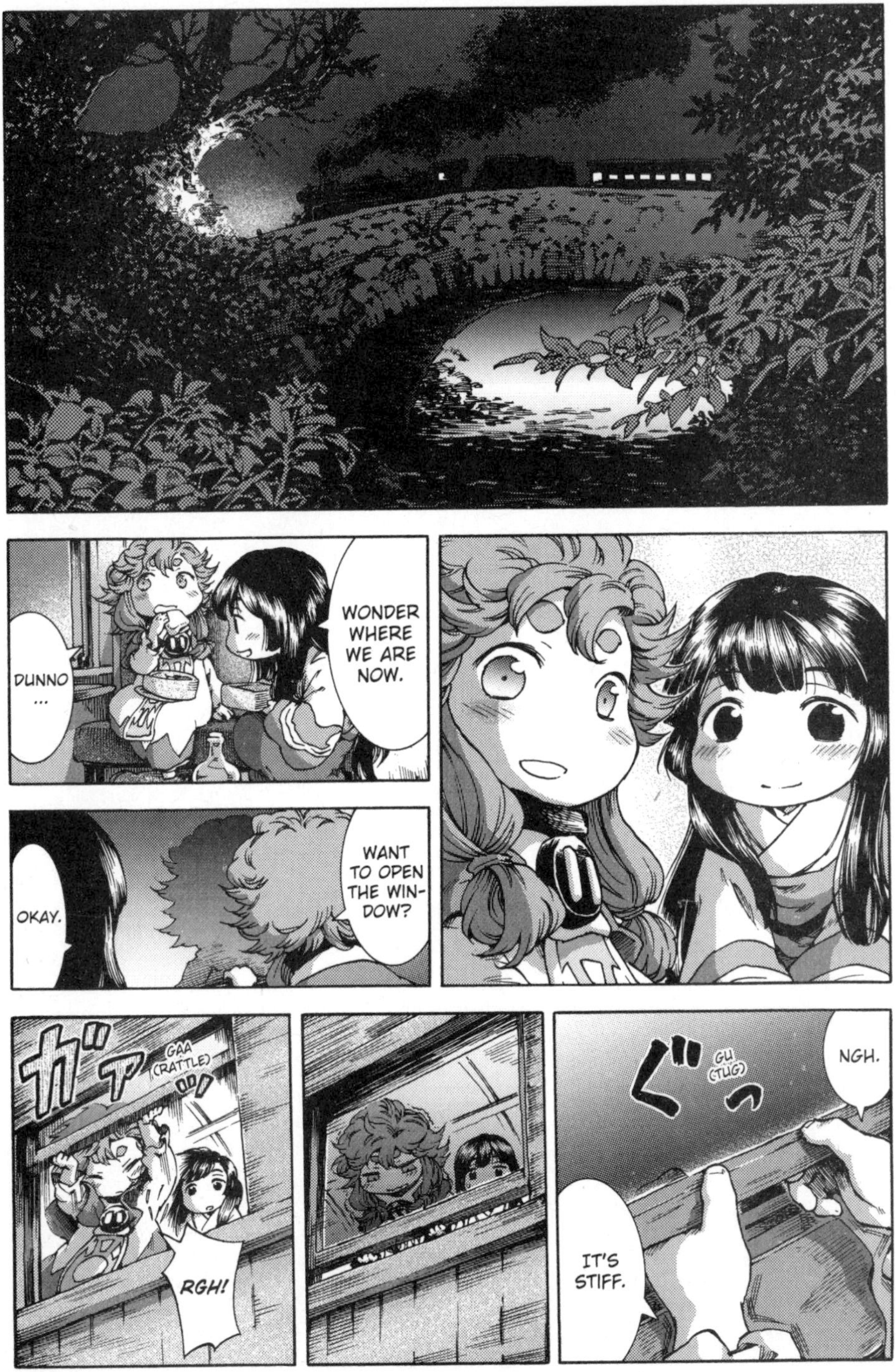
WONDER WHERE WE ARE NOW.
DUNNO...
WANT TO OPEN THE WIN-DOW?
OKAY.
NGH.
ぐっ
GU (TUG)
IT'S STIFF.
ガァ
GAA (RATTLE)
RGH!

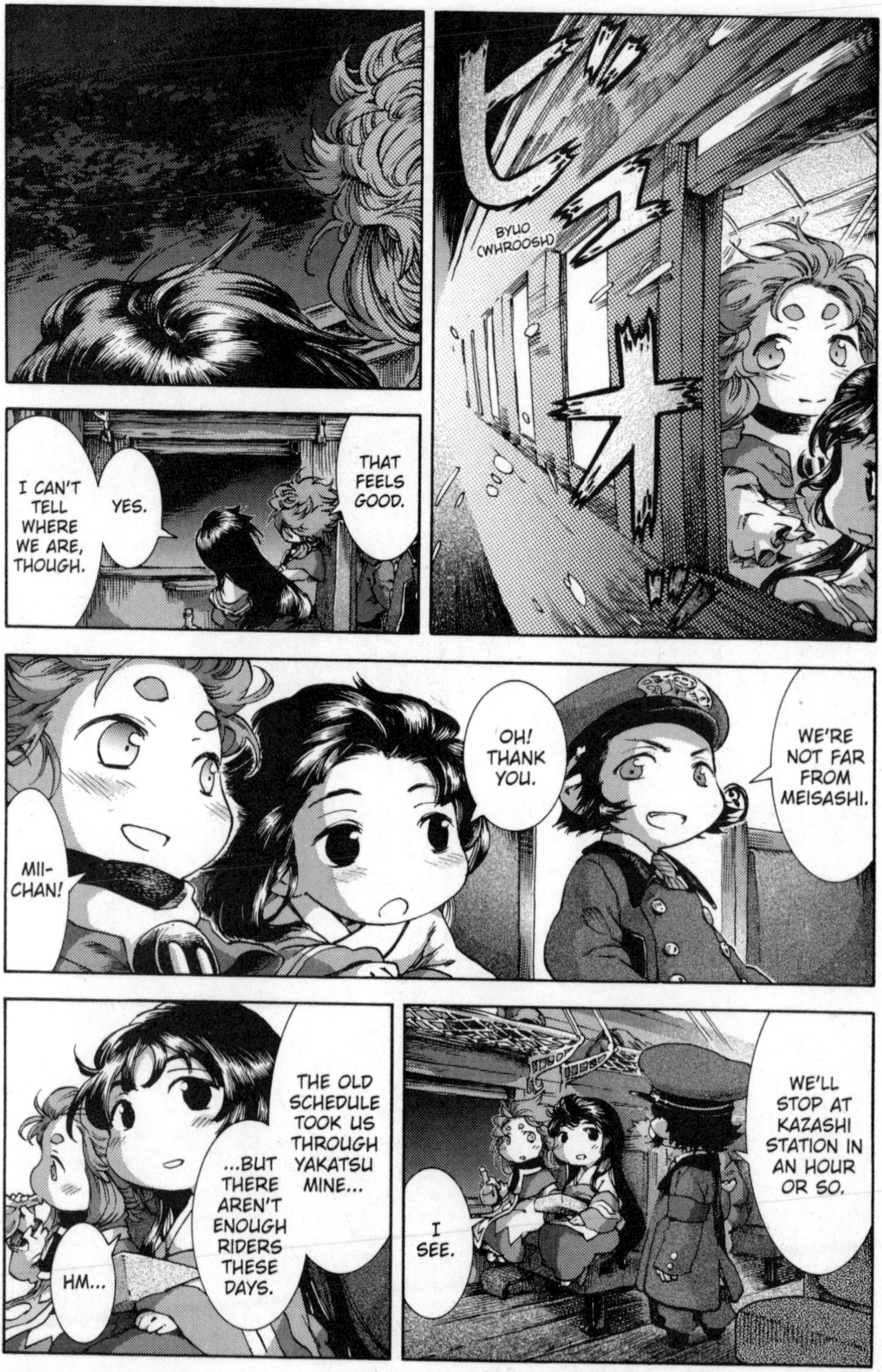
BYUO (WHROOSH)
THAT FEELS GOOD.
YES.
I CAN'T TELL WHERE WE ARE, THOUGH.
WE'RE NOT FAR FROM MEISASHI.
OH! THANK YOU.
MII-CHAN!
WE'LL STOP AT KAZASHI STATION IN AN HOUR OR SO.
I SEE.
THE OLD SCHEDULE TOOK US THROUGH YAKATSU MINE...
...BUT THERE AREN'T ENOUGH RIDERS THESE DAYS.
HM...

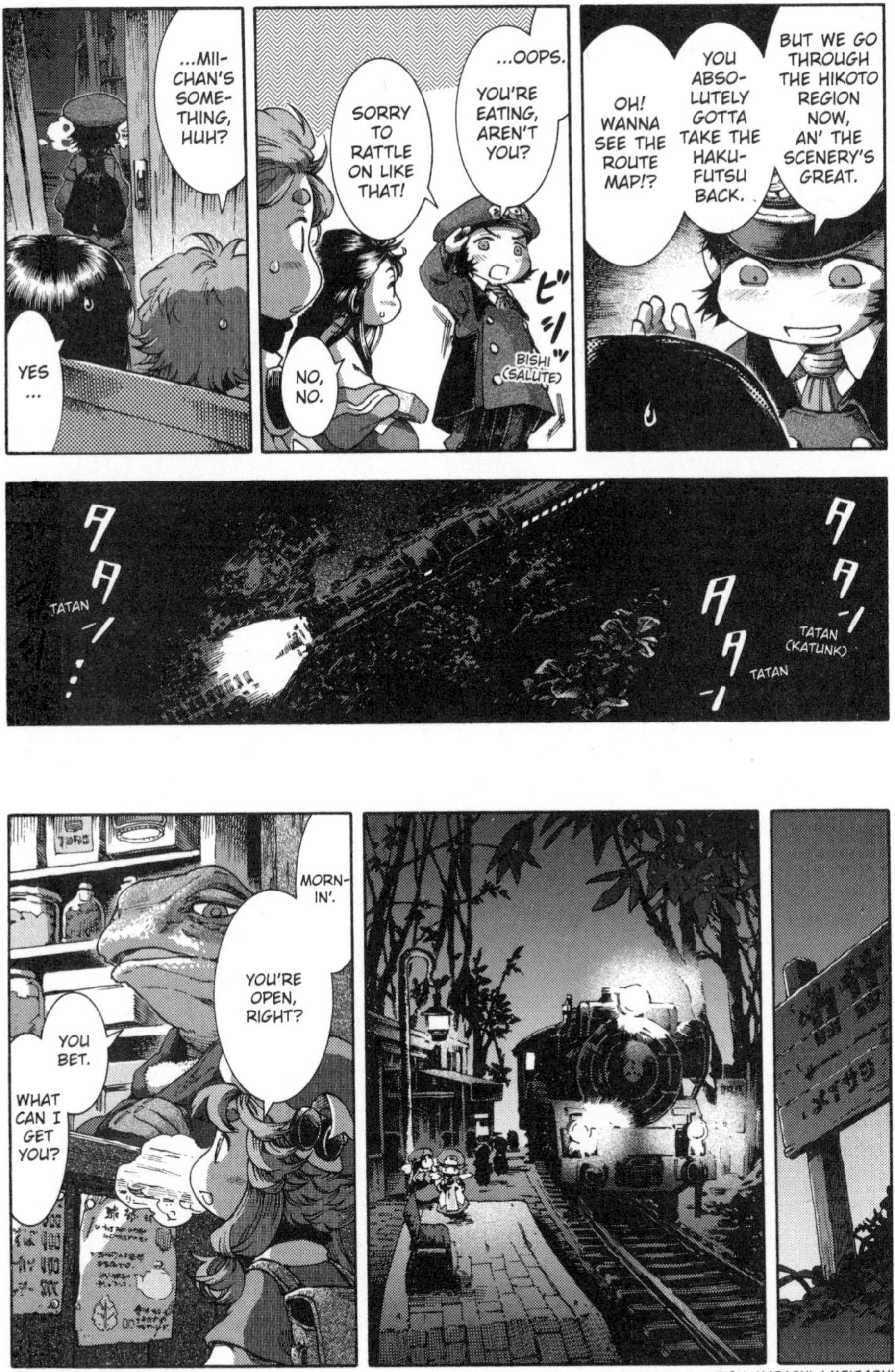
BUT WE GO THROUGH THE HIKOTO REGION NOW, AN' THE SCENERY'S GREAT.
YOU ABSOLUTELY GOTTA TAKE THE HAKUFUTSU BACK.
OH! WANNA SEE THE ROUTE MAP!?
...OOPS.
YOU'RE EATING, AREN'T YOU?
SORRY TO RATTLE ON LIKE THAT!
BISHI (SALUTE)
NO, NO.
...MII-CHAN'S SOMETHING, HUH?
YES...
TATAN (KATUNK)
TATAN
TATAN
MORNIN'.
YOU'RE OPEN, RIGHT?
YOU BET.
WHAT CAN I GET YOU?

SIGN: KAZASHI / MEISASHI

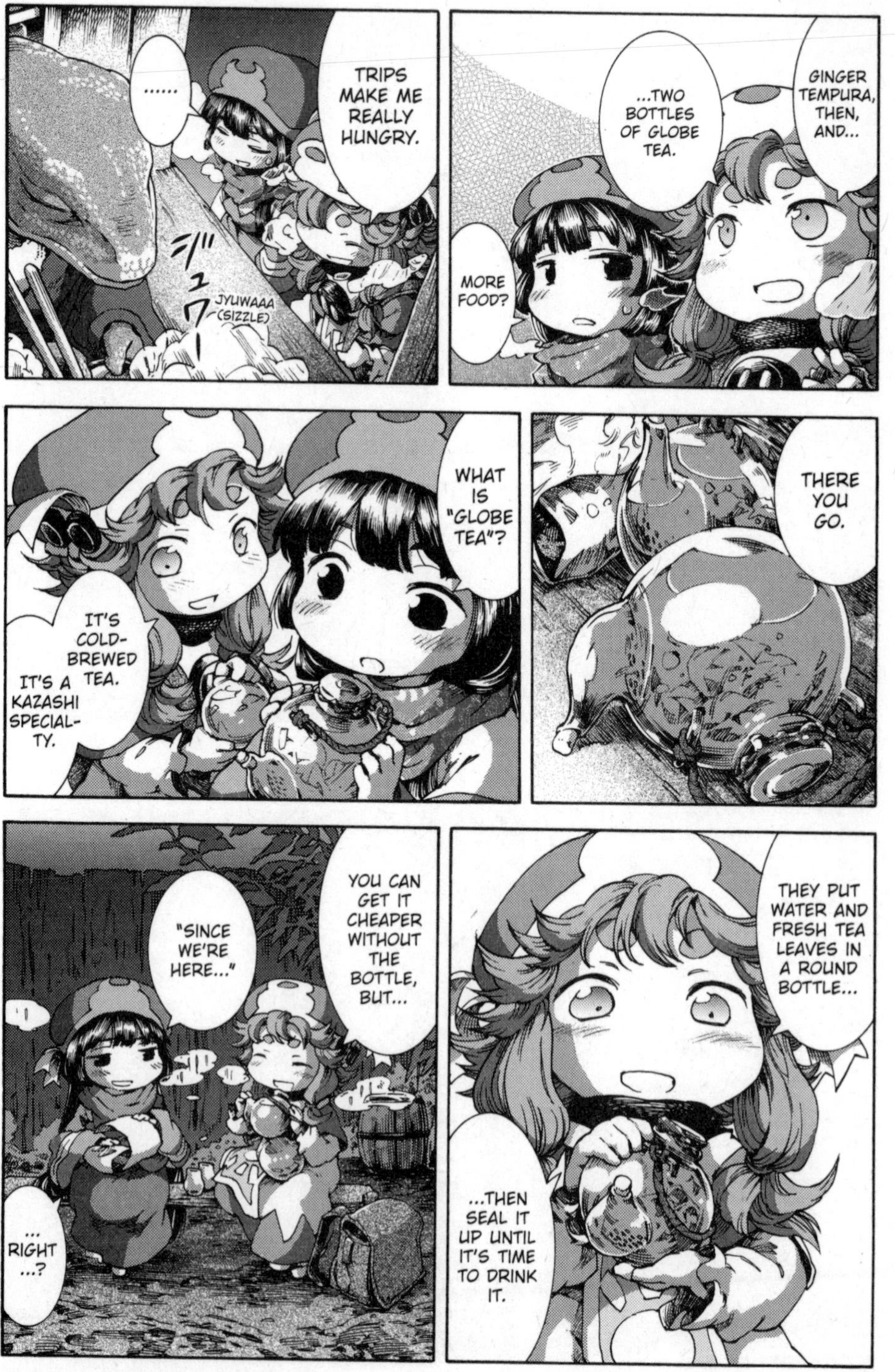
GINGER TEMPURA, THEN, AND...
...TWO BOTTLES OF GLOBE TEA.
MORE FOOD?
TRIPS MAKE ME REALLY HUNGRY.
......
JYUWAAA (SIZZLE)
THERE YOU GO.
WHAT IS "GLOBE TEA"?
IT'S COLD-BREWED TEA.
IT'S A KAZASHI SPECIALTY.
THEY PUT WATER AND FRESH TEA LEAVES IN A ROUND BOTTLE...
...THEN SEAL IT UP UNTIL IT'S TIME TO DRINK IT.
YOU CAN GET IT CHEAPER WITHOUT THE BOTTLE, BUT...
"SINCE WE'RE HERE..."
...RIGHT...?

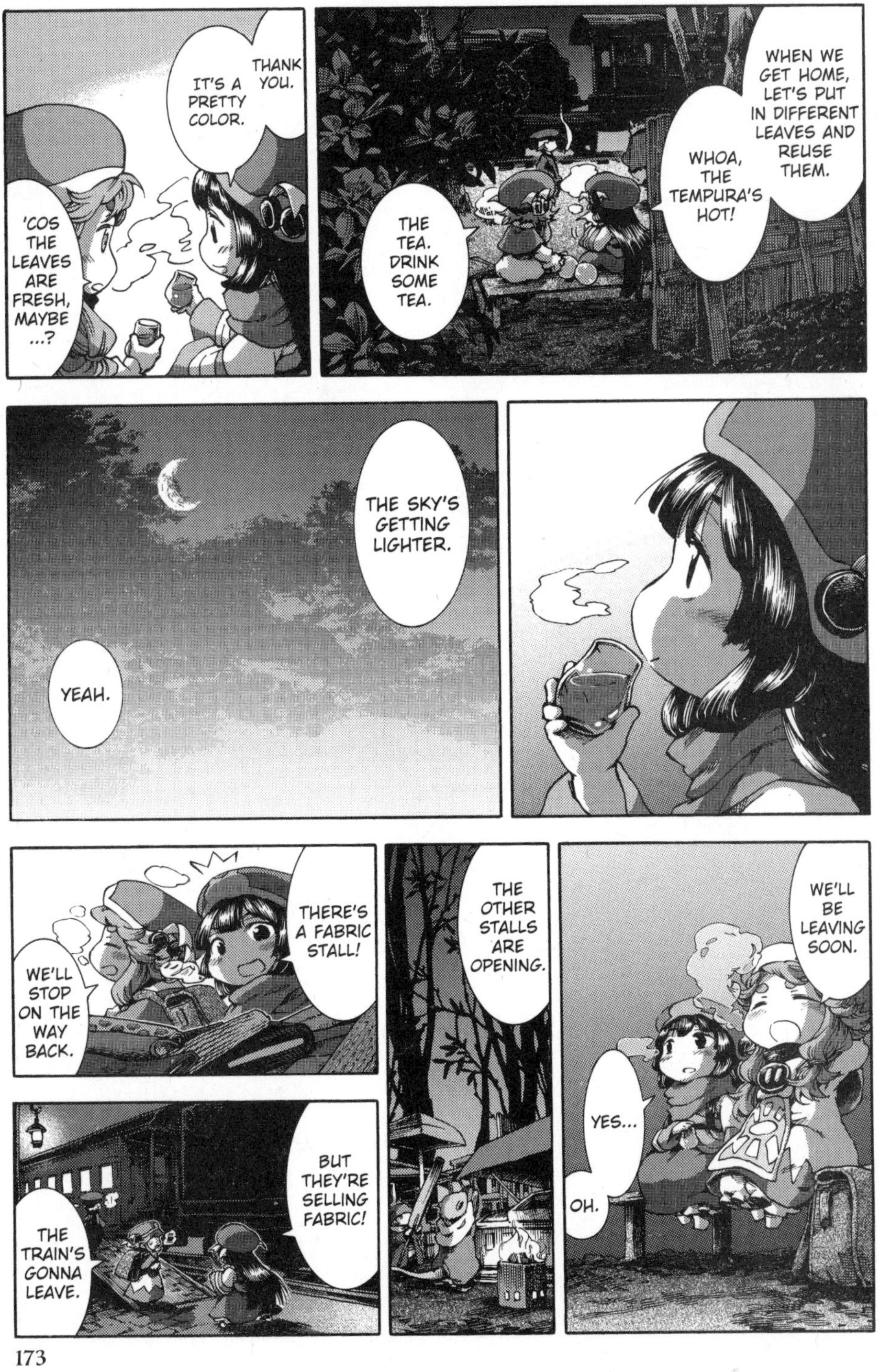
WHEN WE GET HOME, LET'S PUT IN DIFFERENT LEAVES AND REUSE THEM.
WHOA, THE TEMPURA'S HOT!
THE TEA. DRINK SOME TEA.
THANK YOU.
IT'S A PRETTY COLOR.
'COS THE LEAVES ARE FRESH, MAYBE ...?
THE SKY'S GETTING LIGHTER.
YEAH.
WE'LL BE LEAVING SOON.
YES...
OH.
THE OTHER STALLS ARE OPENING.
THERE'S A FABRIC STALL!
WE'LL STOP ON THE WAY BACK.
BUT THEY'RE SELLING FABRIC!
THE TRAIN'S GONNA LEAVE.

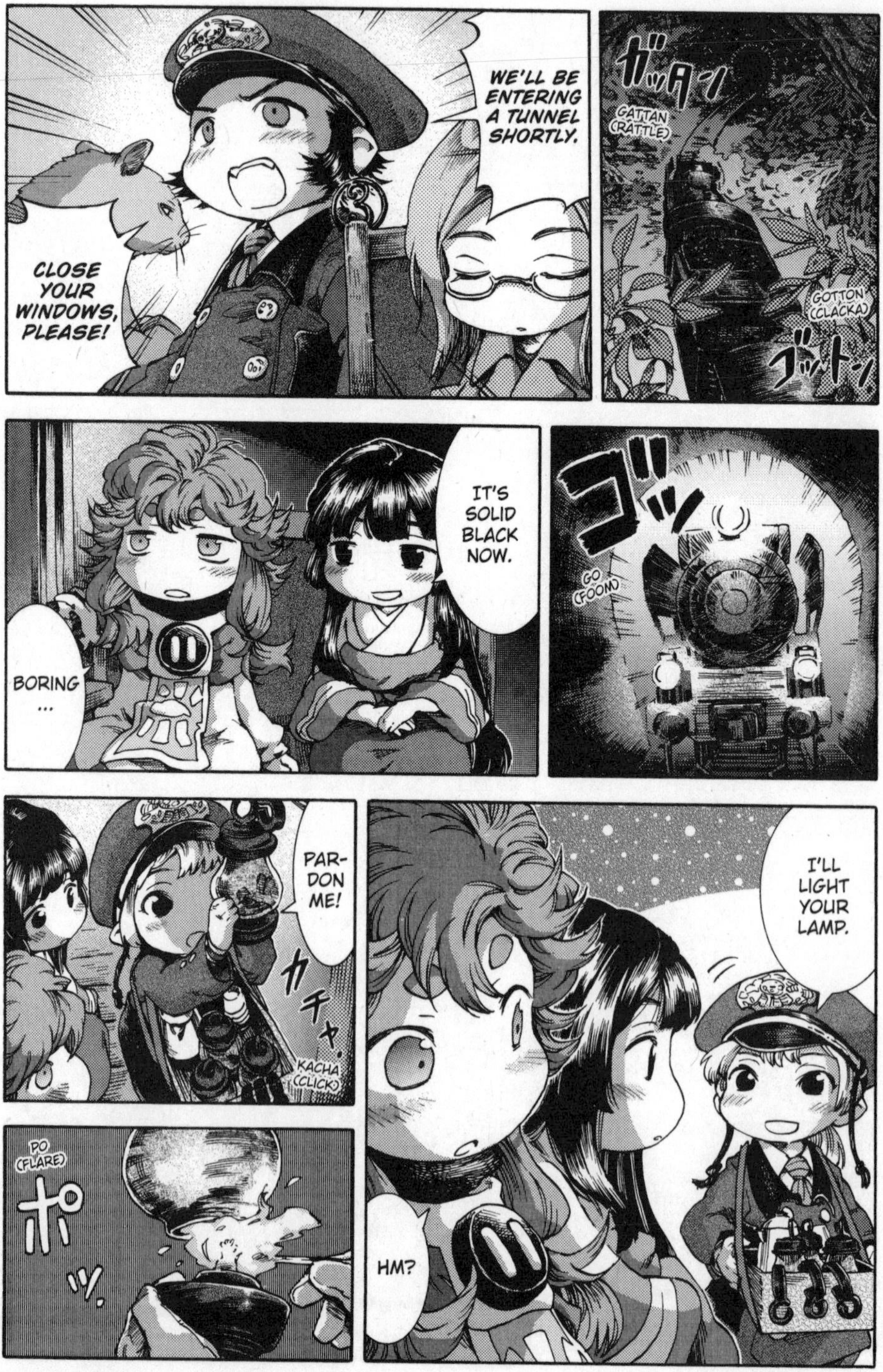
ガッタン
GATTAN (RATTLE)
GOTTON (CLACKA)
ゴットン
WE'LL BE ENTERING A TUNNEL SHORTLY.
CLOSE YOUR WINDOWS, PLEASE!
ゴッ
GO (FOOM)
IT'S SOLID BLACK NOW.
BORING...
I'LL LIGHT YOUR LAMP.
HM?
PAR-DON ME!
カチャ
KACHA (CLICK)
PO (FLARE)
ポッ

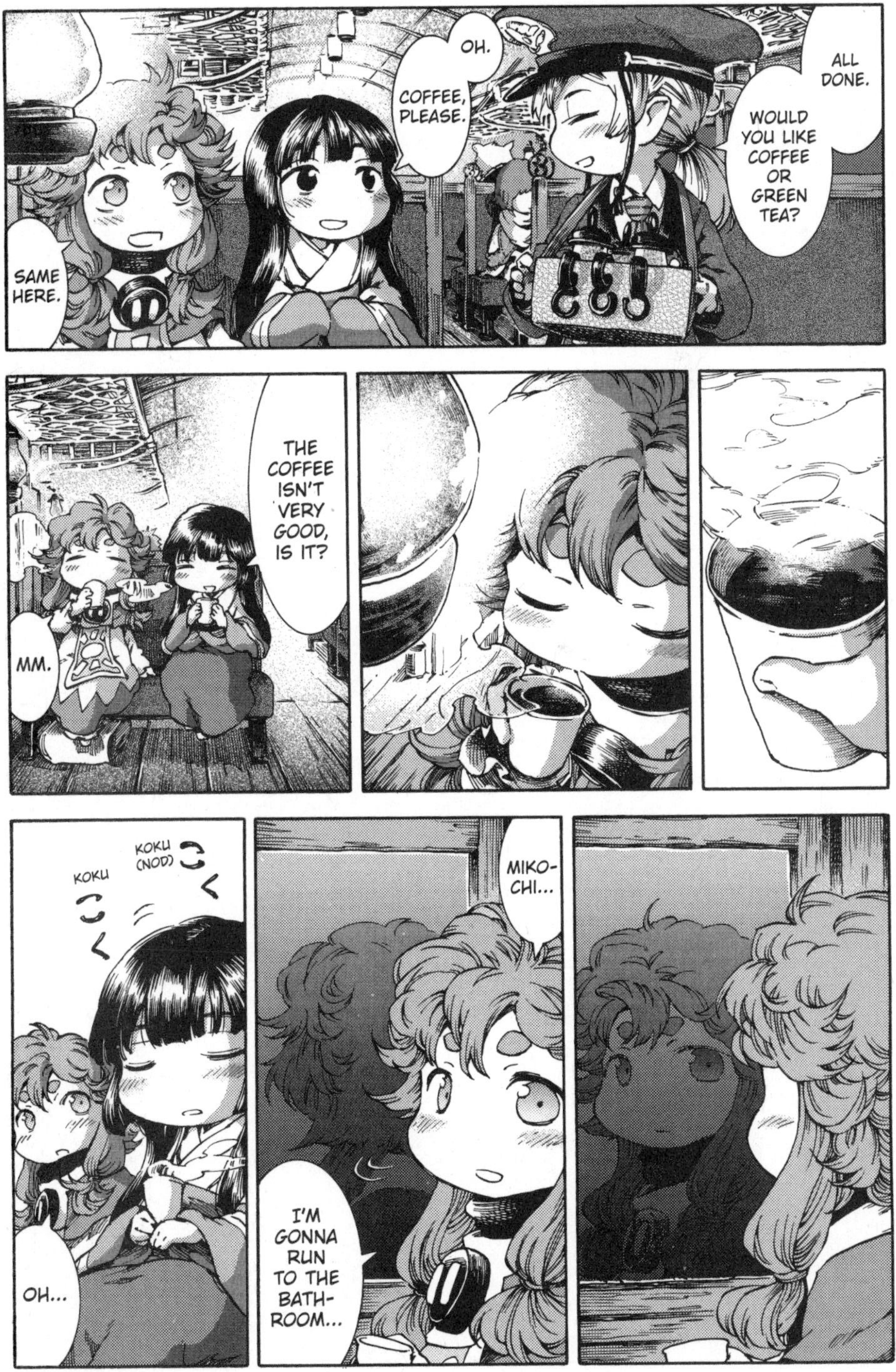
ALL DONE.
WOULD YOU LIKE COFFEE OR GREEN TEA?
OH.
COFFEE, PLEASE.
SAME HERE.
THE COFFEE ISN'T VERY GOOD, IS IT?
MM.
MIKO-CHI...
I'M GONNA RUN TO THE BATH-ROOM...
KOKU (NOD)
KOKU
OH...

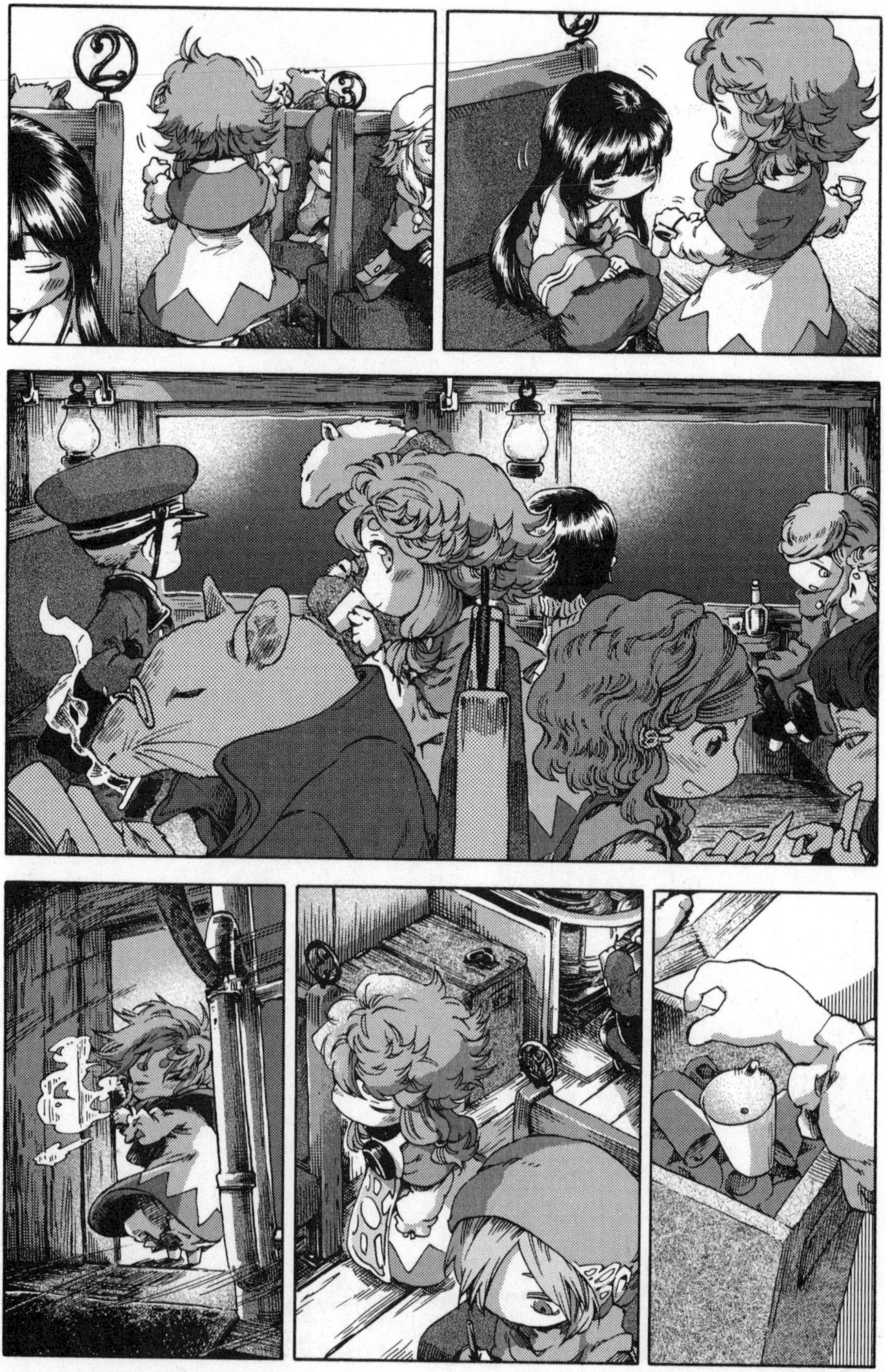

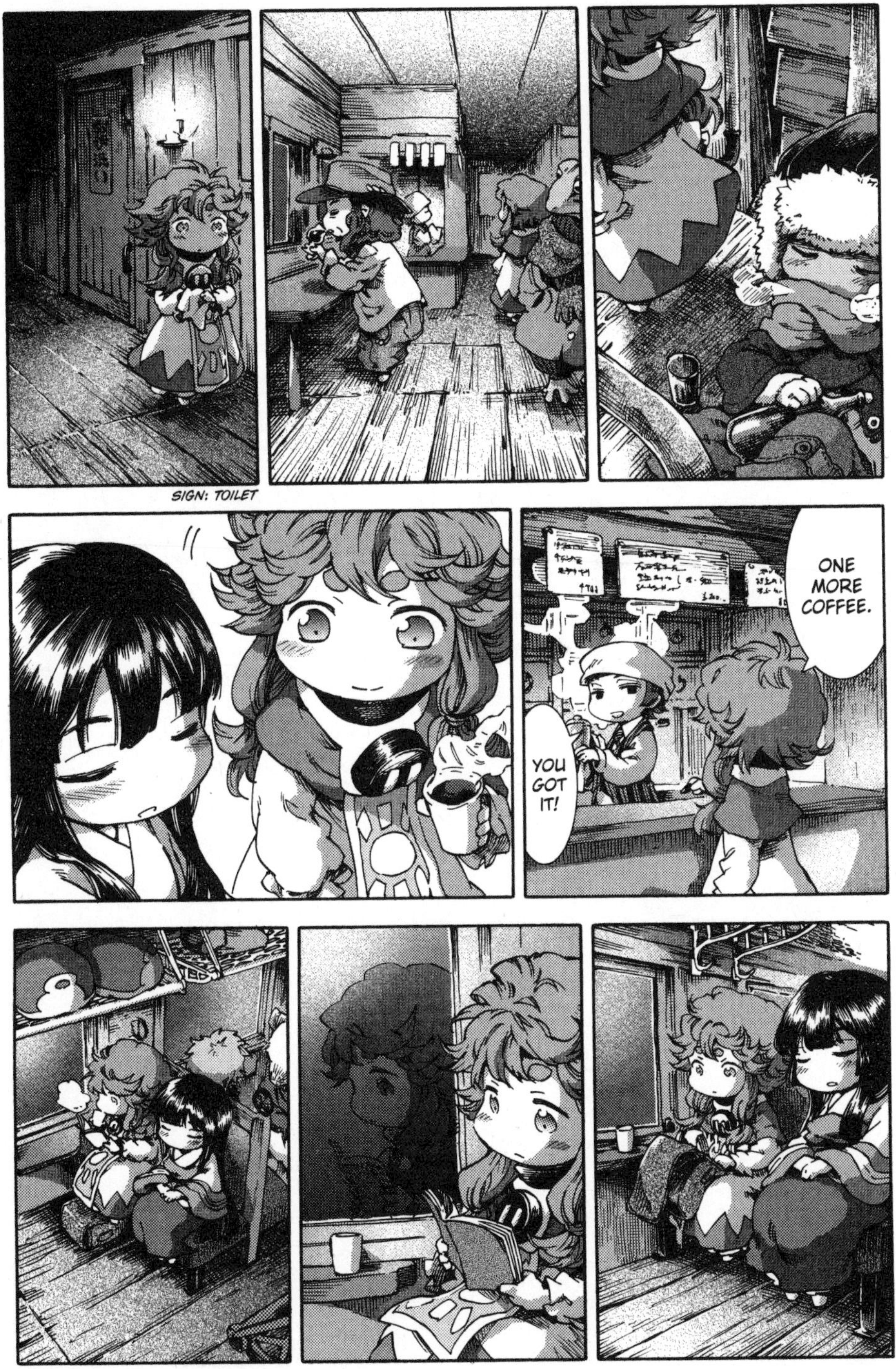
SIGN: TOILET
ONE MORE COFFEE.
YOU GOT IT!

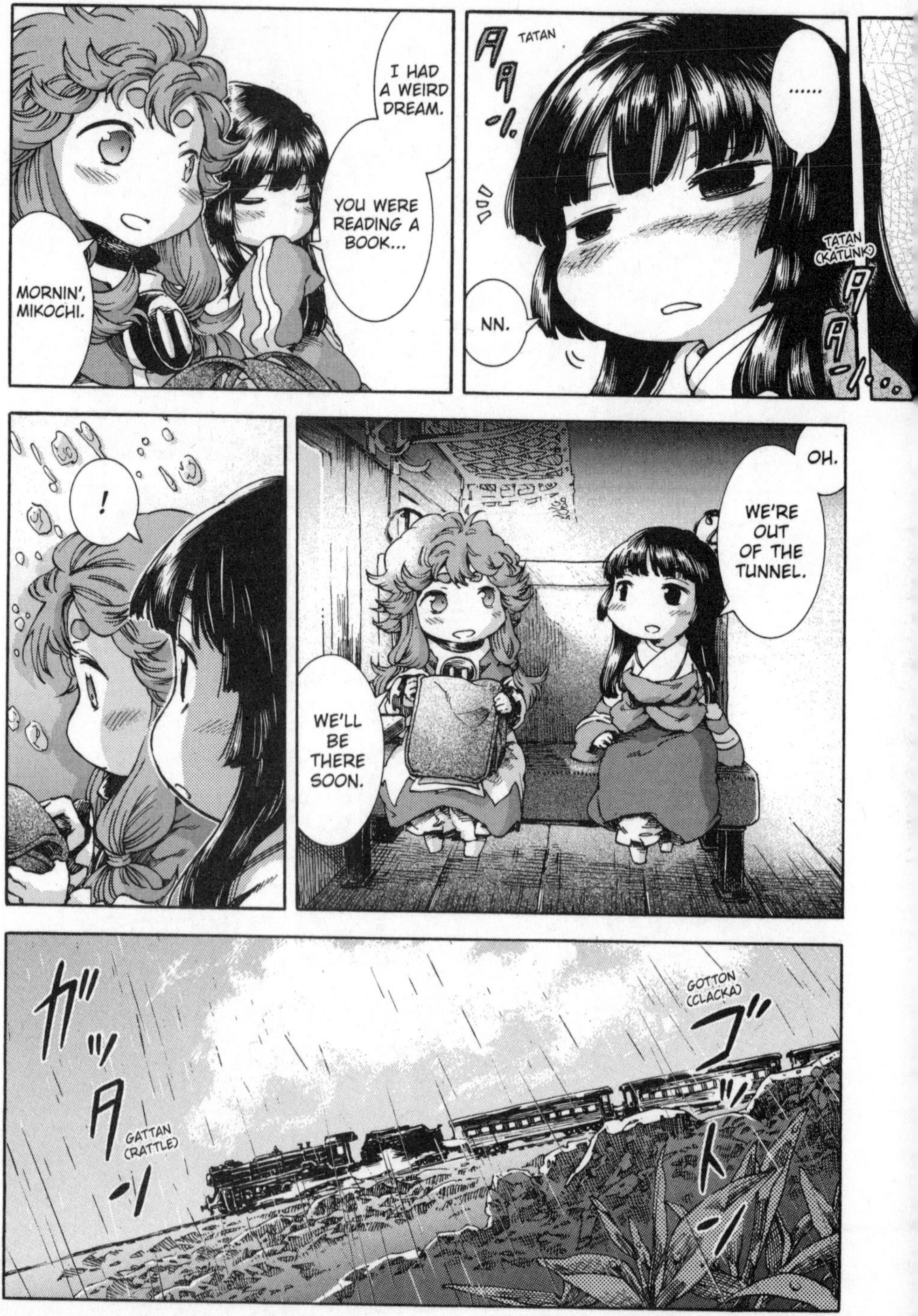
......
TATAN
TATAN (KATUNK)
NN.
I HAD A WEIRD DREAM.
YOU WERE READING A BOOK...
MORNIN', MIKOCHI.
OH.
WE'RE OUT OF THE TUNNEL.
WE'LL BE THERE SOON.
!
GOTTON (CLACKA)
GATTAN (RATTLE)

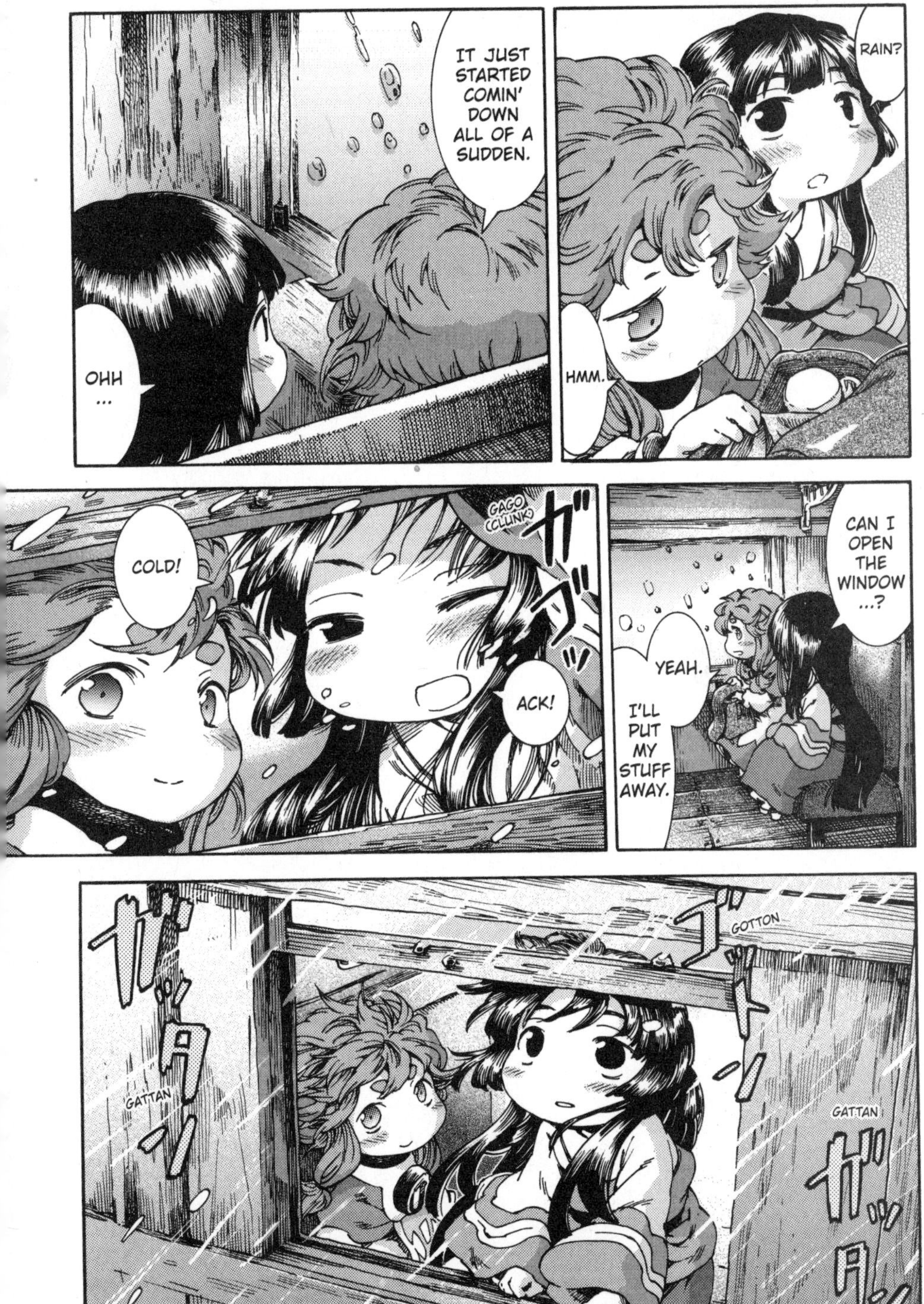
RAIN?
HMM.
IT JUST STARTED COMIN' DOWN ALL OF A SUDDEN.
OHH ...
CAN I OPEN THE WINDOW ...?
YEAH.
I'LL PUT MY STUFF AWAY.
GAGO (CLUNK)
ACK!
COLD!
GOTTON
GATTAN
GATTAN

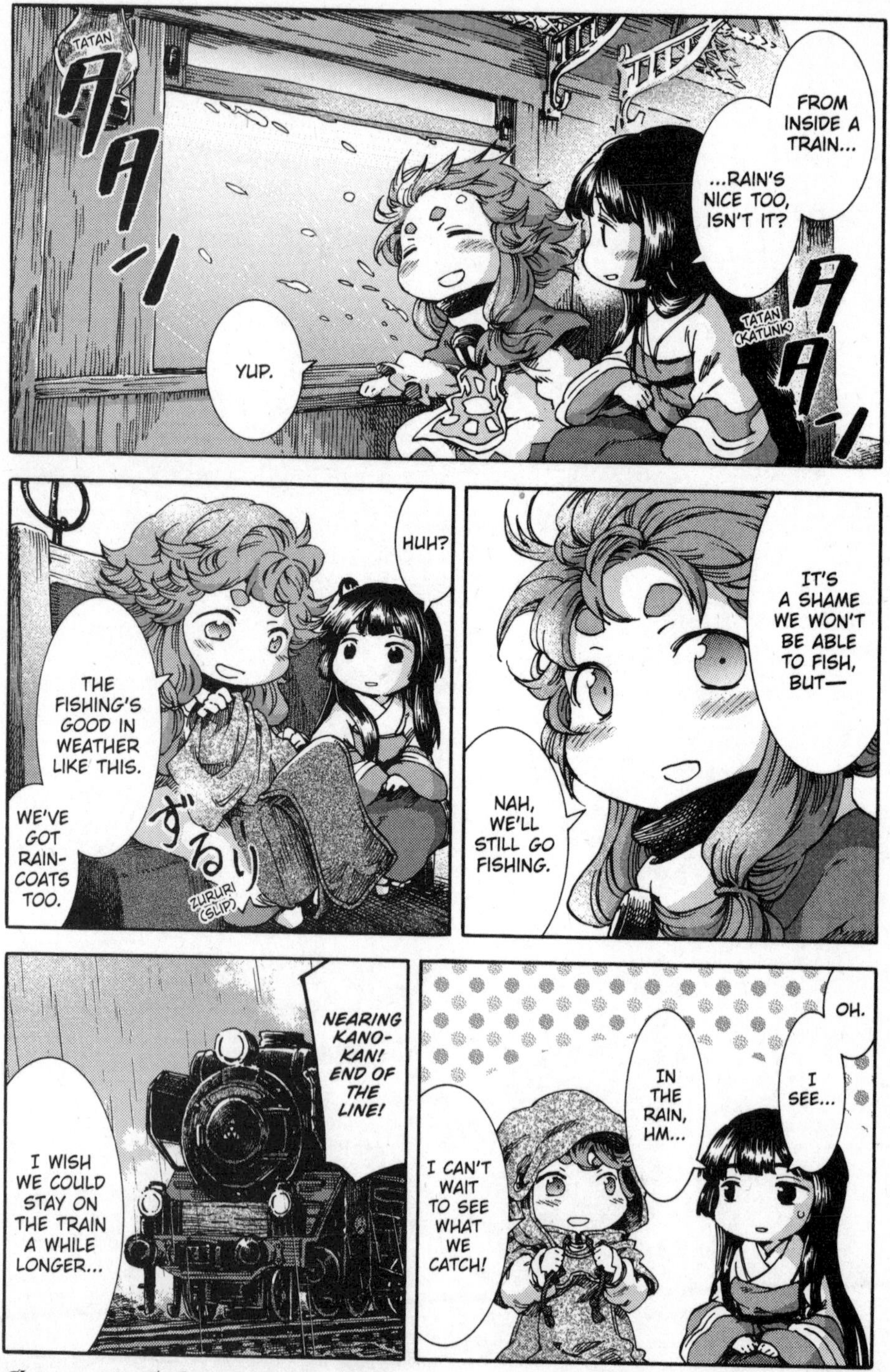
FROM INSIDE A TRAIN...
...RAIN'S NICE TOO, ISN'T IT?
TATAN (KATUNK)
TATAN
YUP.
IT'S A SHAME WE WON'T BE ABLE TO FISH, BUT—
NAH, WE'LL STILL GO FISHING.
HUH?
THE FISHING'S GOOD IN WEATHER LIKE THIS.
WE'VE GOT RAIN-COATS TOO.
ZURURI (SLIP)
OH.
I SEE...
IN THE RAIN, HM...
I CAN'T WAIT TO SEE WHAT WE CATCH!
NEARING KANO-KAN! END OF THE LINE!
I WISH WE COULD STAY ON THE TRAIN A WHILE LONGER...

Chapter 26 • End

•*Column*• Underfoot Steps 26 / The Equal Senpai

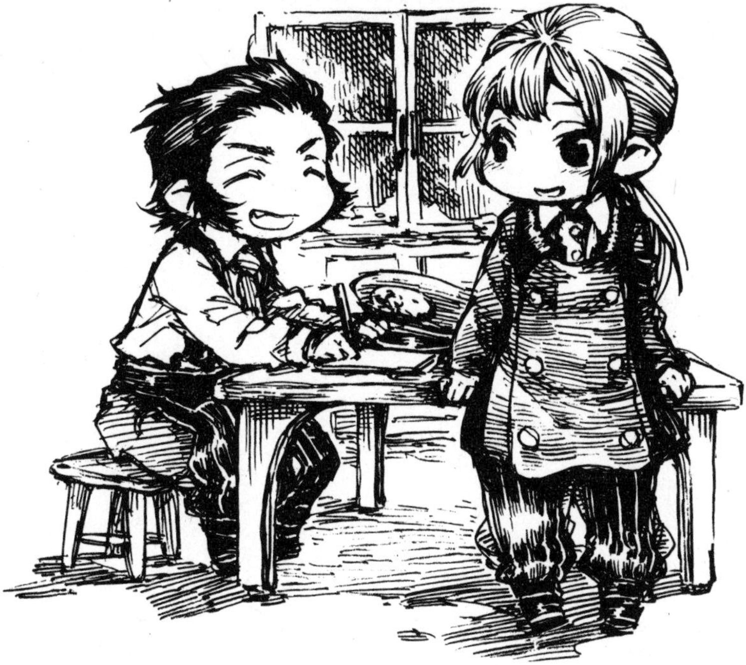

"Mii-chan, let's go have a drink when you get off work."

"Sorry, but I wanna get home an' get down my thoughts on our current timetable."

"I see. Well, 'serious' is good. What about your next day off, then?"

"Sorry. Got plans ta ride the Aobara Railway on the other side of Kanokan."

"I see...Let's go together. I'll tell you about the railway company I was with before."

"That'd be terrific, Senpai! Real educational!"

"I told you, don't call me 'Senpai.' We're equals here."

"You're my senpai when it comes ta railroads!"

"'Zat so?"

"Yeah!"

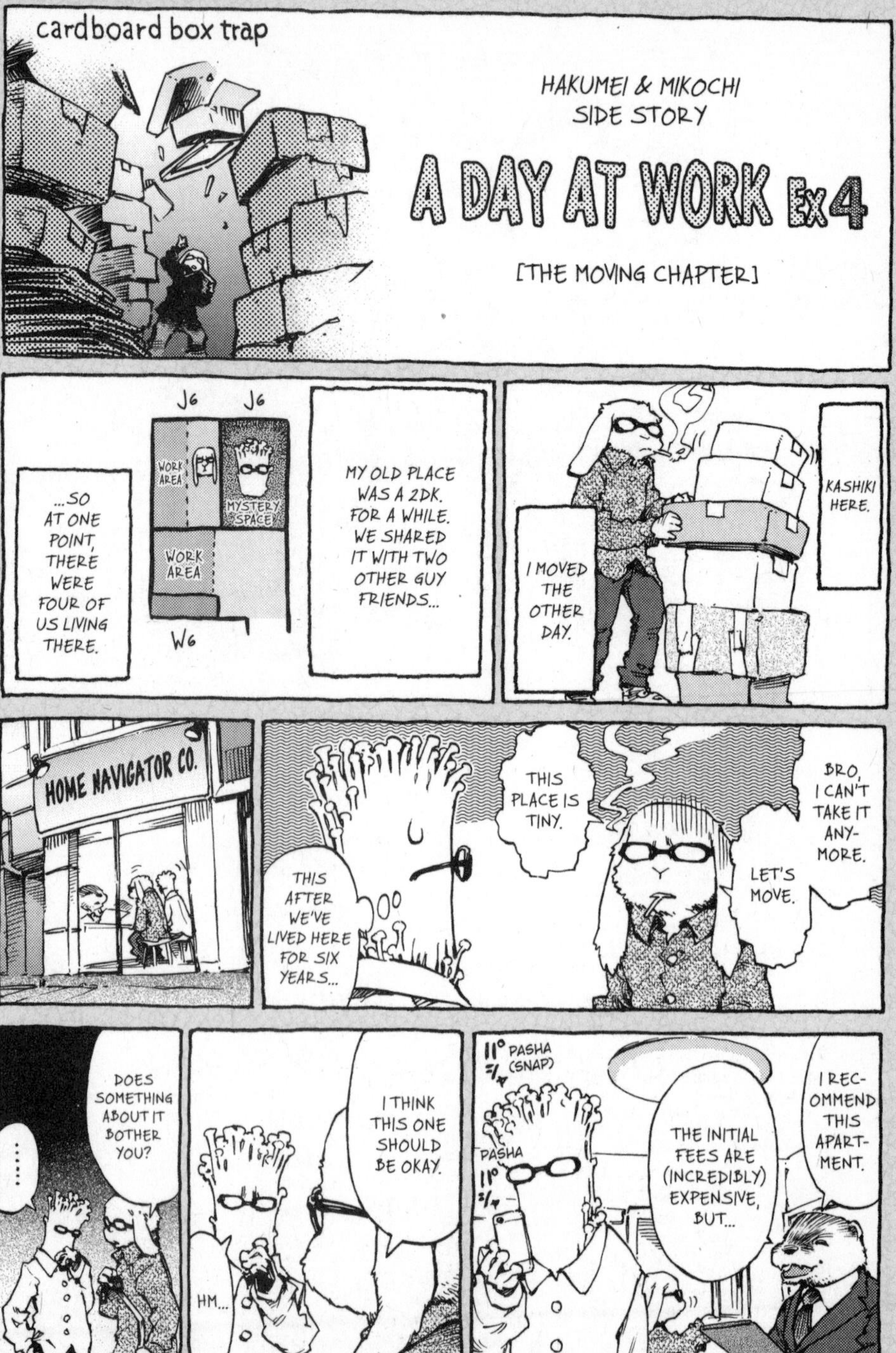

cardboard box trap
HAKUMEI & MIKOCHI SIDE STORY
A DAY AT WORK Ex 4
[THE MOVING CHAPTER]
KASHIKI HERE.
I MOVED THE OTHER DAY.
MY OLD PLACE WAS A 2DK. FOR A WHILE. WE SHARED IT WITH TWO OTHER GUY FRIENDS...
J6
J6
WORK AREA
MYSTERY SPACE
WORK AREA
W6
...SO AT ONE POINT, THERE WERE FOUR OF US LIVING THERE.
BRO, I CAN'T TAKE IT ANYMORE.
LET'S MOVE.
THIS PLACE IS TINY.
THIS AFTER WE'VE LIVED HERE FOR SIX YEARS...
HOME NAVIGATOR CO.
I RECOMMEND THIS APARTMENT.
THE INITIAL FEES ARE (INCREDIBLY) EXPENSIVE, BUT...
PASHA (SNAP)
PASHA
I THINK THIS ONE SHOULD BE OKAY.
HM...
DOES SOMETHING ABOUT IT BOTHER YOU?
......

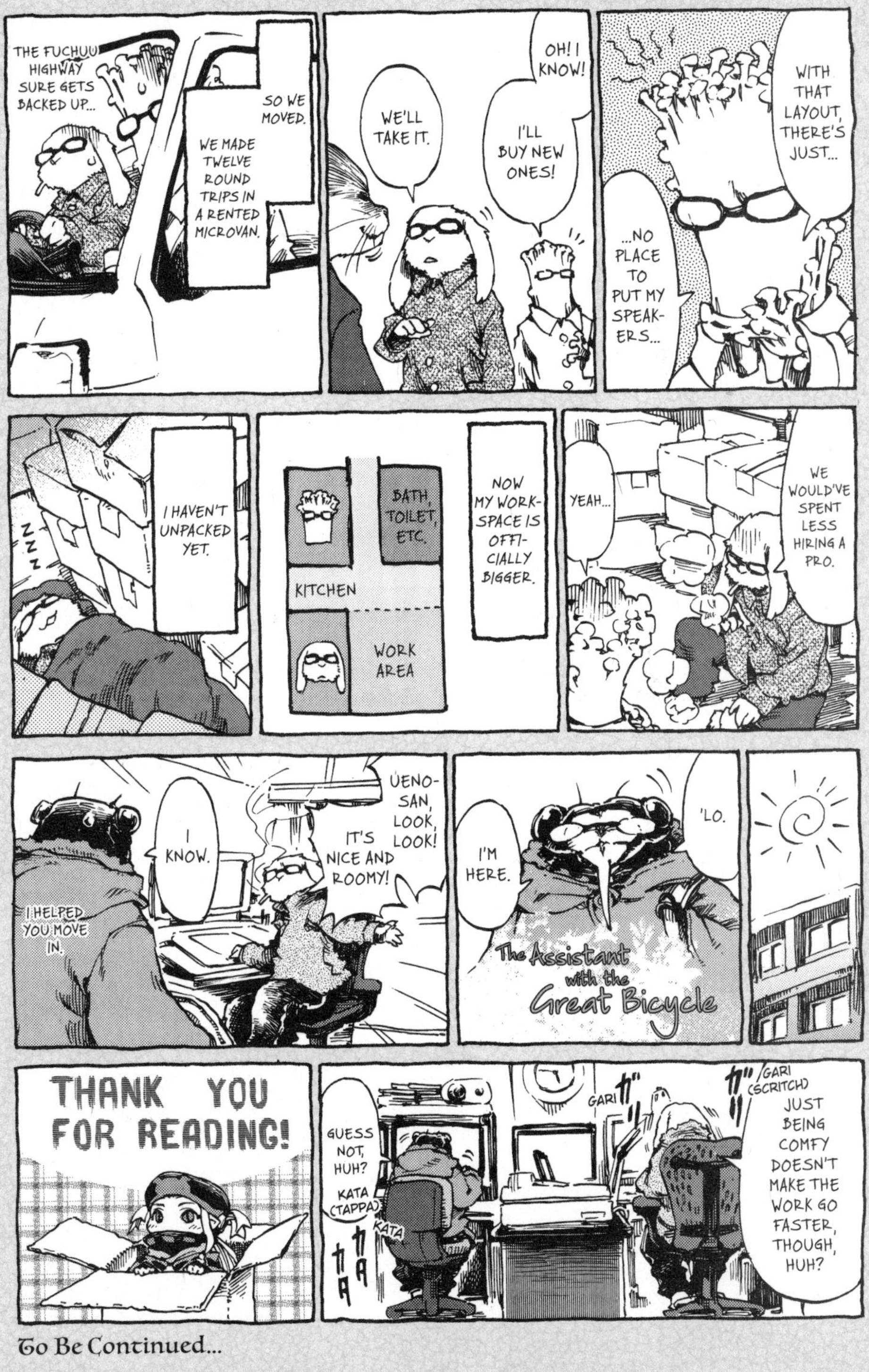
WITH THAT LAYOUT, THERE'S JUST...
...NO PLACE TO PUT MY SPEAKERS...
OH! I KNOW!
I'LL BUY NEW ONES!
WE'LL TAKE IT.
SO WE MOVED.
THE FUCHUU HIGHWAY SURE GETS BACKED UP...
WE MADE TWELVE ROUND TRIPS IN A RENTED MICROVAN.
WE WOULD'VE SPENT LESS HIRING A PRO.
YEAH...
NOW MY WORKSPACE IS OFFICIALLY BIGGER.
BATH, TOILET, ETC.
KITCHEN
WORK AREA
I HAVEN'T UNPACKED YET.
Z Z Z
'LO.
I'M HERE.
The Assistant with the Great Bicycle
UENO-SAN, LOOK, LOOK!
IT'S NICE AND ROOMY!
I KNOW.
I HELPED YOU MOVE IN.
GARI (SCRITCH)
GARI
JUST BEING COMFY DOESN'T MAKE THE WORK GO FASTER, THOUGH, HUH?
GUESS NOT, HUH?
KATA (TAPPA)
KATA
THANK YOU FOR READING!

To Be Continued...

Translation Notes

Common Honorifics
no honorific: Indicates familiarity or closeness; if used without permission or reason, addressing someone in this manner would constitute an insult.
-san: The Japanese equivalent of Mr./Mrs./Miss. If a situation calls for politeness, this is the fail-safe honorific.
-chan: An affectionate honorific indicating familiarity used mostly in reference to girls; also used in reference to cute persons or animals of either gender.
-senpai, Senpai: An honorific used when addressing upperclassmen or more experienced coworkers.

Currency conversion: Although exchange rates fluctuate daily, a good general estimate is ¥100 to 1USD.

Page 44: **Jada's books** (*After the Apples* by her arm and *Like a Starlight* at the top left of the panel) are references to a Kazuya Yoshii album and song, respectively.

Page 65: The actual word used here for **tangerine** is *tankan*, which is a variety of tangerine grown in subtropical zones and generally eaten as fruit rather than being cultivated for its rind or juice.

Page 80: ***Robata-yaki*** is a cooking method where food is grilled out in the open in front of customers. It evolved from a very old style of cooking that was done over an *irori*, a sunken hearth.

Page 113: In Japan, hot springs tend to be categorized by the type and quantity of minerals they contain and their temperature, pH, color, scent, taste, and how they feel against your skin, which is why the water is described as having a "**slippery quality**." At this point, there are ten standard categories, which were set by the Ministry of the Environment in 1978.

Page 113: ***Uruka*** is salt-preserved *ayu* (sweetfish) eggs and innards.

Page 117: ***Soumen* noodles** are sometimes served by being washed down a flume made of half tubes of bamboo (like the water pipe that's feeding the bath in the previous panel); diners catch the noodles with chopsticks and eat them.

Page 119: The **tool** Hakumei is using is technically called a *nata*; it's usually translated as "hatchet" in English, though it has a distinctly different shape. Just like hatchets, *nata*s are used in forestry and for splitting firewood.

Page 123: ***Ginjou* sake** is brewed by low-temperature fermentation from white rice milled to 60 percent. ***Junmai***, or "pure rice," sake is made without adding any alcohol or sugar. ***Kuragakoi*** is a mature sake that has been stored in a dirt cellar at room temperature in the dark for a little over a year.

Page 126: ***Shiokara*** is a dish made of small pieces of meat in a paste made from that animal's salted, fermented innards. It has a very strong flavor and is often served as a pub snack to accompany drinks.

Page 131: ***Oden*** is a type of hot pot that is enjoyed all over Japan during the winter months. It consists of a variety of fish cakes, tofu, seaweed, konjac, eggs, and similar ingredients stewed in broth. Thick, round slices of daikon radish are a standard.

Page 136: **Simmered daikon** is pretty much what it sounds like: Daikon radish rounds are simmered until they are soft enough to slice through with a chopstick, then topped with a sauce made of miso paste, sesame, and rice wine.

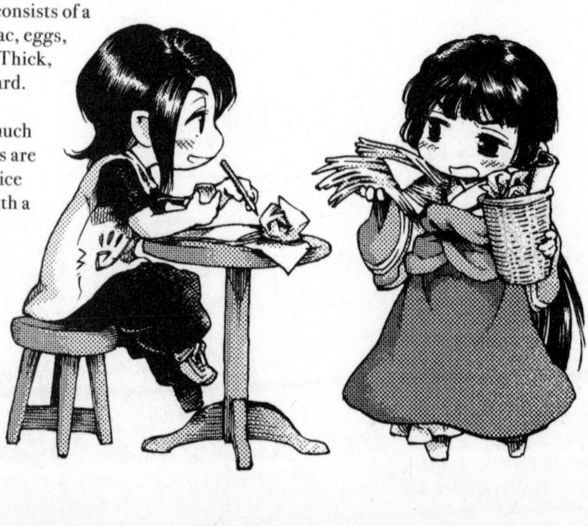

Page 166: *Soboro* is seasoned ground meat, commonly used as a bento topping. *Inari* is short for Inari tofu, or fried tofu.

Page 167: **Bento**, or traditional Japanese box lunches, are something of a classic on trains. They are sold from kiosks at large and midsize train stations all over Japan and from carts on *shinkansen* bullet trains. Every area has bento that highlight that region's particular specialties.

Page 167: As you would guess from the name, **mountain yam** is a type of tuber, but it has a very unique, slimy texture. The actual flesh is light and a bit watery, and it is often served grated as a topping for soba noodles or stirred into soups. The lightly fried yams are indeed crunchy, but if they're left in a bit longer, they develop a texture that's remarkably like French fries, so the characteristic sliminess may disappear when they are prepared this way.

Page 181: When Mii-chan lapses into **casual speech**, he adopts a verbal tic of dropping a syllable so that the ends of his sentences sound noticeably clipped. It's a way of speaking that tends to be associated with young men who are into sports. In her final line of the dialogue, his coworker teasingly mimics his speech, which he seems to miss.

Page 182: A **2DK** apartment has two bedrooms and a (non-separated) dining/kitchen area plus a bathroom.

Page 182: The **J**s along the top of the floorplan and the **W** along the bottom stand for "Japanese" and "Western," respectively. They mean that the top two rooms are Japanese-style (with woven *tatami* mats on the floor) while the bottom room is Western-style (with carpeting or wooden flooring). The number indicates the size of the room in terms of tatami mats (in this case, a little less than 100 square feet).

Page 182: There are generally a lot of **fees** when you move to a new apartment in Japan (a deposit, key money, agent fees, and more), and it's not uncommon for them to add up to the equivalent of six months' rent.

Two girls, a new school, and the beginning of a beautiful friendship.

Volumes 1-7 available now

1
Kiss & White Lily for My Dearest Girl
CANNO

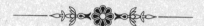

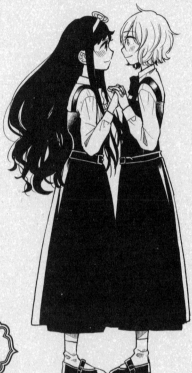

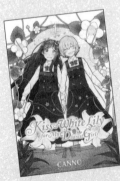

Kiss & White Lily for My Dearest Girl

In middle school, Ayaka Shiramine was the perfect student: hard-working, with excellent grades and a great personality to match. As Ayaka enters high school she expects to still be on top, but one thing she didn't account for is her new classmate, the lazy yet genuine genius Yurine Kurosawa. What's in store for Ayaka and Yurine as they go through high school...together?

Yen Press

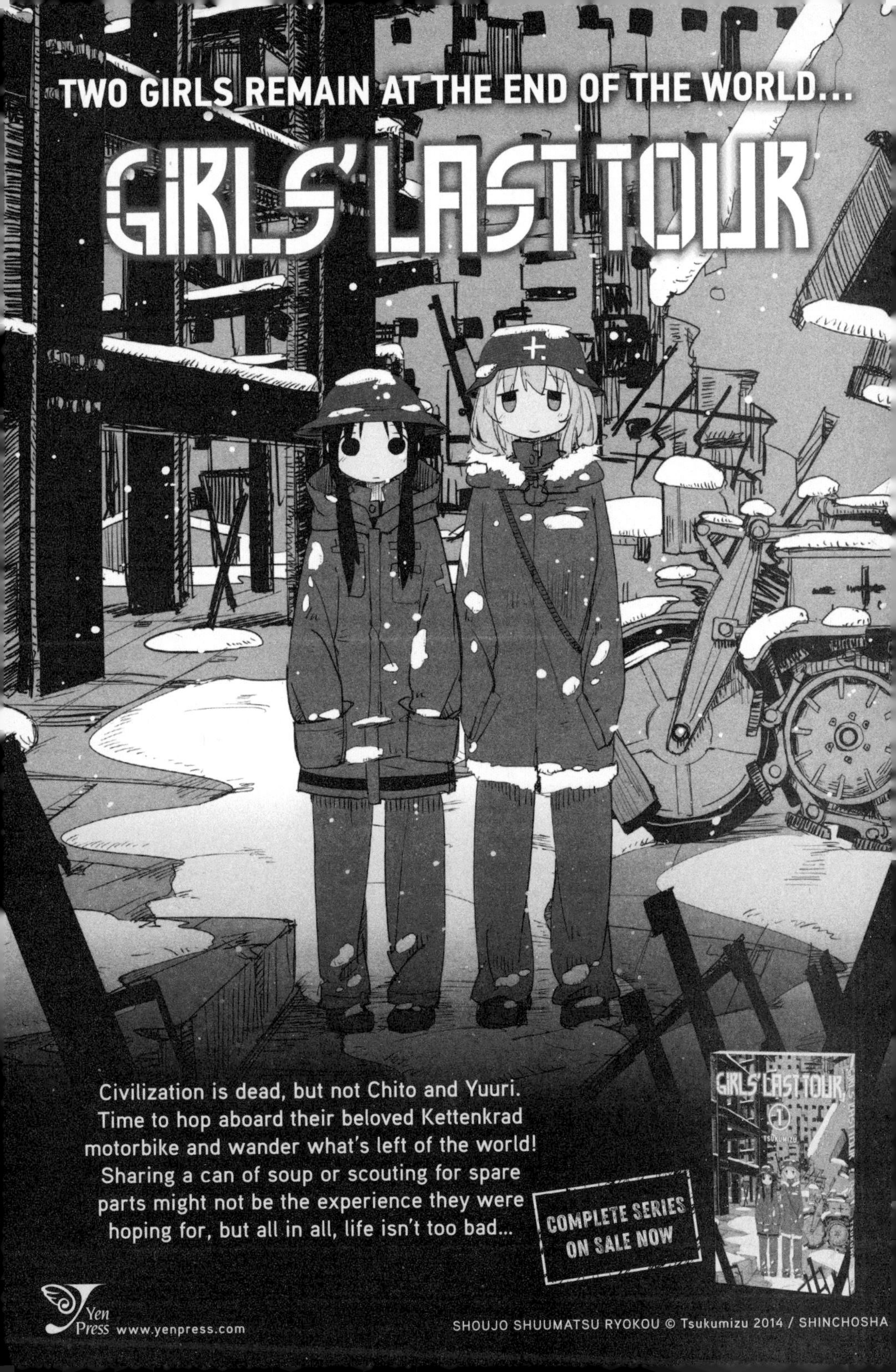
TWO GIRLS REMAIN AT THE END OF THE WORLD...
GIRLS' LAST TOUR
Civilization is dead, but not Chito and Yuuri. Time to hop aboard their beloved Kettenkrad motorbike and wander what's left of the world! Sharing a can of soup or scouting for spare parts might not be the experience they were hoping for, but all in all, life isn't too bad...
COMPLETE SERIES ON SALE NOW
GIRLS' LAST TOUR
1
TSUKUMIZU
Yen Press www.yenpress.com
SHOUJO SHUUMATSU RYOKOU © Tsukumizu 2014 / SHINCHOSHA

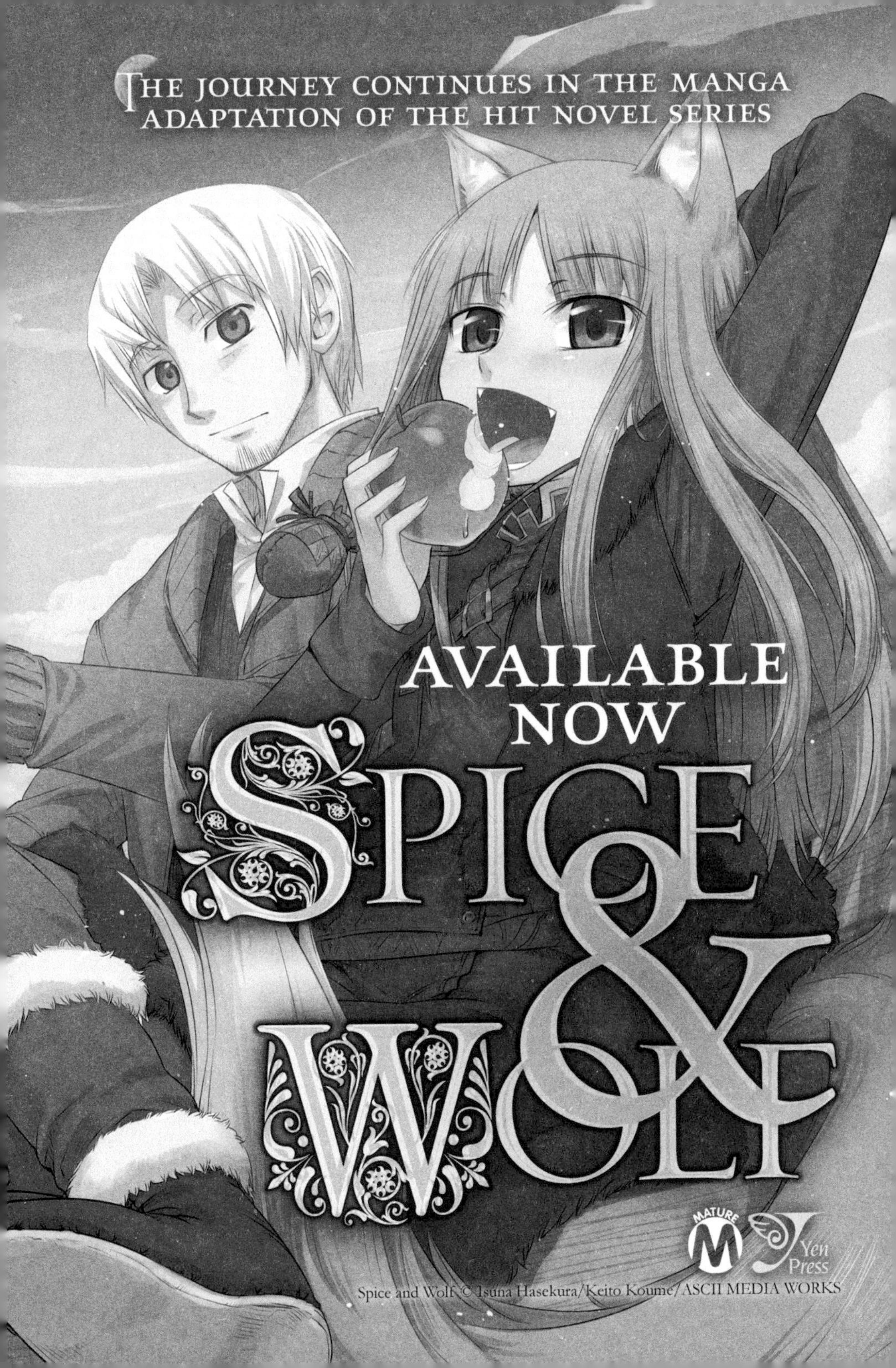

THE JOURNEY CONTINUES IN THE MANGA ADAPTATION OF THE HIT NOVEL SERIES
AVAILABLE NOW
SPICE & WOLF
MATURE
Yen Press
Spice and Wolf © Isuna Hasekura/Keito Koume/ASCII MEDIA WORKS

Hello! This is YOTSUBA!

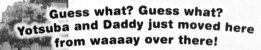

**Guess what? Guess what?
Yotsuba and Daddy just moved here
from waaaay over there!**

**And Yotsuba met these
nice people next door and made
new friends to play with!**

**The pretty one took
Yotsuba on a bike ride!**
(Whoooa! There was a big hill!)

And Ena's a good drawer!
(Almost as good as Yotsuba!)

**And their mom always
gives Yotsuba ice cream!**
(Yummy!)

And...
      And...
            OHHHH!

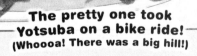

Hakumei & Mikochi 4

Tiny Little Life in the Woods

Takuto Kashiki

Translation: TAYLOR ENGEL *Lettering:* ABIGAIL BLACKMAN

HAKUMEI TO MIKOCHI Volume 4

First published in Japan in 2016 by KADOKAWA CORPORATION, Tokyo.
English translation rights arranged with KADOKAWA CORPORATION, Tokyo through TUTTLE-MORI AGENCY, Inc., Tokyo.

Yen Press
1290 Avenue of the Americas
New York, NY 10104

Visit us at yenpress.com
facebook.com/yenpress
twitter.com/yenpress
yenpress.tumblr.com
instagram.com/yenpress

First Yen Press Edition: February 2019

Yen Press is an imprint of Yen Press, LLC.
The Yen Press name and logo are trademarks of Yen Press, LLC.

The publisher is not responsible for websites (or their content) that are not owned by the publisher.

Library of Congress Control Number: 2018941284

ISBN: 978-1-9753-0294-8

10 9 8 7 6 5 4 3 2 1

WOR

Printed in the United States of America